PRACTICE
TO
DECEIVE

PRACTICE
TO
DECEIVE

by
Patricia Veryan

St. Martin's Press
New York

Design by Doris Borowsky

Library of Congress Cataloging in Publication Data

Veryan, Patricia.
    Practice to deceive.

        I. Title.
PS3572.E766P7   1985   813'.54   85-11728
ISBN 0-312-63553-2

First Edition

10 9 8 7 6 5 4 3 2 1

For Angie—

One of the gentlest, kindest, and
most courageous ladies I know.

Oh, what a tangled web we weave,
When first we practice to deceive!

Sir Walter Scott
"Marmion"

PROLOGUE
England. July, 1741.

Hector John Montgomery, Fifth Baron Delavale, was a gentle and scholarly man, having a deep love of nature and little children. His hopes for a large family were blighted when his beautiful young wife survived a long and painful labour to present him with their second child but, never recovering the bloom of her health, became increasingly frail until she died, some four years later. Desolated, Lord Delavale sought consolation in his children. His fortune was moderate, but no necessity of life was denied them, and many luxuries given without contributing to the overindulgence that nourishes selfishness. At age nineteen, Geoffrey was a handsome, well-built youth of a good-natured temperament. Penelope, four years his junior, had inherited neither her mother's daintiness nor her father's good looks, and on the day she left the schoolroom her Aunt Sybil threw up her hands in despair and informed her spouse that his niece had little to recommend her.

"For she is," declared Mrs. Montgomery pithily, "at least seven inches too tall; she speaks her mind in a most vulgar way, does not hesitate to stare any gentleman out of countenance, and is besides always buried in a book! My heart goes out to poor Delavale! 'Twill be a miracle can he ever fire her off!"

1

It was true that any one of these lamentable qualities was sufficient to condemn a debutante to a place among those unfortunates who occupied the chairs edging Society ballrooms. However, upon receiving an invitation that included his family, it was not the apprehension that his daughter might disgrace him that caused Lord Delavale to hesitate. He would take Geoffrey, of course. The boy was pretty-mannered and would be a credit to him. Penelope, however . . . My lord frowned uneasily. Despite his sister-in-law's occasional waspish remarks, he was very aware that his allegedly plain daughter had an oddly compelling quality. Perhaps it was the warm, welcoming glow that came into her clear hazel eyes when she met someone. Perhaps it was her way of speaking very softly, but evincing an intense interest in what others had to say, or her eagerness to help any creature in affliction. Whatever the cause, my lord had lately become aware that although Penelope Anne did sometimes voice opinions rather more knowledgeably than was entirely feminine, and although her frank gaze was not always demurely lowered as it might have been, young gentlemen did not seem to find her unattractive. It was more than kind of Sir Brian Chandler, the closest friend of his boyhood, to invite them to Lac Brillant for so long as they should be able to stay. The estate was situated in Kent, not far inland from Dover, and was renowned for its magnificence. It would be a joy to present his children to such an old and dear friend after all these years. Only—there were two sons to be considered. The eldest, Gordon, was in his twenty-fifth year. The younger, Quentin, was two and twenty, and rumour whispered he was already a bit of a rascal with the ladies.

One might be pardoned for supposing that a middle-aged widower with a plain daughter on his hands would welcome the opportunity to introduce her to the sons of a close comrade, who also chanced to be extremely wealthy. In Delavale's case, such a supposition would have been unwarranted. My lord had an intense interest in birds. Regrettably, his heir did not share the fascination. To Geoffrey, birds were noisy little pests who woke him at an ungodly hour with their shrieked hymns to the dawn. It was Penelope who accompanied Delavale on his long country walks, who searched with him for nests and kept his records of sightings, migration patterns, and behaviour. It was she who sat with him hour after wintry hour in some damp and chill meadow to catch the first glimpse of wild geese flying south, or who helped him nurse some tiny scrap of fragile bone and scrawny feather that had slipped from a nest until, with care and luck, and perhaps an assist from the Almighty Hand, a sleek young bird was at length released to seek its fellows. No, indeed! Quite apart from the fact that my lord loved his daughter almost as much as he adored his son, he had no wish to lose Penelope. His loss would, in fact, constitute a minor disaster. Not that he was a selfish man. She must marry, of course. Eventually. But—she was only fifteen. And there were those two blasted sons. . . . If they took after their father . . . Thus, it was with considerable misgiving that Delavale yielded to his daughter's importunities and allowed her to accompany him.

When their two carriages turned on to the long, winding drivepath that led to Lac Brillant, Penelope was far too awed by the richly wooded slopes, the sweeping park, the magnificent gardens, the ornamental water and fountains, to pay more than fleeting attention to the young man who rode at the gallop to meet them, his welcoming shouts echoed by Geoffrey's equally exuberant responses. The newcomer drew his black Arabian to a walk and reached up to shake hands with Geoffrey, who rode on the box beside Charles Coachman. Not until he fell back to greet the inside passengers and thus came between her and the view did Penelope withdraw her fascinated gaze from the distant roofs of the three semicircular blocks that constituted the main house.

"Welcome, Miss Montgomery; my lord. I trust you had a pleasant journey?"

As from a great distance Penelope heard her father answer courtesy with courtesy. It seemed to her that the carriage had ceased to rock, or the wheels to rumble. The panelled walls fell

3

away and the door ceased to exist so that she looked unhindered upon a lithe, loose-limbed young man who rode with easy grace. A youth taller than she, to judge from his height in the saddle. He was clad in buckskin breeches and gleaming boots. A riding coat of dark green hugged his broad shoulders, and lace edged the cravat that was secured by a gleaming emerald pin. Thick hair of a rich chestnut colour, waving back from a high brow, was tied in at the nape of the neck. Heavy eyebrows arched at her enquiringly, and laughter danced into the brilliant green eyes. Penelope knew he had said something, but she made no immediate reply, her intent stare drifting down the lean lines of the high-cheekboned face, the narrow Roman nose, the well-shaped lips and firm chin. "How do . . . how do you . . . do," she said faintly.

Curiosity in his eyes, he reached out a gauntletted hand. Her mittened fingers drifted into it. They had come to a stop now, and he bowed in the saddle as gracefully as though he stood in a ballroom, and touched his lips to her hand.

So soft a touch. So gallant and gentle. Yet a warm shiver ran down her back. Something deep inside her stirred and awoke, and she felt a tingling sensation, as though until this moment she had scarcely been alive.

Straightening, he said in that rich, deep voice, "May I introduce myself? I am Quentin Chandler. I'm afraid my brother is in the North for the summer, but my father bids me assure you there will be other guests to spare you from ennui."

His strong clasp tightened slightly, and Penelope awoke to the fact that she had not withdrawn her own hand as she should have done. Drawing back, she felt her cheeks redden, and smiled shyly. Quentin Chandler returned the smile, his innate kindness deepened by interest.

'We have met before,' Penelope thought dreamily. 'Long and long ago. But he does not know it. Yet.' And in that one short interval, irrevocably, her heart was given.

Lord Delavale had viewed his daughter's behaviour with

4

deepening alarm. She turned to him with an odd, almost guilty little start. As though, he thought, she had quite forgotten he was with her. Her cheeks were slightly flushed, and in her eyes was a new look, a sparkling joy that had in it also an awareness of her femininity. He groaned inwardly, and knew his worst fears had been realised.

I

June, 1746

It began to rain in late afternoon and the wind, gusting fitfully over the rivers and scarps and chalk hills of Oxfordshire, carried on its breath the chill of northern ice-floes. Cold held no terrors for Penelope, but there was a limit, and when it became evident she would soon be soaked through, she patted the tired mare's neck gently and turned her into the lane that led towards the eastern boundaries of Highview. Here, venerable chestnut trees met overhead to cast a shade that was pleasant on a hot day. This afternoon was gloomy even under the open skies, and the lane was dark and hushed, but at least they were protected from the rain to an extent and Missy could amble along with less effort than on the sodden fields.

They soon came to the gate and the higher hedges that marked the start of the Highview preserves. Penelope reined to a halt, slid from the saddle, and gathered her wet habit over one arm as she opened the gate. She paused, her small gloved hand resting on the top rung as she looked nostalgically at the weathered wood. How many times she and Geoff had galloped this way. And wouldn't he tease her, could he see her now, dismounting so staidly to open the gate they had been used to jump, neck and neck. She sighed wistfully and glanced up at the lowering clouds, wondering where her brother's valiant spirit wandered today. He wouldn't be here, she decided. Except perhaps out of love for her. Geoff had loathed Uncle Joseph and his opinion of their beautiful aunt had been couched in unequivocal terms. "The woman is a vulture!" he'd declared, his dark eyes flashing indignation. "She and that rascally uncle of mine could scarce wait for Papa to be decently buried before they descended on Highview to manage my affairs. Much I need *their* management! At the rate they spend, I shall be fortunate to have an estate left to manage by the time I reach five and twenty and am allowed to come into my inheritance!"

But Geoffrey, tall, bronzed, and full of health and vigour in his twenty-third year, chafing against the constraints his father's will had placed upon his taking full control of his estates, had quarrelled constantly with his rapacious aunt and uncle and had gone off to fight the King's enemies in Scotland. Frightened by a letter notifying her that her brother had been wounded at the Battle of Prestonpans, Penelope was devastated the following day when a correcting communiqué advised that Captain Lord Delavale had been killed and buried by the Scots in an unmarked grave, following that rout. Still mourning her beloved father, Penelope was left to grieve also for the brother she had mothered and adored since childhood. Fat Joseph Montgomery was the lord of Highview now, and he and his beautiful wife no longer had to brood upon a future that must see Geoffrey taking over his full inheritance, and themselves dispossessed.

A mildly complaining whicker from Missy awoke Penelope to the fact that she was standing motionless in the rain. She squared her shoulders, fighting sorrow away as she led the mare through, closed the gate, then used the middle rung as an impromptu step to assist her climb into the saddle. Geoff had been gone for nigh ten months. It was no use grieving so. She must put her wits to better use than vain regrets. For instance, how much longer she could endure the humiliation of existence at—

7

She ceased to adjust her long wet skirts and glanced about tensely. She was being watched. She knew it as surely as if she could see someone standing in the meadow. There was no sign of life, no movement of anything save for the wind-tossed branches of trees and shrubs. But someone was near, and if it was that horrid Captain Otton . . . ! Her heartbeat quickened. She kicked her boot home with rather more urgency than usual, and Missy snorted and broke into a canter.

The rain had settled into a steady drizzle, but by the time Penelope was halfway across the meadow it became a deluge and, again, she was obliged to change her route. The closest shelter was offered by Nurse's abandoned cottage and a quick dash brought them to the copse and then the broken picket fence and weed-filled garden that the old lady had once kept so meticulously ordered. Penelope dismounted under the now empty woodshed at the side. She looped the reins around one of the support posts, promised the drenched mare that she would come back, and ran to the front door. It was locked, of course, but Nurse had always kept a key above the lintel and, braving dust and crawly things, Penelope groped for and found it.

The door creaked open. Inside, there was a musty smell of disuse. Almost she fancied to catch a whiff of cheese on the air which was, she thought prosaically, mould rather. She went through the small entrance hall and looked about for something to use to rub down Missy. The curtains were closed in the parlour, and a grubby-looking cover of Holland cloth had been thrown over the sofa, this apparently having been judged the only piece of furniture worth protecting. Penelope pulled off the cover. Turning to the door again, she gave a little squeal of fright as something moved in the shadows. Her heart almost stopped. Knees melting with terror, she pressed the dusty cloth to her breast. And then, dimly, she saw the answering flutter and felt weak with relief. The movement that had startled her so had been her own reflection in the old mirror over the oaken sideboard—nothing more.

"Stupid girl . . . !" she gasped, and tottered nearer.

Her eyes were becoming accustomed to the gloom, and she was depressed by the bedraggled vision in the mirror. Her hat hung limply about her face, water dripping from the brim to trickle in little rivulets down her cheeks, and the feather sagging at a ridiculous angle. Black did not become her. She looked washed-out and colourless. "You are not a pretty girl, niece. . . ." Uncle Joseph's unkind verdict rang again in her ears. She put down the Holland cover and rested both hands on the sideboard as she leaned forward, scanning her reflection. She sighed. There was no denying it was truth; she was not pretty. Of course, her hair was a straggling disaster at the moment, but even when it was well-brushed and neatly dressed, it was only a rather mousy brown. Unless she wore powder, which she seldom did in the country. She thought defensively that it *did* have honey-gold highlights sometimes, when the sun touched it. But . . . there were her eyebrows. Too straight, and since she refused to pluck them, lacking the fine, thin line that was The Fashion. Her mouth was full and well-shaped, but the most infatuated of swains could not have termed it a blushing rosebud. And below it, her chin was both too decided and lacking even the suspicion of a dimple. Still, her eyes were really quite good; wide-spaced, well-opened, deeply lashed, and of a rich hazel flecked with blue. Her hopeful look faded. Only yesterday her aunt had scolded that they were 'witch's eyes.' "And if you persist in looking so directly at the gentlemen, instead of lowering your lashes demurely, as any female should, you'll end a spinster, my girl! The Lord only knows your uncle and I try to be patient, but whoever heard of a chit with your looks receiving three perfectly acceptable offers and spurning every one? Your poor papa must have been all about in his head to have borne with such high flights! On the day you put off your blacks, miss, there'll be an end to such nonsensicality. Your uncle will accept the first respectable offer that comes your way—*if* you ever receive another at your age! So if you're taken some unnatural vow to wear the willow all your days, prepare yourself! I've no mind to keep a spinster here, eating us out of house and home, and so I warn you!"

Penelope had taken no such vow. To be a spinster was, in fact, quite the antithesis of her dreams. Her eyes softened and one finger traced a letter into the dust atop the sideboard. The letter Q. Five years ago she had indulged such glorious hopes. Five years ago next month, she and Geoffrey and Papa had spent that wonderful week at Lac Brillant. Despite all that had transpired since, she had only to close her eyes and she could see Quentin Chandler's aquiline features, the beautifully chiselled lips always ready to quiver into a smile, the mischief that lit the deep green of the wide-set eyes, the grin that flashed white and irresistibly across his face, so that one had perforce to laugh with him. How easily he had slipped into familiarity with them, as though he had been part of the family. And what a golden time it had been, one happy day blending into the next while they rode or walked, or played croquet on Lac Brillant's velvet lawns. A boat party and a ball had been given in honour of the visitors. There had been dances at the homes of neighbours, afternoon musicales and card parties, breakfasts *al fresco.* Laughter and joy, and that thrilling excitement that had made her heart race and brought a sweet new shyness whenever Quentin touched her hand, or smiled her way. Always, he had teased her gently, and she had gloried in his assumption that he had the right to do so.

To leave had been the most painful experience of her life. Quentin also had seemed saddened and vowed he would be at Highview before the month was out, to visit the Montgomerys. Papa had despatched several letters urging that Sir Brian and his sons visit Oxfordshire, but they had not come. The following year Geoffrey had heard through friends that Quentin was in Rome, taking the Grand Tour in the company of his father's chaplain. Then, early in the autumn of 1744, Lord Delavale had walked out at dawn to watch his beloved birds, despite the annoyance of a bad cold. He had come home with a slight fever, and a week later was dead. Penelope had not yet put off her blacks when her brother had ridden off to war, so soon to fall. There could be no thought of marriage whilst she was in mourning—nor did she mean to accept any of the gentlemen who had previously courted her. How could she, when her heart belonged forever to Quentin Chandler? If, on some glorious golden morning he should come riding up the drive-path to claim her . . . She sighed wistfully. An unlikely prospect. But even though he would probably never come and thus doom her to spinsterhood, there were worse fates. The lot of a spinster must be infinitely preferable to being the wife of a man for whom one could feel neither liking nor respect.

She took up the Holland cover absently, knowing why she had been so frightened when she'd fancied someone stood behind her. She'd thought it might be Roland Otton. The repellent creature admired her, there could be no doubt of it. The gall of the man! She was the daughter of a baron. Her father's family could trace their lineage to the twelfth century, and Mama's people had been numbered among those brave Saxons who had striven against the invading Normans in 1066. All anyone knew of Otton was that he claimed the rank of Captain (which Geoffrey had said was probably self-bestowed) and that he had a splendid physique and a countenance so darkly handsome that it was a distinct shock when one first beheld him. Scarcely sufficient grounds for a gentleman to look at a lady as Otton had taken to looking at her. But then—Penelope's lip curled scornfully—Captain Roland Otton could not be taken for a gentleman. He had come to Highview two years earlier, in Joseph Montgomery's train. The first time she had met the man she'd been in deep mourning for her father, yet Otton's bold eyes, near as dark as the stuff of her gown, had roved her from head to toe, a gleam coming into them as they drifted back to meet her haughty frown. Unabashed, he had grinned and bowed sweepingly, then reached out to shake hands with her brother. The Captain's impertinence had not escaped Geoffrey, however. He had quite "failed to see" the extended hand, and

11

Otton had been relegated to his list of 'Contemptibles'; a judgement he had not amended to the day of his death.

A growl of distant thunder recalled Penelope to the present and, impatient with her ponderings, she turned to the side door. Her movement was very sudden, and she saw the shadow that whipped across the hall. There *was* someone here! Her blood seemed to congeal, and she felt stifled with dread. *Had* Otton followed her? Was he lying in wait, ready to force his attentions on her the instant she stepped into the hall? A sob of helplessness rose in her throat. She was totally alone. Even if she should scream there was not a soul within hearing distance. 'God help me!' she thought numbly. 'What can I do?' Do something, she must! She could not simply cower in fear and trembling until the wretched man came and ravaged her. The prospect of such an outrage made her blaze with anger, and fear was routed. If Otton attempted to assault her, he would pay dearly for his villainy! Thank heaven that when dear Nurse had been denied the pension Papa had promised, and gone to Exeter to live with her sister, she had left the estate cutlery in the cottage. Penelope slid the top right-hand drawer open. The long-bladed carving knife was still there. Her fingers slipped around the handle, and she took up the Holland cover, concealing the knife beneath it.

Her nerves tight but her resolution unwavering, she marched to the door. All was quiet, save for the pattering of the rain, but as she stepped into the hall she heard a faint sound to her right. From the corner of her eye she could see nothing untoward. Her heart was leaping about wildly, but she continued to the front door. At any second she expected to hear hasty footsteps. The skin of her back began to creep and the knife handle slipped in her wet hand. She was almost to the door. She opened it somehow, praying Otton would not be lounging outside, watching her with his lazy, suggestive grin. . . .

But only a drifting veil of misty air awaited her. Vaguely noting that the rain had stopped, she pulled the door to and made her way to the side of the house. Missy whickered an amiable greeting. Furtively, Penelope slipped her knife into the leather sheath that ran down the stirrup before she went through the motions of rubbing down the mare. Finishing, she draped the sodden cotton over an empty barrel and led Missy around to the front. She was taut with fear, but still there was no sign of the intruder. The front step aided her scramble into the side-saddle, her wet garments hampering her and forbidding any attempt at speed. Not daring to betray fear, even now, she tapped her heels and Missy trotted down the path. Only then did Penelope allow a choked sob to escape her. Her bones felt like jelly, but as soon as they were beyond the garden she urged Missy to a canter.

At first, she was so overwrought that all she could think of was her amazing good fortune. But gradually, as terror faded and the thunder of her heart eased, it came to her that whoever had been in the cottage could very easily have prevented her leaving. Perhaps some poor starving vagrant had taken shelter from the rain, even as she had done, and been just as afraid of her as she had been of him. Or—and more logically—perhaps some wretched Jacobite fugitive, flying desperately for his life and hounded by soldiers and bounty hunters, had used the cottage as a temporary haven of refuge. She drew a deep breath. Either way she had been spared, and she whispered a small prayer of gratitude.

The sky was lightening as she crossed the meadow and, by the time she topped the last gentle rise and looked down upon the misted outline of the great house that was Highview Manor, the sun was slanting a few crimson spears through the clouds. Missy smelled home now and began to canter, and then, as they entered the small stand of birches that ran along beside the stream, a man rode out before them and Penelope had no choice but to rein to a halt.

Roland Otton, clad in a magnificently tailored olive-green riding coat, a small-sword strapped above his lean middle and a tricorne set at a rakish angle upon his thick, elegantly powdered hair, bowed in the saddle. "Thank God you are safe, dear Miss

Montgomery! Your uncle is fairly beside himself, and your aunt is nigh prostrated with anxiety. Is aught amiss?"

"The only thing amiss, sir," she replied tartly, "is that you block my way. Be so good as to move aside."

He guided his tall chestnut to the edge of the narrow drive, but reached out to seize Penelope's rein. "Sweet lady," he began.

Through clenched teeth, she gritted, "Captain Otton . . . let me pass!"

"But of course." He placed one gauntleted hand over his heart. "If you do not wish to hear my news . . ."

The velvety black eyes twinkled. A smile tugged at the corners of his shapely lips, and he waved her on grandiloquently.

Touched by apprehension, she walked Missy past. "I am not so very late," she said in a tentative probing. "I scarce fancy my aunt and uncle are thrown into despair."

Otton reined the chestnut alongside Missy, keeping pace with her. "'Tis more than that, m'dear."

Stiffening at the familiarity, Penelope exclaimed, "How— dare you!"

"Egad!" He put one hand briefly across those dancing black eyes. "A slip of the tongue, merely. My humblest apologies. 'Tis only that—I've so much to tell you."

How gentle and winning the smile. How wistfully admiring the gaze. And how she loathed this ingratiatingly charming, treacherous young man! Yet he obviously was abrim with news, and so she said merely, "Pray see that your tongue does not slip again."

He sighed, and they rode side by side to the ancient stone bridge, she curious and uneasy, he maddeningly silent.

They were clattering up the high-arching structure before she prompted, "Well, sir?"

"You bade me hold my tongue," he responded meekly. "I had thought—"

"Oh, have done with your nonsense! What is it you taunt me with?"

14

"Taunt . . . ? Ah, how can you utter such cruel words, lovely lady? Am I not your slave, your faithful servant, your most—"

"My most fulsome servant, 'twould seem. Speak, or have done. I am soaked, Captain, and would seek my chamber."

"Fortunate chamber," he said yearningly, but noting the angry spark in her eyes, went on, "Did you know there are escaped rebels in the neighbourhood? When you failed to return, Lady Sybil feared—"

"That I had been captured and held for ransom, perhaps?" Penelope gave vent to a small, unladylike snort. "Then she must in *truth* have been distraught! If my captors demanded a high ransom, whatever would the County say did she refuse to pay it?"

He laughed softly. "How well you know her, dear Penel—er, Miss Montgomery. And—how.well I know the depth of your longing to escape."

Startled, Penelope pulled Missy to a sudden halt. "What do you mean?"

He turned his mount and brought up very close, so that he sat facing her, their knees all but touching. The smile was gone from his mouth now, and he looked very earnest. "Dear lady, can you think I do not see the humiliation that is daily visited upon you? Do you think I do not notice how Lady Sybil abuses and degrades you? With my poor bruised heart beating only for—"

She said with chill hauteur, "Let us dispense with the disorders of your heart, Captain. Do you seriously suppose I mean to leave Highview? This is my home. The home of my forebears. And I—"

"Are beyond words miserable." He reached out to clamp strong fingers over her hand on the reins. "Dearest girl— No! Hear me out! You know my feelings. You cannot fail to have seen that I worship your—"

Flushed and furious, she interposed, "Worship my—*what*, sir? I am no beauty. Nor have I a vast fortune to lure such a man as

15

yourself! What is—" But she gave a gasp, really frightened as the hand upon her own tightened so that it was like a steel band around her wrist. His black eyes narrowed smoulderingly. She was jerked closer. His other arm swept around her and in a fluid muscular movement he had dismounted, dragging her with him so that she fell into his embrace.

"Beauty?" he growled. "What have today's vapid beauties to say to me? What care I for their simperings and giggling inanities? You have more character in your little finger than any dozen of today's Toasts have in their entire powdered and scented bodies! Aye, and more sweet passion, I'll warrant!"

Enraged, Penelope struggled to no avail. Inexorably, she was crushed against his chest. He was taller than she and, with one arm trapped between them and the other caught up behind her, she was powerless, however she fought.

"Let me go, you cur!" she panted. "Oh! Did my brother yet live . . . !"

"Well, he does not, love. But I do—and you do! And what I see peeping from those lovely, forthright eyes of yours is not coy modesty, but the naked desire of the lusty heart you hide beneath your prudish posing."

"Beast!" she hurled at him. "Horrid, impertinent—"

The balance of her denunciation was smothered as his mouth came down upon her own. All her attempts to evade him were wasted. His lips seared hers in a long, hard kiss. The arm about her tightened until she could scarcely breathe, and his other hand was wandering down her throat, tracing the shape of her breasts, beginning to unfasten the buttons of her habit. Tears of anger and humiliation stung her eyes, but since force would not serve, she relaxed gradually until she leaned limp and yielding in his arms, her lips parting before the insistence of his.

Otton raised his head, a glow of triumph in the dark eyes that roved hungrily over her backward tilted head and the shapeliness now so lax against his eager body. Easing his grip on her, he began to kiss his way down her throat. "My sweeting," he murmured huskily, "I always knew that—"

16

With all her strength, Penelope tore free and boxed his ear.
He gave a startled yelp and recoiled instinctively. With a pan-
therish spring she got one foot into the stirrup and, desperation
lending her strength, leapt to grab the pommel and pull herself
up.

Otton was after her with a shout, only to pause as she
rounded on him, her face livid, her eyes glinting as deadly as
the steel blade of the knife she held in one purposeful hand.
"Stay back, you filthy lecher! Stay back, or as God is my judge,
I shall use this!"

His eyes hardened as he stared first at the unwavering blade,
then up into the savagery of her eyes. He laughed suddenly. "I
ever loved a maid with spirit."

"I do not doubt it. Go and seek one who is also willing. You
should find many such in the taverns at Banbury or Oxford!"
And seeing the dark brows twitch together over his slim,
straight nose, she added, "I go to my uncle on the instant, to
tell him of how you dared to paw and insult me. Have you any
belongings, I advise you to gather them, Captain Otton—or
whatever your real name is!"

It was a bow drawn at random, but that it hit home was
evidenced by the shock that came briefly into his face. Then he
grinned confidently. "Go to him, then. But he'll not see you
tonight."

"He will see me, never fear!"

"If he does, which I doubt, I can tell you what he'll say, for I
had words with him on the subject of your lovely self, this very
day."

Gathering the reins with one hand, even as she held the
knife firmly with the other, Penelope said, "You lie! Scheming
rogue that you are! You lie!"

"Ask him," he taunted, folding his arms across his broad
chest and laughing up at her. "Or ask her ladyship. She
knows."

"Anything concerning you, Captain, holds no interest for
me."

"Oho! What a firebrand! Yet you'll make me a good wife, nonetheless!"

Speechless with shock, she stared at him.

"Aye—*wife,* m'dear! I told your kindly uncle that I crave, I burn, I shake with the need to wed and bed you. You cannot say there's aught dishonourable in that—eh?" He chuckled to see her face so white, her eyes stunned with disbelief. "You are mine, sweet shrew. And before the month is out, I'll have you, soft and naked, under—"

Quite forgetting the knife in her hand, she lashed at him with the end of the reins. Then, even as he lunged to catch those same reins, she drove home her heels in earnest so that the placid Missy gave a snort of shock and jumped into something resembling a gallop.

Swiftly, they passed down the other side of the bridge and along the winding drivepath, leaving behind an elegant gentleman who laughed loudly as he watched that whirlwind progress before turning to recapture his own mount.

Highview Manor was an imposing flat-roofed structure situated in the centre of a nice, if not large, park, and surrounded by once neat flower gardens. These latter were now in the process of being torn out, for the prevailing admiration of bare lawns suited the new Lord Delavale. He grudged not a penny spent on mansion or house servants, but flowers he held to be a wasteful affectation, requiring the care of far more gardeners than were needed to care for lawns and shrubs. Besides, the great red brick house, rising to a square three storeys and brightened by white ornamented balustrades, was, he declared, sufficiently striking as to require no further adornment.

Riding Missy straight up to the front steps instead of going around to the stables as was her usual fashion, Penelope scarcely noticed the further desecration of the flowerbeds Mama had so loved. She dismounted in such haste that she had to run a few steps to catch her balance. The stable boy, sprinting to take Missy's reins, gawked his astonishment that even so unaffected a lady as Miss Penelope should rush up the steps in such a scrambling way, holding the skirts of her habit so carelessly that almost he could see the tops of her boots.

The lackey who flung open the door gazed at a point two feet above the sagging ruins of Miss Penelope's hat. He had observed her headlong approach with glee, and could scarcely wait to apprise the staff of this latest impropriety.

"Where," Penelope demanded breathlessly, "is Lord Delavale?"

"I believe as his lordship is not to be disturbed, miss," drawled the lackey, his supercilious gaze still fixed upon the invisible midair marker.

"I asked you . . ." Penelope's bosom heaved as she strove to catch her breath, "a question."

Inch by inch, the lackey lowered his gaze until his perpetually bored brown eyes encountered the blaze of her hazel ones. Having discovered that she grasped the carving knife, she now thrust it at him. The boredom left the lackey, abruptly. "Yi!" he yelped, and gave a leap to the rear.

"*Penelope!*" shrilled a feminine voice.

Penelope set her teeth. For the first time since his arrival at Highview the lackey encountered an icy stare that caused him later to advise the staff that Miss Penelope was a blue-blood all right. "Take this at once!" she commanded and, having been gingerly divested of the knife, turned her dishevelled soddenness to face the affronted splendour of Sybil, Lady Delavale.

Her ladyship, having come to a halt on the last step of the staircase, stood with one hand held to the white swell of her magnificent bosom and gazed in horror at her niece. Although she was nearing forty, Sybil Montgomery was still a lovely woman. Small-boned and dainty, she had only to stand near Penelope to make that young lady feel as tall and ungainly as a camelopard, or giraffe, as some people now called them. Her

19

complexion was a delicate pink and white, the fair skin showing no sign of a wrinkle. Her golden hair had been swept up over a pad so that it framed her face, falling into ringlets at each side and threaded by a pink velvet riband that was somewhat at odds with the black brocade of her Watteau gown. Great brown eyes that could, when she so wished, be soft as velvet, were now flashing with irritation, and the cupid's bow of her mouth was set in a tight, vexed line. "Whatever are you about?" she demanded. "Your uncle has been vastly annoyed. I'faith, but you look a drowned rat!"

Penelope glanced to the lackey's faint smirk. The fact that her aunt would be so crude as to make such a remark in front of a servant no longer surprised her. One purpose obsessed her bedevilled mind: to discover if there was any truth in what Otton had claimed. To that end, she started past, saying merely, "I shall see Uncle Joseph at once and apologize."

My lady flung out a white arm and a wrist bright with the sparkle of diamonds. "He is engaged in his study at present and cannot— Girl? Are you deaf? I said he was *engaged!*"

"And I heard you, madam." Penelope walked on. "I shall make myself presentable and then see him."

"You will not! His man of business is here, and my poor husband in a foul humour. He wishes to see no one tonight. You had better get to your bed. You've likely taken a chill, which will serve you right for behaving like any village hobbledehoy! I vow I'll never understand from whence you get your breeding, for your dear papa, however foolish, was a gentleman, and your mama came of good stock . . . so I am told."

Halfway up the stairs, Penelope checked. How *dare* this vulgar, ill-bred woman presume to criticize her parents? She swung around, prepared to do battle, but the front door had been swung open again, and Roland Otton was striding with his slight swagger across the wide hall. Reminded of her purpose, Penelope hurried on up the stairs.

Lady Delavale had seen her niece's expression change, and she turned questioningly. "Roland!" She extended her hand,

20

stepping down to meet him as he came to press her fingers to his lips.

"A word, ma'am, if I may," he murmured, his eyes smiling at her.

Sybil glanced to the retreating back of the lackey. "We can be private in the book room," she said and led the way along the side hall to that large and now deserted chamber.

The instant the door closed, she flung herself into Otton's ready arms, raising her face, her lips eagerly parted for his kiss. He claimed her hungrily, and she gave a whimper of delight when he at last released her mouth only to rain hot kisses over her eyelids and nibble his way down her throat. One hand slipped, unchallenged, below the deep plunge of her neckline. Sybil moaned, her eyes closed, her body straining against him. Otton bent to the breast he had exposed and gave it his full attention, until Sybil was gasping with desire. "Roland . . ." she whispered. "Oh . . . my love . . ."

He looked up and a cynical gleam came into his eyes. "He's not like to find us?"

"No, no. He is too busied with—" She broke off, shivering all at once, and regarded her lover with a trace of horror. "He'll not leave that ghastly room until they've broken the poor fool."

"Which may take longer than your lord fancies." Otton tidied his lady's gown. "I saw Chandler when they hauled him in. I've come up against his type before. Delavale should have let me question him."

Sybil shuddered again, then caught Otton's hands, pressing them against her soft flesh and saying invitingly, "But he did not, and so we are safe, my dearest love."

He smiled down at her. She really was a delightful dalliance, and always so willing. But—"You're a hot little vixen, ain't you, Sybil?" He ran his fingers down her cheek.

She swayed to him. "What would you expect, with Joseph for a husband?"

"Yet you loved him once."

21

She pouted and said pettishly, "He had less resemblance to a whale then. Now, he lusts only after money."

"Aye, so as to keep *you* satisfied, m'dear." He grinned to see anger flash into her wide brown eyes, and added, "His present pursuit of riches may soon be interrupted."

"No, I tell you! I have instructed the servants that he confers on weighty matters with his man of business and that he is not to be disturbed under any circumstances."

He led her to the sofa and, when she had sat down, seated himself close beside her and took up her hand. He began to kiss the fingers, and then the palm. He had progressed to the wrist, and Sybil's eyes were languorous again when he asked idly, "Did you also instruct your niece?"

She frowned and jerked her hand away. "Lud, but you are in a funning mood today, Roland! Yes. I told the chit he was to be left alone."

He chuckled. "I think she will not heed you."

"She had best do so, for her own good! If she—" Suspicious of the sly amusement in his expression, she interrupted herself. "And why would she do such a thing? She despises him."

"Perhaps because . . . I told her, my life."

"Told her? What?"

He kissed her ear and answered with a wicked twitch of the lips, "Why, that I have . . . won her hand in marriage."

The lackey, crossing the hall towards the kitchens, paused as he heard the shriek that rang out from the direction of the book room. He gave a faint snort of mirth. *That devil Otton must be really pleasing my lady.* . . . One of these days milord would catch those two at it, and then . . . *then* the fur would fly!

II

On the second floor of Highview Manor were some four-
teen bedchambers, four having adjacent parlours, and
all containing dressing rooms, some of which could be
opened to an adjoining room to form a suite. The north side
was reserved to the family and consisted of the master suite and
five large bedchambers. One of these latter had been Geoffrey's,
and another, Penelope's. Of late years, however, Penelope had
been dispossessed several times and was now the occupant of a
large but rather shabby room situated in the southwest corner.
She did not turn in that direction when she reached the second
floor because, contrary to what she had told her aunt, she had
not the remotest intention of tidying her appearance before she
confronted Lord Joseph. The knowledge that Roland Otton was
already downstairs and undoubtedly conferring with Sybil
fanned the flames of her rage. It was in vain that she told herself that Joseph, who had hitherto been so determined she
should make an advantageous marriage, would not agree to her
union with his penniless henchman. She had long ago deduced
that her uncle from time to time engaged in activities that
were, at best, shady. Captain Otton's services were obviously
valued; perhaps indispensable. Uncle Joseph's reliance upon the

Captain might well have led to his agreement to such a betrothal. Hurrying along the hall, she decided that if such was the case she would have no recourse but to run away. But—to whom? And where . . . !

She came at last to the door of the room which Delavale had caused to be converted to a private study. Her knock was drowned by an outburst of profanity from within. Seething, she tried the handle, but the door was locked. Well, she would *not* be put off! She *must* speak to him before Otton beguiled Sybil into speaking for him, for if that happened, her own cause was doomed! She hurried to her aunt's bedroom. It was unlocked, and in another minute she stood at the connecting door and, not taking the chance that admission would be denied, flung it open, only to halt, stunned, all thought of her own predicament banished from her mind.

A man lay sprawled on the long sofa beside the hearth. A man of tattered and dishevelled appearance, his clothes in rags, his dark hair a tangled untidiness, his face bloodied and covered with a stubble of beard. Lord Delavale stood behind the sofa, both hands resting on the back as he blinked down on the recumbent figure through the curling smoke of a fat cigar. His bosom bow, that hulking lout Thomas Beasley, was sitting on the edge of the sofa, a dripping rag clutched in one beefy hand. All this Penelope saw in a brief second, even as a half-smothered moan rang out, a sound so tormented that it made her blood run cold. For one bewildered moment she thought the two men were ministering to the sufferer. Then, Beasley cried a triumphant, "There, Joseph! Did I not tell you I could bring him around again?"

"And about time," grunted his lordship, his cunning little eyes glinting in his pudgy face. "Come now, Major. This is most unnecessary. Why put yourself through it? You'll tell us what we want to know, eventually. All we ask is that—"

"That I . . . put the head of my . . . my friends on the block. Alongside mine . . . own, eh?"

Those words of intrepid defiance were spoken in a feeble

24

voice that caused Penelope's heart to give a violent lurch, and so deepened her shock that she stood as though rooted to the spot, quite powerless to move or speak.

The man on the sofa struggled to sit up, an effort facilitated by Delavale, who reached down to grab the ragged shirt and wrench his victim upwards. With all the bluster of the weak man suddenly given absolute power, he snarled, "Would you prefer that we hand you over to the military? They'll be less patient with a damned traitorous Jacobite than we have been, I can tell you! And there are implements in the Tower guaranteed to wring truth from vermin such as you in jig time!"

The prisoner's right arm hung limply at his side, the sleeve torn and stained a dull red between shoulder and elbow. He seemed far spent, but answered jeeringly, "Then—why delay? Hand me . . . over, and be damned to—" But the words were cut off by a gasp as Beasley seized his disabled wrist, jerking it roughly.

"This arm should have a surgeon's care, my friend. We've none at hand, alas, so I shall try to do my best for you. Poor fellow . . . I've had no experience. How do you suggest I begin, Delavale?"

His lordship flung the injured man down and watched without compassion as he writhed in silent agony. "For Christ's sake, Chandler! Why be such a fool? I'd not have Beasley minister to *me*, especially were my arm in such condition! Only tell us where the gold is hid and we'll get you safe to France. I'll even summon my own surgeon to treat you, for to say truth, I am of a gentle disposition and in great distress to see you in such sorry case."

Chandler laughed weakly.

Delavale's hands clenched, and the high colour in his cheeks rose dangerously. It was with an obvious effort of will that he held his temper and went on in a cajoling tone, "If 'tis your friends you fear for, they'll not be harmed, I swear it! Chandler? Blast the fellow, I believe he's gone off again! *Chandler?* Do you hear me? Have some sense, man! Your cause is lost and has no need of the treasure now. What can be more important than your own life? Speak up! Tell us! Where is it hid?"

Chandler roused slightly and panted, "Go to . . . hell!"

With a cry of frustration, Beasley shook the prisoner savagely, then uttered an aggrieved wail as Chandler sagged, lax in that merciless grip. "The fellow means to die!" Beasley complained. "Damn his eyes, he means to die, Joseph!"

"Tush! No man dies for an ideal, save in epic poems!" But Delavale bent lower, peering anxiously. "Do you know what I think, my Thomas? We have sadly neglected our guest. He does look poorly. . . . Ah, that amuses you, does it, Chandler? I have only your good in mind, and I cannot but think your wound should be seared, lest it become infected. . . ." He glanced up at his friend, grinning slyly.

A trace of consternation came into Beasley's face. He drew back and began to pluck uneasily at his lower lip as Delavale tapped the ash from the end of his cigar and bent forward to rip aside the fabric of Chandler's shirt-sleeve.

The sight awoke Penelope at last from the trancelike state she had fallen into. With a shriek of horror, she ran into the room. "Stop! Oh—please do not!"

Delavale jerked back with a yowl of fright. White and appalled, Beasley cried shrilly, "Blast and damn the chit! We are undone!"

Chandler struggled on to one elbow, turning to Penelope so that for the first time she saw him fully. The haggard countenance was scarcely recognizable, the cheeks so sunken, the fine mouth white and twisted. But even frantic with pain, the eyes were unmistakable and into their green depths came recognition. One hand stretched out to her in a mute pleading. Then, awareness faded, the heavy eyelids closed, and he slumped down to sprawl forward over the edge of the sofa.

All but pouncing at his niece, Delavale raged, "*What in the devil—?* Miserable girl! How *dare* you intrude here?"

"She will betray us!" howled Beasley. "I *told* you it was too chancy! Damn you, Joseph! I *told* you!"

"My God!" Penelope sobbed, utterly distraught. "Oh, my dear . . . God! What—monstrous cruelty is this?"

His face murderous, the hard little brown eyes narrowed and threatening in the flabby face, Delavale snapped, "Nothing that would trouble a patriotic conscience, girl. Is a Jacobite dog not worth the hanging and will end with his head on a spike on Tower Bridge when the military get their hands on him!"

Penelope's horrified gaze was still fastened upon the unconscious man, and she scarcely heard the callous words. "How can you hurt him so?" she gulped, wringing her hands in anguish. "Do you not know he is a dear friend of my father, and that we were guests in his home? How—" And she shrank back with a shocked cry as her uncle's hand cracked across her cheek.

"After all that my loved wife and I have endured because of your ungrateful behaviour! After all our forbearance, you have the *gall* to stand there and name a traitorous rebel a friend to any member of this family? Do you know what would happen if we were suspected of Jacobite sympathies?"

"Or—if you were discovered to be concealing a fugitive . . . ?"

The mocking voice came from behind Penelope. Faint with horror, she turned quickly, her repugnance of the tall young rake who stood there forgotten in the nightmare of this development. "Stop them," she begged, tears beading on her lashes. "In the name of heaven—I *beg* of you! Stop them!"

Otton took her by the arms, smiling down into her distressed face. "Now here's a happy improvement. It would be worth much to me to win favour in your lovely eyes, m'dear."

Like a scared rabbit, Beasley darted to close the door and lean against it as though to prevent Otton leaving.

"If I lose the prize," his lordship warned, scowling, "then *you* lose the prizes, Captain. Do not forget that it is because of this"— he gestured to Chandler—"that I gave you—her."

Otton's black eyes glinted. "Ah, but only think how much sweeter is a willing bride than a reluctant one. And—I would win a reward."

27

Beasley mopped his brow, his pale gaze shifting nervously from one to the other of the two men.

His lordship stiffened, then uttered a disparaging snort. "Humbug! You are not the sort to whistle a fortune down the wind in exchange for a handful of coins! This rebel fool must soon break. Before dawn, I'll warrant. And we shall be rich men. You, my dear Otton"—he grinned towards his niece— "doubly so."

Her own anguished gaze fixed on Quentin, Penelope knew he would not tell them. Nothing would induce an honourable gentleman to betray his comrades. But he was so weak, he could not stand much more. If they kept at him, he would surely die. Never had she felt so helplessly at the mercy of her uncle. Reaching out to Otton in desperate appeal, she said, her voice breaking, "If—if you truly love me, Captain Otton . . . oh, *do* not let them do this awful thing. I *implore* you!"

"And I wish I could help, m'dear, but"—he grinned ruefully—"your uncle's up to every move on the board, I own it."

With a relieved sigh, Beasley returned to the sofa.

Penelope caught Otton's arm. "*Surely* you cannot be so lost to all human feelings—to all sense of decency? You are not without breeding, and civilized men do not torment wounded prisoners only for the sake of—"

"For the sake of a king's ransom in gold and jewels, amassed by the Jacobites to save their miserable Cause?" Otton smiled. "Alas, dear lady, for much, much less than this, bloody murder has been done all through the history of our illustrious civilization. And for your sake, I must— Beasley!" His voice sharpened. "Gently, man! The poor fellow is far spent. Would you have a corpse on your hands before we've loosened his tongue?"

Wild with grief and rage, Penelope beat small clenched fists at his chest, sobbing hysterically, "I might have known! You are *just* as depraved! Just as—"

"*Silence!*" thundered his lordship. "Get to your room, miss! And keep a still tongue in your head, or you'll rue it, I promise! I'll deal with you tomorrow, when we've done with this makebait! And you may count yourself fortunate do I not take a whip to your sides!"

Otton frowned but, meeting the distraught eyes of his promised bride, he shrugged, spread his hands fatalistically, and sighed, "*C'est la guerre . . .*"

Penelope fled.

The rain drove stinging drops against her cheeks, and the night was very dark, but Penelope ran on, her breath coming raspingly now and a catch in her side protesting the speed of her going. She was forced to stop at last and rest for a moment. Standing there in the wind and rain, one hand pressed to her labouring chest, she waited for her pounding heartbeat to ease, while thoughts tumbled chaotically through her mind. Sometimes, during the Rebellion, she had heard snatches of male conversation, hurriedly broken off when ladies came near. Hushed talk of captured officers tortured because they refused to divulge military information. She had convinced herself that such remarks were grossly exaggerated, that such hideous things did not really happen in this enlightened age. Now, she had to face the fact that such things *did* happen. She had seen her adored Quentin's suffering with her own eyes. . . . And to think such horror had taken place at Highview! How enraged Papa would have been. How dear Geoff would have exploded with wrath at Uncle Joseph's greed and evil . . . and how in the name of God could she stop it? To whom could she turn for help? The servants, perhaps? But most of the dear, faithful people who had served the Montgomerys for decades had been replaced after Papa's death by individuals Aunt Sybil considered more suitable. Ryan, whose quiet gentility had been an inspiration to every footman with dreams of someday rising to the exalted state of butler, had been a short, rather emaciated man. Lady Sybil had let him go and in his stead hired Hargrave, a tall, broad-shouldered toad-eater who openly admired her, bowed splendidly, and made the life of the downstairs staff miserable. Papa's aging valet, Peterson, had served the new Lord Delavale for exactly one month before tendering his resignation, having advised the housekeeper that his reputation would not survive dressing a man who was not only as fat as a flounder, but had the manners of a wart hog. And so it had gone. One after another, new servants had appeared in place of the old; younger, better-looking, and lamentably less qualified. But even had their own loyal retainers still been at Highview, how could she possibly have asked their help? To give aid to an escaped Jacobite was punishable by death. And if the fugitive chanced to be of noble birth and was judged guilty of High Treason . . . She shuddered at a vision of dismemberment and disemboweling before the final savage mercy of execution. How could she ask any friend or neighbour to risk such a ghastly fate?

The memory of the torment in Quentin's eyes; the way he had reached out to her, as if knowing even in his misery that she would help if she could, haunted her. What were they doing to him at this very moment? Was Uncle Joseph busied with that ghastly cigar . . . ? With a sob of despair, she ran on until, exhausted and near hysteria, she almost blundered into a tree trunk and halted, shocked to find herself in the woods. How stupid! How utterly weak and silly she was being! Not at all as she had fancied she would behave in a moment of real crisis! Whatever had she hoped to achieve by this headlong flight? At the back of her mind she knew that she had followed the impulse of all frightened creatures—to run. But it would not do! She was her father's daughter, and Quentin needed her so desperately. She was his only chance. She *must* find a way. . . . "Please, God—let me be clever. Let me find a way to save him. Oh, dear Lord—I love him so! Guide me. . . ."

And gradually, as she stood there very still in the dripping darkness, reason crept back, and the frenzy of her breathing lessened. She must go back at once—back to her own old bedchamber . . . 'The Passion Pit,' as Geoff had been used to call it. Her heart gave a sudden leap of excitement. The Passion Pit! My heavens! If the Passion Path was still usable . . . ! And Uncle Joseph very likely knew nothing of it, for he had not lived at the Manor as a child. In the winter of 1689, the year before her father's birth, much of the roof of Highview had been blown off during a great storm, and the interior so badly water-damaged that the family had removed to the Dower House. Grandfather Montgomery had been a frugal man, and Highview had not been completely refurbished until his son inherited the properties. Joseph had never lived in the great house until he himself had fallen heir, and Sybil had discharged the only servants who might have known about Great-Great-Grandfather Phineas. A handsome devil, Phineas, and madly infatuated with his brother's wife. So deep was his desire for the lady that he had closed down the house one winter and nobly carried his wife and family out of England's rain and cold to the warm sunshine of Italy. His steward had remained, however, busily occupied with the construction of a concealed passage leading from the master's bedchamber to the room occupied by his love when she stayed at Highview. A century later, Lord Hector Delavale had discovered the tale in some old diaries and had poked about with his son until he found the illicit passage. Geoffrey had been wildly excited, but the passage ran behind the fireplaces and at that time Penelope had been an adventuresome girl of nine. Afraid that her billowing skirts might cause her to be burned while trying to get into the passage, my lord had sworn Geoffrey to secrecy. Not for another two years had Penelope learned about her ancestor's Passion Path, and even then, true to his promise, Geoff had refused to show her how to enter the passage, gleefully taunting her instead with the hair-raising notion that if ever she heard anyone coming down her chimney it might not be a lover of her own, but rather the ghost of Lord Phineas. The forbidden passage had ceased to charm and, down through the busy years, had been all but forgotten. Until now!

Immeasurably heartened, Penelope started back the way she had come. There was hope now. If she could just get— A branch snapped, very close behind her. Her blood turned to ice. She spun around, then screamed as something black and smothering engulfed her. Flailing out blindly, she was seized and swept off her feet. A man's cultured voice muttered, "Don't hurt the chit. Whatever else, she is a lady." Another voice spoke in answer; a gruff voice, less well-bred. "A lady tiger kitten! I'll go bail as she's blacked my eye—if I ain't downright blinded!"

It was, thought Penelope dimly, some small consolation. And with a little sob, she fainted.

Penelope shivered and blinked up into the anxious grey eyes of a man who bent above her. The room was brightened only by a solitary candle, but that glow illumined features that seemed vaguely familiar. A lean face, framed by neatly tied back unpowdered dark hair. She asked, "Do I know you, sir?"

This calm awakening caused the heavy brows to lift in surprise. "No, madam, but I know you. 'Twill suffice. Are you better?"

Bemused, she said drowsily, "Have I been ill, then?"

He peered at her in a puzzled way. From the shadowed recesses of the room another man said, "Mayhap she has taken a chill, Mr. Gor—"

The first man swung around angrily. "No names, fool!" He turned back to Penelope. "May one ask why a lady was creeping about alone at night, ma'am?"

Her brow wrinkled with the effort of thinking. "Yes . . . you may, but . . ."

"Here." A cup was offered. "Drink this. It will restore you."

She sipped and went into a spasm of coughing. Nonetheless, when she wheezingly recovered, she was urged to drink again.

The potent brandy burned through her. Strengthened, she wiped her eyes and, discovering that she lay on a sofa, sat up and ordered her gown before asking where she was and what had happened.

"I think you are, temporarily at least, our prisoner," answered the man whose name was evidently Mr. Gordon.

"*Prisoner?*" echoed Penelope, incredulous. "But—whatever for?"

The second man chuckled and came into the small circle of light. He was less tall than his companion and more sturdily built, broad of shoulder, with long, powerful arms that seemed to strain at his frieze coat, and muscular legs encased in dark breeches and high knee boots.

"You're mighty calm about it all," said Mr. Gordon, perching on the arm of a nearby chair. "I had feared lest you swoon once more."

The room, what she could see of it, looked and smelled familiar. Peering about, she answered absently, "Oh, no . . . good gracious! We are in my nurse's cottage! Ah! Then you must be the man I saw here this afternoon!"

Amused, Mr. Gordon said, "So she did not spot you, eh, Corporal?"

The sturdy man eyed Penelope with grudging admiration. "You did not betray that you'd seen me, miss. Or seem afraid. Perhaps you fancied me to be someone you knew?"

"I thought you might be a poor . . . Jacobite. . . ." With the word came full recollection and she ended with a faint cry of dismay.

The two men exchanged grim glances. Gordon demanded harshly, "You have a fondness for traitors, madam?"

Penelope sprang up and confronted her captors, trembling with agitation. "I have a fondness for honour, sir. In war or peace. And a disgust—a loathing for . . . for cruelty. Oh, you must let me go at *once*, for—for I—" But grief betrayed her, and her voice scratched into silence.

Mr. Gordon had stood also. Very pale now, he fixed her with

33

a piercing stare and asked in a fierce half-whisper, "Have you seen cruelty, then? Is—is that why you were rushing about in so distracted a way?"

Her nerves tightened. He might be a military spy. He might have captured her to discover if her family was harbouring an escaped rebel. However she despised Uncle Joseph, he was her father's brother. If she spoke, she could well be condemning him and his silly, spiteful wife to a traitor's death. And Quentin, beyond doubt, would be hauled to the Tower and executed. It was not to be thought of. She looked away from that penetrating scrutiny. "I have been . . . given in marriage to a man I —very much dislike," she faltered. "I was running away rather than—"

"Fustian!" His iron hands gripped her arms once again. "However grieved you may be, you'd have stayed for a valise, or *some* of your clothing and belongings. And what has your betrothal to do with Jacobites and your dislike of cruelty? Speak, woman! Or—by God—"

The Corporal came over to say urgently, "Easy, sir! There's nought to be gained by terrifying the lass!"

"If she has seen my bro—"

"Mr. Gordon!"

The gruff voice, sharp with warning, cut across the final word, but it had been sufficient for Penelope. She knew now where she had seen Gordon's likeness in the past. As he released her, she demanded with frantic eagerness, "Sir, are you related to Mr. Quentin Chandler?"

He jerked as if she had struck him. Under his breath, the Corporal swore and stepped closer. His face taut and strained, Gordon hesitated, then replied, "He is my brother. Have you seen him?"

"Yes! Oh, yes! He is at Highview."

The Corporal exhaled a hissing breath. "But—he's dead, eh?"

"No! Or—or at least, when I ran from the house he was alive."

"Tell me, I beg you." Gordon Chandler's voice quivered with emotion. "Have they sent for the authorities? Do they mean to give him up? Or are they helping him?"

Aghast, Penelope stared at him, then dropped her face into her hands and sank on to the sofa once more. "If only they were!" She raised a pale, sad face. "It shames me to tell you, Mr. Chandler. Your brother is wounded, and—and it would seem he carries a most deadly secret."

"Here's treachery!" growled the Corporal. "I told you, sir, that the Major should've trusted no man, however he—"

His haggard gaze still fixed upon Penelope, Chandler made an impatient, silencing gesture. "Who told you that, Miss Montgomery?"

"I overheard. They— Oh, sir, you *must* help him! They are—are questioning him. Perhaps, even as we speak! He is in dire need of a surgeon, and I fear that—if we do not hasten . . ."

Gordon uttered a strangled sound and turned away, shoulders hunched. Pacing to stand close before her, the Corporal eyed Penelope grimly. "Are you saying your kinfolk have sunk to torment a wounded gentleman, miss?"

She bowed her head and nodded miserably.

"Do you know how much he has told them?"

Chandler spun around. In a choked but angry voice he cried, "Nothing, damn you! Quentin would not speak. Not with all your lives at stake!"

"That is truth," said Penelope. "But he must be rescued, and quickly. He cannot—he *could* not withstand them for much longer."

With a prideful lift of his chin, Gordon said, "You do not know my brother, ma'am. Now, tell me. Is Quentin wounded to death?"

She said slowly, "I saw only that his right arm was hurt. But he is very weak. He has likely not eaten . . ."

"And very likely lost a deal of blood," put in the Corporal, gloomily.

Chandler drove a fist into his palm. "We must get him clear, Rob. Oh, Lord! To have to *stand* here and not know how to free him! While those bastards—"

He strode to the sideboard, took up a saddle holster, and removed the long-barrelled pistol it contained.

The Corporal leapt forward to grasp his wrist. "Are ye gone daft, sir? You must stay clear of this at all costs! You're no Jacobite, or ever have been!"

"Very true." Chandler wrenched free. "But do you fancy I shall stay clear while they slowly murder him? By God, but I shall not!"

"You would have no chance, sir," Penelope interposed quickly. "Without me to help you, my uncle's people would catch you before you ever entered the house."

They both stared at her. Chandler said a bewildered, "You? Why? Unless—did your papa hold Jacobite sympathies, perhaps?"

It would probably be wise to answer in the affirmative, but lies had never served her well, and so she admitted, "No. He was in disgust of the Prince's Cause. But he was an honourable gentleman and never would have treated your brother so savagely, whatever the inducement."

"Ah, so you know about the—inducement," he sneered.

Penelope met his scornful gaze levelly. "Yes. And that Quentin refuses to tell my uncle where the treasure is hid. If it is just the money, I would think—"

"But it is not just the money. There goes with the treasure a list of all those who contributed."

She paled. "What madness! Sure death for all so named!"

"Aye. And a traitor's death. But for a man such as Delavale, an extra windfall, for it would be a choice gem of blackmail."

Surprised, Penelope asked, "You are acquainted with my uncle, Mr. Chandler?"

His lips tightened. He slanted a glance at the Corporal, then replied, "I believe your father and mine were acquainted, but— well, I've—forgive me—I've heard rumours concerning your uncle. Is why I—we—came this way and watched day and night, hoping to intercept my brother."

Incredulous, she asked, "You *knew* Quentin would come to Highview?"

"He was hounded this way. We knew he was hurt and desperate, so we thought it logical he might seek shelter here. For old times' sake." He saw Penelope wince, and went on quickly, "Each instant we delay likely holds a bitter price for him. We must start now. How can you help us, Miss Montgomery?"

"I'd think," the Corporal put in thoughtfully, "as the lady herself might be Major Chandler's best hope."

Gordon tensed. "By Jove! You're right, of course! What a clod that I did not think of it!" He appraised Penelope's damp person speculatively. "Your uncle, m'dear lady, will pay highly for your safe return."

"Good God! Am I kidnapped, then?"

"Aye. To be traded for my brother."

Perhaps because this had been such a terrible day, Penelope began to laugh hilariously.

"An odd reaction to a kidnapping," Gordon said dryly. "I make you my compliments, ma'am. Most ladies would be indulging a fit of the vapours."

She gasped, "I very well . . . may be. Oh, sir—you cannot know how I pity you. If I thought 'twould serve, I'd agree, I swear it. As it is—alas, my uncle would be delighted did you make him such an offer. Delighted to be rid of me. The only use he had for me was to treat me as an unpaid drudge and to bully me into an advantageous marriage. But now I am to be given to his crony, Captain Roland Otton, in exchange, I gather, for his aid and a still tongue with regard to your poor brother."

"Nonsense! No man could be so base as to refuse the exchange under such circumstances. If nothing else, fear of what his friends and neighbours might say would surely weigh with him."

It was the argument she herself had used with respect to just such a situation, but to admit that now would not serve her at all. "The only thing that weighs with Delavale is gold. If he had any reaction to your demand, it would likely be to laugh for a week."

A trace of bitterness had come into her voice. Watching her from under his heavy brows, Gordon said uncertainly, "The fellow must be a black-hearted rogue if what you say is true. Killiam? What do you think?"

"I think as 'tis likely the lady knows her kinfolk, sir. And that we are drove to the ropes before ever we start."

"No, no—you are not!" Penelope jumped up, her heart beating very fast. "Mr. Chandler, I may be able to get you to your brother. Whether you are able to spirit him away will rest in your own hands. It will be very chancy, but—I will help you . . . for a consideration."

Hope dawning in his eyes, he said eagerly, "Lady, if you can get us to Quentin, you may name any reward it is in my power to give."

"My—my price is—that, if you escape . . . I go with you."

III

"Daffy! What is it?" Penelope closed the door and hurried to the plump abigail who had served her faithfully for the past five years and who now sat in a corner of the bedchamber, her face buried in the snowy folds of her apron.

Phyllis Brooks sprang up, her round comely face alight with joy. "Miss Penny! You've come back! I was sure as sure as you'd runned off and left me!"

Penelope wrapped the girl in a hug and, with a twinge of conscience, said reprovingly, "As if I would do so unkind a thing!"

Despite her prim and sometimes rather Puritanical demeanour, Brooks had been 'Daffy' to Geoffrey and Penelope since she had let slip the nickname during her first week at Highview. She had been hired despite some rather questionable references, due mainly to the kind heart of the housekeeper who had later joined the ranks of the deserters. Her relationship with Mr. Hargrave was an uneasy one, since she had objected to a pinch he had generously bestowed upon her bottom, and the thought of being compelled to ask him for a reference was daunting. Thus, the reappearance of her young

39

mistress lifted a great weight from her troubled mind. Fear lingered in the blue eyes, however, and she pleated her apron with nervous fingers as she wailed, "Oh, miss! I've had the most *drefful* time! You wouldn't never believe what I been through!"

Penelope regarded her distractedly for an instant, then ran to throw open the casement and peer into the rainy night. Below her, the wind tossed the branches of the great oak, but there was no other sound, no sign of life. She thought, 'Whatever shall I do if they do not come . . . ?' and turned back to her astonished abigail, wringing her hands worriedly.

Daffy decided that poor Miss Penny was all about in her head, which was only to be expected, what with the miserable life she led and that oily Captain Otton undressing her with his eyes every time he saw the dear soul! "Come away from there, miss," she urged, trotting over to close the window. "You be fair soaked. Going out on such a night! Whatever next? You'll take an inflammation of the lungs if—"

"No! Pray leave it open. I am—er, rather warm. I was running to—to get out of the rain, you see. Now, do tell me, Daffy, what has so upset you? Has that footman been pestering you again?"

"No, miss." The saucy twinkle so at odds with her manner brightened the girl's eyes. "Bingham has kept his place since I told him straight out to keep his hands in his own pockets."

"Then what has distressed you?"

Daffy lowered her voice. "I heared such a great crashing and banging about, Miss Penny. Like—like the devil hisself was capering about milor's study. Then the gentlemen went downstairs to their dinner—and well in their cups they was, if you'll excuse me for saying so. I was watching from the top of the stairs to see which one would fall down first, when . . ." Her eyes became very round; she said with solemn drama, "—when I heared . . . it."

Trembling with apprehension, Penelope urged, "Oh, *do* hurry up, Daffy! When you heard—what?"

"A . . . ghost . . . !" whispered the abigail awfully. "For

40

there wasn't no one in the study, as I do know. But I heared this drefful sound—like a soul in mortal sin and guilt—coming from in there. I was so *frightened*, miss! I ran—" She broke off with a shriek of terror and threw her arms about Penelope.

Gordon Chandler stood watching them, and Corporal Killiam was in the act of closing the window. Both men looked very grim and in Chandler's eyes was a horror echoed in Penelope's heart.

"You heard?" she asked, gently detaching Daffy's convulsive clutch.

Gordon nodded. "Where is he?"

"I'll take you, but you must let me go first, to be sure none of the servants is about." Here, Daffy uttering a small whimper of dismay, Penelope turned to give her a reassuring hug. "I know this must seem a very odd circumstance to you, dear Daffy. But these gentlemen were—were friends of Master Geoffrey. I shall say no more than that. It is better for you to know none of the business. When we leave, you must go to the servants' hall and stay with the others."

Daffy merely continuing to stare numbly at the two men, Penelope sighed and crossed to her standing mirror. The bedraggled creature reflected there caused her to utter a moan of frustration. To appear thus before the servants could not fail to attract attention. She took a cream shawl from her chest of drawers and draped it around her shoulders. Recovering her wits to some extent, but with many a nervous glance at the men, Daffy hurried to take up brush and comb and urge her mistress to sit down so that she might tidy her disordered locks. When she was done Penelope thanked her and turned to the door, but the abigail again clutched her arm and whispered distractedly, "Oh, miss! Oh, *miss!*"

Penelope kissed her. "Whatever may chance, I ask only that for the sake of any affection you may have for me, you will not tell anyone downstairs that you have seen my friends."

Her eyes blurred with tears, Daffy nodded and turned away, dabbing her apron at her wet cheeks.

Cautiously, Penelope opened the door a crack, gradually widening it until she could see the length of the west hall, past the railing of the stairs, to the door that once had been Geoffrey's. There was no sign of anyone, but a distant burst of male laughter told her that Delavale and his cronies still lingered over their wine.

She beckoned, and Chandler and the Corporal came swiftly to her side. "He is in a room at the other end of the north hall," she whispered. "It is locked, I've no doubt, and if you break it in you'll neither of you leave this house alive. My uncle has four strong manservants besides Otton and his friend Beasley, and any commotion here would be sure to rouse the grooms and gardeners."

Chandler nodded. "We are to enter through the Passion Path you spoke of, eh?"

"Yes. It leads from the room that was used to be the master bedchamber. My mama did not care for the view from the windows, so my father had the three centre rooms converted to a master suite. Do you wait here whilst I go. If I am seen, I will have to make some excuse and return as soon as may be."

She started out, but Chandler caught her arm, looking down into her eyes. "If you betray us, ma'am," he said with stern implacability, "I do assure you we shall take some of your relations to hell with us."

Penelope met his gaze gravely. "Do not forget our bargain," she murmured.

He released her, and she slipped into the hall.

At once, her nerves tensed and she had to force herself not to walk too hurriedly. Expecting at any second to encounter a maid or a footman, she passed one bedroom door, another, and another. The sounds from the stairwell grew louder as she approached the landing. Her eyes were fixed on that crucial point, her hands tight-gripped on her shawl. She almost cried out with shock when she inadvertently trod too close to the large bowl of stocks on the ornately inlaid chest that Grandpapa had brought back from India. As usual, Lady Sybil had stuffed too many blooms into the vase. A large spray became entangled in Penelope's shawl, and she caught the vase just as it toppled downwards. With shaking hands she restored it and then hurried on. The landing loomed up. Penelope forced her reluctant feet to wander past the stairs and pause while, with one hand lightly resting on the railing, she pretended to be about to descend. Luck was with her: there was no maid or footman to bow and watch and wonder. From below came another raucous shout of laughter. The gentlemen were drinking heavily, it would seem; probably, she thought, in an attempt to forget the inhuman things they had done.

She strolled across the landing to where the stairs continued up to the second floor. Again, all was quiet and deserted. Abandoning caution she ran to the northwest door and went quickly inside. Geoffrey's old room. The cold and empty darkness, the dim glow from the hall lamp revealing the shrouded shapes of Holland-covered furnishings brought a lump to her throat. If only . . . But there was no time for grieving. Staying only to whip the window curtains closed, she ran back to the corner of the hall and gestured urgently. Her bedroom door opened wide. Chandler and the Corporal hurried towards her. She held her breath until they were safely beside her, then ushered them into the room and closed the door.

Chandler whispered, "Well done, ma'am! Dare we light a candle?"

"One only. The draperies are closed, but they are not very heavy."

The Corporal took a tinder box from his greatcoat pocket and by the light of the single candle he lit, Penelope led them to the wide hearth. "It is here somewhere. Behind the fireplace."

Gordon bent, peering. "I cannot discern any kind of bar, or handle. . . ."

"Nor I." She knelt and groped anxiously along the sooty walls. "I know it is here, but I was never told just how the door was opened. I had quite forgot about the passage, until—"

"See here, sir!" The Corporal's deep voice rang with excitement. "This part where we stand is much narrower than up above us. The hearth was a sight deeper at one time."

Despite this apparent corroboration there was no sign of a door or anything that might constitute a handle, and Penelope began to fear that the passage had been sealed off.

"Logical enough that so secret a route would have been well hidden." Gordon stepped back, carrying the candle with him. "Feel along the mantel," he suggested. "Try for anything that gives a little, or can be twisted."

They obeyed, twisting, pulling, tapping all along the carven stone, but without success. In desperation Gordon wrenched at a wall sconce above the hearth, and the iron came away in his hand, leaving a chunk of crumbling masonry behind it. Three hearts that had leapt with hope knew the pangs of disappointment.

"Try the other one, sir," urged the Corporal. "Just in case."

Gordon reached across to the second sconce, but his cloak caught the remains of the one he had laid on the mantelpiece and sent it crashing to the hearth. Penelope gave a gasp of fright, and Gordon groaned his repentance. Killiam snatched up the offending article. Straightening, he cracked his head on the corner of the mantel. He had moved faster than he'd realized, and saw stars for an instant. He staggered and steadied himself by grasping an ancient iron brazier mounted on the wall beside the hearth. An instant deep creak resounded through the hushed room. The three conspirators looked at one another in breathless questioning.

All thought of his throbbing head forgotten, the Corporal grabbed the brazier with both hands and pulled downwards. Little by little, grinding with the protest of iron rusted in place for years, it lowered, the sounds becoming so piercing at length that Penelope's heart thundered with the dread that at any instant they must be discovered.

Snatching up the candle that Killiam had replaced in the branch, Gordon dropped to one knee in the hearth, holding the flame high. "Jove! Here's the door now," he exulted. "Good work, Rob! A trifle more, only."

Crouching beside him, Penelope saw a section of the chimney wall sliding jerkily in upon itself, revealing an aperture sufficiently large for a man to step through. "Thank God! Oh, thank God!" she whispered.

A hand gripped her shoulder. Gordon was watching her, an enigmatic expression on his face. "And thank you," he said fervently. "I'll confess I'd my doubts, but— Rob! That's enough! Do you stand guard now, whilst the lady and I go through."

The Corporal's face fell. Penelope hesitated. More than anything in the world, she longed to go with him. But the creaking of the brazier might very well have been overheard. Reluctantly, she offered to stay and wait. "For if anyone comes, you must see that I am the only person whose presence here might somehow be explained."

"The Corporal will deal with whatever chances. Come."

Penelope offered no further argument but, allowing him to help her scramble up through the tiny doorway, she knew that whatever he had said, they still did not completely trust her. She thought, 'Who could blame them?' and, following Gordon's hunched figure, was touched by the depth of devotion that had compelled him to walk unhesitatingly into what he suspected to be a deathtrap.

The flickering candle flame illumined only a very small section of the winding, cobwebbed walls. The air was thick with the smell of soot, the floor was uneven, and Penelope held her breath as they crept past the area of her Aunt Sybil's bedchamber. The tiny passage began to grow warmer, and by the time Gordon came to a halt, it was very warm indeed.

"Here is the other end," he whispered. "Pray, Miss Montgomery."

Penelope had been praying for some time. She heard him fumbling about, and then he swore under his breath and wrapped his coat skirt about his hand and gripped a heavy iron

45

latch. Her heart jumped once more when a sharp thud was followed by an all-too-familiar high-pitched squealing. Gradually, their dim little passage was brightened by a rosy, leaping glow.

Over his shoulder, Gordon whispered, "Hold fast to your skirts, ma'am," and stepped downwards. Beyond him, Penelope saw the wide hearth and generous fire that warmed her uncle's study. She heard a smothered groan from Gordon, but whatever he had seen that so affected him did not prevent his staying to help her. "Nobody about, at least," he whispered, lifting her down the deep step. "Have a care, now. Everything's hot."

As at the entrance, the passage opened directly behind the hearth, and the air struck Penelope's face with fierce heat. She held her skirts close and edged carefully around the glowing logs. The room was dim, lit only by the oil lamp on the desk that once had been her father's. Quentin no longer lay on the sofa and Gordon was running to the desk. She saw then that the prisoner lay huddled beside it, his wrists bound to one of the legs. She flew to kneel beside him. He looked quite dead, and she breathed a frantic prayer as Gordon reached with a trembling hand to feel for a pulse.

Quentin moaned faintly. His dark head rolled back, revealing his face deathly white between numerous bruises. A cut above his left brow had covered his eye with dried blood, but the long lashes of the other fluttered, and he looked up. Penelope's heart cramped with sympathy, and she could have wept with gratitude because he was still alive.

Blinking rapidly, Gordon laid a gentle hand on his brother's sound shoulder. "My poor old fellow," he said huskily. "What a—a damnable fix you've got yourself into this time."

Quentin's lips quivered betrayingly. The solitary green eye was suddenly glittering with tears, and for an instant there was an emotional silence. Then, incredibly, he managed a faint, irrepressible grin. He said weakly, "I thought you'd . . . never come. For Lord's sake, Gordie . . . find my sword. And . . . get me to a chamber pot."

"I'll find the sword," volunteered Penelope, her face very pink.

Quentin, who had not seen her because of his blind side, turned his head painfully. "Oh . . . my God!" he groaned.

Between tears and laughter, Penelope said, "There is a commode in the next room, Mr. Chandler. Quentin—can you stand?"

"Of course." He peered at her curiously. "Ma'am . . . surely you're not little Penny Mont—" The words were cut off by a gasp as his brother slid an arm under his shoulders and began to lift him. His teeth clamped down on his lower lip, his eye closed, and he sagged helplessly.

Whitening, Penelope held his left arm and, between the two of them, they got him to his feet. Quentin swayed dizzily. Watching his face, Gordon asked, "How are you now, halfling?"

"I . . ." Quentin whispered, "shall do . . . thank you."

Penelope flew to the connecting door to her aunt's room. She lifted the latch, inch by inch. Her straining ears could detect no sound from within, and very gradually she opened the door. A small fire flickering on the hearth provided the only illumination in the deserted room, and the open door to the adjoining parlour revealed no light beyond. She gestured to Gordon, and he half-carried his brother over, murmuring softly, "Thank you, ma'am. Do you try to make it appear as though Quentin had escaped through the window."

She turned at once, and heard him scold laughingly, "A fine way to greet me! And in front of a lady!" Faint but indignant, Quentin responded, "*You* should only know the joys of being . . . trussed up for hours!"

Penelope sped to fling open the window. The trees at this side of the house stretched their branches quite close, but it seemed unlikely that Delavale and his cohorts would believe that a man in Quentin's condition could have made the climb without falling. Nonetheless, to emphasize the 'escape route,' she pulled over a chair and set it beneath the window sill. She found the sword-belt on the floor behind the desk. As she snatched it up, her frayed nerves were jolted by the sound of approaching voices.

Lord Delavale proclaimed in an irritated bray, ". . . tell you the fool is too weak by far to free himself! You likely heard something from th' stables, is all. Where's th' damned key?"

Guiding his brother's faltering progress back into the room, Gordon glanced to the hall door and hissed, "Into the passage! Run!"

Penelope flew. Gordon bent, threw Quentin over his shoulder, and followed. Heedless of decorum or the display of her pretty ankles, Penelope scrambled into the Passion Path. Gordon set his brother down and guided him around the logs, and Quentin struggled feebly to climb into the passage. A key rattled in the lock. It was no time for compassion. Penelope seized Quentin's shoulders and Gordon boosted him up. Quentin shuddered and became a dead weight in Penelope's arms, but he made no sound. The door burst open even as Gordon jumped in and began to pull his brother's legs from sight.

Delavale let out a howl of fury. "He's *gone!* The filthy scum got *away!* Well, do not *stand* there, you stupid dolt! Rouse the house! Call the grooms! *Horses*, man! And *fast!* Oh, may he rot in *hell* for this!"

There was no chance to close the passage door. Holding Quentin's head pillowed against her breast, Penelope shrank back, trying not to breathe so rapidly, and listening in terror to her uncle's maddened bellowing. He had only to look this way and he must see them, for the dancing flames must surely light their precarious hideaway. Through those flames she saw several pairs of male legs run into the room. The voices of Otton and Beasley added to the uproar. Milord's blistering accusations against everyone but himself were cut off as Otton said coldly, "We avail ourselves nothing with all this chit-chat! Chandler had help. He was in no case to have crawled as far as the window, much less climbed down the tree! Delavale—your pistols! Hargrave, your master's cloak. Come—we must scour the

neighbourhood before someone else gets—er, claims the reward!"

And with slams, shouts, and curses, they were gone.

"At last!" Gordon stroked back the damp hair from his
brother's forehead. "He's coming round."

Penelope glanced up from her ministrations. Quentin blinked
at her, and briefly there was such weariness and pain in his eyes
that she asked with a pang of sympathy, "Am I hurting you very
badly? I am no apothecary, I fear."

"No . . . you are not. . . ." A trace of the mischief she so
well remembered crept into his eyes. "For which I do not . . .
intend to . . . grieve."

She felt her cheeks grow warm, and bent shyly to her ban-
daging.

Gordon asked anxiously, "How are you, my great looby?"

"Very much better . . . thank you, sir." With an effort,
Quentin peered about. "Where the deuce are we?" And, becoming belatedly aware that he was half-sitting, half-lying in
Killiam's arms, he said with an attempt at heartiness, "Rob, you
old scoundrel! What? Have I . . . dragged you into this, also?"

"Aye. And never try to fob me off with your nonsense, Major. I'd hoped 'twas a clean sword cut you'd taken, rather than
that ugly mess. A musket ball, eh, sir?"

"It went right through, so let us have none of your gloom.
Thanks to—you all, I'm reprieved. And so soon as this lady
is—is finished, we . . ." The brave words trailed off, Quentin's
eyes widening as he became aware of the dainty bed on which
he reposed, and the faint feminine scent that lingered about the
pillows. "The devil! Never say I am—"

Penelope chose that moment to tighten her bandage and as
her patient was thereby bereft of breath, she said gently, "But—
you are, sir. And very improperly, I might add."

49

He stared at her in dismay, his face so white and pinched that fear gripped her anew and she asked that Gordon please produce the flask of brandy he'd brought.

"I'd thought we were—well away," Quentin gasped. "Are we still at Highview, then? Lord—if we are found, this lady—"

Gordon shoved the flask at him. "Take a pull at that, it'll warm you. Hold him up, Rob."

"Here we go, sir. Do you know what I think? We may not be burying the poor Major, after all."

Penelope flashed an irked glance at Killiam's craggy features. "Here, let me plump the pillows and then you may lay him back."

"No such thing!" Quentin blinked a little as the brandy burned down his throat. "We must be away, ma'am." He glanced at his brother. "Can we, Sir Knight?"

Gordon took back the flask and stoppered it, a faint grin curving his stern mouth at the familiar nickname. "We'll contrive, rabble. Though it may be a close-run thing." He turned to Penelope, who had retreated to the washstand to remove Quentin's blood from her hands. "You are a valiant woman, Miss Montgomery. I know of no adequate way to thank you."

She looked at him sharply. "I think you do, sir."

"Well, if he don't, I do," said Quentin. "Get my pestilential self as far from the lady as possible!"

"We'd have been away at once, if 'twere possible," Gordon explained. "We only managed to carry you thus far undetected because Delavale was raising hell's own din outside. But to climb down the tree with all his bounty hunters milling about below would have been sheer folly."

"It was folly to come in here after me in the first place!" Despite that harsh judgement, Quentin's expression spoke volumes, and he added earnestly, "I'm much obliged to you, brother."

"Pish!" His cheeks reddening, Gordon looked to Penelope. "Well, ma'am? I'll get no sense from him. Can he travel?"

Quentin sat straighter. "Have I not said it?"

"You speak gibberish, as usual. You're weak as a cat."

"Starved," declared Quentin. "It grieves me to complain, Miss Montgomery, but your uncle sets a devilish poor table."

His green eyes twinkled at her, his indomitable courage causing a lump to come into her throat. She had been fashioning a square from the sheet she'd torn up for bandages, and she took it up and bent over him. "I cannot deny that, alas. And this arm must rest in a sling." She began to arrange the cloth about his arm, moving very cautiously. Not until she leaned closer to tie the knot did she commit the serious blunder of meeting his eyes again. The smile in them made her head spin, and she paused, staring at him.

He reached up to place his thin hand over her trembling fingers. "You always were a right one," he said, in the deep voice that had brightened her dreams. "Penelope Anne . . . I owe you my life."

Little ripples of a strange electricity were making her skin shiver. Her breathing became hurried and shallow. Dreading lest he see, and know, she looked down and was further flustered to see his hand clasped on hers. She noticed in an absent way that he wore a heavy gold ring on that hand, a beautifully wrought representation of a dragon's head, with two gleaming rubies forming the eyes. She freed her hand and finished the knot. "You owe me nothing, Major Chandler," she said, marvelling that her voice could be so calm when her emotions were so riotous. "I struck a bargain with your brother. I have no doubt he intends to keep his given word."

Gordon bit his lip and avoided her eyes. "You have not answered my question," he evaded. "How bad is his hurt?"

They meant to leave her! Penelope fought down the urge to demand that their agreement be honoured. It had been a nightmarish day, and tears stung her eyes, but she would not cry—she *would* not! 'Let them just try to leave me,' she thought fiercely. 'Let them just try!' And she answered, "It is an ugly wound and much inflamed, but not infected, as I had feared at

51

first. If he has rest and care when he reaches your hiding place, it should heal quickly."

"*Hiding place?* Egad, ma'am, we've no hiding place! We've to ride for our lives! Even do we escape your uncle and his people, Quentin is an escaped rebel with a large price on his head. Every hand will be against us. Every door closed. We have horses well hidden nearby, and if we can but reach them safely, our one hope is to come to Lac Brillant, which is something more than a hundred and fifteen miles from here."

Penelope's heart sank. She had cherished vague hopes that their plans were better made than this. She thought, 'They'll carry a corpse to Lac Brillant.'

Quentin had seen fear darken this valiant girl's expressive eyes. "Stuff!" he said cheerily. "What a piece of work you make of it." He swung his long legs over the side of the bed. "I've had a good rest and shall do very nicely. Have no fears that . . ." He stood, showing more confidence than he felt. And crumpled. The Corporal leapt to catch him and sit him back down again.

Inwardly dismayed, Gordon met his brother's appalled gaze and said with a rather strained grin, "Oh, you'll do, all right! I wonder, rabble, that you do not pop down the oak and toddle home alone! I fancy Killiam and I would have our work cut out to come up with you."

"Here's a fine bumble broth," Quentin muttered unsteadily. "I'd not thought, you know, that I was so . . . so blasted pulled."

The Corporal said with considerable indignation, "And why should you not be pulled, I'd like to know? From the look of you, you've not eaten in a month, to say nought of the loss of blood and misery you've endured."

"Never fret so, old fellow," said Gordon kindly. "I'm a fool for ever thinking you could get to the horses. No matter. We'll simply bring them closer. We'll have you away, yet! Found you, didn't we?"

Quentin passed a weary hand across his eyes. "I cannot seem to think. Gordie . . . how *did* you find me?"

Gordon's eyes flickered to Penelope. "A message reached us."

"I see. And—and is it known then, that I fought for Charlie?" Anxiety sharpened his voice. "If 'tis, Lac Brillant will be watched and you and my father in jeopardy!"

"Easy, easy! We are not watched. Still, we must go carefully."

Penelope, who had been thinking desperately, said in her quiet way, "I think it were better, sir, that we do not go at all."

Three heads turned to her in alarm. Suspicion flaring in his eyes, Gordon demanded, "Ma'am? Are you saying—"

"I am saying that you have no choice," she interposed. "All I could think of at first was to get Quentin out of their reach. I see now that it will not do for him to undertake such a long and hazardous ride."

"Be dead inside a week," the Corporal said with a heavy sigh.

"Quite so," said Penelope, for the first time appreciating this man's apparently habitual gloom. "And thus, gentlemen, it would seem the safest place for Major Chandler is—here. At Highview."

Starting up, his eyes dilating with horror, Quentin exclaimed, "No! Dammitall, you do not know what you invite, Penny! *No!*"

Gordon said thoughtfully, "He'd be found in one day."

"If they were searching," Penelope agreed. "But this is surely the last place they would look. Especially, sir, were you and Corporal Killiam to ride out, leaving a trail for them to follow."

"No, I tell you!" repeated Quentin fretfully.

The Corporal chuckled. "'Twould be a rare trick to serve your gentle uncle, miss. To hide the Major right under his nose, while he scours the countryside for him. Ar, but I'd give something to see his lordship's face does he ever find out!"

Frantic, Quentin demanded, "Have you lost your wits entirely? Think of what will happen to Miss Montgomery if I am

53

found here! *Gordon!* For the love of God! I am sworn to deliver part of a message they'd stop at nothing—"

Gordon blanched. "The cypher?" he gasped. Quentin nodded grimly. Gordon turned a stunned gaze to Penelope. "They'd stop at nothing, all right," he muttered. "I might've known you'd be one of the couriers! God!"

Penelope could not tear her eyes from Quentin. He was wounded, half-starved, exhausted, and too weakened to order his own fate, yet fighting against the one course of action that might save his life, because it must also endanger her. He was gripping his injured arm painfully, and she touched those clutching fingers very gently. "You should be resting, dear sir, rather than worrying so." She glanced up. Gordon was staring at her with an incredulity that brought a dark blush burning into her cheeks. Her chin went up. "There are a dozen places we can hide him," she asserted defiantly. "Places where the servants very seldom go; rooms that have been closed since my papa's death."

Wonderingly, he said, "But—Quentin's hurts will need to be tended. How could you—"

"I'll be here to help, sir." The Corporal clapped a hand over Quentin's parting lips and added with glum pessimism, "And we'd best not jaw here too long, for from what I've seen of your lot, miss, only let one whisper leak out and we'll all die—hidjusly slow!"

Penelope nodded, chilled by the possibly prophetic words. "True. No one must know. We shall have to take the *greatest* care that not a soul—"

The door burst open. Daffy ran in, took one look at Quentin in his bloody rags, and let out a shrill scream of terror.

IV

The Corporal was the first to recover. With a muffled oath he leapt at Daffy and swept her up with one strong arm, his free hand clamping over her mouth.

Gordon ran for the partly open door, but flattened himself against the wall behind it. "Somebody's coming!" he whispered.

"Then—dammit—render me up!" gasped Quentin feebly.

"Be still!" Desperate, Penelope sprang to push him down on the bed and whip the eiderdown untidily over him.

Still holding Daffy, who had ceased to struggle, the Corporal bore her to the dim corner beyond the wardrobe.

Penelope made a dart for the door as a lackey ran up. "Oh!" she cried in a distracted fashion, "thank goodness you are come! There is a mouse under my bed, I think. Please come and—"

"For Lord's sake," the man muttered, barely under his breath. "We are all to go with his lordship, miss. I dare not delay. You should be glad 'tis no more than a mouse in your room."

"Well!" said Penelope, her knees knocking but her voice indignant.

The lackey hurried off, his impatience very obvious. Penelope closed the door, leaning weakly against it. Gordon, one fist still clenched for action, sagged back against the wall. "Whew!"

The Corporal asked dolefully, "What are we to do now? Scrag this baggage, sir?"

"Heavens, no!" Penelope touched her abigail's arm, and Daffy's eyes, huge with fright, rolled to her. "Daffy, dear girl, will you give me your solemn vow not to scream if the gentleman lets you go?"

Daffy nodded. The Corporal released her gingerly. At once she rounded on him and boxed his ear. "Very free you are with your hands, sir!" she said, her fear apparently evaporating the instant she was freed. "Scrag *me*, will you?"

Gordon, who had crossed to uncover his brother, muttered a distressed, "He's gone off again, poor fellow."

Slanting a worried glance at Quentin, Penelope said, "Daffy—I'm so sorry you have seen, for I'd no thought you should be involved, but—please say you will not betray us."

"Of course I won't, Miss Penny. And mighty shocked I am that ye'd need to ask such a question. If you're involved, then I am likewise. Only tell me how I may help the poor gentleman. A Jacobite, is he?"

Lips tight, Gordon exchanged a troubled look with the Corporal.

"Another female party to our secret," muttered Killiam, fingering his abused ear resentfully. "Maybe we'd best take the Major with us, after all."

"In the Lord Mayor's coach, with a troop of cavalry riding escort," said Daffy, throwing a look of scorn his way. "Aye. Ye might as well, for he'd be just as dead at the finish." She crossed to the bed and touched the unconscious man's cheek. "So hot as any fire he do be. I'll not be surprised does the poor soul wake up out of his senses altogether."

Penelope went over to feel Quentin's brow. His head tossed as she touched him and Daffy was right; the skin burned with fever. She turned to meet Gordon's eyes. "That settles the matter, then. He cannot be moved in such a state."

Torn by indecision, he argued, "And what if we leave him here and he starts to rave in delirium?"

56

"We will gag him," she said calmly. "And we waste time, sir. One of the first places my uncle will search is Nurse's cottage. If your horses are stabled there—"

"They are not, never fear. We found a small depression under the riverbank, not too far from the bridge."

"Badger's Hall?" Her astonished gaze fixed on his face, Penelope barely breathed the words. "I've not so much as thought of it these three years. My brother and I used to play there. How on earth did you—"

"Of course I shall find it," muttered Quentin, looking up at them with unseeing, fretful eyes. "D'ye take me for a gudgeon? Won't take me no more time . . . no more than . . ." Sighing, he closed his eyes again and the words trailed into an unintelligible muddle.

The four gathered around the bed looked at one another sombrely, the quiet broken only by occasional gusts of wind that crept through the cracks to dance with the candle flames, and sent rain driving at the windowpanes.

Penelope closed the bedroom door without a sound. "You were not seen?" she asked, her eyes flashing anxiously from one face to the other.

"Lawks, no, miss," answered Daffy. "The gentleman shinned down the tree so easy as winking, and is safely clear of the house. Did the poor Major waken again, Miss Penny?"

"No. Nor stirred when I pulled off his boots, poor soul. He is covered with cuts and bruises. He will rest much easier when we have his clothes off and bathe him."

Corporal Killiam looked shocked. "Cannot do that, miss! Any minute your kinfolk might find us, so we've to run for it, and the Major can't go flitting about the countryside in a night-shirt. He must stay clad."

"We shall find him clothes tomorrow, but first, we must de-

57

cide on a secure hiding place." Penelope said slowly, "I've thought and thought, and the only place that seems logical—"

"Is the attic, eh, miss?" Daffy nodded. "It's not once in a month of Sundays does anyone go there."

"True. And only think how it would be remarked did you and I suddenly begin to make repeated trips up those stairs. Someone would be sure to put two and two together."

Daffy's face fell.

The Corporal said, "You must have a fine basement in this big house, ma'am. Only show me the way, and I'll get the Major down there and stay with him. No need for you two ladies to be popping up and down."

"We have a very large basement," Penelope confirmed. "And it presents the same problems as the attic. Even if you undertook all Major Chandler's nursing, you must have supplies, Corporal. If Daffy or I tried to bring them to you . . ."

Killiam sighed. Daffy said, "Oh, miss! It *is* a fix! Whatever are we to do?"

Her chin lifting in anticipation of the inevitable outcry, Penelope said coolly, "Major Chandler must stay where he is."

"Lawks!" squeaked Daffy, her eyes enormous and scandalized.

"Cor, luvvus!" the Corporal gasped, scarcely less shocked. "In—in your *bed*, miss?"

Well aware that her cheeks were flaming, Penelope said a rather flustered, "No, of course not. But—only think, no one comes in here, and—"

"What about when the maids clean, or change the linens?"

"Since my dear papa's death, I am required to keep my own room clean." He looked incredulous, and Penelope added, "It sounds very bad, I know, but it is true. Daffy and I do everything."

"Cor. . . . But what about when your lady aunt drops in to have a bit of a chat?"

Penelope smiled bitterly. "I wish I may see it! I don't believe she has once set foot in this room since I—"

Even as she spoke a shrill voice arose in the hall. "I shall want it in ten minutes, Simmonds, and be sure it is warm—not boiling. I am going to talk with Miss Penelope for a little while."

Her face white as chalk, Penelope gasped, "Good heavens! Corporal—my dressing room. Quickly! Daffy—tidy the bed."

Killiam sprang to toss Quentin over his shoulder. Daffy straightened the rumpled bedclothes. Penelope flew to her dressing table and began to take down her hair, her heart thundering. The Corporal had no chance to do more than partially close the dressing room door before Lady Sybil swept imperiously into the bedchamber.

"What—not abed yet?" she scolded. "I vow you are slow as treacle, girl! I fancied to find you asleep."

"How fortunate I was not, ma'am," said Penelope, "else you must have wakened me."

"Do not be impertinent. Dismiss your woman, I wish to talk to you."

Sybil seated herself in the one rickety armchair. Glancing nervously at Daffy, Penelope saw her face—frozen. She followed her gaze and her heart turned over. One of Quentin's boots was fully visible beside the bed. Standing, her knees like rubber, she said, "That will be all, Daffy. Please heat some water and bring it up. I must wash." Her eyes met the abigail's petrified stare meaningfully as she wandered closer to her aunt, trying to block that lady's view.

"Wash?" echoed my lady, incredulous. "Do you put water on your face at night? What folly! Have you no creams?"

Numbly, Daffy gathered together the sheeting that Penelope had torn for Quentin's bandages, and contrived to drop her collection over the tell-tale boot. "Clumsy me," she muttered, stooping to gather up the evidence.

Turning to her frowningly, Sybil said, "Stay! What is that you have?"

Penelope's breath froze in her throat.

Daffy gave a little squawk. "Wh-what, ma'am?" she asked in a thin, piping voice.

59

Much shocked, my lady exclaimed, "Did you remove that sheet from your mistress's bed? Good heavens! The thing is in rags! Really, Penelope, one might suppose you to have time for a little simple mending! Oh, go *on*, girl, do!"

Daffy tottered out.

Penelope wielded her hairbrush with a shaking hand.

"You should get rid of that girl," said my lady bodingly. "It's my belief she's short of a sheet."

"N-no, ma'am," stammered Penelope. "I feel sure she took it all."

Quite lacking a sense of humour, Sybil said an impatient, "Do not try to be clever, niece, it don't become you! You know perfectly well what I mean. The girl is little better than a half-wit. And only look at your bed—one might think three men have slept in it, rather than that she has newly changed your linens!"

"Yes, aunt," said Penelope meekly. "But Daffy has been with me for years, and we pay her so little, I doubt—"

"Lud! Do we *pay* the creature? One might suppose she should pay *us* for being allowed to live here in the lap of luxury."

Having recovered somewhat, Penelope said nothing, but looked deliberately around the shabby room.

My lady saw that look and had the grace to blush. "I did not come to bandy words with you." Diamonds glittered as she reached up to adjust a ringlet that had strayed from its appointed place. "Your uncle tells me you intruded upon his privacy this evening. I distinctly told you—"

"So you did, ma'am," Penelope interrupted daringly. "What you neglected to tell me was that my uncle and his friend were busily torturing a helpless—"

My lady sprang to her feet, her face pale beneath its paint, her great brown eyes flashing. "Keep your tongue between your teeth, my girl, or you will rue it, I promise you!"

Penelope stood also. "Do you not mean, ma'am, that my uncle may rue it? Were the authorities to learn—"

Sybil gave a gasp. "Wretched, wretched girl! Your uncle is a *patriot!* He sought only to—to wrest the whereabouts of—er, other traitors from that Jacobite vermin! And if you breathe a word—a single *word,* Penelope Anne Montgomery . . ."

Killiam had laid Quentin on the small truckle bed that was Daffy's occasional resting place, and was listening intently to this conversation. He would have done better to have kept his attention on the Major, for at this point Quentin tossed restlessly, and a faint resultant groan escaped him. The Corporal whipped around, his big hand clamping over the wounded man's lips.

Lady Sybil stiffened. "What was that?"

"Oh, my," said Penelope, having no need to pretend fright. "I pray it was not that horrid mouse again."

My lady frowned uncertainly. "It did not sound like—"

Desperate, Penelope was inspired and gave vent to a gigantic sneeze.

Her aunt harboured no fear of mice and was not, in fact, a timid woman. Of one thing, however, she went in mortal terror—disease. She received the full benefit of the sneeze, and she jerked back with a cry of disgust, dabbing at her cheek with a wisp of cambric and lace. "How *revolting!* I should have known better than to come into this filthy room, only to see how you went on. You have got a cold. And you spread your beastly germs all over me!"

"I ab i'deed sorry," said Penelope, sniffing realistically. "I got so wet this afterdood—but, had Captain Otton not delayed me, I—" She checked, began to wheeze, and let out another horrendous sneeze as my lady sprinted for the door.

In the dressing room, the Corporal bent over Quentin and held a warning finger to his lips. Eyes intent, Quentin nodded.

"Keep to your room!" commanded my lady shrilly, retreating to the hall with her little handkerchief clasped to her nostrils. "Wretched girl! We cannot have everyone in the house stricken with a putrid cold—especially now! Oh, I pray I may not have contracted it!" She slammed the door, wailing, "Simmonds!

61

You must make me a poultice! And I shall take a paregoric draught. *Simmonds!* Do you hear me . . . ?"

The querulous voice faded.

Penelope fairly flew to the dressing room.

Quentin was rational again, but the flush of fever highlighted his gaunt and battered features, and as soon as he saw her he demanded fretfully, "*Now* do you see why I cannot stay here?" He struggled on to one elbow. "Penny, in the name of reason, let Rob help me to—"

"To your death?" she said, smiling as she crossed to his side. "No, sir. I cannot think that at all reasonable. And, do you know, I believe we shall go on famously now that my aunt thinks I've a bad cold. In fact . . ." she added thoughtfully, "were I to become quite ill, she would avoid me completely, and no one would think it odd for Daffy to be running up and down the stairs with hot soup and an invalid diet."

Obviously unconvinced, Quentin again tried to speak, but she laid cool fingers across his lips and said gently, "Never worry so. This little room has its own window, as you see, so you will have fresh air and not be obliged to suffocate when the door is closed. I own it will be inconvenient for you, but—"

"*Inconvenient!* What fustian you speak! Madam—*will* you listen? I am—"

"You are weak and tired and ill, sir. If it is the—the proprieties that concern you, never fear. Corporal Killiam will protect me." She slanted a blushing glance at the dour man and surprised a look of admiration on his face. "And I have my maid, who will chaperone me most respectably. No, no, Major. It is not the least use your scowling so. Your brother has gone, *and* your horses, so—like it or not—here you stay."

Joseph Montgomery had viewed with indifference the ousting of his niece from the luxurious bedchamber she had previously occupied. In the matter of Geoffrey's room, however, he was adamant. He lost no opportunity to inform guests that he "still mourned the boy." And, he would add sadly, although his wife often requested that the bedchamber at least be tidied (for "dear Geoff," one had to admit, was never known for neatness), he forbade it. Aside from one or two Holland covers, the room must remain exactly as his gallant nephew had left it. True, months had passed since word of Geoffrey's death had been received but—and here the new Lord Delavale's voice would break—but there was always hope. It was not beyond the realm of possibility that an error had occurred. These things *did* happen in battle. Suppose the poor lad had been badly wounded, perhaps to the point that his mind was impaired? Suppose he should suddenly recover and come home, only to discover that all his familiar belongings had been disposed of and his room beautifully restored but thus rendered quite foreign to him? Such a shock it would be! No—my lord would not hear of it! Not until a full year had elapsed would he admit the folly of optimism. Not until September had come and gone would he abandon the hope that his "beloved nephew" might still return to reclaim the title and the inheritance which Joseph would "so joyously" relinquish.

Depending upon the nature of his hearers, his lordship might be obliged at this point to turn away and blow his nose. It was a moving performance and one that had caused several kindly souls to admire such unselfish devotion. The first time Penelope had chanced to witness it, she had been so astounded she had laughed, shocking the company and earning for herself a later reprimand so furious that she had retreated to her chamber and wept. She had never again commented upon the little drama although it had been frequently re-enacted, but that Joseph should bother to stage so hypocritical a scene, being fully aware of how Geoff had loathed him and his wife, disgusted her.

Tonight, for the first time, she was grateful for her uncle's duplicity, and she sent Daffy to commandeer one of her brother's nightshirts. The abigail scurried off and came back in a few minutes with a nightshirt and dressing gown hidden amongst a pile of sheets and blankets. "To be mended, miss," she said with a conspiratorial wink.

Killiam answered Penelope's scratch at the door. "How is he?" she asked, as Daffy handed him the bedding.

"I got him stripped down and bathed, ma'am." Killiam eyed the nightshirt uneasily. "I still think as how it'd be best was he fully dressed, just in case."

"Are his clothes wearable?"

For answer he excused himself, closed the door briefly, then reappeared holding the clothes Quentin had worn. Penelope flinched as she took those dirty bloodstained rags. "We shall certainly manage to find something better than these," she promised in a rather cracked little voice.

He thanked her, but after he had closed the door she still stood there, staring down at the rags she held.

Watching her, Daffy's loyal heart sank. She was deeply fond of her young employer and scarcely a night passed but that she asked St. Francis to please send Miss Penny a good husband. Someone in heaven must have become muddled. She'd put in a request for a strong, kindly, reasonably well-circumstanced man—not for a hunted, badly hurt fugitive with no future but the gallows. The sooner Major Quentin Chandler left Highview, she thought, the better for all concerned.

Penelope looked up, saw her abigail's concerned expression, and smiled rather lopsidedly. "Dare we burn these, do you think?"

"I don't think we got much choice, miss. Here—I'll do it. You get ready for bed. Proper wore out, you look."

"No, I'll be all right, but the Major must have food. Gruel would be best, but—do you think you could bring something?"

Daffy said staunchly that she could bring up a suckling pig did she set her mind to it, and hurried out.

Not until the abigail mentioned bed had Penelope realized how tired she was, but she could not prepare for sleep yet. She carried the rags to the grate and poked up the few coals that glowed there, contriving to awaken a flame. She had to dangle the garments on the end of the poker to get them to burn, and the shirt slid off at one point, smothering the fire and sending a great gout of smoke billowing into the room. She was still coughing and rubbing her reddened eyes when Daffy came back, carrying a laden tray.

"Oh, crumbs," she exclaimed, setting her burden on the small table. "You got 'em to burn all right, didn't you, miss? Best open the window a minute." She hurried to do so, admitting a cold blast of air, and flapping her apron at the smoke.

Penelope investigated the contents of the tray, discovering a large bowl of soup, several thick slices of bread and butter, a plate of sliced cold pork and mustard pickles, two pieces of gooseberry pie, and a pot of tea. "How splendid!" she cried. "However did you manage it? No one suspects?"

Daffy gave a disdainful snort. "That lot? There's a new kitchenmaid named Betty who's a nice little thing, but the rest of 'em got more hair than wit. They're all conflummerated because the word's got out there was a rebel in the house. Most of the men are out hunting and hoping to get rich, and Mrs. King's so busy making eyes at Hargrave she don't see anything else! I told 'em that you was feeling poorly, and that milady was fearful of your germs, so you'd be like to keep to your bed for a day or three." She closed the window and turned with a grin. "That Bessie Simmonds come upstairs with me, fetching a poultice for her la'ship. She heard you coughing, miss. Lor', but you should've seen her run! Fair galloped past your door, she did, like you'd got the bucolic plague rather than a cold."

"Oh—*what* a piece of luck," exclaimed Penelope, overlooking the medical lapse.

"Aye, miss, and about time!"

They delivered the soup and half the food to the Corporal, who received it gratefully, then returned to the small fire to share their supper. They had not quite finished when a knock sounded. Daffy gave a squeak and sprang up, snatching her apron to her mouth as was her habit when distressed. Fearing her uncle had returned, Penelope also started up in alarm, then realized the knock had come from the dressing room, not the hall. Weak with relief, she called, "Come in," and the Corporal entered cautiously, apologizing for disturbing the ladies and expressing the hope he'd not startled them.

"Oh, no," said Daffy with heavy sarcasm as she pressed one hand to her bosom. "Me poor heart jumped right up into me head, is all!"

"Likely more room for it up there," the Corporal allowed, his interested gaze on the affected area. Daffy's flood of indignation brought a twinkle into his blue eyes, and he said to Penelope, "Major Chandler sends his respects, ma'am, and would take it kindly could you look in on him for a minute—seeing as he's presentable now."

When Penelope crept into the tiny room, however, Quentin had dozed off. The truckle bed was too short for his height, and his feet stuck over the end. She crept closer, scanning him anxiously. The thick auburn hair was still wet from the Corporal's efforts and clung in damp curls against his forehead. Suffering and hardship had etched deep lines beside his nostrils and between his brows; he looked older, and so ill and exhausted that her heart twisted. Who would have dreamed, she thought sadly, that the dashing carefree youth of five years ago could be reduced to this frail and helpless fugitive? He was certainly a far cry from the dauntless hero she'd dreamed would ride up some-day to claim her for his bride. . . . And yet, if anything she loved him the more and could only be grateful that she had been here to help when he so needed her.

As though he sensed her presence he opened his eyes, and the immediate frown of pain eased into a warm smile. He stretched out one thin hand and, grasping hers, touched it to his lips, murmuring such an abject flood of gratitude that she warned him to desist before she was obliged to have such a pest removed from her room.

A faint echo of his remembered chuckle sounded.

She said, "Oh, Quentin, you should have a physician. If only—"

"No need," he interposed weakly. "You cannot guess how—how magnificent I feel. Clean and dry and well fed—and 'twixt linen sheets again! Paradise! I . . . I never . . ." His eyelids drooped. "Never thought . . ." And he slept.

Penelope gently replaced his lax hand on the blanket and crept back into her bedchamber.

Killiam and Daffy were huddled close to the dying fire, and she joined them to map out their initial strategy. The Corporal, of course, would sleep in the dressing room. The concern of the two girls to provide an adequate bed amused him. He would be far more comfortable lying on the floor of a snug room, he assured them, than when he'd "kipped" in the fields of Flanders, with rain coming down in buckets and a freezing wind, to boot. "Quieter here, too," he added. "Unless—" An arrested expression came into his eyes.

Penelope said understandingly, "I expect you have lost many friends during your campaigning, Corporal."

He agreed that was the truth and no mistake, then clapped large hands onto his knees, and stood. "You'll be needing your beauty sleep, ma'am, so I'll be off. P'raps you'd be so kind as to give the door a scratch when the coast is clear, as y'might say, in the morning, Miss Brooks? If the poor Major lasts through the night, we—"

"Good gracious!" exclaimed Penelope, aghast. "Of course he will last through the night! I had thought he might be in a raging fever by now, instead of which he is peacefully asleep. And *I* shall waken you after I get up, for Daffy will not stay with me tonight."

Up went the snowy apron again. Round with horror grew Daffy's big eyes. Her protestations were brushed aside, nonetheless. Penelope pointed out that it would not do to have her 'ailment' become severe too suddenly. "In the morning I shall go about my tasks as usual," she said with a tired but mis-

67

chievous smile. "By afternoon I give you my word the entire household will be heartily glad to see me take to my bed for a week!"

Killiam looked troubled. He started off, checked, and returned to stand at attention and clear his throat before launching into a disjointed but intensely sincere speech of thanks. "It don't never mind 'bout me," he said, by now rather red in the face, "but—him"—he jerked a thumb towards the dressing room—"he's—true blue, he is. Best officer I ever served under. One of the right 'uns. Always out in front, he were. When we went into action it was all the men could do to catch up with him." His blue eyes fixed on the worn rug, he finished, "Hadn't been for you, miss, he'd be dead by now, 'cause that uncle o' yours would've kept at him till they'd killed him. No doubting. If—if we come through this alive . . ." He looked up, his face very red now, but his gaze steadfast. "What I means is—I'm your man, Miss Penelope. Whatever. Whenever. I'll never forget 'twas you as saved him. Never!" His eyes flickered to Daffy's solemn face. He gulped bashfully, "You, too, ma'am," and bolted for the dressing room.

Penelope was so weary that her head no sooner touched the pillow than she was fast asleep. Her last thought was that she must be up early, but she was surprised to open her eyes and find the room pitch-dark. She lay there between sleeping and waking for a few seconds, vaguely aware that something of great importance had changed her life, but not quite able to recall what it was. Abruptly, Quentin's drawn face was before her mind's eye. She gave a gasp and sat up in bed, wondering if she had woken because he had cried out. But the Corporal was with him, of course. It was silly to be so apprehensive. He was going to be all right. He was going to make a rapid and complete recovery . . . please God.

She lay down again, staring into the darkness, her mind at once grappling with the many details that had yet to be worked out. Of immediate concern was the matter of suitable clothing for Quentin. The Corporal was right; he should at all times be prepared to run for his life. She considered and rejected the most logical source. Dear Geoff had been of shorter stature. His nightshirt had served, but the sleeves had been midway up Quentin's forearms. No, she would have to look elsewhere, unless—

Her schemes were interrupted by a sound she'd not heard since she and Geoff were children and had crept into Papa's bedchamber early one morning to surprise him with their birthday gifts. She could still remember how surprised they had been, and how they had stood beside the bed giggling hysterically until Papa woke up and caught them. Papa had been a powerful snorer, but the emanations from the dressing room would have put Papa's efforts to shame. She remembered then that the Corporal had started to say something about it being quiet in the dressing room, and then that oddly guilty look had come over his face. No wonder! It was to be hoped that Quentin would be able to sleep through all the uproar. But perhaps the senses of a hunted man were alert to sounds that spelled danger, and something so innocuous as a snore would not disturb him.

Settling herself cosily in the warm cocoon of her blankets, she pulled the eiderdown higher about her ears, but it was of no help. The next rendition was clearly audible; she wondered in fact that the windows did not rattle. She might be forced to suggest to Corporal Killiam that a clothes peg be applied to his nostrils, for that gargantuan snore could very well spell disaster for all of them.

Yawning, she drifted back to sleep.

V

The bedcurtains were drawn aside and sunlight flooded in. Blinking into that brightness, Penelope saw Daffy smiling at her.

"What a nice sleep you had, miss! Half-past ten o'clock of a fine—"

Penelope sat up with a shocked cry, but she was at once advised there was no need for concern. She'd slept late, which was natural enough for a lady with such a "bad cold." As Daffy balanced the breakfast tray across her knees, Penelope's glance flashed to the dressing room.

Daffy said, "I already gave Corporal Robert Killiam hot water and Master Geoffrey's shaving things, miss, and the gentlemen had their breakfast half an hour since."

"Thank you, Daffy." Penelope accepted a cup of tea gratefully. "Now, please draw a chair closer and talk to me for a little while. How is Major Chandler? Was he able to sleep last night?"

"Like a top, the Corporal says." Daffy dragged a straight-backed chair near the bed and perched on the edge, hands primly folded in her lap. "He's feeling quite hisself again, s'morning, says Corporal Robert Killiam."

"Thank heaven for that!" Penelope applied herself to a toasted crumpet. "What of my uncle? Is he come home? Is there any news of the hunt?"

The corners of Daffy's mouth pulled down. She said scornfully, "That slipperyshanks come back."

Penelope lowered the crumpet and stared at the abigail with frightened eyes. "Captain Otton? Alone?"

Daffy nodded. "The master sent him back to bring his man and his clothes. They been a'scurrying and flapping about this hour and more. One might think his lordship was going away for a year!"

"Would that he were! But—why does he not come home?"

"Mr. Hargrave says he heard the Captain tell my lady as they're hot on the trail of the rebel." Daffy giggled and added saucily, "I don't rightly see how that can be, Miss Penny, being as he's right here in your bedchamber."

It was very probable, reasoned Penelope, that her uncle in his arrogance had chanced upon the trail of some quite innocent traveller and was hunting the wrong man. Poor Uncle Joseph! She smiled into her teacup, finished her breakfast and very soon afterwards, washed and dressed, was seated before her mirror, looking at Daffy's reflected frown and echoing, "What won't do?"

"You, miss. Only look at yourself."

Penelope did so. Her thick hair was neatly pinned up, and she did not appear to have thrown out a spot during the night. Everything seemed as it should be. She said questioningly, "I—do not see . . . ?"

"You mayn't, miss. But *she* will. Any woman would." Daffy glanced to the dressing room.

A blush crept up Penelope's throat. Her gaze returned to the mirror, and she surveyed the whole rather than the various parts. She discovered a girl who glowed with happiness, whose cheeks were becomingly pink, and whose eyes sparkled joyously. She stammered, "I—er, do not look ill—is that it?"

Daffy folded her arms and pursed her lips judicially.

Penelope said, desperate, "I know you—do not approve of all this, Daffy."

"No, miss. I doesn't. For your sake."

"But—you said—I mean, I thought you were willing to help the Major."

"I was." Daffy sighed. "But—I didn't think, then—"

Penelope swung around. "You wouldn't betray him?" she cried imploringly. "Please stand by us, Daffy. *Please!*"

Distressed, Daffy clasped her outstretched hand. "You do know as I'd do anything for you, miss. Anything!"

Penelope jumped up and hugged her. "Thank you, my dear faithful friend. Now—tell me what I must do? Shall I paint my face so as to be pale?"

"Not you, miss. Me. I'll go and get some things." Daffy hurried out, to return very shortly carrying some tablecloths, ostensibly to be mended, from amongst which she unearthed sundry pots, bottles, and brushes. She wrapped a sheet around her young mistress, tilted up her face, and set to work with such confidence that Penelope said an astonished, "Why—I have never seen you use—"

"Mustn't talk, if you please, miss. Be so still as you can." And Daffy resumed her task, delicately wielding brush and pencil and hare's-foot until at length she drew back, scrutinized her handiwork, and nodded. "That'll do, I think."

Penelope turned eagerly to the mirror and gave a gasp. The glowing girl had vanished, and in her place was a sickly-looking young woman with a bright pink nose, deathly pale face, and darkly shadowed eyes. "Oh, my!" she exclaimed. "However did you manage it? I look positively *ill.*"

Daffy blushed with pleasure. "I used to work for a—a actress, once. I was fair took aback when I first watched her change her face, but after a bit I began to help her. She—she said I'd a real knack for it."

"You have, indeed! But how comes it about that I did not know you'd worked for an actress? Is she famous? Would I know her?"

72

"Oh, no, miss. She's—er, she's dead these five years. I didn't speak about it 'cause—well, me mum didn't approve of me situation with her. Nor I didn't, neither. 'Cept, she paid very well, and—" perturbed, she said in a rush, "oh, miss—I hopes as ye won't think bad of me now?"

"*Bad* of you! I think it splendid!" Penelope stood, removing the sheet. She glanced towards the dressing room, hesitating, knowing she should delay no longer in putting in an appearance downstairs.

Daffy said, "I think Corporal Robert Killiam's shaving him, miss."

"Oh," said Penelope. "Well—into the fray! Wish me luck."

Daffy did so and ran to open the door. She ventured to give her mistress an encouraging little pat on the back as Penelope stepped into the hall but, having closed the door, she leaned against it, her own words coming back to her. "I'd do anything for you, miss. Anything!" She muttered, "And there's not nothing I wouldn't do to keep you from being hurt, neither!"

"Not now, Sybil!" There was a hint of irritation in Captain Otton's voice as he removed my lady's little hands and did up the buttons she had so eagerly unfastened.

She flounced to the window seat of her boudoir and sat there pouting. "You said you wished to talk to me."

"Exactly so." Straightening his laces, he laughed suddenly. "I meant—talk, believe it or not."

"Pon rep! Something new, Roly. You are becoming staid. Perhaps you and Penelope will suit, after all."

She was jealous. Amused, he said, "Our proud maiden is far from staid. Her blacks make her look dowdy, but—Gad! You should've seen her when she pleaded with me for Chandler. *There* was passion, my Sybil. Deep and fiery and . . . pure."

"Passion!" My lady sprang to her feet, flushed with anger.

"The chit despises you! Besides which she is untouched. What does *she* know of passion? Any more than *you* know of purity?"

He bowed low. "*Touché!* But—it will be jolly to teach her what I *do* know."

She gave a little squeak of rage and flew at him, clawing for his face. Laughing, he caught those dainty wrists, swung her to him and kissed her long and deeply. When he lifted his head she lay lax against him, her eyes closed.

"None of which," he murmured, very aware of how his cards must be played, "has anything to do with our delightful, ah . . . liaison, m'dear."

My lady leaned back her golden head and blinked languorously up at him. "Devil!"

He chuckled and held her at arm's length. "Now you must listen, for this is of an urgency, Sybil—for all of us." He led her to the window seat, sat beside her and went on in serious fashion, "Delavale fancies us hot on the trail of our valuable rebel, and—"

"And you do not?" She pulled away, her great eyes wide and scared. "Does Joseph follow a false trail, then? I might have guessed it. They are clever, those Chandlers. I met the father and the elder brother once at a soirée. They engaged in a quoting match or some such thing with that dandy Thaddeus Briley and—oh, I forget who else. I was bored to death, but Boudreaux thought them very well-read, so—"

"Boudreaux?" Otton intervened sharply. "Lord Boudreaux?"

She nodded and, with a flutter of lashes and a pert shrug, said, "He was—very interested in me at one time, you should know."

"*Boudreaux* was?"

The note of incredulity in his voice brought a spark to my lady's eyes. "You find that remarkable, perhaps?"

"I find it remarkable you did not snag him! He has half the money in the world, so they say."

She made a little moue. "How vulgar you are. But—yes, I could have had him save for that wretched de Villars, who took

74

a maggot in his head and turned his uncle against me, may he rot!"

The last three words were ground out between gnashing little pearly teeth, but although the inference was obvious, Otton did not tease her this time. "I've had a few brushes with de Villars myself," he said thoughtfully. "A very nasty customer. But never mind that now—the thing is that if we do corner our man, we'll likely not haul him back here, so it's possible we shall be gone for some days. If I know Chandler, he'll be hard to break." He paused and muttered, "Poor devil."

"Good God!" exclaimed Sybil. "Pity? From *you?* Will wonders never cease?"

His mouth hardened. He threw her an angry glance, but said only, "The whole damned countryside's up. It's very obvious we're not the only ones who know this fugitive is worth his weight in gold."

"You m-mean," she faltered, "they may seek him . . . *here?*"

"It is apparently known he came this way." He took her hand and went on intently, "You must receive any callers yourself, and instruct the servants they are to give out no information at all."

"But—what shall I say?"

"That your husband and many of his people are hunting a traitor who was said to have been seen in these parts. Try, if you can, to ensure that no one discovers Chandler was inside the house. *Especially* if his kinfolks should come nosing around."

"They would not dare! Their estates—including that magnificent place in Kent—would be forfeit if they were thought to be Jacobite sympathizers." Curious, she asked, "Are they, Roland?"

"I rather doubt it. Quentin is the hothead. Gordon's a real sobersides; the type never to have done a foolish thing in all his days. But—there's a fondness, I believe, between them. Gordon *may* come, so—be careful."

My lady nodded but with reluctance. "Oh, how horrid it all

is! And with Joseph's wooden head we're liable to end in a pretty mess."

He patted her hand. "Or rich, my pretty. Enormously rich, for there's enough to ensure each of us a life of luxury for the rest of our days." She looked at him, her eyes shining at the thought of such a glorious future, and he smiled and added, "Worth the spilling of a little blood—eh?"

The glow faded from her eyes. She said with a trace of unease, "So long as it is not mine!"

Penelope went drearily about her appointed tasks, sneezing at an alarmed Mrs. King as she conferred with the housekeeper regarding the week's menus, sniffing through an interview with the silversmith who called to offer an estimate on repairs to the large epergne that had been dropped by a drunken footman, and succeeding in generally wheezing, coughing, and choking back sighs in so doleful a fashion that twice she saw parlourmaids turn aside into nearby rooms rather than encounter her in the hall.

At half-past one o'clock, she started down to the stables to look at Missy. The mare had been thoroughly soaked yesterday. Cole would take care of her, of course. Thank heaven they still had Cole. The tall, stooped, elderly man was as knowledgeable as he was devoted and had stayed on through all the changes at the main house, even Joseph having sufficient sense not to upset such a jewel of a groom.

"Good afternoon, m'dear."

Her heart lurched with fright. Even as she spun around, her elbow was seized and she was swept breast to breast with Roland Otton.

"Alas, you look not in the height of bloom this morning," he said, his black eyes gleaming as he bent over her. "Never say you hold a grudge because I sided with your uncle yesterday.

One has to know on which side one's bread is buttered. And with a wife to support, I—"

"*Sided* with him?" she interpolated, her heart hammering but her scorn fierce. "I would say you aided and abetted him, rather! How proud you must have been, Captain Otton, to watch him burn and torment a wounded man! Faith, one can but admire such valour!"

He stiffened, then crushed her closer, his arms iron bands about her shapeliness. "You've a naughty mouth," he murmured. "I shall silence it."

His lips parted, his head lowered. Expecting a desperate struggle, Otton noted only that his captive was breathing oddly.

In the second before he claimed her unwilling mouth, Penelope sneezed with all her might, her head coming into sharp but gratifying contact with his front teeth.

He swore and released her, stepping back to clap handkerchief to lips. "By Jupiter—" he began, furious, but muffled.

Penelope sneezed again, snatched the handkerchief and blew her nose with a great noise, pinching her nostrils so hard that her eyes watered realistically. "I seeb to hab caught a liddle cold," she gasped, mopping at her tears.

"So you do." He took another step backwards.

With horror, Penelope saw that her efforts had left pink and black stains on the handkerchief. "Oh, dear. I'b afraid by dose is bleedi'g, just a little," she lied. "Here you are." She proffered the violated handkerchief. "Thag you very buch."

"No, no. You keep it." He smiled without much enthusiasm since his lips were starting to swell. "My betrothal gift."

Penelope swept into a low curtsey, saw the glitter in his eyes and, even as she rose, sneezed again. It was a magnificent sneeze, but she had acted too well; her hair came loose and fell in a thick cloak about her shoulders.

Intrigued, Otton caught a silken strand and twined it about his finger. "I never knew you had such glorious hair. . . ."

Penelope stood very still, her eyes watchful above the hand-kerchief.

"What a pity I must leave. . . ." He sighed, and allowed the captive strand to slip through his fingers. "Oh, well, the time will pass quickly enough, I fancy, and then I'll come riding home to claim my—eager bride."

"Sooner," Penelope murmured sweetly, "would I be dead."

"Easily said, m'dear. But do you not keep your pretty mouth still regarding what transpired here last evening—your wish may be granted right speedily. And we *all* may be dead!" He bowed. "Think on it, beloved. Adieu."

Despite her aversion to the man, his words haunted Penelope as she made her way back to the house half an hour later. Nothing would have induced her to have acted differently with regard to Quentin. Her worry was not that his presence con-stituted a deadly threat, but that he might not survive his wound and the brutal handling he had endured. Nonetheless, she was not so selfish as to ignore the fact that others were involved. Her decision to shelter him did indeed bring the shadow of axe and block over Highview, and even if she argued that her unprincipled uncle had brought the situation about and that his wife was little better, there was Daffy to be con-sidered. The faithful abigail was guiltless, and if *she* should be arrested . . . Penelope shivered and blotted out the ghastly spectres that sprang to mind. If the unthinkable *did* happen, she would swear that Daffy had been unaware of the presence of the rebel. And if the judge should demand to know how a maidser-vant could possibly be ignorant of the fact that two strange men were occupying her mistress's dressing room, it could be ex-plained that Penelope had kept her away by professing to have contracted some highly contagious— She had opened the side door to the house, and her reverie was interrupted as, from somewhere close by, a feminine voice was upraised in com-plaint.

The worthy housekeeper—Mrs. King. And the complaint was, it would seem, directed to her ladyship. Penelope entered the hall, tiptoed to the point at which it turned into the main entrance, and stood there, out of sight, listening unashamedly.

"—filthy creature, ma'am. And likely et up with fleas and vermin. I've told and told the girl to get rid of it, but all she'll say is Miss Penelope give her leave."

"I'll own I do not care for birds," replied Sybil, impatience in her tone. "But I really fail to see why Brooks's canary should create such havoc. Heaven knows, the master and I have enough to worry us without fussing about a small pet."

"But it is horridly dirty, ma'am," argued the housekeeper in the whine that so irritated Penelope. "Throws its food and its— er, other things—all over the place. To say nothing of the diseases it likely spreads. They do say—"

"*Diseases?* Faith, I never thought of that! Yes, yes—you are perfectly right. Tell the girl to get rid of the pest. Oh, and before my husband's man leaves, send him up to my sitting room."

The housekeeper murmured a humble acknowledgement, and Penelope heard the jingle of her keys as she hurried away. Triumphant. Horrid creature! Well, Daffy should *not* have to part with Jasper. How much trouble could a tiny canary cause? The poor girl had little enough of joy in her life, and she loved that silly bird devotedly. Penelope peeped around the corner. She saw the departing flutter of the black gown as Mrs. King hurried towards the back stairs. Lady Sybil stood looking down at something she held, then she walked along the hall and entered the breakfast parlour. There was something almost furtive in her manner, and why in the world would she go in there at this hour? Whatever the reason, however, such a move fitted very well into Penelope's schemes. She followed, treading as softly as possible. When she drew level with the door, she discovered her aunt, standing by the far window, engrossed in reading a rather battered document. Penelope walked in, edged as close as she dared, then emitted one of her best sneezes. She had become rather good at it, she thought, and the result was shattering.

Lady Sybil uttered a piercing shriek, leapt into the air, and lost her grip on the letter. She juggled with it frantically and, having somehow regained it, whipped it behind her back and spun around. Penelope had hoped to alarm the lady, but was considerably astonished by so violent a reaction.

Sybil was deathly pale, and an expression of stark terror lit those dark eyes. "*Wretched* girl," she shrilled. "Must you creep and slither about, spreading your germs to every corner of this house? I wonder you did not startle me into a spasm!" She clutched at her heart and sank into a nearby chair.

Despite these manifestations of weakness, Penelope noticed that there was no trace now of the document she had been reading. Perhaps it was a love note. The question would then become—from whom? Otton, most likely. Although, with Sybil, one could never tell. The only person *not* likely to have sent such a missive was her husband.

"I was goi'g to ask," Penelope mumbled, taking a dutiful step backwards, "if I might be excused frob talki'g to the architect this afterdood. I ab feeli'g rather—"

"Yes, yes! Did I not tell you to keep to your room?"

"Yes, ma'am. But—I thought you just me'd last dight."

"Oh—well, I did. But—for heaven's sake, we shall likely not add the new ballroom until next Spring at all events. Get to your bed, do! You look perfectly horrid. And whatever happened to your hair? Cannot your stupid woman pin it better than that?"

Penelope lowered her eyes and imparted meekly that she'd had an encounter with Captain Otton.

With oblique logic and inward fury, my lady scolded, "Do not be crude. You may stay in bed for a day or so, at least. *I* have no wish to become ill."

"Thag you. But—suppose U'cle Joseph cobs hobe . . ."

"Your uncle will likely be gone for several days." My lady rose, her eyes cold. "And you had best hope his mood improves before he discusses *your* conduct of yesterday!"

At any other time those ominous words would have thrown

Penelope into an agony of dread that she was soon to be subject to another of her uncle's shouting rages. Today, however, she didn't give a button. Quentin would have several days in which to recover; several days of rest and warmth and care. Hope burgeoned in her heart, and it was all she could do not to dance her way up the stairs.

Her bedchamber was empty and, despite her efforts to bring a little cheer into the stark room, it looked drab and shabby. Penelope scarcely saw the worn rugs, the ill-matched furnishings, or the faded curtains. Her eager gaze flashed to the dressing room, and she swung shut the hall door and tiptoed across the room, only to halt in alarm.

From inside came the sounds of strife: voices low and rasping, stumbling, feet, a thump as something fell. Otton must have come! He had crept up here to waylay her, perhaps, and discovered the fugitive! Frantic, she scanned the room for some kind of weapon. Daffy had not yet removed the large copper pitcher in which she had brought up the hot water this morning. Penelope snatched it up and wrenched open the door.

She had maligned Captain Otton unjustly. Quentin and the Corporal were the two who struggled so desperately in the tiny room. Penelope was amazed to note that the invalid was dressed in shirt, breeches, and stockings, but no boots, and that this man who had seemed at death's door yesterday afternoon now strove so effectively that the Corporal was hard put to it not to hurt him.

"Sir," wailed Killiam. "Oh, sir—let be! For Gawd's sake, Major—I don't want to hit you!"

"Then give over," snarled Quentin. He wrenched free and up came his left arm, the fist knotted and looking competent, no matter how thin.

The Corporal dodged, saw Penelope, and cried, "He don't know what he's about, miss! Help me—else I must knock him down, surely!"

"Nonsense," said Penelope, recovering her wits. "Step on his toe, merely."

Killiam trod down hard. Quentin swore and doubled over, clutching his foot, then sank on to the edge of the bed, head down, panting heavily.

Penelope exchanged a worried glance with the Corporal. "Did you mean to leave us so soon, Major Chandler?" she asked formally.

"Naturally . . . enough . . ." he gasped, without looking up.

"I'd dozed off in the chair, miss," the Corporal confessed miserably. "Woke up to find him all dressed and trying to pull on a pair of boots. Don't ask me where he got the duds—I dunno. But he was ready to creep off, just like you said. And him no more ready to walk than any infant!"

"What folly," she declared, frowning. "Quentin—I gave you credit for—"

"For what, ma'am?" His head jerked up. He was very white about the mouth, his bruises vivid against his pallor. "Did you credit me with—with some belated . . . sense of responsibility, perhaps?"

"Had you that, sir," she said, sitting down beside him, "you'd not be trying to rush out before you are strong enough! I'd give you an hour, perhaps less, before you blundered into my uncle's men. Faith, but I'd not fancied you so enjoyed his care on Sunday that you yearn to return to it!"

"I do assure you, he'll not get his hands on me again. Not while I live."

He spoke softly, but there could be no doubt that he meant it, and Penelope quailed, a terrified feeling of helplessness chilling her. She managed a scornful look. "La, but here's a high flight! And quite unnecessary. My uncle is off chasing a will-o'-the-wisp, and not expected to return for some days, so you may be easy until—"

"*Easy!*" His voice sharp with emotion he cried, "How may I be easy whilst I skulk here like—like a damned Judas goat, knowing I bring the shadow of death over you all? Can you guess how I felt when I looked out of the windows and saw that bastard pawing you—and you not daring to so much as slap his filthy face?"

So that was what had brought all this about! She hid her elation that he would care so much that Otton had forced his attentions on her, and said, "Did you suppose I was pleading for your life in exchange for my virtue? It would not work, I think. Otton's by far too mercenary."

Quentin scowled at her. "For Lord's sake, Penny!"

"Have I disappointed you?" She investigated the top of her head with a cautious hand. "Oh, dear. And I'd thought I did rather well . . ."

"You little wretch," he said uncertainly. "*What* did you do?"

"Such a pity you missed it. But I suppose you were too busy breathing fire and smoke, dragging on your purloined clothes, and"—she fluttered her lashes at him—"and vowing to avenge my outraged innocence."

The Corporal grinned and folded his arms across his deep chest. Not to be so easily fobbed off, Quentin demanded, "What did I miss, Penelope Anne?"

"When I was clasped against his heart," she said demurely, "and he bent, panting with passion, to claim my reluctant lips . . ." Quentin was scowling again, with such delicious grimness, and she said with a sigh, "I sneezed all over him. Dreadfully. Wherefore the wicked Captain has a badly swollen mouth."

Killiam laughed delightedly, then clapped a hand over his mouth. "Jolly good, miss!" he said in a more subdued tone.

Quentin smiled. "I'll wager he was ready to strangle you. Would I'd seen it. Nonetheless, with that foulness lurking about—"

"But he will not continue to lurk. My uncle merely sent him here to bring clothing and his man. Even now, they pack for an absence of several days. They appear to labour under the delusion they have you cornered, dear sir."

"Well, *that's* a slice of luck," said the Corporal.

Quentin muttered thoughtfully, "Unless my brother is this will-o'-the-wisp Delavale follows."

"Oh, how splendid of him," cried Penelope, clapping her hands. "Yes, he is just the type to thoroughly enjoy leading Uncle Joseph on a wild-goose chase."

Reverting to his glum manner, the Corporal grunted, "And liable to become a *cooked* goose!"

Quentin winced, and Penelope could have shaken his devoted but disastrous minion. "Mr. Gordon Chandler seemed to me a most capable gentleman," she said swiftly. "And I do think one of you might have noticed how ill I look."

Her small diversion succeeded. At once remorseful, Quentin said, "Yes, I did notice you looked hagged when you first came in, poor girl. Have you truly taken a cold, then? Lord knows, with all this worry and uproar, I'd not wonder at it."

"The only trouble is," said Penelope, taking out Otton's handkerchief and inspecting it, "my illness comes off rather easily. I shall have to be more careful."

Curious, the two men moved closer, and she showed them the pink and black stains. Staring at her, Quentin exclaimed, "Jove! It's masterly. Do you say that you are perfectly well?"

"Not very loudly," she answered, twinkling at him. "My 'cold' won my freedom from that pestilential Otton, and a happy exile to my bed. Oh, my performance was superb, I'll own, but without Daffy's talents I doubt I could have convinced my aunt."

Awed, the Corporal said, "Miss Brooks did it? Cor! I don't see how she—"

The outer door flew open with a crash. Penelope leapt up, her heart in her throat. Killiam whirled around, and Quentin struggled to his feet, prepared to fight for his life.

Someone was running for the dressing room. Penelope sprang to the door but it was too late, and she uttered a shocked little cry as it was wrenched open.

Her eyes reddened, tears streaking her cheeks, her hands

wringing frantically, Daffy sobbed out, "Miss Penny . . . they're going to take him! Oh, but they mean to take him!"

Blanching, Penelope cried, "Are we found out, then? Are they coming here?" From the corner of her eye she saw that Quentin had produced a serviceable-looking dagger. Beside him, the Corporal gripped a large horse pistol. Both men looked grim and desperate.

"It's so cruel," sobbed Daffy. "He shouldn't have to die . . . just 'cause he's got some naughty habits."

"Wh-what . . . ?" breathed Penelope.

"Only last night he sung so sweet to me whilst I lay in bed. Even with the cover right up over him."

"Good . . . heavens . . . !"

The corners of his mouth twitching, Quentin murmured a pious, "I deny everything!"

Bewildered, Killiam stared from the Major to the distraught girl.

"Mrs. King says I can either give him up, or—or I shall be turned off," wailed Daffy. "Oh . . . miss . . . !" She threw her apron over her face and wept copiously.

Penelope drew a deep breath of relief. "It's all right, gentlemen. Her canary is at risk, merely. Do please lie down again, Quentin."

It was clear that the two men were strangling on suppressed mirth, and she left them, closed the door, and led Daffy to a chair. "Sit here. And try to compose yourself."

Something about that quiet voice broke through the girl's woe. She lowered her apron and blinked through her tears. "I—I don't want to lose that little rascal, Miss Penny," she said hoarsely. "You—you will help me?"

"As you were willing to 'help' Major Chandler?"

Briefly, Daffy looked frightened, then she lowered her reddened eyes. "I went in there to take their bowls and—and the Major begged as I should fetch him something to wear. I was only looking for to help—"

"You know how desperate he is to be gone from here—for our sakes. And you knew he was much too weak to leave here today. Yet when you saw me downstairs you said no word of this."

"Corporal Robert Killiam was there, and—"

"And fast asleep. Which you also knew."

The abigail was shaking visibly, but Penelope hardened her heart. "I cannot abide treachery, Brooks. I am of a mind to—"

With a wailing moan, Daffy flung herself to her knees. "Don't ye say it! Dear Miss Penny, as I do so love—don't ye never say such a awful thing!" And burying her face against Penelope's skirts, she wept again; a different sobbing this time, less frantic, but revealing a deeper grief.

Penelope looked down at that desolate figure, wondering remotely why it meant so much to the girl to stay in a house where she was treated badly and paid such a penurious wage.

"I'll own up," Daffy mumbled. "You're right, miss. I did it—deliberate, like." She slanted a frightened glance upwards, saw Penelope's frown, and whimpered, "I see a look in your eyes, Miss Penny. A look I'd never seen before. And—oh, miss! He couldn't never bring you *nothing* but fear and sorrowing. And a cruel horrid death, mayhap. I'd sooner see you wed to that horrid Otton, than— Your dear papa and—and Master Geoffrey, they wouldn't want *that* kind of a man for you, miss! They wouldn't!"

Appalled, Penelope sank into a chair. "You would have sent him to his *death*? To try to protect me?"

"No, no! He's much stronger already. And—and he would have the Corporal and likely—"

Penelope leaned forward. Very softly, she interrupted. "If you truly love me, Daffy, listen to me. If anything—*ever*—happens to Quentin Chandler because of you . . . for so long as I live I shall never, never forgive you."

Daffy's sobs ceased. For a moment they remained thus, silent and intense, looking into each other's eyes. Then Daffy said, not as servant to mistress but as woman to woman, "I didn't know. It was so soon, I didn't think . . ."

"I met him five years ago, you see."

"Ah. And I didn't understand how it were. I am so sorry. So very sorry." She made the sign of an X across her bosom and said very solemnly, "Cross my heart and hope to die—nothing won't happen to the Major 'count of me, Miss Montgomery. Not though I'm tied twixt two mad horses and torn asunder, it won't!"

The unlikelihood of such a gruesome fate brought a furtive smile into Penelope's eyes, but the use of her surname affected her almost as much as Daffy had been stricken by being addressed in such a way, and her vision blurred. The two girls fell into each other's arms and embraced tearfully, then drew back, each drying her eyes in some embarrassment.

"You do forgive me, then?" Daffy asked timidly.

"Now that we understand each other, of course I do."

"And—and you won't *never* call me—Brooks—again, please, miss?"

"Not unless you give me cause—dear Daffy."

With a sigh of relief, Daffy stood up, shook out her rumpled skirts and straightened her apron. "In that case, Miss Penny— what about my Jasper?"

VI

espite his insistence to the contrary, Quentin's brief period of activity had exhausted him, and when Penelope went in later to change the bandages, he was fast asleep. With an inward sigh of relief, she decided not to waken him, but stayed for a little while, holding a whispered conversation with the Corporal before returning to her room and settling down to some mending. The afternoon was cool, and she would have liked to start the fire, but her aunt would likely suppose her to be in bed and warm enough, and there would be trouble if she dared use too much coal at this season of the year.

Quentin awoke when Daffy brought up a late luncheon, and half an hour later Penelope again gathered her salves and lint and bandages.

Watching her, Daffy saw the white hands tremble. She said compassionately, "Let me do it this time, Miss Penny."

Penelope struggled to overcome her dread of treating the wound again. "I do not quite know why I am so—so overset today," she said threadily. "I did fairly well . . . last evening."

"'Course you did. You was wonderful. But we was all so frightened that the Major would be killed, or that we'd all be

88

found. I think we sort of—outdone our selves. Still, there's no reason you should have to—"

"Yes. There is." And knowing that her dread was rooted in the fact that the hurt was Quentin's, that *his* was the flesh so cruelly torn, Penelope pulled back her shoulders. "I must not be a coward. Heaven knows, the Major is not."

Despite those resolute words, she prayed for strength as she cut through the bandages. The Corporal had told her that Quentin had been shot by a lone trooper early on Friday morning. His desperate ride for life, his capture two days later by her uncle, and Lord Joseph's subsequent brutality had done nothing to expedite the healing process, but at least the inflammation was reduced today. Penelope worked as carefully as she was able, but it was impossible not to cause her patient considerable discomfort. He endured bravely, but each time he flinched, she did. She could not know how white and stricken she looked and, glancing up, was surprised to find his eyes upon her filled with such anxiety that she could not keep from smiling. At once his pale lips curved into an answering smile. The awareness that he had been worried for her sake gave her the strength to master her nausea, and she chattered easily, drawing from him an occasional breathless response.

When she finished, the Corporal had ready a glass of wine for all of them, and they toasted one another in grateful relief that the ordeal was over. Afterwards, Quention dozed off, having thanked her for her care of him, those thanks echoed by the Corporal when he opened the door for her.

"I don't know many ladies would be able to face that," he whispered, glancing back over his shoulder at the injured man. "Them damned musket balls! Asking your pardon, ma'am, but it'll be months afore he's himself again, specially with the burns what your uncle—"

"No, no," Penelope intervened hurriedly. "Major Chandler is young and basically in excellent health. I doubt he would be so pulled were it not for all these weeks of being starved and

89

hunted. Even so, I fancy he will heal fast enough can he but have three or four more days here."

"Much chance there is of staying here that long," he grunted. "All the Major can think of is to get himself away from you, miss. And how I'm to keep him here once he starts to get well, is more than I know. He's so stubborn as any ox, Miss Penelope, once he sets his mind to something. By tomorrow, or the next day, there'll be no holding him, and so I warn you. I knows him!"

"To leave here before Thursday would be madness! You cannot even think—" She checked. The Corporal was listening intently. Penelope heard the footsteps then and ran frenziedly for her bed, whipping the supplies under it, and barely having time to pull the eiderdown close up around her chin and think that it was probably only Daffy again, before the door opened.

But it was not Daffy. A housemaid carried in a tray with a pot of tea and biscuits and a bowl of fresh fruit. She was a pretty creature with glistening red-gold hair, friendly blue eyes, and an air of gentility that was intriguing. Her name, she said, was Betty, thus confirming Penelope's thought that she must be the new housemaid of whom Daffy had spoken. She had asked permission to bring up the tray, and she said sympathetically that she knew what it meant to be sick and all alone. Kindness had become a rare commodity in Penelope's life, and she was touched. She was also alarmed, because it had been a very close call that must not be repeated. After the maid had gone, she got out of bed and went to the dressing room to reassure the Corporal. She then changed into her nightdress, determined to wear it constantly from now on, so as to be prepared in case somebody else paid her a surprise visit.

All was quiet, however, until Daffy arrived in a short while, carrying the cage with her reprieved canary. She was aghast to find her mistress clad in night rail. It was in vain for Penelope to point out that her flannel nightdress with its high collar and long sleeves covered her far more decorously than had many of the pretty gowns she'd worn before going into blacks. Daffy was

90

much shocked. "Only think, miss," she murmured, as they sat mending together, "if it should ever become known as ye'd been in this room—all night. On your *own!* With not so much as a lock 'twixt you and . . . *them!*"

Her face hot, Penelope straightened the pillowcase she was hemming. "Well, it will not become known. And whatever you may imply, Daffy, you certainly are aware I came to no—er, harm, for they are honourable gentlemen, both."

Daffy sniffed, unconvinced.

"Besides," Penelope went on, soothingly, "you will be sleeping in here tonight, so I shall be properly chaperoned and we all may be comfortable."

It was not to prove her most successful prediction.

Quentin continued to sleep throughout the evening. After Daffy had brought their dinner upstairs, the Corporal, a gregarious individual, engaged Penelope in a whispered colloquy and they chatted for over an hour, formulating elaborate plans for their escape, each of which eventually had to be discarded for one reason or another.

Daffy reappeared with an armful of books that were gratefully received. However, in snatching the volumes from the shelves of the book room, Daffy had not taken time to read the titles. She had brought a treatise on *The Occasional Onset of Baldness Following an Interval of Fever*; a *Life of Pedro Arias de Avila*; a dissertation upon the trials of a missionary group attempting to teach dressmaking to a tribe of head-hunters in Equatorial Africa; and an epic poem detailing the struggle of an Archbishop against his lust for a flower seller. Penelope selected the biography, and with a hopeful gleam in his eye the Corporal retired to look into the activities of the lustful Archbishop, aided by a candle.

Penelope had supposed that the story of Señor de Avila would contain some of the colour and customs of a distant land. Instead, it proved to be a particularly gruesome recounting of the deeds of a gentleman who had evidently spent most of his ninety years executing anyone who might in some field of endeavour prove superior to himself. An hour later, Penelope set the book aside with a shudder and snuggled under the covers.

She was tired and soon fell asleep, to wake briefly when Daffy came in. The abigail was extremely nervous about disrobing "in front of Corporal Robert Killiam," and although Penelope reminded her drowsily that the Corporal would not think of opening the door without first knocking and receiving permission, Daffy spent ten minutes of painful struggle shedding her garments from beneath the protective but encumbering folds of her voluminous nightdress.

Penelope drifted back into slumber. She was again jolted awake at some later hour. At first she entertained the notion that Daffy was talking in her sleep, but a moment afterwards a throaty gobbling informed her that the 'talker' was Jasper. It was a small annoyance, she thought, to which one could quickly become accustomed. Her eyes opened a good deal wider when the gobbling became a soft chirping, interspersed by occasional but quite shrill warbles. Gritting her teeth, Penelope pulled the eiderdown higher about her ears and at last fell asleep.

Daffy slept like a log, but she was prone to making sudden violent turns during which she sat halfway up and lay down again, taking most of the bedding with her. Penelope was wrenched awake by two such upheavals and, having considered the benefits of strangling her faithful abigail and rejecting the notion, was once more wooing sleep when a new disturbance brought her sitting bolt upright in bed.

Someone was throwing gravel at the windowpane. Her heart leapt. Perhaps Gordon Chandler had come back! Perhaps he had managed to get through the patrols and had brought a fast coach in which to bear them safely away!

She threw back the blankets and sped eagerly to the lighter grey square that was the window. Before she reached it, however, she gave a squeal as her bare foot came into excruciating contact with something hard and sharp. Moaning softly, she limped over to the window seat where she knelt and parted the curtains.

The moon rode high on the wings of a wide-spreading cloud;

the night sky was jetty black close at hand, but with a greying edge at the eastern horizon that told of the inexorable creep of dawn. The empty flowerbeds beneath the window and the patch of lawn between it and the drivepath were quite visible and completely deserted.

Puzzled, she brushed from the sole of her foot whatever it was she had stepped upon, only to tense, her attention caught by a movement at the corner of the house. A man's tall figure appeared. So it *had* been Gordon! She threw open the window and leaned forward, but the call she prepared to utter was stifled abruptly. A pipe glowed red as the man strolled nearer, and the moonlight revealed that his coat was also red. Penelope stared, appalled, as the soldier waved a friendly hand. Jerking her head around she distinguished a second man approaching from the east face of the house; a man who carried a musket slung across one shoulder, with above it the deadly gleam of a bayonet. She shrank back, and knelt there, her brain spinning. So Highview was under guard! Did they know, then, that Quentin was in the house? Were they here to keep him from escaping? Or did they hope to apprehend him if he *did* come?

She wrung her hands distractedly. Surely, if they suspected he was here, the soldiers would hesitate not an instant to arrest him. To arrest them all! They could not know. And there had seemed to be no urgency about their movements. They had behaved more as men mildly bored than as men guarding—or preparing to apprehend—a dangerous fugitive. Biting at her knuckle, Penelope considered waking the Corporal. She decided it would be better to let him get a good night's sleep. He might stand in need of all his wits tomorrow. In the morning she would try to discover why the soldiers were here. . . .

Preoccupied, she started back to her bed and did a small anguished dance as she again trod on some sharp particles. Bending to dust them from her feet she encountered more of the same. It came to her that the window had been closed when first she had reached it. And besides, there had been no sign of anyone flinging gravel to awaken her. Where then had this dreadful stuff come—

A sudden scrambling sounded above her. As she started up, she was deluged by a flying shower of debris from the bird cage. Her gasp of shock was echoed by a shrill squealing, for all the world like avian mirth.

It was Penelope's first experience of Jasper's 'naughty habits.'

"Wake up, miss," cried Daffy cheerfully, pulling back the bedcurtains. "I know as you slept so snug as a bug in a rug, for there was not one peep out of you all night long." It occurred to her then that her mistress lay staring at her with a rather odd expression, and she added confidently that Miss Penny would feel better after she'd et her nice breakfast. She then tripped off to deliver some smuggled bread and sliced ham to their guests and to exchange some pleasantries with the Corporal. Returning, her cheeks pink and her eyes very bright, she stood guard while Penelope washed, and assisted her to change her nightdress while observing in a pleasantly flustered way that one could always tell a military man "because they do all be such owdacious flirts!"

"Speaking of which," said Penelope, searching her face anxiously, "have you noticed any soldiers loitering about Highview?"

Daffy gave a gasp, and gripped her apron convulsively. "Oh, miss! You know, then? I'd not said nothing 'cause I couldn't find out what they're up to, but Betty's spoke with them. Quite a flirt she be, and not what I'd first thought her, I must say."

"Did she learn anything?"

"Only that there's two of 'em what comes at sundown and prowls about the grounds after dark. Only . . . today there's another pair, miss. Trying to make their silly selves invisible. As if everyone hasn't seen 'em lurking about in the shrubbery!"

Penelope's heart sank. "But—Betty doesn't know *why* they're here?"

"She says they're likely keeping a eye on all the big estates, thinking the poor Major, being Quality, might be given shelter." Brushing out Penelope's long hair, Daffy sighed heavily. "Not going to make it any easier to get him away, is it, miss?"

Penelope agreed and was lost in gloomy introspection until a shriek from Jasper reminded her of his nocturnal activities, and she put his owner in full possession of his behaviour.

Daffy was remorseful. Jasper, she admitted, *did* scratch about "just a little," but she was quick to clean up after him, and she would put the cage where he wouldn't bother miss again.

"In the south meadow?" enquired Penelope.

"Maybe I could tuck him in with the gentlemen," Daffy proposed innocently.

"You most assuredly could not! Major Chandler must have every possible moment of rest and quiet."

"Aye, well, he be a new man today, though that great foolish Corporal Robert Killiam would likely have you believe as the funeral's next week! Would you like me to put your hair in ringlets like you used to—"

"Good gracious, no! This is no time for me to try to improve my looks. Pray put on my 'illness' again, and tell me—is there news of my uncle?"

Daffy fashioned the thick tresses into a braid and wound it around her mistress's head. Through a mouthful of hairpins she mumbled, "If there was, I s'pose her la'ship would've cancelled her dinner party. But she hasn't, so—"

"Her—*what?*" Startled, Penelope exclaimed, "She cannot give a dinner party! We are in mourning!"

"Milor's away, miss," said Daffy with a cynical shrug. "And Lady Sybil's always complaining how lonely it is here. Though, was you to ask me, she finds her share of company."

Furious, Penelope muttered, "I suppose she would say that in three months she can put off her blacks."

Daffy uttered a scornful snort and took out her paints and

brushes. They did not converse while the wan look was under construction, but Penelope's mind was busy. She decided that she must put in an appearance downstairs later on and try to come at why the soldiers were here and for how long they would stay. The prospect was a dismal one, for once she resumed her usual routine she would be expected to take her meals in the dining room with her aunt, and it would be so much more difficult to smuggle food up here. Troubled, she put on her dressing gown when Daffy was finished, and went to the dressing room.

Her soft knock was answered by Quentin, wearing Geoffrey's dressing gown over his nightshirt, the sight of which brought a momentary grief to her eyes. Quick to note that changed expression and to divine the reason for it, he threw her a courtly bow and replied to her protest by declaring breezily that he was in excellent point and ready to race from Land's End to John o' Groats if need be.

Penelope laughed at him, her heart soaring because the glitter of fever had left his eyes, his grin was as carefree as she remembered and, although he was still thin and pale, the bruises did not look quite so lurid.

His own gaze had become intent also. He said with a trace of irritation, "You are tired, I think. I doubt you slept well with your maid sharing your bed." He ushered her to the chair and, apparently not hearing her request that he lie down again, instead sat on the neatly made bed.

Penelope glanced around curiously.

"If you're looking for my batman," he said whimsically, "he's stepped out to the barber."

A derogatory snort wafted from behind the sheet that had been stretched across one corner of the little room to form a private area.

"Good heavens," cried Penelope in exaggerated dismay. "Never say we are—all alone, sir?"

It was a return to the lighthearted raillery they had indulged in five years ago. Entering her drama at once, Quentin said menacingly, "*All* alone, fair lady! And both, mark you, in our night rail! Faith, but were I not a thorough rogue, I'd be most shocked!" She chuckled and he went on in his normal voice, "You really are thoroughly compromised, you know."

She knew she was blushing, and said lightly, "Fustian. You and the Corporal have been more than gentlemanlike. I doubt either my papa or my brother would have called you out."

Despite her denial, her pulse had quickened, because in point of fact, what he had said was truth. She'd not realized she was pleating her sash until his hand closed over hers for an instant, stilling her nervous fingers. She raised her eyes shyly and encountered such a tender expression that she could only be glad she was sitting down because her knees had melted.

"Wherever either of those fine gentlemen may be at this moment," he said gently, "I pledge them my word that I shall not abuse my trust. Indeed, Penelope Anne, you must know how I—love and honour you . . ."

Penelope's heartbeat was deafening. She felt choked with joy, overwhelmed by the sure knowledge he was about to declare himself.

". . . as deeply," went on his deep, kind voice, "as though you were my own dear sister. The sister I never had, alas."

It was like a blow to the heart. She felt quite frozen, and for a moment it took all her resolution not to betray her hurt. Somehow she responded, marvelling that her voice could sound so calm. "In which case, I mean to exercise a sisterly right. Oh, I—I know you are concerned for my safety, but just because your strength has begun to return does not mean you dare overtax it. It would be enough to sit up in the chair a few times today, and perhaps walk a little tomorrow."

"A little!" The Corporal uttered a derisive, "Huh! Walked a mile already he has. And made sorry work of it!"

"Oh, Quentin," exclaimed Penelope. "Please do wait until tomorrow to walk about."

"I shall be gone from here by tomorrow." The words were quiet, but his eyes were steady and determined.

97

Dismayed, she cried, "You *cannot!*"

Once again, he reached for and clasped her hand. "Dearest Penelope Anne, I was as good as dead and you gave me a priceless second chance at life and freedom. There are no words to thank you for what you've done—the risks you have taken, but— No!" He relinquished her hand to cover her parting lips. "You do but waste your words. I'll not be talked out of it this time. We leave at full dark this evening."

Stunned, she stared at him in silence. She had mentally relegated him to the role of passive invalid, and had assigned to herself the task of arranging his deliverance. Only yesterday she had judged him too weak to do more than bow to her decisions. It was borne in upon her now that this resilient young man was not the kind to bow for very long, and that she would have to use all her wiles to prevent him from running himself into another disaster.

He lowered his hand, watching her rather sadly.

She said, "I repeat—you cannot, Major. There are military guarding the house."

Quentin's breath was indrawn with a faint hissing sound, but he said nothing.

The Corporal, in his shirt-sleeves, little mountains of white soap beside his nose and cuddling against one ear, rushed out from behind the sheet to demand, "You've seen 'em, miss?"

Penelope nodded and told them the circumstances.

Killiam groaned, sat down on the bed, took up the towel that was draped across one shoulder, and began to wipe his face, quite forgetting that a lady was present and he wore neither jacket nor cravat.

Watching Quentin's stern face anxiously, Penelope added, "So you see, it is not to be thought of."

"To the contrary," he muttered. "It is become even more imperative."

Exasperated, Killiam demanded, "Now, sir—how a'God's name can you leave here if they're outside, waiting for you to show your phiz? Likely, they're all slathering for promotions."

"Or the reward," said Quentin slowly.

"If they knew you were here," said Penelope, "they'd come in after you, do you not think?"

"Most decidedly they would. No, m'dear, they're unaware as yet of my illegal residence. 'Tis far more likely your kindly uncle's conscience wrought upon him. He may have fancied I'd reach friends or family who would be eager to avenge my—less than gentle treatment at his hands. Or perhaps he thought I might swing back myself and fire the house, or some such deed."

"But whatever could he tell them without betraying his own part in all this?"

"Probably he concocted some tale to the effect he'd been called away and was uneasy about leaving his ladies unprotected, with murdering rebels in the area."

"In that case, we are safe for a time," said Penelope, hopefully. "After Uncle Joseph returns and the guards are withdrawn, you can slip away."

"Thank you, ma'am," he said with a slow smile. "But it will not do. I leave tonight."

"Gawd!" groaned the Corporal. "What'd I tell you, miss? Major, with the price that's on your head, it's like as not the whole countryside's up. Tell me how you mean to get clear. Only tell—"

"Hold your tongue!" snapped Quentin, suddenly all haughty authority.

"You shan't make me hold mine," Penelope stormed. "If I'm to be dragged to my death, I mean to—"

"*You!*" he cried, patently horrified. "By God, but you'll not be dragged by me! Why in the deuce would I remove the threat of my presence from Highview only to carry you into greater danger? Have some sense, do, Penny!"

The brotherly candour of those words acted on her overwrought nerves like a fan to flame. "Forgive me, sir." She stood, chin high and her voice scornful. "I am too filled with disgust at this moment to be sensible, I doubt."

Standing also, he said with a faint, fond smile, "I know what you're about, Penelope Anne. It will not do. Surely you see why I cannot—"

'Penelope Anne.' He had been used to call her that years ago and had always said the name in a way she had come to think of as tender. That he should speak it now, having named her his sister, further infuriated her, and she turned on him, pale with anger. "I agreed to this—this risky business on one condition, Major Chandler. And your brother took an oath to abide by my terms. Now you seek to break his given word and foul his honour. For shame!"

His pale cheeks reddened and he turned away from her for an instant, but when he faced her again, his jaw was set. "Think what you will," he said quietly. "But I'll *not* drag you to the gallows. No more would my brother have done. If that causes you to despise me, or to repent of your bargain, why"—he smiled wryly—"the soldiers wait outside. You have only to call."

He knew she would not. In that moment, almost she could have struck him. She met his steady gaze, her own eyes blazing wrath. Then, she flung around and walked out, her head held high, but unhappily aware that it was difficult to look regal while clad in a flannel nightgown and a much-patched and faded dressing gown.

"After all we have done," raged Penelope. "After all we have risked! How can he be so stupid? So arrogantly determined to throw it all away?"

"Never weep, my lamb," said Daffy, tucking Penelope back into bed and placing the neglected breakfast tray across her lap. "He is only a man after all. And there's not a one of 'em as won't drive a woman distracted sooner or later."

The prosaic words shocked Penelope. She realized suddenly

100

that she had not thought of Quentin as a human being, but rather as a godlike creature, perfect in face and form, with a serene sweetness of disposition and an unwavering gentleness, at least insofar as she was concerned. She had caught a glimpse of steel just now when he had flown out at the poor Corporal. She had been hurt when he had spoken to her so sharply. . . .

Watching her expressive face, Daffy wielded teapot and cup deftly, and murmured, "Changed, has he, miss?"

Had he changed? Or was it simply that she had never really known him? Had she imbued him with qualities he did not possess? That no man possessed? She thought in a detached way, 'I am a silly, naïve girl who fell in love with a dream that does not exist.' And at once, she began to enumerate his good points. His courage and warm-heartedness. The way he had of watching her when she spoke, as though what she had to say was the most important thing in the world to him at that moment. His ready sense of humor, the set of his lips that was so instant an indicator of his mood; the lurking smile in his green eyes. She smiled faintly, tenderly, thinking, 'and the way that one lock of hair persists in tumbling down over his brow. . . .' And she knew it didn't matter if he was less than she had thought him, that the fault was hers for having visualized him as being so godlike—and in supposing she could live with perfection, even if she won it. She was learning about Quentin Chandler—good and bad—and she loved him just as much. . . .

"You'll feel better after a nice hot cup of tea," said Daffy kindly. "Oh, misery! It's not very hot, miss."

Scarcely hearing, Penelope accepted the cup and stirred sugar into her lukewarm tea. "He means to leave *tonight,* Daffy," she said. "He will be caught, or killed. . . . Oh, whatever shall I do? He is so stubbornly set on it!"

"Always been the same, by what Corporal Robert Killiam says." Daffy darted a glance to the closed dressing room door and perched on the edge of the bed. "Only say the word and me and Corporal Rob will knock the Major down and tie him 'fore he can wake up. Rob knowed as he meant to do this, and he don't like it above half. He told me—"

Surprised out of her despair, Penelope said, "He did? When?"

"What? Oh—er, well it were last night, miss. The Major was asleep when I come up, and so was you. Corporal Robert Killiam heared me open the door, and he knocked very soft and asked—most polite like—if he could perhaps have a drop more water." She blushed to see Penelope's astonishment. "Well—well, it's as you said, miss. They'm honourable gentlemen both. And I thought, so long as you was sure o' that, then—"

"Why, you deceitful little baggage! I suppose by the time I woke up and saw you disrobing, you had sat in there half the night playing Patience with the man!"

"No, no, miss! Only for a very little, and—oh, whoops!"

"Oh, whoops, indeed! Rascal! Pretending all the time you disliked the poor Corporal, but having clandestine card games with him the moment my eyes are closed!"

"You *knows* as I'm a good girl," pleaded Daffy. "And anyways, much use I've got for that great, clumsy creature." Her small plump fingers began to twist the end of the snowy but much abused apron into a tight roll. She went on in a rather distant voice, "Though . . . he don't seem to be such a bad chap, and . . . and . . ."

"And has a fine pair of shoulders, nice blue eyes, and a fine head of hair—eh, minx?" said Penelope, laughing tremulously.

Daffy's eyes flashed to her face and began to twinkle. "Why, as to that," she said in her prim way, "I'm sure I couldn't say, Miss Penny. I'll own I've not heared him use evil words—or not many. But I don't see as how a girl could be interested in a man what's always so gruff and gloomy-like. Even if he is loyal as he can stare and would give up his life for the Major."

"Good gracious," muttered Penelope, who had selected a piece of cold toast from the rack, and now detached a small, folded sheet of paper that had adhered to it. "What—in the world . . . ?"

Butter had dripped on the page and, as she unfolded it curiously, she saw that some of the writing was so blurred as to be almost gone. With some difficulty, she was able, however, to read the message aloud.

Greetings, R, on this your special day. Looking back over the years I wonder if you remember the Flying Dutchman? What a fellow he was! I've always thought he imparted his own sad lack of *semper paratus* to you. I hope you've overcome it. Can't recall how old you were, but just today I was chuckling over the time you bit Mars. May your troubles, like the years, roll away. Affectionately, S. K.

"How very odd," she murmured, baffled.

"Well, it can't be for you, miss. Your name don't begin with R."

"But how do you suppose it got onto my tray? It almost looks as though it was deliberately hidden."

"What difference, Miss Penny? It don't say anything what makes any sense. Whoever this R is— Oh, I 'spect it is for that Captain Horrid Otton. He's the only R I can—" Daffy's eyes became very round. "Oh—my!"

"Corporal Rob!" Penelope was out of bed in a trice and running across the room, forgetting her dressing gown until, with a little scream, Daffy flew to wrap it around her.

The Corporal answered the scratch at the door, and Quentin turned from the window, a frown in his eyes.

Penelope thrust the message at Killiam. "This was in amongst my toast, Corporal. We think it is meant for you."

The Corporal shook his head in mystification over the message, but Quentin, who came up to take and scan it, said with sudden intensity, "My brother writ this to me! R stands for Rabble." He glanced at Penelope, his eyes ablaze with excitement. "You'll have noted with what irreverence he addresses me."

"Are you sure?" she asked dubiously. "It is signed S. K."

103

"I couldn't mistake his hand. And he'd not dare to put his own initials for fear it was intercepted and someone put two and two together." His brows twitched together. "S. . . . K. . . . Ah! I have it! Sir Knight—of course! I was used to call him that when we were children, because he's the eldest and will inherit the title."

"But whatever do it all mean, sir?" asked Daffy. "Who is this Dutch gent what Mr. Gordon speaks of?"

The Corporal grunted, "If 'twas a cove as sprouted wings, I'd think the whole world would know his name."

"Not wings," Penelope said eagerly. "Sails, I think. Isn't that the legend of the foul-mouthed ship's captain who was doomed to sail on forever and never find harbour? A ghost ship—no?"

"Right," said Quentin, continuing to frown thoughtfully at the blurred message. "My 'special day' baffles me, however. This is not my birthday."

"Unless your brother means to imply it will *become* a special day," suggested Penelope. "But—how is the Flying Dutchman involved?"

"He was our coachman. My father dubbed him thus because he was always losing his way." Chandler sighed with faint nostalgia. "Such a very good fellow. . . . But—as for him having been *semper paratus* . . . Gad!"

"What's it mean, Major?" asked Killiam. "Latin—is it?"

"Yes. And my Latin always so damnable." Quentin turned ruefully to Penelope. "Dear lady, did you study Latin? *Semper* means ever—or forever—I think. . . ."

"Yes, I'm sure it does. But . . . *paratus* . . ." She clutched her temples in a desperate effort at concentration. "Oh, dear! I know it—but . . . I cannot recall . . ."

Frustrated, Quentin asked, "Dare we send Daffy down to your book room?"

"If I show me nose down there, sir," said Daffy, "I mightn't be allowed to come back up. They're all of a state, getting ready for her la'ship's dinner party, and—"

"Ready!" Jubilant, Penelope interpolated, "That's it! *Semper paratus* means 'always ready'!"

"Good girl!" He threw his good arm around her and gave her a strong hug, but released her rather abruptly, returning his attention to the letter, while Penelope prayed he had not noticed how her cheeks blazed around the edges of her applied pallor.

"What's this about you biting someone, Major?" asked the Corporal.

Quentin read softly, "'Can't recall how old you were, but just today I was chuckling over the time you bit Mars. . . .' How old I was . . ." He thought back, his brow furrowing. "Must've been about—eight, I suppose. No! I was nine, for I'd just come home for the holidays. Mars was our dog—a silly great gentle animal, always more paws than brains. I tripped, trying to avoid him because he'd gone berserk when he saw me come back. I fell over the old fool and smashed my mouth on a chair. There was blood from here to breakfast—all mine. But my papa would have it that I'd bit the dog!" He grinned at Penelope. "To take my mind off things, you know."

"Yes, how kind of him. But to what does your brother point, do you fancy? The dog? Or . . ."

"Oh, no. I suspect he means my age at the time. Let's try to put it together, shall we? Today . . . a coachman . . . the warning that I must be ready. And the number nine." He looked gravely at their intent faces.

"Oh, my!" exclaimed Penelope. "Your brother is sending a coach here! At nine this evening!"

"Heaven bless us all!" Daffy said, marvelling. "Who'd have guessed that's what it really means?"

"No one else—I trust," said Quentin, winking at her.

Distressed, Penelope cried, "How shall we ever stop him? Poor man—he will drive right into a trap!"

"Aye." Killiam nodded dolefully. "The troopers'll get him and it'll be off to the block before the coach can run!"

105

Quentin said musingly, "I wonder . . ." They all stared at him, and he went on, "I'm very sure the troopers seek to keep me *out*. They may search the coach when it arrives, but I'll not be in it, don't you see? All I'll have to do is pop in once they've finished."

"And—just how," said Penelope, "do you think you can manage that without being seen?"

"It won't matter if I am seen—by the troopers at all events." He paced restlessly to the window. "I could stroll nonchalantly around the side of the house after the coachman has made whatever enquiries he's been primed to make, and . . ." He swung around, his arm flinging out, his eyes bright as he started back to them. "My dear friends, never look so apprehensive. I'll only have . . . have to . . ." He checked, looking bewildered, then swayed.

The Corporal leapt to steady him, guide him to the bed, and sit with his arm about the thin, sagging shoulders. "Been on your feet too long. Whatever did ye expect?" he growled ferociously, scanning Quentin's white face for all the world like a concerned parent.

"Oh . . . no," argued Quentin, faint but indomitable. "I'm just . . . a little tired, perhaps."

Penelope filled a glass from the water pitcher they'd stood on the pile of books. "If you cannot stand for a few minutes, Major Chandler, I wish I may see you trip down two flights of stairs, walk around the back of the house, and"—she handed him the glass—"stroll nonchalantly to the coach."

"Be flat on your face 'fore you'd come to the foot of the stairs," said the Corporal, predictably.

Humbled by the concerned faces about him, Quentin drank the water and was silent.

"'Course," murmured Daffy through the troubled pause, "if the Major's a touch weak in the knees and cannot walk . . . he could always totter. With a walking cane."

They stared at her.

"What d'ye mean, lass?" asked Killiam in a tone Penelope had never before heard him use.

Blushing, Daffy answered, "I mean—was he to be . . . a *older* gentleman."

They looked at one another speechlessly, scarcely daring to entertain the scenario those words suggested.

In a breathless voice that trembled with renewed hope, Quentin asked, "Daffy—you never could . . . ?"

She all but pounced at him, eyes sparkling. "Yes, sir! Oh, yes, I could indeed!"

"Ye could make my Major into a old gentleman?" asked the Corporal, awed. "So as people would *believe?*"

"You may believe as they'd not know the difference," she boasted.

"God love you, girl!" said Quentin, enthusiastically accepting her claim. "But—faith! What about clothes? Friend Otton's boots are adequate, but his flamboyant style would not befit an older man."

Penelope said, "Never mind that. My papa's garments will serve, with little if any alteration at your present weight."

The Corporal, who had developed a healthy respect for this girl's calm good sense, watched her curiously. "You've a thought or two in your head, I think, miss."

She smiled at him. "Yes, I have. This is better and better. Quentin, my aunt gives a dinner party this evening."

"Aha!"

"Just so. It is likely to begin at about five o'clock, though I doubt they will sit down to table until half-past seven, or eight o'clock. With luck we can get you downstairs by the time the coach arrives and an 'elderly' guest can leave my aunt's party early."

He asked intently, "How shall I get past your butler? Surely he will know who were the guests."

"Yes. So we must manage to be at the side door before the coachman draws up, and we will walk out as though we had

107

been strolling whilst awaiting him." She clasped her hands and did a small, elated jig. "Oh, Quentin! How splendid if—together, we can bring it off!"

The adverb caused him a momentary unease, soon banished by his customary optimism. "By God, but we shall!"

Not until she and Daffy were back in the bedchamber did Penelope interrupt their busy plotting to say thoughtfully, "Whoever put that note in with my toast must know the Major is here."

"Lawks!" shrieked Daffy, and vanished into her apron.

"It must be a friend," Penelope went on, "else we'd have been arrested before this."

"Why—that's so," faltered Daffy, her eyes reappearing. "But—who can it be?"

"I think we should not try to guess. We have a friend who does not dare risk being identified. We must respect that wish." And she thought, 'And pray this is not all a trap. . . .'

VII

Much of the responsibility for their desperate plan rested on Daffy's shoulders. It was she who had to slip up to the attic where Lord Hector's trunks were stored, and she who must select suitable raiment for Major Chandler's proposed *alter ego.* His late lordship had been a conservative gentleman in many respects but, being possessed of an excellent physique, had enjoyed his clothes and had owned quite a nice wardrobe and several wigs that were still in good repair. Daffy filled a laundry basket with garments and accessories, threw a sheet around her spoils and delivered them to Penelope's bedchamber before going downstairs to resume her less criminal pursuits.

Fortunately, an iron was kept in the dressing room. Penelope lit the fire and soon had the iron heated. She set to work and spent the next hour pressing several of her late father's full-skirted coats, knee breeches, and half a dozen shirts. The pile of cravats and ruffles seemed endless but having completed this rather wrenching task, she left the dressing room so that Killiam could help Quentin try on his borrowed finery.

Penelope waited hopefully, but when at last the Corporal ushered in the prospective 'old gentleman' for her inspection, her heart sank. The wig was rather out of the present style, having thick curls loosely arranged about the head and worn long at the back, tied in with a wide black satin bow. The blue satin coat and knee breeches fit well enough, but despite his drawn countenance and the silky white curls, Chandler contrived to look elegant, dashing, and not a year older. "We shall have to place all our reliance on Daffy," Penelope sighed.

That skilled maiden, arriving a short time later with a tray containing their lunch, was not so much dismayed by the Major's youthful appearance as by his lack of qualms at wearing a dead man's clothing. "Does it not make you feel . . . crawly-like, sir?" she enquired, passing Quentin a slice of seed cake.

Patently surprised by the question, he answered, "Why, no. I liked Lord Hector in life. Why should I fear him in death? He was a most good-natured gentleman who'd not in the least object, I feel sure."

"No more he might," she said, tucking in her chin and looking solemn. "But—to wear his clothes! Even his *wig*! Lawks! 'Twould make me feel proper haunted."

Quentin stared at her, then laughed so hard he was obliged to stifle the sound. "A—a haunted wig, by Jupiter," he said merrily. "How shall I survive it?"

Watching him, her heart brightened by his mirth, Penelope thought, 'Just survive, my dearest. Somehow . . . survive.'

She prevailed upon him to rest after their shared meal, so that he would be better prepared for the evening's activities, but when she left, although laid down upon the trundle bed, he was busily occupied in supervising the Corporal's selection of clothing. Killiam was determined to accompany Chandler in the guise of 'the old gentleman's' manservant, and he was as convinced they must fail, as his Major was confident of a successful conclusion. Penelope closed the door upon Killiam's mournful listing of the odds against his attaining his next birthday, and went into the corridor.

Walking slowly down the stairs, for perhaps the hundredth time she considered her own schemes. She had confided these to Daffy and had so frightened that damsel that she could only be glad she had first secured a vow of complete secrecy. If a certain handsome young fugitive were to get wind of her schemes there could be no doubt of *his* reaction! Penelope smiled faintly. 'Sufficient unto the hour,' she thought.

She was very sure she was in for a fine scold from her beautiful aunt and was mildly astonished, upon encountering that lady in the downstairs hall, to be met with a look of dismay, rapidly replaced by a veritable flood of solicitude, apologies for not having visited the sick room "as often as I should have wished, but you know how terribly susceptible I am to illness," and the assurance that she looked "positively hagged" and must not even think about doing anything save to return to bed and rest. "You will likely be quite recovered by tomorrow," appended my lady, remembering that the Curate meant to call and that she had no least intention of dealing with the questions the man would doubtless have to ask.

Penelope coughed her way through profuse thanks and said with noble martyrdom that she would just go to the kitchen and make sure that everything was in order there.

Lady Sybil's white hands flew to close in a remarkably strong grip about her niece's arm. She would not dream, she declared, of allowing "poor Penelope" to subject herself to so tiresome an endeavour. She herself would see Cook. "And I'd best not find her lollygagging with those wretched soldiers," she muttered, frowning.

It was a golden opportunity, and Penelope seized it at once, exclaiming as though greatly alarmed, "Soldiers, ma'am? Oh— never say we are under house arrest?"

"For heaven's sake, why should I say such a thing?" her ladyship replied, throwing a nervous glance up and down the hall. "What*ever* will you think of next, stupid girl?"

"But—but why would soldiers be here, save to—"

"They are come to *guard* us," hissed Sybil, irritated. "When he left, your uncle had the good sense to request protection— what with the neighbourhood positively swarming with traitors,

111

and—" She broke off, eradicated her frown and pinned a rather strained smile to her lips. "At all events, it is nothing to worry about, and will allow us all to sleep at night without fearing to find our throats cut when we wake up in the morning! Get to your bed, girl, and I will tell Cook to send a maid up with a tray, so that you may have your dinner early."

"You are too good." Penelope sniffed loudly. "Faith, I do not know how it can be, but I am fairly famished."

"An excellent sign. Now—run along, do."

Penelope 'ran along' at a slow, wearied trudge, marvelling at the lengths to which Sybil would go to conceal her illicit dinner party. Upon entering her bedchamber, she went at once to scratch on the door of the dressing room. The Corporal opened the door a crack and whispered that the Major was not dressed. Penelope called mischievously, "Well, you may tell him that the soldiers are here only to guard against his cutting my throat whilst I sleep."

She heard a muffled laugh, and the Corporal grinned broadly.

"Who told you that, Penelope Anne?" asked Quentin.

"My aunt. And I know her well enough that she has no least idea you—loiter about my bedroom, sir."

He chuckled and imparted that she was a sister in a million. Bristling, Penelope crossed to the window and seated herself in her battered but comfortable old rocking chair.

It was a pleasant afternoon, the breeze urging a cluster of small clouds across the sky so that they looked like so many hurrying sheep. Watching them, Penelope was reminded of how she and Geoffrey had been used to create faces or objects, or sometimes entire beings out of the shifting cloud formations. She tried to picture her brother perched on one of those celestial sheep, looking down at her perhaps, with loving eyes, but she found, as she'd often found in the past, that she could not associate Geoff with so saintly an occupation; that she could not, in fact, associate him with death at all. Which was ridiculous, for had he survived he would most certainly have been in touch with her long before this.

Her thoughts shifted to the venture ahead. The Corporal was right, alas; their chances of bringing Quentin safely away were terrifyingly slight. A dozen possible disasters chased one another through her bedevilled mind. If he was cornered, he would fight, she knew that. Suppose he was hauled away in chains to face a traitor's death? Whatever would she do? How could she go on living—without him? She began to tremble and put a very cold hand over her eyes, seeking to shut out such terrible imaginings.

A familiar and yet unfamiliar voice growled, "Madam—you are my prisoner! Do you surrender?"

With a gasp, Penelope looked up. An horrendous figure stood beside her. A lurching, leering creature with enormous black moustachios. A vivid neckerchief was tied around his head, a patch covered one eye, and an expression of depraved lechery glinted in the other.

Penelope's mouth fell open and she stared, too astounded to respond. Her wrist was seized in a surprisingly powerful clasp. She was jerked from the chair, whipped around, bent backwards, and, quite off balance, held in that undignified position while that one green eye laughed down at her. The moustachios appeared to constitute a considerable impediment to her captor, who was obliged to spit them out a time or two as he snarled ferociously, "Dast ye keep the Scourge o' the Spanish Main waiting, wretched woman? You are in me—me power! Ah, ye do well to shake in yer shoes! Anger me, and I'll have ye hung by yer thumbs from the yardarm, or keelhauled—or—er, something like that. Please me, and I'll shower ye with gifts, such as—"

At this point the Scourge of the Spanish Main was considerably startled to find himself showered with gifts. A muffled, gobbling squeak had preceded a most vigorous scratching, and now a hail of gravel, seed, and other debris rained down on the dastardly pirate. Astonished, the Scourge was so ill-advised as to look up. He received the second deluge full in the face. With a yelp of disgust, he released his captive and leapt clear, dragging a sleeve across his sullied countenance, thereby twisting his moustachios sideways. "Curst . . . little pest . . . !" he snorted, picking at his hair and blinking at Jasper with an expression of loathing.

Penelope was giggling hilariously. Scowling at her, Quentin realized he had allowed her to fall and, with a remorseful apology, helped her to her feet.

"Well you may mock, heartless girl. But that meagre luncheon has left me ravenous. I'm just primed to devour a roasted bird."

"Never mind about your murderous plots, sir. I should like to know what in the world you think you are about."

"Making you laugh," he declared, his vexation promptly forgotten. "I remember what a particularly delightful little laugh you had, Penny, and I've heard not much of it."

Rather hurriedly removing her hand from his warm clasp, she scolded, "So only for that you must needs endanger us all with your silly play-acting?" His grin faded, and he took off the patch and the sideways moustachios. Repenting her harsh words, she went on, "Besides, I might perhaps be able to explain the presence of an elderly gentleman in my bedchamber, but how on earth could I account for a villainous pirate?"

"You could say I was so sunk in depravity that as an act of Christian charity you felt obliged to throw me a lifeline. As indeed you did, dear little Penelope Anne."

His lips were grave now, but the smile had returned to his eyes, causing them to crinkle at the corners and sending such a pang of yearning through Penelope that almost she was glad to hear rapid footsteps approaching.

Quentin heard, too. With a leap he was in the dressing room and had swung the door closed. Penelope straightened her gown and slipped into the chair and the door opened to admit the maid, Betty, carrying a tray laden with many covered bowls and tureens.

"Milady told me to be sure and bring you a nice lot, as you was very hungry, Miss Penelope," she said in her soft, shy voice.

Penelope thanked her and lifted the lids. She uncovered baked chicken, sliced beef and ham, a piece of pork pie, green peas, beans with cream sauce, some chocolate gâteaux, fruits and nuts and cheeses. All the portions were large. Taken aback, she exclaimed, "Good heavens! There's enough here to feed me for a week!"

The girl blinked in rather bewildered fashion. "Did I do wrong, miss? I know your abigail takes her meals up here with you, so I thought . . ."

Penelope looked levelly at her. Betty looked back and ventured an uncertain smile. If she had been going to identify herself, this, thought Penelope, would have been the logical moment. She said, "I must admit I am very hungry. Thank you so much."

Betty curtseyed gracefully and departed. Penelope carried the laden tray to the dressing room and tapped her shoe against the door. Killiam opened it and took the tray. His thick brown hair was neatly dressed. He wore a severe brown coat and beige breeches and on his feet were buckled brogues that looked familiar but that had certainly never belonged to Lord Hector. Standing beside the bed, watching her with a half-smile of anticipation playing about his mouth, Quentin was clad in a coat of cerulean blue velvet over a waistcoat of blue and silver brocade. White knee breeches fitted surprisingly well, and silver buckles gleamed on his high-heeled shoes. Leaning on an ebony cane with a carven silver handle, he said, "Now who's this pretty creature come bearing gifts for a poor old gentleman?"

Recovering her breath, Penelope admitted, "I'll own I'm tall, but I fancy our new maid has mistook me for Gargantua!" She managed to appear critical and added, "Daffy should be up soon, to add some years to you, Major. As it is now, you seem more likely to fence with that stick than to lean upon it."

"It wouldn't be the first time," he said, passing her one of the plates they had hoarded for their meals. "You'd be surprised, Penny, how well a man may defend himself with a strong cane."

She answered that she prayed the need would not arise, and carried her plate to the chair by the windows. She had little appetite and had set the food aside, her nerves tingling with tension when the first carriage came bowling up the drive, to be followed in a few moments by a second vehicle. Penelope did not see the guests alight, since the entrance was on the west face of the mansion, but, leaning to the open casement, she heard a sudden flurry of laughing voices abruptly cut short and guessed that her conniving aunt had begged her guests to be as quiet as possible to spare her 'ailing' niece.

Penelope glanced to the clock on the mantel. It was a small work of art, fashioned from gilded marble, whereon a talented artist had painted happy nymphs and shepherdesses in a sylvan glade. The colours and the superb craftsmanship brought a wistfulness to Penelope's hazel eyes. In the last days of her short life, Lady Hector had asked that the clock be kept for her little daughter. Together with a strand of pearls and a fine topaz-studded hair comb with matching earrings, it was all that Penelope had managed to keep of her mama's belongings once Joseph and Sybil Montgomery had descended upon Highview. She pushed nostalgia aside. The filigreed hands of the little clock informed the interested that the hour was a little past six. It was time to commence her plan.

Slipping to her knees, she pulled from under the bed the valise she had ordered Daffy to bring from the attic. She laid it on the bed and began to pack, selecting the articles with care. It was close to seven o'clock, and she was tucking her few cherished items of jewellery in amongst some undergarments when she heard someone coming. The valise was very heavy now, but she lifted it down and pushed it under the bed again.

Daffy hurried in, carrying the usual pile of laundry that served to conceal the many items the faithful girl was required to smuggle into this room. Closing the door behind her, she threw Penelope an anguished glance. "Oh, miss! Please say as you've changed your mind. Please do."

Penelope shook her head. "No, dear Daffy. This is my chance. I mean to take it. But there is no reason for you to feel obliged to come with us."

"'Course there is, miss. If you go—I go. Anyways, I've got two band boxes all packed, though it would take three or four trunks to get all your gowns—"

"My poor clothes are all out of the style, I fear. I shall have to manage as best I can. Now, tell me—when does my aunt lead her guests in to dine?"

My lady, said Daffy, had ordered dinner to be served at eight. She carried her cosmetics to the dressing room, scratched at the door and, having directed another worried look at her mistress, went inside to age Quentin as best she might.

Penelope changed into a black gown she usually wore only when journeying into Oxford or on rare trips to Town. She pinched some colour into her cheeks, but her fingers were like ice from nervousness, and she took down a warm cloak to wear outside. She then took up the unpleasant book she had rejected yesterday evening, and went back to her rocking chair, determined to compose herself. After what seemed an eternity she was no calmer, nor could she recall one line she had read, although she had turned several pages. She set the book aside and went over to look at the clock. It now showed twelve minutes past eight. Her heart gave a leap of excitement. Less than an hour until Gordon's Flying Dutchman would come. She prayed a short but fervent prayer that all would be well, pulled out the valise and tucked her precious clock inside, then returned to the window.

The sun was setting, throwing long shadows across the park and awakening golden gleams from the winding ribbon of the stream. Softened by the mellow light, the little bridge swooped

117

gracefully over the hurrying water, and on every side the hills rose in darkening green sweeps against the blushing skies. A lump came into Penelope's throat. This was her birthplace; the only home she had ever known. Looking past the recent memories, she could call to mind so many happy moments—carefree days with Papa and Geoff. Squandered days, taken for granted because she had not dreamed how soon they would be snatched away. Her roots were here. Was she mad to risk everything, even her life, on this wild adventure? She heard a low chuckle from the direction of the dressing room and her pulse quickened. She had no roots, really. Papa and Mama and her brother were gone; she had no claim on the estate, and memory she could take wherever she went. Her only hope for happiness dwelt with the man who had just laughed. Her lips twisted wryly. The man who thought of her as the dear sister he had never known. . . .

Self-pity was revolting. She straightened her shoulders. Possibly, the pot of gold did not wait at the end of her rainbow. Possibly her only reward would be to have helped Quentin Chandler escape savagery and death. If that was her fate, she would have to accept it and be grateful that she had been of some small aid to him. She sensed rather than heard someone behind her, and spun around.

An elderly gentleman watched her. A proud gentleman clad in blue and silver, whose lined countenance was marked by the pallor of age, but showed no trace of cuts or bruises. Great grey eyebrows bristled ferociously over green eyes that sparkled with amusement and were decidedly too brilliant for those elderly features. Still, the gentleman bore so little resemblance to the pathetic fugitive they had carried in here on Sunday night that Penelope clapped her hands softly, and cried, "Oh, well done! Well done!"

Daffy gave a rather wan smile. "I did as best I could, Miss Penny. But I couldn't do a blessed thing about the Major's eyes."

"Lord knows what you're grumbling about," said Quentin indignantly. "Feels like there's five or six tons of twigs hanging over 'em! I cannot think how anyone could tell I *have* eyes!"

"Well, they can," said Penelope. "And however well my clever Daffy may have worked her magic with the rest of your person, you would be well advised, dear sir, to keep your eyes lowered."

"Was I to go about like this," he said, hobbling along on his cane, his head twisted sideways and eyes drooping grotesquely, "people are like to think—"

"That you are well over the oar," Penelope interpolated merrily.

He straightened, grinning at her. "Then you are simply going to have to put up with my ancient self, as it is."

"And not for long, at that," the Corporal put in. "Time we was getting downstairs, sir."

Briefly, it was as though a blight had touched them, and everyone stood very silent and still.

His face unwontedly grave, Quentin stepped forward and took Penelope's hands. He said softly, "If this should fail, there are still no words to thank you for all you've done. But if, by the grace of God, I come safely away, so long as I live do you ever need help you've only to call on me and I shall come." He bent and kissed her gently on the brow.

Penelope's heart turned over, and the room swam and faded into a rosy haze.

"Farewell, dearest of sisters," said Quentin, drawing back.

The room straightened, and Penelope's rosy haze was dissipated.

Corporal Killiam came over. "What the Major just said," he mumbled. "Well, I feel the—the same, Miss Penelope. You and Miss Brooks. You—been so—so—"

Penelope reached up, took his face between her hands and stood on tiptoe to press a kiss upon his cheek. The Corporal became beet-red and stood in bashful silence.

Turning from pressing a similar salute upon Daffy's blushing

119

face, Quentin exclaimed an indignant, "Hi! I wasn't given one of those!"

"No. But then you are my brother," said Penelope meekly. "Now—come, gentlemen. The coast should be clear, for the servants will be having their dinner or serving at my aunt's table." She opened the door cautiously.

The hall stretched away, dim and quiet and cold. She stepped into it, beckoning the men to follow and, with a last meaningful look at Daffy, she led the way. Reaching the main stairwell, she motioned for a stop while she paced slowly past the descending flight. Quentin and the Corporal pressed against the wall, watching her tensely. There was no sign of anyone, only the distant sound of conversation interspersed by Lady Sybil's occasional shrill giggle. Reaching the far side, Penelope beckoned urgently, then continued to the back stairs.

This she judged the most hazardous part of their flight, for the stairs were almost constantly in use and terminated at the ground floor, perilously close to the kitchen and the servants' hall. Had Quentin been stronger she would have judged it far safer for him to climb down the big oak at the rear of the house, as Gordon had done, but she was very aware that, for all his brave nonchalance, he was weaker than he seemed and the effort of coming downstairs would likely tax his strength to the utmost. She stopped again and peeped around the corner. And still luck was with them, for the narrow stairway was deserted.

She started down. Behind her, the Corporal shifted the heavy valise to his left hand and gripped Quentin's left arm. Quentin grinned at him insouciantly, but he did not pull away and went down with his right hand, now removed from the sling, resting on the banister rail.

Her nerves quivering with tension, Penelope trod down the last step. From the servants' hall came a mumble of conversation, with Hargrave's strident tones predominating. It would seem that luck had deserted them. The door stood wide. Penelope could see Simmonds and Mrs. King seated with their backs to the hall. Her hopes plummetted as she heard Cole's voice. The groom had been slavishly devoted to Geoffrey, and his loathing of the Jacobite cause had deepened since her brother's death. Her hands gripped tight with indecision. Each instant they delayed built a greater threat of discovery, but to venture forth with that wretched door wide open would be fatal. Quentin and the Corporal waited on the stairs, watching her. She motioned to them to wait and walked sedately along the corridor. As she drew level with the servants' hall, the door was flung wider open. Cole came out, remarking in a dour way that he would "ask 'em." Looking back into the room, he added, "But if you was to ask my opinion they're a pair of regular knock-in-the-cradles and about as much protection to us as any two choirboys would be."

Cole prided himself on being a well-read man. The butler, who had never been seen to read anything more complicated than a menu, responded sharply that the troopers were not at Highview for their intellectual abilities. "All as is wanted of them, is that they can shoot straight, or be quick with a bayonet. But if you care to take the matter up with her la'ship . . ."

Cole grunted, started down the hall, but stopped as he saw Penelope. A fond light came into his faded blue eyes. "Evening, miss," he said, touching his brow respectfully. "Was you wishing to see Mrs. King, I'll call—"

"No—pray do not disturb her," said Penelope hastily. "I—er, had come down to be sure the soldiers were invited to take dinner, but it seems Hargrave has already attended to the matter. Do you know where they are at the moment?"

He grinned. "Probably blowing a cloud in the shrubbery. They'll not want to be too far from the house, miss. Just in case they was to be invited to eat, and couldn't be found. 'Sides—they're taking no chances of collecting any bounty that might come their way."

"Are there just the two of them?" she asked. "Is it allowed that they both come in at the same time?"

"Just the two until nine, miss. Then another pair come on.

121

And don't you never be afeared, one on 'em will wait by the door till his mate's through eating, and turn about."

She assured him she was much relieved, and turned back towards the stairs, her mind racing. What she'd at first fancied to be a blessing had become even more of a curse. With the troopers both safely ensconced in the servants' hall, she could have whisked the two men outside with less fear of their being seen. As it was, with one trooper inside, and one waiting outside, they were likely to be delayed for upwards of two hours; the coach would arrive and leave with no chance of getting to it. The only hope was to get out now—before Cole returned with the guards.

She heard the back door click shut and flew towards the servants' hall again. Cole had swung the door a little more closed than it had been, but it was still too wide. Standing away from the opening, she reached for the handle, only to whip her hand back again.

Mrs. King's voice was very near. ". . . inconsiderate is not the word," she said ingratiatingly. "Do you just sit there, poor Mr. H., and rest yourself. *I* shall go upstairs."

Penelope knew distractedly that she must somehow divert the wretched woman. But how could she hope to keep her from noticing the two men waiting on the stairs?

The door opened wide. There came the swish of bombazine.

"There is not the need," Hargrave called in his oily fashion, "though much do I appreciate your kindness, dear Mrs. K. The chit and chat is flying heavy, and my lady bade me leave 'em to their cakes and ices. They'll likely gabble for a hour yet, so I've set Forbes to wait outside of the dining room door. When milady rings her little bell, Forbes will run down and fetch me."

Murmuring tributes to Mr. H.'s sound common-sense, Mrs. King rustled away but she left the door wide open.

Penelope bit frantically at one knuckle. Cole might come back with the soldiers at any second, especially if they had already started to the house. Alternatively, clumsy little Jenny

Forbes might come galloping down the back stairs to fetch the omniscient butler.

Quentin was peering around the corner at her, and she waved to him urgently. Leaning on his cane, either in his new character, or out of need, he trod swiftly towards her, Killiam tiptoeing after him.

"I shall go in and close the door," Penelope whispered. "Directly I do, you must go outside and make your way as quickly as possible to the west drivepath. The soldiers are on their way here to eat, but they have to do so one at a time, so that there is always a guard watching. Hurry—do hurry!"

He nodded, eyes grim. "Go on then, brave girl. We shall do nicely, never—" He broke off with a startled gasp.

Betty hurried down the back stairs and came lightly along the corridor, humming to herself. She glanced up, saw the three who stood in a frozen tableau, and halted abruptly.

Penelope seemed quite numb. In a detached way she saw the girl's big blue eyes grow bigger. Killiam made a grab for her. She whispered, "Ssshh!" and eluded him to slip into the servants' hall, saying brightly as she closed the door, "I'm sorry to be late, ma'am. But if you're still of a mind to it, I'll sing for you now. . . ."

Penelope's knees were shaking. She thought distantly that her suspicions of Betty had evidently been correct, and she walked along unsteadily, scarcely able to credit this wondrous reprieve.

The Corporal murmured in her ear, "If you could just see if the coast is clear, Miss Penelope," and he opened the side door.

Penelope was vaguely aware of cool evening air scented with blossoms; of a crimson-streaked dusky sky, and of brisk footsteps approaching from the direction of the stables. She whispered, "They're coming! Quickly!" and plunged down the steps and into the bushes beside the house.

Quentin growled a curse, but there was no chance for him to restrain her and he had perforce to follow. Surrounded by foliage, they stood motionless. Penelope scarcely dared to breathe and, with a branch poking in her ear and a cobweb an inch from her nose, heard Cole grumbling, ". . . sent here to guard the estate, not sit around making eyes at the maids."

A deep laugh rumbled out. "Is it shaking in yer shoes ye are, then? Never worrit, my cove. Me comrade's got his peepers fixed on the road, and nought'll get past him, I dare swear."

Cole wrenched open the door and grunted a profanity. The door slammed shut.

'We did it!' thought Penelope. 'Oh, but we are almost away!'

"Excelsior!" exclaimed Quentin. "You see, Gloom and Grim—did I not tell you that . . . it would go well. . . ."

His voice was thready. Killiam asked anxiously, "You all right, sir?"

"I am very well," murmured Quentin. "But—just for a moment, perhaps, I think I shall . . . sit down. . . ." And he descended with a rush onto the valise the Corporal had dropped.

Penelope fell to her knees beside him. "Mon pauvre! You are so weak still."

He peered blurrily at her and with a weary smile declared, "No such thing. Run you a—a race, my girl. And win, begad."

The Corporal, who had crept through the shrubs to the point at which the drivepath neared the mansion, now returned, hissing urgently, "Coach coming!" He pulled Quentin to his feet, and they all three repaired to the edge of the lawn. Penelope could neither hear nor see a vehicle. "Are you sure, Corporal?" she asked.

"Never doubt old Rob, m'dear," said Quentin. "He's got the ears of a sparrow hawk."

For a moment they all stood listening. Then Quentin nodded, and Penelope heard the distant drumming of hooves, becoming gradually louder until she dreaded lest the servants hear the carriage. And then, from the house she heard a sweet soprano voice singing, "Blow, blow, thou winter wind, Thou art not so unkind as man's ingratitude . . ."

"Bless your heart, sweet songstress," muttered Quentin, his gaze fixed on the rapidly moving carriage.

"Is it your brother's man, sir?" asked Killiam.

"I cannot quite . . . tell. . . . Devil take it!"

A shout rang out. A soldier strode onto the drivepath, musket gripped before him. With a gasp, Penelope shrank closer to Quentin, and his arm went around her. The Corporal swore under his breath. The coach slowed and stopped, and the soldier strolled to call up to the coachman.

"Better there than in front of the house," Quentin whispered. "But if we're to pull this off, we'd best get around the corner while that trooper's occupied."

Penelope glanced anxiously to the back door. Daffy had not yet come. If the girl was detained, their scheme might yet fail. And then, even as she turned away, she saw Daffy slip down the back steps, two cloaks over her arm, a valise in one hand and the bird cage in the other. 'Jasper?' thought Penelope, and then they were around the corner and creeping towards the main entrance.

Good-humoured shouts rang out, and the team was moving again. The carriage came into view. Quentin murmured, "It *is* our Flying Dutchman, by thunder! Dear old Gordie's come to the rescue, as always! God love the man!"

"Now, sir?" asked the Corporal.

Quentin nodded and strolled out onto the drivepath. At once, the coachman pulled up his team. The Corporal snatched up the valise and followed Quentin. Penelope glanced back. Daffy came around the corner of the house but stayed amongst the shrubs, waiting until the last moment. Penelope walked to the coach, praying that no zealous stableboy would come running.

The creature that ran across the drive was no stableboy, but a sleek black cat, disturbed by Daffy, and voicing his displeasure as he darted under the heads of the leaders. Back went their high-bred ears, and snorting and squealing, they plunged on, the coachman snarling curses as he pulled at the reins. He brought his team under control within seconds, but they halted almost level with the front doors—the very spot they had all prayed to avoid. Penelope's heart was racing. The Corporal groaned, "The wolf's in with the sheep, now!" Quentin said coolly, "There was no horn sounded. We may still be safe," and with the aid of the cane he led the way to the coach.

The guard jumped down from the box, swung open the door, and let down the steps. Killiam handed over the valise. The coachman, a ruddy-faced squarely built individual, leaned over to grip Quentin's upreaching hand and gulp, "Master Quentin! God be thanked!"

"Be damned if you've changed a bit, Dutch," said Quentin gladly. "I wonder you recognized me, though." He glanced at the guard, who had thrown the valise onto the roof. "Up with you, man. Quickly! Inside, Rob!"

The Corporal knew better than to argue, and he clambered into the vehicle. Quentin started up the steps, then turned about. Daffy gripped her burdens and prepared for the last-minute dash. Quentin reached out to touch Penelope's pale cheek. "Bless you," he said fervently.

"Hurry, hurry!" cried Penelope, and as he stepped back, she jumped onto the step.

"Hey!" said Quentin.

"I go with you," she cried, determined.

"*Penelope!*" In strident and outraged accents, Lady Sybil demanded, "What on *earth* are you about?"

VIII

Gripped by despair as all her hopes crumbled, Penelope still had the presence of mind to back down the steps so that the coachman could whip up his team. She turned to face her aunt, grief like a knife in her breast, but her eyes flashing defiance. Quentin would be safe—that was all that really mattered.

But the coachman was not whipping up his horses. A hand was upon her arm; a deep, courteous voice was saying, "There is not the need for introductions, my little Penelope. I have heard sufficient of the beauty of Lady Delavale to know who this ravishing creature must be."

Penelope gasped an instinctive, "No!" but Quentin stepped past her.

"Do not be ridiculous, niece," said Lady Sybil, looking with favour upon this discerning gentleman. A fine pair of shoulders, for all that he leaned so heavily upon that cane. And what mischievous green eyes. A rascal, if ever she'd met one! "I am unmasked," she said, extending her white hand and smiling because the gentleman's lips lingered a shade too long upon her fingers. "I think we have not met . . . ?"

"I am John Macauley Somerville," said Quentin blandly.

"You doubtless will have heard of my brother Andrew. A charming fellow, but—famous brothers can be so tiresome. He sent me forth to poke about in search of traitors. A most taxing endeavour, ma'am, which has resulted in a recurrence of gout. Since I found myself close to some relations, I decided to inflict myself upon you. But my grand-niece tells me that poor Hector has passed to his reward."

Penelope stared at him, marvelling at the ease with which his inventive mind had fabricated a new identity, wishing with all her heart that he had gone when he might have, yet foolishly grateful that he'd not abandoned her to face alone the nightmare that must have followed. In the carriage the Corporal waited, listening frowningly and with one large hand gripped about the pistol in his belt. Daffy had started her dash for the carriage, only to retreat even more precipitately when she heard Lady Sybil's voice. Peeping through the leaves, she set Jasper's cage down and watched breathlessly.

"Do you say you are related to my husband?" asked Lady Sybil. "I have not heard him mention a Somerville branch, I think."

"Likely not, dear lady," Quentin acknowledged, his eyes travelling her with frank admiration. "My mother was aunt to the mother of the late Lady Hector. My wretched brother seldom stirs from his desk at Whitehall, and I have been much abroad of recent years, on affairs of State, you know." He sighed. "Pray accept my condolences upon poor Hector's passing. I had best be on my way now, and will leave you with—"

"No such thing," said my lady, taking his arm and smiling up at him coquettishly. "You must stay as our honoured guest. At least until my dear husband returns."

From the corner of his eye Quentin saw Penelope's aghast expression. He had, he thought ruefully, overdone it again! "I wish I might, lovely lady." He patted the small hand on his arm. "But—alas, my brother—" And Fate thwarted him, for as he drew back a wave of dizziness caused him to stagger.

"You there!" shrilled my lady, considerably alarmed as she slipped a steadying arm about 'John Macauley Somerville.' "Come and help your poor master! His gout troubles him."

Recovering her scattered wits, Penelope said, "Aunt, really I think Lord Joseph would not wish to keep my great-uncle from his mission. Perhaps—"

"For shame," cried my lady with splendid vehemence. "Would *you* turn an ailing kinsman from our door, I assure you your sainted papa would never have done so! Whatever must Mr. Somerville—" She paused. "It *is*—Mr.?"

"As a matter of fact," said Quentin, not one to settle for half-measures, "it is Sir John."

Lady Sybil beamed. So much better to entertain a titled relative than a commoner. And besides, once her dinner guests left she would be bored again.

She led the way up the steps, Quentin, very tired, following with Killiam's assistance, and Penelope bringing up the rear, plagued by apprehension over what this unexpected development might lead to.

About to cross the threshold, my lady halted, flinging up one white hand. From the shrubs beside the house had burst forth a silver ripple of song; a full-throated paean of praise.

'Jasper, you little beast!' thought Penelope, terrified.

"Only listen," said my lady, her voice throbbing with emotion. "Only listen to the *dear* birdie!"

In the shrubs, Daffy dealt the dear birdie's cage a sharp rap which effectively put a stop to his ill-timed serenade. She threw on her cloak, striving to conceal as much as possible of her burden beneath it, and retreated to the south door.

Having stepped gracefully into the entrance hall meanwhile, Lady Sybil sent one lackey running for Hargrave and another for Mrs. King. When those retainers arrived, they were notified that Sir John Macauley Somerville, one of my lord's distinguished relations, was to be shown at once to the best guest chamber, and a bed installed in his dressing room so that his man could remain close by. A lackey was despatched to arrange suitable accommodations for his cattle and servants. Her invitation that Sir John join her dinner guests having been politely refused, my lady sank into a stately curtsey.

"You will honour us, Sir John," she cooed, "if you treat this house as your own. Should you desire anything, you have only to pull your bellrope and my servants will wait upon you."

'Sir John' responded appropriately. My lady desired Penelope to ensure all was as she herself would have wanted because he was *her* great-uncle, after all, and having wished her new guest a sweet good night, she rustled off to rejoin the guests she neglected.

She was smiling as she entered the drawing room. It had not been her dear husband whose coach she had fancied to have heard, she told them. It had instead been one of Joseph's kinsmen. An emissary, in fact, of Sir Andrew Somerville—of whose exploits *everybody* knew. She perceived that her guests were impressed and when one of them asked dutifully just what it might be that Sir John was 'emissary-ing,' Sybil answered with a delicious shiver that he stood very high in government circles, and that his task had to do with "these wretched traitors in our midst." The explanation would, she thought, please her husband, for if a Jacobite hunter stayed at Highview, no one could suspect anything underhanded of being conducted here.

The guests exchanged sober glances. Sybil all but purred as she seated herself amongst them. Behind her gracious smile and her easy chatter, she was titillated. The gown she wore tonight was very décolleté. When she'd sunk into her curtsey, the old gentleman's eyes had lingered with appreciation upon the view that she was aware revealed most of her breasts. Sir John was quite decrepit, but in his younger days he must have been a very well-featured man. A harmless flirtation with him would help pass the time until Roland came back, and it might brighten the poor old fellow's dull existence for a day or two. . . .

130

"A day or two!" Penelope uttered an unladylike and irate snort. "Do you not comprehend, Don Quixote, that in *a day or two* my gentle uncle will return? What shall you do then?"

Lying full length upon the bed, one arm behind his head, Quentin answered with a slow smile, "Be gone, I trust. But—until then . . ." He laughed softly. "Gad, Penelope Anne—can you not see the lovely irony of it? Here I lie, an honoured guest in the home of the man who without a *soupçon* of conscience planned to torture me to death. The man who, even now, scours the countryside for my valuable head, so as to stick it on a pike! And while he stamps and searches, suffering innumerable inconveniences and privations and furies, here am I, regaining my strength in pampered comfort. Fairly wallowing in luxury; eating his food, drinking his wine, and consorting with his family." He chuckled and quoted, "'We need greater virtues to bear good fortune than bad. . . .'"

There was a glint in his eyes Penelope did not at all like. She said crossly, "Good God, Quentin! You gloat like a naughty little boy. Are you forgetting that my uncle spent much time with you? He'll not be fooled by a wig and a few bits of paint and cotton!"

"True. But never mind about that." He sobered, and sat up, watching her with a frown. "What's to happen to you if they discover you aided and abetted me in deception?"

"You should've thought of that, sir," the Corporal pointed out bodingly, "afore you had such a lovely time making up Sir John Somerville."

"Damn you—you're right," Quentin said wryly. "At the time, it was all I could come up with, but I see now that Rob's come at the root of it, for I've dragged you into my masquerade, poor lass."

"What stuff," she exclaimed, at once on the defensive for him. "I had jumped from the carriage steps. One shout from you and the coachman would have been well away before my aunt could have sent the soldiers after you."

His thick lashes lowered. "But surely you must know I could not leave once I'd glimpsed that incomparable golden-haired witchery. . . ."

Penelope glared at him, saw the quirk at the side of his wide mouth, and said, "Wretched creature! I vow you're as much a tease as ever you were! You did not leave because they'd have known then that you were *going*, not coming. And that I had helped you."

"Lor'!" exclaimed the Corporal, pausing as he hung up a fine green velvet coat with broad, pleated skirts. "I'd not thought o' that. They'd have had you off to the axe in no time, miss!"

The harsh reality of it all suddenly overwhelmed Penelope. She turned quickly to the window, but Quentin had seen her lips tremble, and he was off the bed and striding after her.

She was swung around. The brilliant eyes were smiling down at her. He swept her into a tight, consoling hug. Tears blinded her as a long, gentle hand stroked her hair. "Do you fancy I'd allow them to harm one hair of this funny, untidy little head?" he said.

At once irritated, she pulled away and stood with her back turned.

"Easy enough to say, sir," Killiam grunted. "But after we're gone it's liable to go cruel hard with Miss Penelope. Like as not they'll blame her for the whole and charge her with treason before you can say—"

With sudden and rare fury, Quentin rounded on him. "Blast your eyes! Do you *never* say anything cheerful? 'Fore God, but I'd be better off alone than listening to you moan and whine day and night! If you are so damnably out of curl, why in hell do you not take yourself off and cast your gloom over some other unlucky fellow?"

His eyes a green blaze in his white face, he glared at Killiam, who bowed his head and stood in silence with the air of a faithful dog inexplicably kicked by his god.

132

Her heart wrung, Penelope protested, "No, how can you talk to him so, when he has been so very good and loyal to you?" She turned to the stricken Corporal. "Major Chandler is very tired, you know. He did not mean—"

"By your leave, ma'am," snapped Quentin, "I'll make my own apologies." He stepped closer to the Corporal, who continued to gaze down at the carpet in abject misery, and said in a contrite voice, "I should be flogged for speaking so, after all you have done, old friend."

His head still bowed, the Corporal gulped, "Not your fault, sir. I—I'm sure I dunno how you put up with all me miseries. Only . . ." He lifted pleading eyes. "I allus sort of thought as ye knowed I didn't mean nothing by it. It's—just my silly, stupid way. Can't help it. . . ." His gaze flashed to Penelope, who had walked over to straighten the bed, her back to the two men. With a small gesture towards her, Killiam mumbled, "I know why you was so provoked, but—"

"There was no cause for me to lose my temper." Quentin clapped a hand on the Corporal's drooping shoulder and added with his warm and endearing smile, "I ask your pardon, Rob."

The Corporal said nothing, only he reached up to cover those thin fingers with his own strong clasp.

Fighting tears, Penelope plumped up the pillows. It was silly to be so hurt because he had used that harsh tone with her. He was still very much the invalid and under normal circumstances would have been confined to his bed for several more days at least, before venturing a few steps, much less coping with the exhausting events of this day. It came into her mind that had Geoffrey dealt her such a scold, she would have taken not the least offence. 'But Geoff loved me,' she thought, 'and he was my brother.' A sly inner voice taunted, 'Which is exactly how Quentin Chandler thinks of you, foolish chit! As your fond but careless brother.' Love, she reflected sadly, was a painful business when it was so one-sided. . . .

She turned from the bed and, trying to keep her voice calm and dispassionate like the bloodless creature he evidently supposed her to be, said, "I suppose this *contretemps* may have one redeeming feature—it will give you another day in which to rest, Major."

Penelope Anne Montgomery was not noted for the infallibility of her predictions.

Lady Sybil lost no time next morning. A note was delivered with Quentin's cup of hot chocolate, inviting him to join her at ten o'clock in the breakfast parlour. This presented a problem. His 'age' must be reapplied and, although Daffy, who had brought the chocolate, was able to commence her task at once, it was not a speedy process. When at last she was finished, it was a scramble to don Sir Hector's clothes and a freshly ironed wig, and Quentin was already late when he proceeded cautiously down the stairs.

Clad in a naughty pink silk gown, Lady Sybil waved away his apologies and greeted him warmly. Rather too warmly, he thought uneasily, meeting the flirtatious look she bestowed on him after he kissed her hand.

My lady's coquettishness vanished when Penelope joined them. She could see that her niece was shocked because she'd not gone into her blacks again, and she became rather irritable. It very soon dawned on her, however, that Penelope, with her pale face, mousy hair, and quiet manners, presented a delightfully dowdy contrast to her own blooming beauty, and she cheered up enormously.

"I mean to take your great-uncle for a drive, dear Penelope," she declared. "It must be many years since you visited the estate, Sir John. I fancy you will enjoy to see it again."

Her long eyelashes were fluttering at him, and he assured her politely that he would enjoy it excessively, but his heart sank. In a hundred ways she could trip him, for actually he knew very little of the Montgomerys. With a distinct shock he realized that he didn't even know what Lady Hector's Christian name had been. Sybil prattled on, and he responded appropriately. When the opportunity arose, he slanted a desperate glance at Penelope. She interpreted that silent plea correctly, but when

134

she attempted to accompany him upstairs she was foiled. It was my lady who offered her arm to "dear Sir John," and my lady who walked with him to his bedchamber door, so that it was not until a few minutes later that Penelope was able to slip in and join him.

She found him looking very distinguished in a green coat and a handsome white waistcoat embroidered with green *fleurs-de-lis*. He was most apprehensive, however, and begged that she tell him as much as possible of her late mother. "For I dread lest I betray us all by my lack of knowledge."

Penelope rather doubted that her aunt meant to discuss family matters, but she did all she might to help, providing pieces of information that someone in "Sir John's" position might be expected to know and describing various relations until Quentin groaned that he would never be able to remember them all.

"Never worry so," she said as she walked with him to the door. "Just remember that my mama's name was Margaret, she was held to be very beautiful, and they called her Meg. You told Sybil that your mother was great-aunt to mine. What was *her* name?"

"Margaret," he said promptly, and added a pleased, "sometimes Meg."

"No, no. I mean *your*—Sir John's—mama."

He clutched at his wig. "Oh, egad! She'll have to have a name, too, will she? Very well—er, Petrouchka. I'll not forget that one."

"Nor she believe it! Quentin—*do* be serious!"

His eyes slanted an emerald twinkle at her. "Catherine, then. Better?"

"Very nice. But you must *remember* it. Your mama was Catherine Macauley."

"Where'd you get the Macauley? Whoops! It's my middle name. I'd forgot."

"Good God! Now—listen. . . . You are Sir John Macauley Somerville. Your mother was Catherine Macauley, and she was great-aunt to *my* mama who was . . . ?"

"Margaret." He beamed at her proudly.

"Correct. And your brother . . . ?"

He stared blankly. "Brother . . . ?"

It was Penelope's turn to tear her hair. "Your *famous* brother, Quentin. Sir Andrew. The one who sent you here!"

"Heaven help us all," groaned Sir John Macauley Somerville.

That small prayer was to remain in Penelope's thoughts for the rest of that long morning. She performed a few household duties, but excused herself from staying downstairs after one o'clock, on the grounds that she still felt rather pulled after her bad cold. Truth to tell, she was as nervous as a cat and, once upstairs, she closed her door and flew to the window, scanning the drive in vain for a glimpse of the returning carriage.

She knelt in the window seat, knowing it was senseless to worry so. Quentin was not on top of his form, but he was an intelligent man. He'd go along famously and probably charm Sybil out of any suspicions she might hold. She would very likely find him handsome despite his 'years' and flirt with him even though he might have one foot in the grave. Penelope scowled and went to the press to look over the gowns she'd had packed away for the past year and a half. She must be ready with her new plan whenever the chance might offer . . . and there was not much time.

"But we have lots of time, dear—cousin." Lady Sybil edged a tiny bit closer to the old gentleman. They had left the carriage and wandered through a pleasant copse of trees before sitting here on the wall that divided the south meadow from the park. It was a low wall, but she'd convinced Sir John that she must be lifted onto it. He had seemed breathless when he'd perched beside her, but the hands that had encompassed her tiny waist had been deliciously strong, despite his age. On this sunny morning, my lady had worn a full-skirted gown of blue and violet floral silk. The neckline, swooping very low, was edged with tiny pleats of lace. Her hair was powdered and pulled high on her head to fall in thick ringlets onto her creamy shoulders. She knew she looked very well, and she pouted and went on, "Lud, but one would think you anxious to leave us. And here am poor I"—she leaned to him coyly—"so lonely for the company of a gentleman now that my husband has gone from me."

"About the King's business, I understand," said Quentin, unpleasantly aware that he should have pleaded age and infirmity rather than swinging the lady onto this blasted wall. "You must miss him sadly, poor child."

"Child, is it?" Playfully, she rapped her fan on his knee. "I doubt that very many years separate us, dear sir. Nor . . ." She spread the fan again and held it just below her big eyes. "Nor do I fancy you so *very* feeble."

"Why—at my age, you know, one has to be—"

Entranced by his smile, she leaned closer, whispering, "Careful?"

Her ripe lips were parted as she lowered and folded her fan. Delicate, blue-veined lids drooped provocatively over those great brown eyes. And her bodice, what there was of it, was sagging so that one might easily—

Quentin recovered himself with an effort and drew back. "I was—going to say," he stammered, "that—that one has to remember we are—related, ma'am. And I a—very old fellow. Not up to your—er, playfulness, my pretty."

"How is it, I wonder," she said thoughtfully, "that your face may be just a trifle—middle-aged, let us say. And yet your eyes are so very . . ."

He stiffened. "Very—what, ma'am?"

She giggled. "I'll not flatter you, you rogue. Tell me of Peggy. What was she like? I never knew her."

'Peggy . . .' he thought desperately. 'Who the deuce is Peggy?'

His hesitation was noted and the obvious interpretation placed upon it. "Penelope's poor mama," my lady prompted.

"Joseph always called her Peggy. She was a beauty, he said, so she could not have resembled my niece who is so plain as any pikestaff." His frown and the slight lifting of his chin warned her, and she amended, "Not that she ain't a good enough gel—in her way."

"A very good girl, indeed," said Quentin austerely. "But I fancy you are correct, my lady. Margaret did have a look of young Geoff about her, now that you mention it. Especially about the—ah, eyes, y'know."

"What a memory! Why, she must have been gone these . . . how many years?"

'Good God!' thought Quentin. "Now—er, let me see," he muttered.

With a sudden trill of laughter, she leaned to him. "See what, you naughty boy?"

Her white, rounded bosom was scant inches beneath his chin. He thought faintly, 'I am a . . . sick old man . . .' and clung to the wall, answering threadily, "I . . . forget."

Edging ever nearer, she murmured, "Not—everything, I trust?"

'Help!' thought Quentin.

Sybil stretched up to place a moist kiss upon his chin. "My goodness," she said, peering at him curiously. "You do use a lot of paint, dear sir. I wonder it—"

Quentin fairly leapt from the wall. Flung off balance, my lady squealed and tumbled. He grabbed for her instinctively, then gritted his teeth, reeling and sickened by the resultant stab of pain.

Sybil gripped at his arm to steady herself, then gripped tighter, laughing provocatively. It was either free himself or fall at her feet. He thrust her away and, to cover the fact that the landscape wavered before his eyes and that Sybil herself was a blur, he croaked, "Madam, I remind you that I am kin to your husband, and a guest in his home."

Enraged, Sybil drew herself up. "How—*dare* you! Be assured that I—" But she did not finish her threat. The old gentleman's eyes were positively glazed, and tiny drops of perspiration trickled down his temples. With a little cry of admiration, she flung herself into his unready arms. "What iron control," she breathed huskily. "Do you think I do not see how you desire me? Dear, foolish fool. I knew the moment you arrived that you were a wicked rogue. And I have ever . . . loved a rogue. So—you may have just one little kiss, my poor gallant gentleman."

Despite his throbbing arm, a bubble of mirth rose in Quentin's throat. The strumpet! She really fancied that no man could fail to lust after her! He had begun to hope his noble renunciation would have so irked her she would demand he leave Highview at once. Now, however, another and even more tantalizing notion tickled his fancy. His eyes began to dance, and he bent lower. She lay against him, her eyes half-closed, her smiling lips parted invitingly, and that fantastic bosom surging against the slight restraint of her gown.

'It would,' thought Quentin, 'be such a pity to let it all go to waste. . . .'

It was almost half-past two o'clock before the carriage came into view, moving at a leisurely rate along the drivepath to disappear momentarily around the jutting side of the house.

Penelope, who had been sitting at the window of 'Sir John's' room, called a tremendously relieved, "They're coming!" The Corporal and Daffy left their cards and ran to join her, and all three peered anxiously as the carriage came into sight once more.

"So long they've been gone," murmured Daffy.

Penelope said a worried, "Poor Major Chandler must be quite exhausted. I only pray he has not made some dreadful blunder. My aunt is very shrewd in some ways."

Having formed a fairly accurate opinion of my lady's character, the Corporal's thoughts had taken a different direction, but he said nothing.

The guest bedchamber faced west and thus the carriage came to a stop almost directly beneath the windows. The groom sprang down and opened the door. He did not let down the steps but, having glanced inside, stood back and waited in a patient, wooden-faced way. The fear in Penelope's heart deepened. Why did they not get out? Was Quentin so ill he could not walk? She was on the brink of running into the hall when the steps were put down and Quentin descended to hand my lady down. Sybil leaned to him and they wandered slowly up the steps together, she clinging to his arm and gazing up at him in what Penelope thought a disgracefully bold way.

'Wretched woman,' she thought, hurrying into the hall. 'She thinks to enslave every man who comes within her orbit!'

By the time she reached the lower flight of steps, the travellers were in the front hall. My lady's little hands were on the old gentleman's chest, and he clasped them tightly, though whether to support her or keep himself from falling would have been hard to say.

Seething, Penelope trilled sweetly, "Did you have a nice drive?"

They both jerked around to face her. She thought that Quentin looked positively haggard, yet his eyes glinted brightly. My lady Sybil wore an expression in which surprise and another emotion seemed to struggle for supremacy. Penelope could neither identify that emotion, nor did she very much care. Running down the last few stairs, she cried, "My goodness! Such a long drive has been too much for you, Uncle John! I trust you have not made yourself ill."

Quentin uttered a mumbling jumble of refutation, but my lady gave a little rippling laugh. "'Twould take considerably more than a long drive to tire this . . . magnificent gentleman," she said huskily. "Nonetheless, I think we both should rest, dear Sir John." She smiled up into Quentin's face with that same expression that Penelope now recognized as a sort of awed admiration. "We'd a silly little accident," Sybil rushed on, having seen Sir John's gaze slant with some apprehension to her

140

niece. "I was so clumsy as to fall, and your great-uncle was so gallant as to catch me, but I fear it has been rather a—er, strain on him."

"Not at all," murmured Quentin.

"Small wonder you are so wearied, sir," said Penelope in rather a brittle voice. "May I help you to your room?"

Sir John thanked her and said jauntily that he was not so decrepit he could not manage to negotiate a few stairs. My lady leaned to his ear and whispered something that so amused him he tripped, and Penelope slipped a supporting arm about his waist.

"Sweet child," he murmured. "Damme if I ain't developing a liking for all this pampering."

When they reached the second-floor landing, my lady clasped Sir John's hand and promised she would have luncheon brought to his chamber. "You must have a nice long nap," she urged, "for we cannot be deprived of your exhilarating presence at the dinner table. Until seven, then. . . ." She withdrew her clasp, smiled dreamily at him and murmured a soft and caressing, "Adieu, dear . . . cousin. . . ."

"What a revolting performance!" snarled Penelope the moment Sybil was out of earshot.

Quentin darted a startled glance at her.

"That horrid, horrid woman," she went on. "Only look how exhausted you are. Quentin—why *ever* did you let her keep you out so long?"

"She is—something hard to withstand," he asserted, studiously avoiding her indignant eyes.

"Especially when she wants to captivate some hapless gentleman! Did she really fall?"

"Oh, she fell, right enough."

Quite aware of that betraying quirkish grin, Penelope said scornfully, "Very revealingly, I've no doubt. Faith, but she's a—" She cut off the sentence in the nick of time, and finished, "I suppose you hurt your arm?"

Leaning against the wall as she opened the door, Quentin

141

said, "Not to speak of. And—I could not very well let her just—crash down, now could I?"

He could not, of course, Penelope acknowledged as she relinquished him to the Corporal's care and went to her own bedchamber. But—oh, how she wished he had! It was very apparent that Lady Sybil was completely captivated, in which case it would take all Quentin's diplomacy to escape the lady's clutches before Lord Joseph returned. She sighed. At least he would be able to rest for a little while. From the look of him just now, he was likely fast asleep at this very moment.

She was quite mistaken. Far from sleeping, Quentin lay on the bed, convulsed, his mirth so hilarious that Corporal Rob, grinning broadly, was finally obliged to put a pillow over his face.

Penelope's best mourning gown was of black velvet, trimmed with white lace, having a square-cut neckline and rounded hoops, the great back Watteau pleats swooping into a small train. It was a charming dress, but Penelope had not worn it since she had been included in a small dinner party at Sir Thomas Beasley's house the previous Christmas. She gasped for mercy when Daffy tugged relentlessly at her stay laces, but when the dress was fitted to her trim waist she was quite pleased with the effect.

Daffy brought out Lady Margaret's pearls but, having slipped them about Penelope's slender white throat, whisked them out of sight again. "Too fast, by far," she decreed primly. "It's bad enough that milady cavorts in her bright colours only nine months after dear Master Geoffrey's passing aloft. We want no tongues wagging about *you*, Miss Penny."

Penny agreed at once, feeling wretchedly disloyal to dear Geoff's memory. "But"—she touched the hair which Daffy had dressed so severely that it caused her eyebrows to feel stretched to the crown of her head—"do you not think I might curl and—and powder my hair? Just for—"

"Heavenly whiskers, miss!" Much shocked, Daffy cried, "Whatever next? We must go slowly. I dast not think what my lady will say when she sees you looking so prettily in this gown. Slow and careful, Miss Penny. Like a tortoise with the ague." She sprayed a discreet puff of Spring Morning behind the ear of the reluctant tortoise. High heels clicked in the hall at that instant and, turning to her maid in dismay, Penelope received Spring Morning in her face instead. She sneezed violently just as my lady entered the room with a rustle of satin and laces.

All dainty femininity from the top of her high powdered wig to the tip of her tiny begemmed slipper, Sybil raised a lace-edged handkerchief to her little nose and surveyed her niece uneasily. "Lud, girl—have you that horrid cold, still? Heaven knows you've lain about doing nothing long enough that I'd fancied you were over it."

"So I am, ma'am. Though I thank you for your concern."

Penelope's irony went right over Sybil's pretty head. "You do not look almost well. You look horrid. Wherever did you find that antiquated gown? I vow it makes you look older than Sir John. Go and sit over there and try to breathe in the other direction. Saffy—or whatever your name is—fetch a chair for me, and then you may go."

Daffy pulled the chair to the point at which my lady felt relatively safe from any of Penelope's lingering germs. It was as well, thought Daffy, yearning to tug the chair a foot or two to the rear as my lady settled herself upon it, that she'd not allowed poor miss to wear her mama's pearls, for they certainly would have drawn attention to her flawless complexion. And had she piled up and powdered her curls . . . ! She suppressed a shudder. Not that Miss Penny was a beauty, nor ever would be. But there was something about her . . . something that drew all the gentlemen's eyes. And my lady knew it!

She slanted an encouraging glance at Penelope, bobbed a curtsey and took herself to the door, wondering what Lady

Tickle-Me-Quick—as she'd long ago apostrophized Sybil—wanted here. She certainly looked a dasher in that pink gown, the bodice cut so low it almost reached her waist, and enough to make any man's head swim. Daffy closed the door, her heart heavy. She longed to arrange Penelope's luxuriant hair into a more becoming style, to dress her in the pretty gowns that had looked so well on her tall, slender person, to busy herself with rouge and powder. Instead of which, obedient to the Major's orders, she'd done all she might to render the dear girl as unattractive as possible. There'd been nothing she could do about the gown of course. Short of tearing it "accidental" which might have made her mistress suspicious. And it would be cruel to get her hopes up, when Major Chandler might not be able to pull off his scheme.

Penelope said, as the door closed, "You look very well, ma'am. Are you expecting Uncle Joseph home?"

Lady Sybil levelled a cold stare at her. "Do not be impertinent. You know very well he would not like me to put off my blacks. Indeed, I would never have done so had not your great-uncle been so sadly in need of cheering up. He seems most depressed, poor old fellow."

This intelligence surprised Penelope, but she said nothing.

My lady slanted an oblique glance at her and began to flutter her fan. "It seems strange," she observed idly, "that no one in the family has spoken of him before this."

With a twinge of nervousness, Penelope said, "I doubt anyone has even thought of the gentleman for years. There was some—er, scandal, I believe. I don't know what. The Somervilles are related in a distant way to my mama."

"So the old gentleman said. He has . . . never married . . . ?"

"I really could not say."

"How odd."

"Odd?" echoed Penelope, frightened.

"One might suppose so exceeding attractive a man would have been snapped up long ago." Watching her niece, Sybil

144

murmured, "He is old now, of course, but—exactly how old is he?"

Desperate, Penelope stammered, "I do not know. Near seventy, I would think, to look at him."

"What rubbish!" Irked, Sybil contradicted, "In his early sixties at most. And even at that . . ." She broke off, staring at the empty grate, then went on in a softer voice, "It is remarkable that he should be so amazingly . . ."

Penelope said, intrigued, "Amazingly—what, ma'am?"

"Eh?" Sybil turned dreaming eyes on her niece, recollected herself, and stood, smoothing down her satin. "Nothing you are ever likely to understand, poor creature," she said unkindly. "I shall ask my husband, since you appear to be so sadly uninformed as to your dear mama's relations. Lord Joseph has ever been vastly proud of her side of the family." She opened the door and said over her shoulder, "I have told Cook that we will dine at eight. There is no need for you to come down until then." And she was gone, leaving behind the heavy fragrance of her perfume.

Penelope, who had politely risen, gazed with considerable anxiety at the closed door. Sybil had come here only to try to get information about 'Sir John.' He had properly bewitched her, which had been most unwise. She gave a rueful sigh. As if he could help himself. It was as natural for him to attract the ladies as it was for she herself to fail to attract him. "There is no need for you to come down until then. . . ." She took up her fan and began to ply it abstractedly, although it was chilly in the room. My lady wanted to be alone with her fascinating guest. . . .

IX

"I make it a practice," Quentin murmured into the warm curve of Sybil's throat, "never to answer questions when there are better things to be done." She offered only a breathless little giggle by way of resistance, and he kissed her long and thoroughly. They sat on the sofa in a cosy saloon that was rich with crimson and gold. Because of the coolness of the evening, a fire burned in the marble hearth, the air was warm and scented, and Quentin had seen to it that my lady's glass was always filled. Sybil responded to him with a dismaying ardour, and he proceeded as he knew she wished, taking more and more liberties until Sybil was moaning faintly, her eyes closed, her head thrown back in eager submission.

"Go on," she gasped blissfully. "My darling . . . my superb lover . . . why do you stop?"

Shaken, he lifted his head from her fragrant bosom. "I am—a mere man, lovely one."

Soft with passion, her eyes opened. "You are magnificent," she said, her voice just above a husky sigh. "Never have I been loved with such fire . . . and virility."

"For an old fellow I do not so badly, eh?" he asked, his eyes twinkling.

She took his hand and pressed it to her lips. "You are wondrous—even for a young man! Indeed"—she smiled coyly—"when my husband returns he will be hard put to it to—"

It was the chance he'd waited for. With an exclamation of repugnance, he put her from him and sprang to his feet. "Do not so reproach me!" he cried dramatically. "Oh, do not!"

"Eh?" said Sybil, sitting up and blinking at him. "How should I reproach you?"

"How should you not?" he cried, beginning to stride up and down and wave his arms about. "Coming here . . . accepting of my kinsman's hospitality. And—and in return, seducing his wife! Oh!" Up went one arm in a wild gesture that caused my lady to draw back uneasily. "Wickedness, thy name is Somerville!"

"Good gracious!" exclaimed Sybil, not overpleased by this new side of Sir John. "You are very hard on yourself, I think."

His arm lowered with slow drama. He sighed, "They will be harder . . . in the monastery."

Her jaw fell. "M—monastery?"

He hung his head. "I take the vows . . . next week."

"You . . . do?" gasped Sybil, failing but single-minded. "What a dreadful waste!"

Vastly amused, Quentin could almost have liked the wretched woman. She was wholly immoral, cruel, and without a vestige of faithfulness, but at least she did not feign either reluctance or repentance. With difficulty he responded heavily, "My entire life has been a waste."

"Surely not, dear sir? You have spent it in the service of your King and country, after all, and—"

"And—sinned excessively, alas." His shoulders slumped. "Even now, I sin. On this—my last mission. I had hoped to end my career with a fine coup. But having reached here—instead of tending to business—" He sighed again.

147

Sybil had tensed and now said keenly, "But I understood you to say you *chanced* to be travelling this way."

"Did I say that?" He averted his face, then said forcefully, "It will not do, ma'am! Do you not see? You are not to be blamed. I took advantage of you. I was bewitched by your beauty, alas!"

She had been a little alarmed, but at his last words she relaxed a little, smiling.

"I cannot enter the Order with such a flagrant abuse of hospitality on my overburdened conscience," he said with resolution. Watching her reflection in the mirrored sconce above the mantel, he added, "I shall have to confess."

She was growing bored, and her irritation showed when she said pettishly, "Oh, I do not know why you must make such a piece of work of it."

"When will your husband return?" he asked, turning to her, solemn-faced.

Sybil brightened. "Never fear, my love, I do not expect him until tomorrow at the very earliest."

"Ah. That decides it then. I shall wait and try to find words that will mitigate my offence."

"*What?*" Whitening, Sybil sprang to her feet. "You never mean to confess to *Joseph?*"

He spread his hands. "To whom else, dear lady?"

"My God!"

"Oh, yes. To Him, certainly."

"No, no! What I mean is— I had fancied you meant to confess to the—the High Priest, or whomever—"

"The Abbot," he inserted gently, grateful that her knowledge of such matters was even less than his own. "But that would be a cowardly evasion, my lady. If your husband wishes to reproach me—"

"*Reproach* you?" she squeaked, a hand pressed to her heaving bosom. "He will rend you limb from limb!"

Under the circumstances, Quentin thought this would be a quite logical reaction on Lord Joseph's part. Trying not to grin, he said with saintly humility, "I should deserve it, I fear." He groaned and put a hand over his eyes. "I must have been mad!"

It came to Sybil that this was an eccentric old gentleman, after all. She was very frightened but, before she could respond, the door opened. "Oh, come in, come in," she said crossly.

Penelope obeyed, flashing a quick glance from her aunt's petulant frown to the dramatic pose of Sir John Macauley Somerville. A little glow of mirth crept into her eyes. Now what was he up to? She dropped him a curtsey and said demurely that she hoped he was rested.

Quentin frowned at her. He had distinctly told Daffy to attire Penny as unattractively as possible, instead of which here she was looking as fresh and sweet as a flower by comparison with Lady Sybil's paint and posturing. "My soul cannot rest," he said mournfully. "Not until I have words with your Uncle Joseph."

Taken aback, Penelope exclaimed, "Good gracious! What about, sir?"

He came forward and ushered her to a chair by the fire. "Alas," he sighed, "were I to tell you—"

"Fie upon you, Sir John," Sybil interpolated shrilly, fear gleaming in her eyes. "'Twould be most improper of you. And at all events, I cannot say exactly how long my husband will be away. It—it may be several weeks."

Quentin uttered an artistic moan and went over to gaze morosely into the flames.

"Weeks?" echoed Penelope. "But—I thought you said—"

Sybil made an imperative gesture, then tapped her temple and nodded suggestively to Sir John.

Penelope viewed the droop of Quentin's shoulders with admiration. How the rascal had managed it, she could not begin to guess, but it was clear her aunt's infatuation was cooling. "I hope," she ventured, praying she was saying the right thing, "it will not be impossible for you to wait such a time, sir? I know my aunt and I would be most delighted if you can do so."

Sybil, whose frantic signals to her niece had apparently gone unseen, now said, "Your uncle has a most urgent appointment, Penelope. He is to enter a monastic Order next week."

Quentin could not resist turning his head to witness the effect of this solemn pronouncement. He was rewarded. Penelope's big eyes were almost as round as her pretty mouth. Well aware that his own eyes were all too apt to reflect his amusement, he lowered them and murmured humbly, "You may fancy it is too late."

"Not if you leave at first light," said Sybil, misinterpreting.

"I—do not think I can," he said, rather muffled. "How very much more pleasant it would be to spend these last few days in the company of a lovely lady. And besides, if your husband does return, I can—"

Desperate, Sybil babbled, "You can enjoy the company of a lady on your journey, dear sir."

Quentin turned to her, doubtfully.

"My poor—Penelope," said Sybil, groping at any straw that offered, "has been in blacks for nigh two years. It has been in my mind these many weeks to send her to Town to stay with her Aunt Mary for a change of scene."

Stunned, Penelope stared at her.

"My route lies north, to the monastery at York," said Quentin. "But first, I've to return to Town, of course."

"Why, then," Sybil purred, "you could kill two birds with one stone, dear sir. Penelope could travel safely under your escort. She is a bright girl and would, I am sure, enliven your own last few days of—of civilian life."

Her eyes alight, Penelope ran to clasp Sir John's hand. "Oh! Dear sir, I do not mean to impose, but—do—*do* please say I may go with you!"

Hargrave announced sonorously, "Dinner is served, milady."

Sybil excused herself and hurried to engage him in a brief, murmurous discussion.

Penelope whispered, "You magician! How ever did you do it?"

150

"With brilliance, insight, and intuition." He grinned. And as Sybil turned to them again, he patted his grand-niece's hand and said, "How can I refuse? Very well, little Miss Montgomery. You may accompany me to Town."

They went in to dinner, two people who were secretly elated, and a third who thought rather wistfully that, although Sir John had been superb in some ways, it was as well to end the idyll here.

Daffy was waiting eagerly when Penelope went up to bed two hours later, and when she learned how things had evolved, she gave a little squeal and hugged her mistress ecstatically. "Just like the Major hoped, Miss Penny," she cried. "Look, look! He bade me get ready, just in case." She led Penelope into the dressing room where two portmanteaux, already packed, lay on the bed Quentin had lately occupied.

Bewildered, Penelope said, "He . . . hoped this would happen?"

"Aye, miss. More'n that. He *meant* it should happen! He never had no thought to leave you!"

Her heart swelling with thanks, Penelope blinked down at bright silks and satins. "But—why these? Daffy, we have three months yet of mourning. I—I could not."

"The Major says your blacks will be sure to attract attention wherever we go, miss. So once we'm safe away you must become a young lady travelling with your grandpapa."

Daffy chattered brightly on. She and Corporal Robert Killiam were to go with their respective employers, of course, for now everything was perfectly proper.

At such a joyous moment, how could Penelope refuse permission for a fifth passenger? It was firmly stipulated, however, that Jasper was to travel on the box with the Flying Dutchman and the groom.

As it transpired, when they left Highview the following morning, it was in two carriages. Quentin had persuaded Sybil that on a long journey he must support his "gouty foot" on the opposite seat and that, while he was willing to share the interior of the carriage with his grand-niece, he could not view with equanimity the additional presence of her abigail plus his man. Dreading lest he revert to his planned confession, Sybil had hurriedly agreed to the loan of Lord Hector's rather shabby old travelling carriage, in which could be piled the luggage, plus Daffy and Killiam, with Sir John's groom assuming the role of coachman.

Having parted tearlessly from her aunt and been settled in the well-sprung coach, Penelope looked out of the window and watched Highview vanish from sight. Sadness touched her briefly as she wondered whether she ever would return to this loved home, but she was so overjoyed because Quentin was safely away that her spirits could not for long remain depressed. The morning was chill and misty, with dripping leaves and vapours curling up from the meadows towards low hanging grey clouds, but she exclaimed happily, "Oh, how glorious it all is!"

Quentin, seated beside her, was as pleased by her delight as she was pleased by the passing countryside. But he teased, "One would think you'd never seen a soggy summer morning before."

She turned to him eagerly. "Not such a morning as this. Oh—not for almost two years. Do you understand, dear friend? I am free! At last! I am free of them all!"

He did understand, and he squeezed her hand in silent sympathy. Penelope was mildly surprised by the grimness in his eyes, but almost at once he drew back, laughing. "Was there ever anything more exquisite than when those confounded troopers helped me into the carriage?"

"Or anything more terrifying than when they first marched up?" She shuddered. "I was sure they were going to arrest you."

He turned his head against the squabs, the better to scan her animated face. "You did not look terrified, my intrepid ex-grand-niece and present grand-daughter. In fact, you've behaved throughout like a regular Trojan. Lord knows how I shall go on without you."

152

Just for an instant his eyes were sombre, but then his lashes swept down, and he turned away again, saying lightly, "Speaking of which—where do we seek this aunt of yours?"

The thought of leaving him banished her brief sense of confusion. She replied, "Aunt Mary has a dear little house in a village called Hampstead, north of Town. But for the present, sir, should I not be putting off this habit?"

It had been her initial thought that they might stop at some secluded tavern where she could change clothes. Early that morning, however, Daffy had brought word that Major Chandler respectfully suggested she wear a light coloured travelling gown beneath her blacks so that at some opportune moment she would merely have to shed the outer garment. Were they to stop at an inn, he'd pointed out, a lady who arrived in mourning and departed in everyday dress must inevitably be remembered.

Quentin had already given his coachman instructions, and very soon the carriages turned on to a quiet lane leading through a grove of poplar trees. Here, Quentin alighted and walked back to confer with the groom who drove the second carriage. Penelope quickly divested herself of the black habit and thrust it into the small bag she had brought for the purpose.

No sooner had she accomplished this than she heard hoofbeats, and there was just time enough to settle herself before a masculine voice called, "Are you in some trouble, coachman?"

Dutch, as the coachman was known, rumbled a response, and a moment later a rider came up to the window. Penelope thought he would perhaps nod and go on his way. Instead, he glanced in curiously, promptly removed his tricorne and bent his powdered head to the open window.

"Good day to you, ma'am. May I be of any assistance?"

He was a pleasant-seeming young man whose light complexion and sandy eyebrows hinted at red hair. His eyes were blue, his undistinguished, rather snub nose dusted with freckles. He had a firm chin and a generous mouth that now smiled en-

153

gagingly at her. She was very sure that Dutch had told him they required no assistance, and was more than a little elated to realize that (after all this time!) a gentleman was flirting with her. "It is indeed kind in you to offer," she replied, as usual quite forgetting to be fashionably shy and simpering. "We have stopped for a moment so that my grandpapa may confer with our second coachman."

He glanced back, saw an old gentleman stamping up fast, and bent again to the window. "May I introduce myself? I am Duncan Tiele, and—"

"Did you wish to speak with me, sir?"

That growl of a voice amused Penelope. Mr. Tiele sighed and drew back, dismounting and extending a gauntletted hand. "Tiele, sir. Duncan. At your service."

Quentin scowled at the proffered hand and took it with an obvious lack of enthusiasm. "Thank you. But we require no service at the moment." He turned to the carriage, and opened the door. "You all right, m'dear?"

Behind him, Mr. Tiele lifted his brows ruefully.

Her eyes full of laughter, Penelope assured her 'dear grandpapa' that she was quite all right. "Mr. Tiele fancied we might be in difficulties, you see."

"Don't see at all," said Quentin, turning to glare testily at the would-be Good Samaritan. "Can't a man talk to his coachman for a minute without his grand-daughter being pestered by every young upstart from here to Jericho?"

"No, really, sir," Mr. Tiele objected. "Not pestering. Do assure you. There are groups of varmints hunting down rebels hereabouts and they're apt to shoot first and ask questions later. So I—"

"And so they should, sir! England stands in no pressing need of rebels. Nor I in need of your much vaunted service." Quentin started to swing the steps down, recollected his age, and fumbled the business so convincingly that the eager Mr. Tiele had let down the steps in a flash and all but lifted the 'old gentleman' inside. Quentin had not expected such a burst of energy and, resenting the powerful boost, attempted to wrench away from it, thereby contriving to twist his hurt arm. "Con-confound you, sir!" he panted, but was too breathless to say more, and had to content himself with wheezing, infuriated gasps, and a wrathful shaking of his cane at the well-meaning young gallant.

Mounting up with a lithe swing, Mr. Tiele again bent to the window and surveyed Quentin anxiously. "Poor old fellow," he said sympathetically. "Heart—is it, ma'am?"

"Gout," Penelope answered. "No, Grandpapa, you really must not so excite yourself. It is more than kind of you to try to help, Mr.—er . . ."

"Tiele, ma'am. Silly name. T-i-e-l-e. No one ever knows how to spell it if they hear it said, nor how to pronounce it if they read it." He grinned. "Cannot think how my papa was so foolish as to inherit it. I—ah, fancy your own name is less difficult, Miss . . . ?"

"Montgomery," she said, amused by such astute impertinence.

"And none of your affair," roared Quentin, recovering his breath and lunging forward to snatch Penelope's hand away before the eager Mr. Tiele could grasp it. "Devil take you, you young jackanapes! Be off about your business! Drive on, coachman!"

He drew up the window and resumed his seat as the whip cracked, the horses leaned into their collars and the great coach rolled forward, leaving poor Mr. Tiele looking wistfully after it.

Penelope laughed merrily. "Unfortunate young man! You were something hard on him, Quentin!"

"Be damned if I know what the world is coming to," he asserted with rather questionable justification but considerable indignation. "Fellow lays eyes on a pretty girl, and forgets whatever manners ever were bred into him!"

Penelope's betraying heart had given a happy leap. She asked hesitantly, "Am I—pretty, Quentin?"

"Don't be such a goose. 'Course you are. Likely a lot of men

155

would find you downright—" He checked abruptly. "Gad, that fellow had a silly face! If I'd behaved in such a way at his age—"

"*You!*" She gave a trill of mirth. "You *are* his age! And you've no room to criticize after the way you flirted with my aunt!"

He reddened and looked quickly away. "A different matter, entirely."

"And perfectly justified," she agreed warmly, laying her hand on his arm.

He smiled at her, covering her hand with his own and saying softly, "What a jolly good trooper you are, Penny. Always were. Most girls would likely have raised a very great fuss."

"How could I do so," said the 'jolly good trooper,' "with you entering a monastery next week?"

He threw back his head and shouted with laughter. "Oh, faith! Do not remind me. Shall I ever forget Sybil's expression? Like a landed trout!"

Penelope joined in his mirth until he added breathlessly, "And your own face not far removed from it."

"What a horrid thing to say! I'll own I was a trifle taken aback . . ."

He at once imitated her astonishment so exaggeratedly that she cried an indignant, "Oh! Wretched beast!"

He chuckled. "You named me so once or twice before, as I recall. At Lac Brillant."

"What happy days they were," she said with a sigh.

He glanced at her sharply. What a fool to have made her think of the good old days. "Speaking of names," he said, "it is time for you to change yours, m'dear."

"It is?" she said, suddenly short of breath.

"Aye. Unless we are to set the pack properly on our heels!"

The dream faded. Frightened, she asked, "You think they'll be after us, then?"

"I do, Penelope Anne. And it will set them on the right track at once if they discover Miss Montgomery now wears a pretty green gown."

156

"Oh, heavens! Of course! I should not have given Mr. Tiele my true name! What a widgeon I am."

"It's as well you realize it," he teased, but her answering smile was wan. He went on cheerfully, "I pray you do not fall into a deep decline over one small error. When do you suppose your uncle will return to Highview?"

"I had feared . . . today, perhaps. They certainly have not recaptured you. And Uncle Joseph is a man who likes his creature comforts. I doubt he will stay from home much longer."

"Hmmmnn. Still—you are not positive, wherefore we may have as much as two days' head start. And at that, it could be another week before they guess who Sir John MacTavish Somerville really was!"

"I wish *you* might guess! You are *Macauley*—not MacTavish!"

"I hesitate to contradict a lady, but I think the poor gentleman is gone to his reward." He bowed as elaborately as the swaying carriage would allow. "Permit me to present m'self, dear lady. Mr. Martin, at your service."

Penelope put one slim finger beneath her chin and ducked her head. "And I am Miss Anne Martin."

"My grand-daughter?"

She appraised him thoughtfully. "You do not really look very much like a great-uncle, or a grandpapa. Perhaps you should merely be my uncle."

Illogically pleased by this, he hesitated. "There'd have to be quite a spread in our family. You don't look a day over five and twenty."

"*Five—and—twenty!*" Her eyes flashing indignation, she saw his covert grin. "Oh—wicked boy! Are you never serious?"

"Never."

She started to scold him, half seriously, half in amusement. Leaning back against the squabs, Quentin closed his eyes and smiled good-humouredly. But he was thinking that they would be fortunate indeed if Lord Joseph and that bastard Otton did not return until tomorrow, and even more fortunate if Sir John Macauley Somerville was not very soon identified as the rebel

157

fugitive. The hunt would be on then, with a vengeance, and likely the reward on his head doubled, since they'd think he had deceived this innocent girl and run off with her as hostage. An unhappy prospect. Of one thing he must make very sure. Penelope Anne must be safely deposited with her Aunt Mary long before the hue and cry came thundering at his heels.

The skies darkened in late morning, and they approached old Oxford town through a light rain. Quentin had fallen asleep, and Penelope was looking out of the window, still enchanted by the constantly changing scene and wondering if she had ever been so happy. It was a happiness inspired by other things than her release from the dreary drudgery of her life at Highview, she realized as she turned to the man beside her.

Asleep, the humorous quirk was gone from his lips, and his mouth drooped wearily. Many of the lines in his face and the excessive pallor had been applied, of course, but he looked defenceless and vulnerable, and her heart twisted. She leaned to tuck away a curling lock of auburn hair that had escaped from under his wig. An unexpected sound caused her hand to jerk back, and she stared in stunned disbelief at the finely chiselled parted lips of her beloved. She had, it would seem, maligned poor Robert Killiam unjustly, for there could be no doubt now that the snores that had so disturbed her slumbers had not been uttered by the Corporal, but by Quentin. Incredulous, she watched him, then drew back with a little chuckle. Whoever would have thought that such a figure of romance could be so unromantical as to snore?

A sharp rapping on the roof sent her gaze flashing to the window. A mail coach was pulled off to the side of the road ahead, several soldiers standing in the rain, arguing with the irate coachman and some flustered-looking passengers. Their own coach slowed and came to a stop. Dutch Coachman shouted a vexed, "What's to do, my cove?" and was answered by an officious, "Never you mind. Pull to the side!" Dutch grumbled a response. The carriage lurched forward again and wheeled to the side of the road.

Quentin was still noisily asleep. Penelope reached out to alert him, then paused. Those snores seemed to enhance the image of an older man. She straightened his wig carefully and tucked away a few more betraying strands of his bright hair, then composed herself to wait, rehearsing what she must say to these soldiers.

Her pulse began to race as the door was swung open and a tall, cold-eyed officer ran a frigid glance around the interior. His dark gaze lingered on Quentin's sprawled figure for a few seconds, then he turned his attention to Penelope, saluting her with chill politeness.

"Oh, Colonel," she cried in a nervous voice, "whatever is it? My uncle and I are in a very great hurry to reach Town, on an urgent family matter. Whyever must you stop us?"

"For nothing that need worry you, I suspect, ma'am," he replied, his tone as cold as those hard, dark eyes. "Nor am I a Colonel. As yet. Though I thank you for the promotion."

Penelope smiled. She had a frank and winning smile, and the officer's expression warmed a little. "Major . . . ?" she said, looking uncertainly at his epaulettes.

"Major it is, ma'am. Fotheringay. Mariner Fotheringay."

"Oh, dear," she murmured, before she could stop herself.

He laughed outright, and Quentin stirred, mumbled incoherently and was still again.

"Dreadful, I know," said the Major, unknowingly becoming the second man that day to apologize to her because of a disliked name.

"Well, it may be a trial to you now," she said. "But only think—when you are famous, everyone will find General Mariner Fotheringay a splendidly high-sounding name."

This cold hunter was not, it seemed, proof against flattery. Grinning broadly, he thanked her, enquired as to her identity,

159

whither in Town they were bound, and from whence they had come, then glanced at Quentin as another cacophonous snore rent the air.

Awed, he said, "Good Gad! Your uncle is a prodigious explosive sleeper, Miss Martin."

"And with an even more explosive disposition, Major. Would you wish that I wake him?"

He hesitated. "Has he slept the entire time, ma'am, I fancy you can answer my questions well enough. We seek an escaped Jacobite. A very desperate rogue who would cut your lovely throat as soon as look at you." Being interrupted by a violent and prolonged outburst, he was obliged to pause, and then went on in a softer voice, "Have you noted anything suspicious along your way? A beggar or tramp, perhaps. Tall, thin, aged about thirty or thirty-five. Reddish hair and likely in very poor condition."

Penelope's hands were icy cold. She knit her brows and said thoughtfully, "We did pass some men skulking along in the ditch about five or ten miles back. But—although I recollect that one was quite tall and thin, I could not vouch for the colour of his hair, for he wore a hat."

"About five or ten miles back, you say?" His eyes narrowed. "That would be just this side of Blenheim, if you have kept to this road?"

She said they had. The Major stepped back and closed the door, calling to her as she opened the window, "I'd caution you against stopping if any man begs for food, ma'am. We know our rebel came southwards, and we're warned he may now head east for Town and try to lose himself there. Have a care, Miss Martin, and a safe journey to you."

His eyes quite friendly, he waved the coach on, saluted again, and was lost to sight as the vehicle creaked and swayed and rumbled forward.

Limp with relief, Penelope glanced at Quentin. He was watching her, looking disgruntled.

"Five and thirty, eh?" he grumbled. "Now damn his eyes."

160

"So you were not asleep."

"I was until I awoke to find I was betrayed by my undisciplined nose." He grinned wryly. "You should have woken me, Penelope Anne."

"Your noisy slumbers seemed to verify your extreme age, dear sir," she said with a rather tremulous smile.

"Wretched girl! I've been plagued thus since a villain broke my nose for me a year or so ago." He was silent for a moment. "A fine cutthroat they paint me. . . ."

His lips were tight, an unfamiliar bitterness in his eyes.

Penelope said soothingly, "Naturally enough, they seek to frighten people into giving you away."

"How well I know it. Next time we're stopped we must endeavour to discover how much this empty head of mine is now worth. The more valuable it becomes, the more hazardous our journey."

Penelope pressed his hand. "Do not speak so, I beg. In only a few more days you will be safely at Lac Brillant, and—"

"Lac Brillant! God forbid! You never think I mean to go *there?*"

Bewildered, she said, "But surely your brother and your father will be—"

"My *father?*" He laughed rather wildly. "I thought you knew— No, of course, how could you? The dear old fellow is far from well. The shock would not help his health, you may be sure."

"Good heavens! Do you say he doesn't know you fought for Prince Charles?"

"I say precisely that. Nor, I pray, will he ever know. Frail he may be, but—he'd have my liver out!"

"How on earth did you keep it from him?"

"I fought under another name. My brother knew, of course. Gordon and I keep few secrets from each other. But my father . . . Jupiter! I shudder to think of his reaction did he learn what would be to him of all things most repugnant. He is

161

fiercely loyal to the crown." He said with a cynical laugh, "No matter how unfit the man who wears it."

Penelope's thoughts drifted to her brother and his firm convictions of the unwisdom of the Scots Prince. What would Geoff think of her alliance with this man who might have faced him on the field of battle? Who might even— She thrust away that hideous conjecture. Geoff had been deeply fond of Quentin. However he may have despised the Jacobite cause, he would certainly have raged against the present savage persecution of the survivors.

The carriage rolled steadily on through the rainy afternoon. The wheels sang a sharper song as they rattled over a bridge. They were following the Cherwell, the countryside rich and green, and cottages and farmhouses becoming more numerous. Penelope was absently aware of thatched roofs, whitewashed walls and neat gardens; of the distant loom of the graceful spires of the venerable city. She turned troubled eyes to Quentin. He was looking out of the window also, his face stern.

She asked gently, "Where do you mean to go?"

His bright grin flashed at her. "To London Town," he answered. "To deposit you in the loving arms of your Aunt Mary."

"And—then?"

"First, to deliver my message. After that—elsewhere. Now, never look so anxious, dear girl. I've friends who will help me to take ship, since, however I may love her, old England, it would seem, can do without me."

His smile was unwavering, but she sensed the desolation behind the cheerful words, and she put her hand on his arm sympathetically. He stared down at her hand in silence. "Have you funds?" she asked.

"My brother will provide some—along the way. But how very kind of you to enquire, Penelope Anne."

"Will he bring sufficient? I have—" She thought of Mama's pearls with a pang, but went on resolutely, "I can help a little."

The thick white brows lifted haughtily, the proud chin tossed upwards, seeing which, she added a hurried, "Just a loan, you understand. I shall expect to be repaid—with interest."

He chuckled, raised her hand to his lips and kissed it. "Truly, I am fortunate in those—in my friends. But Gordon sent a very full purse along with the Flying Dutchman, and I shall manage very well, I assure you. Now—what of this niece of mine? Shall your Aunt Mary be willing to house you on an indefinite basis? Will she stand up to your uncle should he demand that you return to Highview?"

The thought of pale, shy little Aunt Mary standing up to anyone was laughable. And her son, cousin Donald, was a fine figure of a man but—as Geoff had been used to remark—all show and no go. Uncle Joseph would only have to bellow at him once, and Donald would suddenly recall an urgent matter of business and take himself off, leaving the women to handle things as best they might.

Some of these thoughts must have shown in her face, because Quentin tightened his hold on her hand and asked, "*Will* he compel you to go back?"

She replied slowly, "He wants me to marry Roland Otton."

"As if you would!" He laughed. "Much chance that greedy hound has with you. I'd sooner— Oh, damme! Not again?"

There was a barricade across the road ahead, and once more they were stopped and the carriage searched, although this time the sergeant in charge of the troopers was of a different mold to Major Mariner Fotheringay and recoiled from the wrath of 'Mr. Martin.'

Resuming their journey at last, they did not stop again until they reached High Wycombe, where Quentin decided to rest the horses and take luncheon. Dutch Coachman pulled in to the yard of a pleasant inn called The Golden Goose, and they were at once surrounded by shouting ostlers. The host, a small, slightly built, nervous individual, welcomed them excessively, his delight increasing when he saw the second carriage turn into his yard. Penelope was shown to a cosy little bedchamber and Daffy hurried upstairs after her, bringing Jasper, who was, she declared, frightened out of his feathery little wits. No sooner were his covers removed, however, than the canary let out a shrilling flood of sound that could only be interpreted as rage, and proceeded to rush madly about his cage, flapping his wings and pausing frequently to scratch with much vigour so that birdseed and etcetera flew in all directions.

The two girls looked at each other and broke into a laugh.

"He is really vexed with us," said Penelope.

"Ar, miss. Well," said Daffy, going to the door to accept a large travelling bag from a maid and deposit it on the bed, "if we be getting a fine scold from little Jasper, you may be sure the Major's getting a finer one from Corporal Robert Killiam. Shall you wish to change your gown?"

"I think not." Penelope sighed. "I only wish I had some nice scent to wear."

"Never you fret about that, Miss Penny." From a rolled towel tucked carefully into a corner of the bag, Daffy produced a silver-chased little bottle and flourished it triumphantly.

"Plaisir d'Amour!" gasped Penelope. "My heavens! That is Lady Sybil's!"

"She'll never miss it," Daffy said nonchalantly. "Twenty bottles of scent has my lady on her dressing table, and this one never used because she says it don't please 'the gentlemen.' Roland Otton isn't no gentleman was you to ask me!"

"Oh—Daffy," said Penelope, dismayed, but eyeing the little bottle longingly, "you could be transported!"

"Oooh!" Daffy snatched for her apron, discovered she was not wearing it, and faltered, "Well . . . well, I won't be. And—and they owe you a sight more than one teensy bottle of scent, miss."

There was, Penelope decided, more truth than fiction in that remark, and she accepted the bottle gratefully. Applying the fragrance behind her ears, she asked, "What did you mean about the Corporal? Is he put about with Major Chandler? I had fancied we went on fairly well today."

"Fairly well if we do not count the fact that the Major runs his neck into a noose."

"But we all knew that, Daffy. I warned you this morning how great was the risk, and I'll own to be dragging you deeper into this danger has greatly troubled me."

Busily pouring water into the washbowl, Daffy paused to smile fondly at her mistress. "Stuff, Miss Penny, there's little risk for me. All I've to do is say that the gentleman properly pulled the wool over my eyes—and yours for that matter. 'Tis for himself the Major challenges the odds—or so says Robert Killiam. Fair warned, he was, and would pay no heed. I thought me poor heart would stop when that horrid Major come marching up to our carriage. Did *ever* you see such eyes? Like icicles all froze over. I says to the Corporal, Corporal, says I—"

"What do you mean—warned?" interrupted Penelope, taking the soapy cloth Daffy offered and beginning to scrub her face.

"Why, Betty, o'course, miss," said Daffy, ready with the towel.

Penelope straightened abruptly, peering at her. "Betty! I had so hoped to thank her before we left, but I daren't go down to the kitchen and call attention to her. I cannot think why she didn't identify herself to me when she came up to my chamber. Who is she, do you know?"

"I know as she's no kitchen maid, and that she's a true friend to all Jacobites—and that's all I know, miss. As to telling you who she was, p'raps she wasn't sure you was helping the Major—or p'raps 'tis a case of least said soonest mended lest either on ye should ever be questioned, may the Lord forbid! A right brave lass she is, though, and come to Highview hoping to get a message to Major Chandler. If I'd but known it. But she dassen't say anything, no more did I. She guessed, I s'pose, and she whispered to him yesterday that the road to London was fair bristling with troopers. So did Mr. Gordon. He sent word with Dutch Coachman how the Major was to keep away from Town like it was full of Plague, and go straight to Kent. Would he? No, he would not! Stuck out his chin, says Corporal Robert Killiam, as he does when he be set on something, and off we go, hell for leather—if you'll excuse so wicked of a expression—and never a fig for the consequences! Now—come and sit ye here by the mirror, Miss Penny. At long last Daffy's going to get her hands on your pretty hair and make it look lovely again. Oh, how I have wanted and waited to dress it proper for you."

Penelope sat obediently before the dressing table as Daffy fastened her wrapper tightly about her throat, but she was worried and said in vexation, "Mr. Chandler went to all that trouble, and Betty took such fearful risks to warn the Major, and he would not *listen?* Good God! Is he totally irresponsible?"

"I'll allow as he's reckless," said Daffy, busy with brush and comb. She giggled suddenly and removed three hairpins from her mouth. "But—lor', miss, he's a lovable scamp. When I think of how he played up to milady Tickle-Me—er, I mean—your poor uncle cuckolded by the very man what he's hunting so cruel."

Penelope stiffened, the colour draining from her face, but Daffy, brushing out the thick hair, did not see and went on, "Oh, how I laughed! Me and the Corporal, we . . ." She chattered on, her voice a background for Penelope's distress.

It all made sense now. Sybil's adoring gaze when she and Quentin had returned from that overlong drive. The look of covert amusement on Killiam's face when his master had been restored to his care. What a fool she'd been! Worrying and fretting for fear Sybil was tiring him. *Tiring* him! Looking back, she could see again that odd look he'd slanted at her when they had walked together towards his bedchamber; a look of mingled guilt and mischief she now comprehended. Hot tears of rage and hurt scalded her eyes. A fine villain she'd chosen as the man of her heart! A man who could stand firm against persecution and suffering, but was not proof against the invitation in a pair of wanton eyes. To think of how *fearful* she'd been that interminable morning . . . terrified lest his weakness over-

166

whelm him. And all the time he had been wooing Sybil, kissing Sybil, even— Her cheeks blazed. Major Quentin Chandler might be gallant and brave, but he cared not whose heart he trampled on, so long as his animal appetites were assuaged. It mattered nothing to him that *she* had risked everything to save him. *She* was the "sister he'd never had." Little better than a piece of furniture, in point of fact, to be used and discarded without a flicker of remorse.

And so she sat there, lashing herself into a fury of hurt and disillusionment until she at length began to hear what Daffy was saying,

". . . so stubborn as any two mules, or so says Corporal Robert Killiam, what is one as should know. It were the same when Mr. Gordon begged him not to follow the Bonnie Prince. Not that Charles bean't the most handsomest prince as ever was, and *that* charming, they do say. Turn your pretty head this way now, if you will."

"Stubborn indeed," muttered Penelope, scornfully. "To rush into a doomed Cause with never a thought for his loved ones."

"Well, as to that," said Daffy, about-facing, "Corporal Robert Killiam thinks the sun rises and sets in him, for all his wildness."

"Nor is he the only one to be so gulled," fumed Penelope. "My aunt thought the same, 'tis very evident."

A slow smile came into Daffy's eyes. She demurred, "Why, I do not think as the Major—er, dallied with my lady willingly, miss. He—"

"He is a *man!*" flared Penelope, incensed. "And never tell me he did not enjoy every minute of it!"

Daffy closed her lips and finished her task in a meek silence while Penelope seethingly recalled every least flaw in the character of the late Sir John Macauley Somerville.

X

The Golden Goose was a popular posting house and, as Penelope descended the staircase prepared to deal harshly with one lascivious rake, she heard a rumble of conversation from the coffee room and saw blue smoke drifting across the parlour where Quentin waited. As usual, she thought, her lip curling, he played his part well, for he looked the picture of aristocratic stateliness politely enduring the bluff, red-faced individual who appeared to be a successful farmer.

". . . and if they'd of had a stronger man leading 'em," the gentleman expounded firmly, "the tale might've had a far different ending is what I says. Mighty different. But be that as it may, 'tis over now and no cause to slaughter the poor misguided idjits. And what d'ye have to say to that, Mr. Martin?"

"Each man to his own opinion, sir," drawled Quentin.

"Ar. Well, them's mine. You axed fer 'em. And if they doan't suit, 'tis no one to be blamed but yerself."

"Just so. Now, if you will excuse me, my niece should be coming—" He glanced up, saw Penelope standing on the stairs, and stood.

She continued downwards, remembering in the nick of time the bewildering stranger who had confronted her in the mirror

168

just now, and contriving to walk with a provocative sway of her hooped skirts, fluttering her fan as Daffy had instructed.

Sir John's jaw was sagging. Oh, dear! It wasn't Sir John any more. She *must* try to remember all these various identities. Lud, but how he stared! She frowned at him, reminding herself that she had caps to pull with Major Quentin Chandler, *whatever* his name was at this moment!

Coming to the last step, she gave him her hand and said with flashing eyes but soft-voiced humility, "Dear Uncle—I hope I have not kept you waiting too long?"

"Ecod . . ." said Quentin, feebly. "What a'God's name have you done to yourself?"

She had gone to all this trouble! Daffy had gone to all this trouble! For the first time in years she looked halfway like a personable young lady, and all he could say was "What have you done to yourself?" The heartless wretch! One supposed he was attracted only by middle-aged harridans!

Her fan beginning to flutter at a more rapid rate, Penelope glanced at the farmer and found him goggling at her, his pale blue eyes starting out from his red face. Startled, she ventured a shy smile. The farmer dug his elbow into Quentin's ribs. "Arhumph!"

Quentin blinked at him. "Oh," he muttered. "Ah—my niece, sir. Miss Martin—Mr. Johnson."

The farmer bowed as low as his waistline would allow. "Delighted, ma'am. 'Tis no wonder your uncle awaited you with such impatience. No wonder at all, ma'am. Your uncle tells me you travel to Town. Are you fond of city life, Miss Martin?"

His eyes gleamed at her, and his red nose and cheeks looked bright and jolly. Penelope decided she liked his admiring smile and warm friendliness, and answered in her pleasant, unaffected way.

Her efforts succeeded in enchanting Mr. Johnson. Almost as much did they infuriate Mr. Martin. Fastening a crushing grip upon his niece's elbow, he snarled his farewells to the disappointed farmer, and Penelope's feet all but left the floor as she was wrenched towards the coffee room. "Do not *do* that!" he raged as they started into the crowded room. "If *ever* I saw so revolting a display!"

Indignant, she protested, "I was instructed, dear Uncle, to assume a new identity!"

"I did not mean *that* new!"

"You said people must not recognize me."

"I'd meant people should not think you a lady in mourning— not that people should take you for an opera dancer!"

An *opera dancer!* Of all the crude, ungrateful, insulting— A waiter was bowing before them, his admiring eyes fastened upon her face. Penelope smiled brilliantly at him. The waiter, who had been about to offer a table near the kitchen door in hopes of a bribe to secure the last remaining fireside position, conveyed them at once to the latter table. He drew out Penelope's chair with a flourish and contrived to bend over it as he assisted her to draw it closer to the table. Straightening dreamily, his head swimming with the fragrance of Plaisir d'Amour, he encountered a glare from the old gentleman that congealed his blood. He fled to the kitchen.

"I am very sure," Penelope hissed between her teeth, "that Daffy would not have allowed me to step out of our room had she fancied I looked unladylike."

"Oh, you are, are you," he retaliated with wrath if not originality. "Do you tell me it was that proper maiden who fastened that vulgar patch below your eye? By God, I wonder half the men in this room ain't gawking at us!"

He glanced around and determined to his increased choler that considerably *more* than half the men in the room were gawking at them. Or, to be more precise, at Penelope.

His niece, having arrived at the same conclusion, smiled triumphantly and retreated behind her fan. Several muffled exclamations were heard.

Quentin's exclamation was less muffled. "I've half a mind to make you go upstairs, miss, and wash your face!"

170

"The state of your mind does not surprise me. And I'll have you know, sir, that I am of age."

"And I'll have *you* know, madam, that your father was a friend of mine, and what he would say to this— Ah, host. What have you to offer us? My niece has a somewhat finicking appetite which ain't improved by all these curst clods ogling her. In about another minute I shall have recourse to my horsewhip!"

Quentin's fierce glare swept the room, and there were a few titters, but mine host, trembling lest this ferocious old gentleman provoke violence in his dining room, murmured timidly that he was sure no one had meant to offend.

Her eyes very bright, Penelope fluttered her fan and looked anywhere but at her fuming 'uncle.'

The roast beef Quentin ordered was excellent, but he proceeded to attack it as though it had been served up alive and must be slain as expeditiously as possible. Penelope picked her way daintily through the meal, very aware of the furtive but admiring glances that still came her way and pointedly ignoring Quentin's sporadic attempts at conversation.

His own ill humour having evaporated as swiftly as it had arisen, he lowered his voice and murmured with a beguiling grin, "Oh, come down out of the boughs do, Penelope Anne. I'd not the right to upset you, I'll admit. God knows, I owe you my life and will never forget it."

"Your opinion of my appearance, dear sir," she said coldly, "has absolutely nothing to do with the fact you feel indebted to me. Nor does it compel you to be civil, although I'll own I was upset to be named—vulgar!" And her eyes, which had thus far avoided his, darted to him with so flashing an anger that he blinked.

"Yes, that was very bad. But—I cannot like all this fluffing and flirting."

"Flirting! With whom have I flirted, Major?"

"Uncle!" he hissed.

171

She was shocked into the realization that if she flirted, it was with death, and she stared at him, pale with dismay.

He winked. "No harm done. Do not look so gut-foundered."

His use of so outrageous an expression restored her spirits, as he'd intended. She strangled an instinctive smile and, breathing a little easier, said, "But—truly I was not flirting." She thought, 'I would not know how.' And in that moment she caught the eye of a nearby gentleman, resplendent in a coat of purple velvet, who at once slyly raised his glass to her. She blushed and lowered her lashes.

"There you go again!" Exasperated, Quentin exclaimed, "Not flirting, indeed! I should like to know what else you'd call it! Damme if you don't look just like Sybil!"

Outraged, Penelope gasped, "Oh! I am at least twenty years her junior!"

"I did not mean in age, but in behaviour. Besides—your powder ages you."

How she could ever have been so foolish as to fall in love with this monster was beyond understanding. "Does it indeed," she said airily, favouring the purple-coated gentleman with a coy sideways glance. "Well, if I do resemble my aunt that must be a compliment, since all the gentlemen think her beautiful."

"She is very beautiful. In a hard, calculating— Good Gad! What am I saying? My apologies to the lady. And allow me to inform you, miss, that if the coxcomb in the lurid coat rolls his greasy eyes just once more in your direction, I'll shove his quizzing glass down his silly throat, so you will do well to stop luring him on."

"Lu—ring—him! Of all the—"

"Yer name, hif y'please," demanded a loud, abrasive voice.

They had been so engrossed in their quarrel that neither had noticed the sudden hush as an army Sergeant entered and approached their table.

Schooled by his long and desperate flight, Quentin's expression did not change by one iota. Penelope, however, became white as a sheet and stared at the burly military man in horror.

"Why the deuce should you want my name?" demanded Quentin irascibly. "Unless you've a message for me, perchance. What's *your* name, for that matter?"

The Sergeant, who enjoyed frightening people, was somewhat pulled up short by this attitude, but he made a quick recover. "Me name's Dexter. And Hi ain't in the business o' carrying messages. Me business, as Hi'd think any fool could see by this 'ere uniform what Hi'm a'wearing, is ho-fficial!" He threw a portentous glare around the quiet room and bellowed, "We'm searching out traitors. One traitor in p'ticlar. A escaped rebel. A desprit, bloody-minded cove as any fool what aids him has found out." He returned his truculent glare to the old gentleman and the girl, mildly gratified to note that the latter looked pale.

Quentin was both aware of and angered by the air of fear in the room. He leaned back and, hooking one thumb into the pocket of his waistcoat, said with a broad smile, "And you think I am this—er, bloody-minded traitor, do you? Faith, but you're a brave man to approach me, Sergeant."

Through a flurry of smothered laughter, the Sergeant fixed his intended victim with a hard stare. He allowed, in a voice that must have been heard in the stables, that he hadn't thought no such thing. "Me orders, which Hi do so 'ope don't hinconvenience yer noble self, be to question anyone strange what comes inter this 'ere inn or tavern or posting 'ouse. You"—he jabbed a large wart-ridden finger under Quentin's nose—"and the lady is the only folk Hi 'asn't yet questioned. Unless Hi be deaf and blind, which Hi ain't, though there's a sight of folks as wish Hi was."

"My good clod," said Quentin, waving that intimidating hand aside, "I do assure you that m'niece ain't at all bloody-minded. Well—not as a general rule."

Penelope took refuge behind her fan as every eye turned towards her and more laughter was heard. And she thought frantically, 'Oh, *why* must he take up *every* gauntlet that is thrown?'

"Very hamusing, Hi'm sure," snarled the Sergeant, flushing

173

but taking out a battered notebook. "Hi'll 'ave yer name now, *hif* y'please."

"Devil take you for a nuisance," said Quentin, sitting up straighter and frowning haughtily. "I do not please."

The Sergeant, a stub of pencil poised above his notebook, looked up. The expression in those small eyes appalled Penelope. "Uncle," she intervened, "you should not be obstructive, you know."

"Oh—very well," said Quentin fretfully. "My name is Martin."

"Mar—tin . . ." quoth the Sergeant, printing laboriously. "Martin—what? *Hif* it ain't too much ter ask in 'is Majesty's name."

"Martin," said Quentin, with a sly wink at the amused company.

"Yus, Hi got that." The Sergeant glared at him. "Hi means yer *last* name."

"I told you my last name. Are you indeed deaf, my poor fellow?"

A gentleman in the corner who had imbibed freely began to laugh hilariously. Penelope, however, was terrified. This nasty Sergeant was clearly becoming more furious by the minute.

Her reading of the Sergeant's mood was correct. His was a brooding disposition wherein was combined a hatred of the aristocracy and a love of his own authority—very often misused. The frail old gent and the pretty girl had looked easy prey. He'd expected to intimidate them both thoroughly. He had intimidated several occupants of this room who trembled at the very mention of the word 'Jacobite' and did not dare stand up to his bullying. As a result, the sympathies of most of those present were with the old man and the girl. They were in fact delighted by the Sergeant's embarrassment. Becoming very red in the face, he ground his teeth. "Hi'll take a minute o' me valuable time ter warn yer, sir. It don't do ter come no 'anky-panky with a member of 'is Majesty's armed forces."

174

Quentin smiled upon him. "How you do terrify me, Sergeant."

In a near roar, His Majesty's minion demanded, "His you saying as yer name be Martin Martin?"

"Jolly good, by Jove!"

The laughter this time was sustained. Through it, the Sergeant glared at his prey. Frightened, Penelope said, "Dear sir, the poor man does but try to do his duty." She smiled at the Sergeant's belligerence. "This gentleman is Mr. Martin Martin of London, and I am his niece, Miss Anne Martin."

Quentin said laughingly, "There you are. Does that satisfy your curiosity?"

"No, it don't. You likely got a calling card, 'as yer, Mr. Martin Martin?"

Penelope's heart skipped several beats.

"Of course I have a calling card, Sergeant Impudence," said Quentin, frowning. "And if you expect me to give you one to verify my identity, you may go soak your head! Dammitall, what's England coming to when a gentleman mayn't take supper with his own niece in a public inn, without being pestered by you military scalp hunters? Who the devil is your C.O.? If it's my old friend Mariner Fotheringay, he shall hear about your insolent behaviour!"

There was widespread public distaste for the persecution of Jacobite fugitives, and the laughter in the room was supplanted by a muttering that clearly supported Quentin's stand. The Sergeant was rendered even more uneasy by this horrid old cove's apparent acquaintance with a officer what had the most cutting tongue in the whole army. A officer what could make a man's life not worth living, was he displeased. "Now, now," he said in clumsy apology. "There ain't no cause to take into a huff. Like the young lady says, a man must do 'is duty. Sir."

"There ye go, Mr. Martin," shouted a wit at the rear. "Shake hands and give 'un a kiss."

"Buy 'im a 'eavy wet, why dont'cha, guv'nor," suggested another. "An' maybe he won't chop off yer head."

"Ain't no need o' that, sir," said the Sergeant, eyeing the tankard of ale with longing.

"Perhaps not," said Quentin, having no wish to chance another demand for his calling card. "But I rather fancy my niece is right as usual and I was hard on you. Join us for a moment, Dexter. I suppose you've a thankless job, eh?"

The Sergeant put away his notebook. "Ar, yer in the right o' that, Mr. Martin," said he, seating himself and watching approvingly as the waiter hurried up with another tankard. "Your 'ealth, sir and miss!" He drank noisily, wiped foam from his lips with the back of his hand, and went on, "You'd think as folks'd be grateful to us fer hunting down they vermin, but—no! 'The war's over,' they whine. Enough to make yer—" He glanced at Penelope's shocked face and continued, "Scum of the earth they is, Mr. Martin. Flocking down here like vultures. Slit a man's throat so soon as a wink. And no woman's safe from—"

"Just so," Quentin interrupted brusquely. "But there's no call to frighten my niece with such horrors. Lucky for us we've brave men like yourself to stand between us and the—er, villains."

"Yussir. But we won't stand between yer fer long. No need. Ain't many left." Sergeant Dexter patted his sabre with a broad grin. "And some as was caught won't never be took to trial, Hi can tell yer!"

The green eyes facing him suddenly flamed, but the Sergeant's gaze had lowered and he missed that murderous glare. "You know what, Mr. Martin," he said in a slow, taunting way, "Hi noticed it just now, and Hi notice it again, fer Hi'm a very hob-servant hindividual. And what Hi says is—fer a very old man, you got awful young hands." He lifted triumphant eyes. "Now just 'ow might yer explain that there very odd fack, sir?"

Once again cold with fear, Penelope considered how she could delay this wretched savage if Quentin decided to make a dash for freedom.

176

Quite unruffled, Quentin shrugged. "I do not usually explain it at all." He glanced around and leaned nearer. "However, since I see you've the same curst trouble that plagued my younger days, I'll tell you."

"Will yer now?" The Sergeant dropped one beefy hand to the hilt of his sabre. "Hi'd be powerfully diverted, as the nobs say, to 'ear this 'un, so—*please* don't you make me wait, sir. . . ." He inched the sabre from its scabbard, his sneering gaze fixed on Quentin's expressionless face.

A deathly hush prevailed, everyone's attention turned on the little drama.

Quentin hesitated, then said with disastrous clarity, "Manure."

Penelope stifled a gasp.

The Sergeant's cruel eyes widened. "Wot?"

Quentin nodded soberly.

"Manure . . . ?" echoed the Sergeant. "Now—what the 'ell—"

"Hush!" Quentin leaned closer. "Do you want to be rid of those warts, or not?"

He had touched a sore point. The Sergeant gave a start, glanced down at his unsightly hands and snatched them from sight.

"Know just how you feel," said Quentin. "Had the same trouble. Dreadful."

With a lightning swoop the Sergeant gripped Quentin's wrist and stared down at the graceful white hand and neatly manicured nails. "You tryin' to be funny, or summat?" he growled, lifting narrowed suspicious eyes. "You never 'ad the same trouble as wot Hi got!"

"Worse," Quentin averred with a sober nod. "Much worse. Had to wear gloves most of the time, which is most difficult," he embellished artistically, "when one is a musician." He lowered his voice yet again, almost whispering. "Not a doctor could help me. Silly fellows; they're all quacks, you know."

"Ho, yus," said the Sergeant. "Hi'll trot wi' yer on that one.

Paid over me groat many a time, Hi done. Not that it were a bit o' good. 'Ow did yer find out, then? Gypsies? Hi tried 'em. Thieving maggots! Should be 'ung, the lot of 'em. If you're a'going to tell me as they—"

"I'd not dream of fobbing off an intelligent man with such rubbish. I—" Quentin glanced around in so conspiratorial a fashion that Penelope, torn between mirth and terror, was hard put to it to keep her face straight. "I bought the secret from . . ." Quentin hissed, "a—witch."

"Cor!" The Sergeant crooked the first and middle fingers of his right hand in quick defence against such foul frights. "You never did!"

Quentin nodded solemnly. "When a man's desperate, Sergeant, he has to take desperate measures."

"And—and what she told yer—it worked? It made yer hands look . . . like that there?"

"Well, you're not blind, man. You see the evidence of your own eyes! And I'm rising five and sixty."

"Love a duck!" A crafty gleam coming into the Sergeant's eyes, he said, "Sir—Hi didn't mean ter cause yer no trouble jest now. Duty, y'understand. Hi could—er, pay yer. A little bit."

"No, no. I bought the secret and it's mine to give out as I choose. But—I very seldom choose, and that's a fact."

"Right y'are. No more would I. But—there's this young woman Hi've sorta got me eye on, sir. And she's got a 'ead full of maggots like all women does. Only it's time Hi was a'settling down, says me ma. Hi—er, well, she might find me a touch more to her liking did Hi not 'ave all these warts." He scanned Quentin anxiously and, finding only a dubious look, went on, "If there's anything wot Hi could do fer you, sir. In exchange . . . like . . ."

Quentin pursed his lips and looked at the ceiling. "I fail to see what. We're simply trying to reach London as soon as possible and there's nothing you could help us with in that."

"Hi could 'elp yer by telling yer it'll likely take a week. They got troops so thick as ants round a treacle pot from 'ere to

178

Chelmsford, down to Wrotham, crost ter Reading, and back up ter 'ere again. Ain't a gnat will get through 'thout bein' stopped twenty times a mile, belike."

His heart sinking, Quentin said, "Well, that's of no help to me at all. However"—he shrugged—"I know your predicament, poor fellow. So I'll share my secret. Drink up!"

The Sergeant drained his tankard gleefully and bent forward so as not to miss a word.

"You take a pound of lard," said Quentin softly, "and you mix it well with—er . . ."

"With . . . ? With . . . ?" the Sergeant prompted.

"With the droppings of a sheep."

"Droppings of . . . a *sheep?*"

"But only a *black* sheep," cautioned Quentin, slanting a warning glance at Penelope's quivering lips.

"Why . . ." breathed the Sergeant, "must it be a *black* sheep?"

Quentin frowned. "Be damned if I know. I think the old woman mumbled something about black magic."

"Ar—well, that'll be it, right enough," nodded the Sergeant importantly. "*That* makes sense, so it do. Go on, sir. Go on!"

Quentin went on.

Propped by many lace-trimmed pillows, Lady Sybil held up her jewelled hand mirror and scanned her reflection glumly. She tweaked a stray curl into a little ringlet beside her left ear and sighed. "The house is like a tomb, Simmonds."

Simmonds held the heavy tray beside the bed and wondered why in the name of all that was holy the stupid woman worried about her face when there wasn't a man to see it. "Belike his lordship will come home today, marm," she intoned in a listless voice.

"Is possible," said Sybil with another sigh.

"And—Captain Otton," murmured Simmonds.

Sybil brightened. "How nice that would be. Er—to have the gentlemen about again," she added hastily, and launched into a one-sided discussion as to which gown should be selected for the morning. What she would like of all things would be to wear the cobalt blue *robe battante,* or perhaps that delicious orange *robe à la française,* or the white taffeta with that luscious red embroidery.

Simmonds paid little heed to this monologue. My lady would have no choice but to put on her blacks again, as they both knew. If she descended the stairs before noon, thought poor Simmonds, whose corns were making her more than ordinarily miserable, 'twould be a miracle!

There were no miracles that morning. It was a quarter to twelve and Sybil just leaving her dressing table when the imperative summons of a coaching horn was heard, followed by shouts, the grinding of wheels and the pounding of many hooves.

Simmonds flew to peer eagerly through the rain-splashed windows.

"Who is it? Who is it?" wailed my lady, patting frenziedly at her dainty cap and half hoping it was a certain elderly gentleman with wicked green eyes and a most remarkable virility.

"'Tis my lord." Simmonds added joyfully, "And Mr. Treadway!"

"Good heavens, girl, what care I if my husband's bailiff accompanies him? Is there no one else?"

My lady might not be elated by Mr. Treadway's return, but Simmonds's bored eyes had taken on a marked sparkle. Her corns quite forgotten, she added saucily, "And Captain Otton, of course."

"Wicked jade," said my lady with a little giggle. "Hurry then—my mauve fan, if you please. Ah, that will do nicely."

Thus it was that when the gentlemen, tired, muddy, and disenchanted with one another, their ill-fated quest, and their various and seemingly doomed hopes, came into the hall, they

180

were greeted by a vision in a billow of black lace over mauve satin; all feminine daintiness from the frill of her little cap to the buckle on the slipper that peeped from beneath her gown.

"Welcome home, my lord," trilled Sybil, extending both hands to her husband.

My lord gave a grunt, deposited a kiss on his wife's smooth cheek, and allowed she looked hale and hearty. "Which is more than I can say for m'self or Otton," he added sourly.

"Had you a—er, successful journey?" Sybil asked, giving Captain Otton her hand and a meaningful glance.

"No, we had not," declared Joseph flatly. "I am starved for some decent food, my head aches like the deuce, and I yearn to have the dirt removed from my person."

My lady summoned butler and housekeeper. A bucket brigade was organized, the cook indulged himself in a palpitation when required to furnish a hot lunch within the hour, and servants rushed up and down stairs with valises, portmanteaux, decanters, and dressing cases.

In the midst of the uproar, my lord having disappeared in the direction of his bedchamber, my lady discovered a pair of dark eyes smiling at her. She turned away with a flutter of her fan and the flirt of one satin shoulder.

"All this fuss and feathers," murmured Roland Otton in his deep, pleasant voice, "and not one word as to *your* welfare, ma'am. Have you managed to keep from falling into the doldrums during our absence?"

A tiny smile played about my lady's red mouth. She covered it with her fan. "I have managed . . . tolerably."

He knew that gleam in her eyes and his own sharpened. "Sybil," he murmured, stepping closer to her as they trod up the stairs together, "what the devil have you been up to?"

She giggled. "Oh . . . I have been—entertained. But never mind that. To judge from Joseph's demeanour he has made mice feet of the business, eh?"

Otton scowled. "We were led a merry dance, I can tell you. Chandler has—" He checked to the warning touch of her

181

hand. A maid he had not seen before was crossing the hall. A winsome lass with a nice shape and hair of reddish gold. She looked up as though she felt his eyes on her, and, with a shy half-smile, hurried on her way. 'Hmmmnn . . .' he thought, and resumed, "Chandler has friends, and we were led like a group of fools chasing a will-o'-the-wisp till we were miles from anywhere on a heath swarming with gypsies and other cut-throats. And damned lucky to have got out of it!"

She turned to face him, astonished. "Not—literally?"

"Oh, I give you my word. I've a score to settle with that accursed rebel—and will settle it—do not doubt!"

"It would seem to me you settled it before he escaped you," she said dryly. "How the man could have eluded you in the condition he'd come to, I cannot fathom."

They had reached the top of the first flight of stairs. Otton, glancing about, responded with an edge to his voice, "Well, he did. I'll tell you of it when I've bathed and changed clothes. Where's Penelope?"

My lady wandered towards her husband's bedchamber, from whence could be heard the grumble of his voice. "Oh—she's . . . somewhere about," she called airily over her shoulder.

"Of course I am . . . laughing," said Penelope, sighfully drying her tears. "Nonetheless, 'twas a dreadful risk to take, and so needless."

"Do you think so?" Quentin handed her into the waiting carriage and climbed in to sit beside her. "Just goes to show the different outlooks of man and maid. You thought it a needless risk, and I thought it a very vital duty to so—er, develop Sergeant Dexter's personality."

She strove to look at him severely, but was quite unable to keep the mirth from her eyes.

Quentin chuckled and took her hand. "No, really, Penny.

182

The fellow's a brute and a bully. 'Twill do him the world of good to make an ass of himself."

"I doubt he will agree when he discovers how you've hornswoggled him."

The carriage jolted its way over the cobblestones of the inn yard and began to bowl along the lane.

Quentin mused, "Do you think he will discover it? He really believed my tale of the witch, you know. As if such creatures existed."

"If they do not, very many people are misled."

"Well, of course, for there is ignorance—" He broke off, peering at her curiously. "*You* don't believe in witches and warlocks and all that sort of gibberish, do you?"

"I never have seen one." Penelope detached her hand gently. "But I agree with whoever said 'There are more things in heaven and earth . . .'"

"Shakespeare, I think," he murmured, glancing idly out of the window. "It was in— Good . . . *Gad!*" He sat up straight, then burst into hilarious laughter.

Leaning forward to look around him, Penelope saw a broad slope dotted with a flock of sheep. The red uniform was startlingly out of place in such a setting. "Ooh!" she squealed, clasping her hands with delight. "It *never* is?"

"Be—be damned . . . if it ain't," Quentin gasped. "And— oh, Lord, that I was permitted to see it! Look—only *look!*"

Impervious to the bleating animals that milled around him, Sergeant Dexter followed one creature with marked determination. A small black lamb.

It was too much. They fell into each other's arms and laughed until they cried. Coming to the belated realization that he held Penelope to his heart, Quentin released her abruptly and collapsed, breathless, against the squabs. "He'll likely be following that lamb in the rain for a week," he said.

She turned her laughing face to him, and he watched her for a long moment until for some reason the silence between them became fraught with tension. "Will you tell me, please," he asked quietly, "why you were so very angry with me?"

Her lashes swept down. Not until danger threatened him again had she realized how unjustified had been her anger. She had no right to censure him. *Wives* were taught to pay no heed to their husbands' little *affaires*. And she was not a wife. She was not even a betrothed. She was only a sister. And sisters are not jealous . . .

With one slim fingertip he touched her hand very gently. "Penelope Anne?"

She looked up. No man, she thought weakly, should have such beautiful eyes. It was unfair. She answered rather unconvincingly, "Because you take such dreadful and—and unnecessary chances. As if life was just a game. As if your own life did not hang in the balance."

He'd feared she might have discovered—and been offended by—the fact that he'd seduced her aunt. "Oh, dear," he said with a relieved grin, "you begin to sound just like my father. He has dubbed me a hot-headed here-and-thereian."

"I have always thought Sir Brian a most sensible gentleman."

"No, really, Penelope Anne! How can you be cross? Only look at me." He sat back, folding his hands piously. "Am I not the picture of respectable senility? And what could be further from recklessness than our staid and proper journey?"

"*Proper*—journey? The last route we should follow is the London Road. You saw how many times we were stopped this morning. You ignored the warnings you were given before we ever began, but you must know the Sergeant spoke truth." She placed one hand on his sleeve and said pleadingly, "I beg you will turn aside. You can leave Daffy and me at some nice inn and we will manage very nicely, I am sure. Only—do not, do *not* rush into the trap they set for you."

She was in dead earnest, and her concern for him very plain. That this course was reckless he was all too well aware. He knew also that Penny would be a good deal safer without his perilous self for an escort. But he was uneasy about this Aunt

184

Mary and meant to see for himself that the lady had sufficient backbone to stand up to Joseph Montgomery. If she proved an unreliable ally, he'd be damned if Penelope Anne would be left in Hampstead to be forced into a marriage with the likes of Roland Otton! He shrugged and said in a bored manner, "Foolish child. They search for a battered young man, near death. How shall they connect such a fugitive with an affluent old gent who travels with his niece?"

'If Uncle Joseph had returned to Highview and learned of Sir John Macauley Somerville's true identity, they would *very* soon connect an older man with the desperate fugitive,' thought Penelope.

Covertly watching her, Quentin lied, "Besides, I have business in Town. Relax, my child. We are making better progress this afternoon, had you noticed? Why, at this rate we'll be safely in Hampstead this evening, and I shall be away before nightfall."

Penelope said nothing. If he did have business in Town, which she doubted, it couldn't be of a vital nature or Gordon would not have warned him away. It was as well she had told Daffy to give Dutch Coachman his new direction. Quentin would very likely be furious when he learned of it but, God willing, by that time it would be too late to turn back. She felt a light tap on her hand again and looked up.

"Are you still angry?" he asked, transferring his fingertip to the corner of her mouth and gently trying to coax it into a smile.

He looked so uncharacteristically humble that she could not withstand him. "No. I am not angry."

He sighed and lay back. "Good. Then I can rest easy." He appeared to fall asleep, and she watched him lovingly. After a moment, one eye opened, twinkling with mischief as he peered up at her.

A hot tide of crimson burned up Penelope's throat. She closed her own eyes hastily and turned her head away.

For another moment, Quentin was very still, gazing at her. Then he went to sleep.

XI

"What I cannot understand," said Lady Sybil, toying with the fruit on her plate and trying not to notice how noisily Lord Joseph consumed his food, "is what convinced you it was Chandler who fled before you."

"His friends convinced us, madam," said his lordship rather thickly. "Always just a short way ahead of us. Calling out, 'This way, Quentin,' or 'Hang on, old fellow—almost there,' or some such fustian."

"Fustian we heeded for four damnable days," muttered Otton, his dark brows fixed in a frown. "When I think of my feet sinking into that loathsome mud . . . And now my fool of a man cannot find my new shoes!"

His lordship waved his knife at his wife, his florid face purpling. "When I get my hands on young Chandler again—he'll rue the day, dammim! I'll skin him alive!"

"To expedite that glorious occasion," said Otton, his thin lips sneering as he watched my lord's gluttony, "we might perhaps have an—ah, discussion with Miss Montgomery."

Sybil tensed and bit her lip.

Lord Joseph exclaimed, "Yes, by God! Where is the chit,

186

Sybil? Have her in here at once. She knew Chandler, so she said. She may be of some use for once."

"You do not ask how I have been managing, all alone here, while you were gone," she evaded, pouting.

Joseph looked at her. She flirted her fan, her eyes provocative, and he chuckled. "Madam witchery! Very well, then. How did you manage? Not much for you to do, poor gel. Egad, but I'll be pleased when this blasted mourning period is done! How much longer is it?"

"Three months, officially. But, 'twas none so bad, Joseph. I'd company. However decrepit."

"Old Lady Burrows, was it? Shouldn't call her decrepit, m'dear, though I'll own—"

"*Not* Lady Burrows," Sybil interposed with an arch air of mystery. "A relation of yours, my love. Somewhat distant, 'tis true, but—"

"Good God! Who's come fuzzing around you whilst I was away? From what I know of the distant lot it was likely cousin Amos—a Jeremy Diddler if ever I saw one! I hope you were not gulled into—"

"Good gracious, my lord! Whatever are you talking about?" Sybil put down her wine glass and imparted, "It was Sir John Macauley Somerville. A most splendid gentleman and one you might well be proud to have in the family."

"Somerville . . . ?" murmured Otton. "Don't recall your mentioning his name, sir."

"No more do I. Sure you ain't bosky, Syb? Ain't been on the tipple while I was beating the countryside for that damned gallows bait, have you?"

"I do not 'tipple!'" she repudiated with magnificent indignation.

"And you *did* say . . . Macauley Somerville?" said Otton thoughtfully. "From whence came he, ma'am?"

Ignoring him, Lady Sybil said, "I doubt you've heard of him for years. His mother was some kind of aunt-in-law, and his brother is Sir Andrew Somerville. You surely know of *him!*"

"Why, I—er . . . I may have heard the name," said his lord-ship cautiously. "Cannot remember every dirty dish in your family, m'dear."

"Oh, do *pray* attend me, my lord! I refer to your poor brother's wife, Lady Margaret."

Her life's companion lowered his laden fork and stared at her. "Margaret, you say? She was a *Halsted!*"

Captain Otton inserted curiously, "What like was this—'splendid gentleman,' my lady? You said . . . decrepit, I believe."

"I know all Margaret's kinfolk," muttered my lord, scowling. "Be damned if they include a Macauley Somerville. What's he look like?"

Exasperated, but by now uneasy, Sybil replied, "He is elderly and a trifle feeble, but—not, er, wholly infirm. And a very well-bred type of man. As to looks, he was—"

"Short and fat, with a Friday face, gravestones for teeth, and half-blind so he could not appreciate your looks, I'll warrant," said Otton with a chuckle.

Angered, she fell into his trap. "To the contrary, Captain! He was a fine-looking old gentleman, tall and slender with white teeth, a gentle, mannerly voice, and extraordinarily vivid green eyes that—"

"*Green eyes?*" Otton's chair went over with a crash. "Chandler!" he cried, leaping up and driving a fist into his palm. "*Chandler,* by thunder! Cavorting about here whilst we scoured the countryside for him!"

Shrinking back, one hand going to her throat, Sybil gasped, "You—you're mad! 'Twas an *old* man, I tell you!"

"He's gammoning you, Sybil," said his lordship, grinning broadly. "Can't you see it? Chandler, indeed. That's a good one! The man was all but a corpse!"

"How came he here?" demanded Otton, his jaw grimly set as he turned on Sybil. "Did you see him arrive?"

"Yes! I went out onto the terrace, for I heard a vehicle and thought you might have returned and could not wait for the servants to tell me. Penelope was just helping him into the carriage when—"

"Helping him *in?*" said Lord Joseph sharply. "You mean he was *leaving?*"

"Yes— No! That is— He had come thinking to find my late brother-in-law, and when Penelope told him that Hector was dead, Sir John would not stay."

"Only you persuaded him, eh, ma'am?" sneered Otton. "Had he papers? Identification? Calling cards, at least?"

Sybil's fear was intensifying. A hundred little details rose up to plague her, not the least of which was the old gentleman's lovemaking prowess. "Since . . . since when do we demand identification when . . . when relations come to call?" she demanded threadily.

"By Jupiter, I begin to think Otton has something here," cried Lord Joseph, flinging down his knife and fork. "Are you gone daft, madam? To let in any Tom, Dick, or Harry, just because they claim kinship?"

"But P-Penelope . . . knew him! And—and he *was* old. Besides, do you think I did not get a look at poor Chandler? Sir John showed no signs of having been beaten. His face was lined, his hair and eyebrows white, and—"

"Cosmetics and a wig," rasped Otton.

Shaken by the memory of Sir John's heavy use of paint, Sybil argued desperately, "No! I tell you—*no!* You said yourself Chandler could not even stand. Sir John was somewhat shaky upon his feet, true, but no more a wounded man than—" And she checked abruptly, one hand flying to her mouth.

"Speak up, blast it all," roared her lord.

Thoroughly terrified now, she yet retained a strong instinct for self-preservation and chose her words with care. "I do remember that there was—one incident. We were walking in— in the shrubbery and . . . I tripped over a flagstone. Sir John caught me, and just for a second looked—as though anguished. But he had gout, so Penelope said, and I thought it natural enough. Oh—it *cannot* be!" She turned to her husband, her hands outstretched pleadingly. "I have my faults, my lord—I'll not deny. But I am not a foolish woman. In truth, I am not."

Tears glittered on her lashes, her lips trembled, and she was very beautiful. For all his bombast and bluster, my lord was deeply fond of her. "Oh, pish," he said with a gesture of impatience. "We make a lot of nothing, Otton. Let be. Sybil's no maggot-wit."

"I grant that," said Otton. "But—Miss Montgomery knew this Sir John Somerville, you said, ma'am?"

"Yes, yes. It never occurred to me to doubt him because she vouched for him. In fact, when I questioned her about him later, she said there had long ago been some scandal involving Sir John. It must have been shocking, for her papa would never speak of it."

Outraged, my lord shouted, "Fustian! Wasn't no breath of scandal *ever* touched Margaret's family. Heaven help us, her grandpapa was so strait-laced, he'd have strangled anyone so much as breathed the word!"

"How much—ah, later was it that you questioned Miss Montgomery?" enquired Otton.

"Lud—I don't recall." Sybil fluttered her fan distractedly. "A day or two, perhaps."

"A *day* or two? When precisely did he arrive?"

"Oh, my heavens! Let me see . . . I have it! 'Twas the evening of my dinner party. Tuesday. And I—"

"Dinner party?" howled my lord, dragging his bulk from the protesting chair and glaring at his wife. "You had a *dinner party?* Are you all about in your head? We're in *mourning*, woman! You said yourself we've—"

"Never mind about that!" His eyes ablaze, Otton intervened curtly, "If I'm right, Montgomery, we've been gulled by as neat a Canterbury trick as ever I heard!"

Annoyed at being addressed in such a way, Lord Joseph was half-inclined to give Otton a sharp setdown, but greed got the better of his pride. "I do not see it," he grumbled. "If Chandler

190

was somehow able to escape, why the deuce would he come back here?"

"I always wondered how he managed to get out of that damned window," muttered Otton.

"Well, he did," said my lord emphatically. "He certainly wasn't *in* the room, dammitall! And the door was locked."

Scowling, Otton turned to the trembling Sybil and demanded, "Did anything else happen that struck you as odd? Was Miss Montgomery suddenly inspired to clean attics or basements? Were any large amounts of food used?"

"No. Nothing like that. My niece was quite ill, in fact. She took a dreadful cold and was confined to her room."

"Ah-h-h . . ." breathed Otton. "And her food carried up to her on trays, no doubt!" His eyes narrowed. "By whom?"

"Her abigail, of course. That wretched Saffy."

"That's how they did it, then!" Otton rounded on his lordship. "Do you not see? Chandler *never left* here! He was carried out of your study while we ate that night and hidden in some other part of the house!"

"But—they would've been *seen!* And I tell you, I locked the damned door!"

"Devil take it, who knows how they managed it? Somehow, they *did!* We have been gulled, I tell you! Thoroughly, damnably gulled!" He turned to the tearful Sybil. "What manner of clothing did this alleged old gentleman wear?"

"M-most elegant," whimpered Sybil. "A trifle out of the c-current vogue, perhaps, but fine velvets, satins, and laces most costly."

"Not mine, then," he muttered. "Chandler's taller, I fancy, by half a head, and skin and bone. My clothes would not suit. Though my shoes did, evidently!"

"He certainly couldn't have worn mine," said my lord.

"There are some of your—your late brother's trunks in the attic," ventured Sybil.

"Then *that's* where they shopped," said Otton. "Lord Hector

191

was—" He paused as the door opened. The servants had been instructed to leave them alone, and he scowled as his lordship's man crept in.

"Your pardon, my lady," said this scrawny individual, distraught. "My lord—I am desolated, but—we have had thieves in the house, I do swear! Your lordship's new cloak that was but delivered last month, and a pair of your boots, Captain, have—"

Joseph's pained yowl was heard in the kitchens, and his valet, a nervous man, fled.

As the door closed, Otton said grimly, "We've enough now to confront her." He started towards the bell pull. "Let's have Miss Montgomery in here, sir."

"No . . ." said Sybil, faintly.

Two enraged countenances turned to her.

"She is . . . gone!" she wailed, and burst into tears.

Quentin stretched, yawned, glanced out of the window, and sat up abruptly. The bustling streets and tall houses did not resemble the pleasant, rambling little hillside village of Hampstead. "The devil!" he exclaimed. "Have we passed it, then?"

"Passed what, sir?" asked Penelope, innocently.

"Where the deuce are we? And what time is it?"

She regarded him calmly and said a tranquil, "It is nigh six o'clock, and we are on the outskirts of Reading."

"*Reading?* Has Dutch lost his wits?" He grabbed for the check string, but Penelope moved as fast to intercept his hand.

"No, sir. He is responding very dutifully to my orders."

His brows pulled into a dark bar across the bridge of his nose. "You told him to change direction? Now—blast it all, Penny—"

"Your brother also instructed him to do so."

He removed her fingers and, mouth grim, reached again for the check string. "That's soon remedied. We shall turn about."

192

He was again thwarted. The carriage was already stopping, for they had pulled into the yard of a large posting house and ostlers were running to unharness the horses. "Very well, ma'am," he said angrily. "We shall change teams, *then* return to Town! By God!" he exclaimed with a sudden and unexpected grin, "one can appreciate why my coachman chose this place!"

Following his gaze Penelope saw the sign that swung gently on its iron bracket. A fine four-masted merchantman ploughed through foam-crested billows, the name emblazoned upon her bow reading *The Flying Dutchman.*

"You see," Penelope cried triumphantly. "'Tis an omen, Quentin!"

"Let us hope it is a good one."

The main building was an Elizabethan sprawl. Latticed windows sparkled in the pale sunshine of late afternoon. Hollyhocks bloomed in stately splendour around the heavy oak doors, and the air was fragrant with the scents of flowers and hay and horses, all pervaded by the appetizing aroma of dinner cooking.

"I am very wearied and—quite famished, dear Uncle," said Penelope, sighing, as Quentin led her towards the door.

His grip on her arm tightened. Dutch Coachman, a broad grin on his weathered face, clambered down the far side of the box.

"You little wretch," growled Quentin. "You think to turn me aside, but—"

"I think," Penelope answered meekly, "that we have not once been stopped by patrols since we turned westward, is that what you mean?"

"No, it is not. I do assure you that I mean to have you safe in Hampstead by nightfall!"

Irritated, she cried, "*Why* must you be so ridiculously stubborn? If you persist, I warn you I will—"

Laughter, seldom far from his eyes, banished his vexation with her. "Do what, wicked wench?" he asked softly. "Enchant the nearest gallant and— Oh, my God!"

"I give you good even, Miss Montgomery, Sir John," called a vaguely familiar voice.

"How providential for you, niece," muttered Quentin.

"Mr. Stee—er, Tiele," cried Penelope. "How pleasant to encounter you again."

"*Most* pleasant, ma'am." Duncan Tiele's blue eyes were warm as he bowed over her hand, but the look he threw at Quentin was less apprehensive than measuring. "We meet again, sir."

"So I see," drawled Quentin. "Might one ask whither you are bound, Mr. Tiele?"

The old gentleman, thought Tiele, was nothing if not direct. Amused, he replied, "If you mean—was I following you, sir— the answer is no. I was of a mind you'd be headed for London, whereas my own business takes me to Salisbury."

"Does it?" said Quentin, dryly. "How fortunate."

Tiele looked irked, and Penelope inserted a swift, "Yes, indeed, sir." She turned her bright smile upon the hapless young man, having not the remotest idea of how totally she thus enslaved him. "We follow the same direction, for my un—grandpapa and I travel to—" The words trailed off as Quentin's hand closed sharply, but belatedly around her wrist.

Tiele had noted both the stumble over the relationship and that quick and powerful grip. "Is something wrong, ma'am?" he asked, his eyes, suddenly frigid, fixed upon Quentin's detaining hand.

"No, no," Penelope said hurriedly.

In harsh opposition Quentin growled, "Yes, there is. The 'wrong' thing is yourself, sir. I resent your trailing after Miss— Montgomery. She stands in no pressing need of—" He checked momentarily as an officer rode into the yard with two troopers behind him, then continued, "—of the attentions of a persistent pest! Good day to you, Mr. Tiele!" And he marched Penelope to the doorway where mine host waited eagerly.

He could, averred this rotund, merry little individual, show the lady to "a most hospitable chamber under the eaves, wiv a nice trundle bed for my lady's abigail. And there's a very fine

194

room for yerself, milor', proper cosy-like, jest down the hall from yer pretty . . . er . . ."

"Niece!" snapped Quentin. "With whom I've caps to pull, so show us up at once, if you please."

Mr. Duncan Tiele, having started off to greet an arriving friend, changed his mind and returned to the cosy lobby in time to hear the end of this final remark. Troubled, he noted that the old gentleman had not relaxed his grip on Miss Montgomery's arm, and that his ascent of the rather precipitous flight of stairs was surprisingly spry. He was frowning after them when he heard the host enquire, "And how long will you be with us, if I might be so bold as to ask, Mr. Martin?"

Sir John Macauley Somerville answered with curt impatience. "Only a few hours, host. We shall dine and then push on, for we've urgent business in Winchester."

"Well . . . I'll be damned!" gasped Mr. Tiele.

"Never doubted it in the least," said the officer, coming up beside him. "What's to do, Duncan?"

Tiele looked grim. "I think there's something unsavoury about that old devil, Jacob."

Captain Jacob Holt was a broad-shouldered young man of no great stature. His powdered hair was austerely tied back with a thin black riband. His features were notable only for a dominant chin, a rather small mouth, and eyes of blue ice. His friends were few but his friendship, once given, was unwavering so long as it did not interfere with his career. He had met Duncan Tiele at Eton and, unlike that carefree individual, had worked hard at his studies, well aware of the sacrifices his family had made to ensure his education. But if his house might be impoverished, the Captain's ambitions were very grand indeed. A flame burned behind his cold exterior; the driving need to succeed, to become a power in the military world. He followed his dream relentlessly and already had made his mark in his chosen profession; and, as inevitably, had made enemies.

He glanced at the now empty stairs, then slipped a hand onto his friend's shoulder. "Were I you, old fellow, I'd stay well to the lee of that lovely creature. I saw her grandpapa, or whatever he is."

"Whatever, indeed," muttered Tiele grittily.

"What do you mean?"

Tiele hesitated. What he suspected was not something to be bruited about on so little evidence. Especially when a lady was involved. He shrugged, slapped Holt on the arm, and said ruefully, "Wishful thinking, likely enough. The old boy has warned me off in no uncertain terms."

They turned into the well-patronized tap and sat together at a corner table. Holt called for two tankards of Kentish ale. "Going home, are you, Duncan?"

"No, matter of fact. I'm off to Salisbury to see my uncle before Brooks does." He grinned. "You know him, I believe?"

Holt gave a rather brittle laugh. "Captain Brooks Lambert? The Adonis of St. James's? Jove, but I know him. And does *he* know you're bound to Salisbury, he'll get there before you if he has to desert to do it."

"I fancy he's not *that* desperate. But enough of me and my deplorable cousin. Why are you in these sylvan solitudes? Change of station? Or just rebel hunting?"

Something about the tone of voice sent Holt's eyes slanting to him unsmilingly. "You dislike the occupation?"

For a moment Tiele did not answer. Then he said with quiet candour, "Yes. Do you?"

"They sought to overthrow the crown. The price comes high. As it should."

Tiele said *sotto voce*, "But—only look at who *wears* the crown, Jake."

"Guard your tongue, for God's sake!"

Glancing around the dim room, Tiele distinguished several red coats. He said musingly, "Cannot recall when I've seen so concentrated a hunt. What is it, old boy? Are there fears of another Uprising?"

"Your word, Tiele?" This being at once given, Holt said very softly, "We're after a small group. Four—perhaps six men at most. Each carrying parts of a cypher."

"What about? Where do they take it? And for Lord's sake—why? The Rebellion was crushed, the Cause lost. What could be so important as to justify such desperation?"

Again, Holt's keen stare raked the room. Speaking barely above a whisper, he leaned closer. "A king's ransom in gold, silver, and jewels. More than enough to finance another Uprising. At least—to start things going."

Tiele whistled soundlessly. "Jove! Don't blame you, dear old boy. Only say the word, and I'm with you. Always fancied a treasure hunt, and how satisfying it would be to spend one's spare moments counting out 'a king's ransom.' Let us hie forth and become corrupted with wealth!"

"Idiot," said Holt, his stern face lit by a rare grin.

"Tell me more. Whence came this king's ransom? Jacobite contributors?"

Holt nodded. "Charles Stuart called for it, hoping to run the blockade and hire mercenaries on the Continent. A list was kept of contributors and each donor was promised lands or recompense when their war was won."

"'Sdeath! You seek the *list?*"

Holt nodded once more. "They're traitors all, who've spun their webs and written their own doom. And what the devil do you scowl at?"

Drawing back, Tiele said an austere, "I think it damnable. The treasure's one thing. Every man for himself, there. But—to destroy a man's family, to confiscate home and lands—"

"And heads," the Captain put in with grim emphasis.

"—and all for a Cause lost this three months? That rankles with—"

The Captain made a sharp, warning gesture, and Tiele was silent as the waiter came up and set out two brimming tankards. Holt raised his in salute. Tiele stared at him for a moment, then grinned and returned the salute, and both men drank thirstily.

Tiele asked, "Is that why you've been in Berkshire? Hunting these poor devils?"

Staring into his tankard, Holt asked without inflection, "How did you know I was in Berkshire?"

"Someone chanced to mention they'd seen you. I can't recall— Yes, I can! It was Trevelyan de Villars."

"Was it?" His expression bland, the Captain murmured, "Are you well acquainted with the gentleman?"

"Good Gad, Jake! Treve ain't a gentleman! Women, cards, duelling—dreadful rascal!"

"But you like this—ah, rascal?"

"Yes. He's rather hard to get to know, but really he's the best kind of man. His uncle's a close friend of my sire. Lord Boudreaux. Bit of a stately old fellow. Not like—" Tiele's amiability faded. "You ever hear of a fellow called Sir John Macauley Somerville?"

The Captain considered the question in his unhurried, meticulous way. "No. I've never heard the name. Why?"

"Nothing important. I'd like to know more of the fellow, is all."

There was a short silence, each man lost in his own thoughts. The Captain stirred at length, took up his gauntlets and whip and said that he must be about his business. "I'll likely return later. Do you plan to overnight here, Duncan? If so, I'll take dinner with you."

Tiele, who was hoping to see a charmingly unaffected girl with the most speaking hazel eyes he'd ever encountered, evaded awkwardly, saying that he was undecided. "But if I should stay, why, I'll be glad to join you."

They walked outside together. In the yard, the Captain hesitated, then said reluctantly, "One thing, Duncan. It's none of my bread and butter, of course, but—take my advice. Do not cultivate the acquaintance of de Villars. Nor his uncle, for that matter."

198

Astonished, Tiele expostulated, "The devil! Why not?"

With a faint twitch of the lips, the Captain murmured, "They say—if a man lies down with dogs, he gets up with fleas." He clapped his stunned friend on the shoulder. "Take care, old fellow. I'd not care to be obliged to haul *you* to the Tower!" And he stepped back, tossed a small salute, and strode away, shouting for his orderly.

Tiele, his eyes very troubled, watched Holt's erect figure disappear into the stables, then he turned back to the inn. Wandering to the stairs, deep in thought, he muttered, "De Villars . . . by Jupiter!"

"I fail to see why you are so very put about," said Penelope, as Quentin followed her inside and closed the bedchamber door. "And really, Uncle," she added severely, "it is not proper for you to come in here!"

"Habit," he said, accepting the cloak she handed him. Penelope seated herself at the dressing table and began to tidy her windblown hair. He watched the graceful way she had with her hands. She had lovely hands. And it really was incredible how those high-piled powdered curls became the chit. During those first rather ghastly days at Highview, she'd seemed a combination of angel of mercy and a modern Jeanne d'Arc. More than ever then, he'd realized— He pulled himself together and tossed the cloak onto the four-poster bed. "You know very well why I'm provoked," he fumed. "To see that blasted chawbacon panting at your heels is downright disgusting."

"Do you find it so?" Still awed by the poised lady in the mirror, Penelope pinched her cheeks.

"What the deuce you doing that for?"

"I forget you have no real sisters, poor soul." She smiled at him kindly. "It is to put some colour into my poor face."

He sat on the bed and, not rising to the bait, grunted, "The only *poor* thing hereabouts is that thimblewit, Tiele. I fancy you're primping so as to go down and further captivate the fellow at dinner?" Penelope returning nothing more than a saintly smile, he went on, "You may be assured 'tis the last you'll see of the young mushroom, for so soon as you are rested, we drive to Hampstead."

"I am far more rested at this moment, dear Uncle, than are you. Only look at yourself and stop being so silly."

Stunned by this rank insurrection, he glanced into the mirror. A haggard-faced old gentleman looked back at him. "Well, what d'you expect? With all this curst paint on my skin, I vow I'm drying up."

"Oh, yes. I'd noticed you were a bit crusty."

He grinned at that, then jerked to his feet, startled, as the door swung open.

Daffy came in, followed by Killiam, who carried the bird cage and a large valise. "Praise be, we've come this far safely, miss," said Daffy, betraying not the least surprise at discovering Quentin in her mistress's bedchamber. She took the bird cage and set it on a table. "You'll be wanting to change for dinner, so I've brought a pretty gown up."

"Then you wasted your time," growled Quentin. "We do not overnight here, Daffy. So soon as you ladies have refreshed yourselves we will take dinner and turn about for London."

The Corporal regarded him glumly.

Daffy, busied with restoring light to Jasper's world, exclaimed, "Oh, no! Miss—we must not!"

"If you are concerned about my reputation, sir," said Penelope, rising and turning to Quentin, "pray remember I travel with my uncle and my maid, and am not likely to be reproached."

He threw out one hand and said in vexation, "Be reasonable, Penny. Just give me one—"

He received considerably more than one. Jasper, profoundly annoyed, had been squawking from the moment of his arrival, and now that he was once more reprieved from his darkened little world, went into his full war dance. Scratching as vehemently as he shrilled, he sent debris flying in all directions. Quentin's hand, palm up, received a generous donation. He gave an exclamation of revulsion and threw it back at the screaming bird. "Damn your beak and feathers!"

"Poor little creature," said Penelope, secretly glad of this diversion. "Do not vent your wrath on him, Uncle Martin. Only look how you have terrified him."

Since Jasper was screeching at the top of his small but powerful lungs, his tiny legs fairly flying, and his beady eyes fixed wrathfully on the 'old gentleman,' this latter statement was debatable.

The Corporal intervened. "Dutch Coachman begs a immedjit word with you, Major. He's waiting in the stables."

"Why in the deuce couldn't the block come up?" snarled Quentin, wiping his sullied hand.

Penelope shook her head at him. "He has only risked his life for you," she pointed out reproachfully.

He flushed scarlet, and his eyes fell. "As have you all. May God forgive me. I shall go down at once." He looked at them one after another. "My poor friends," he said, the picture of remorse, "however do you endure me?"

He was reaching for the door latch when Daffy said brightly, "I just saw that very same nice young gent we met this morning, miss, so I've fetched up your pink brocade Watteau gown and the pannier petticoat. Seemed like the gentleman had a twinkle in his eyes, and—"

"A whole dashed bonfire, more like!" exclaimed Quentin, instantly restored to wrath. "And one I mean to extinguish without delay." He stamped out and slammed the door behind him.

The three left alone exchanged a grin.

"Is a something volcanic gentleman," said Penelope ruefully.

"Aye, miss," Daffy agreed with a flash of dimples. "And scarce to be wondered at, things being what they is."

The Corporal, his gaze fixed upon those same dimples, said,

"How has he gone on, miss? I fancied he was rather pulled when I come in just now."

"He slept on the way here, but I doubt all the jolting over those dreadful roads has made his arm more comfortable. He'll not admit it, of course. Corporal, we *must not* turn back to London."

"He's worried for your sake, miss. He'd be less than what I know him to be, if he didn't try to bring you out of this mess— never mind the consequences to hisself."

Penelope's anxious eyes softened. "We cannot allow him to destroy himself out of a foolish concern for my good name."

He pursed his lips. "I don't know as it be all that foolish, Miss Penny. You *have* runned off with us. What your aunt and uncle will say—"

Up went her chin. "I care not! I never shall live with them again! Only to look at them would make me remember what they did to him!" She went back to the dressing table and sat down, resting her chin on her hand wearily.

Daffy jerked her head to the door and the Corporal slipped out.

"You'm tired, my dearie dear," said Daffy gently. "Come now and let me take off that gown and get ye bathed and rested 'fore your dinner. Then you shall go downstairs and show our Major he's not the only fish in the sea . . . eh?"

It was close to half-past seven o'clock before Penelope was rested, bathed, her hair brushed out and dressed in long pow-dered ringlets that fell to her shoulders. The Watteau gown with its tiny waist and stomacher, and the box pleats that swept down at the back from shoulder to hem, was a glory she had scarcely remembered. Papa had allowed her to have it made shortly before his sudden death, and she had never worn it. When the laces were sufficiently tight and the dress was on at last, Penelope turned, gasping, to the mirror and stood quite still, her eyes becoming very round. "Oh, Daffy," she breathed. "I do look—quite nice. I—may die of suffocation, but—I *do* look nice . . . don't I?"

Daffy scanned the tall, graceful figure in the mirror. The ringlets were thick and luxuriant, and the little tendrils that wound down beside her ears added breadth and softness to the rather long oval of the face. The pale pink brocade was enriched by darker threads woven into a subtle floral design, the colour further emphasizing her perfect skin. Daffy went to the jewel box and took out the single strand of pearls, and for a final touch, pinned a spray of tiny pink silk roses amongst the soft curls.

Slightly dazed by her own reflection, Penelope whispered, "He *will* like me a little tonight . . . do you think?"

The abigail blinked. "Any man would be a simpleton not to like you *very* much, miss," she said. "He's likely waiting for you in the downstairs parlour."

"Oh, my!" Penelope snatched up reticule and fan and tripped to the door, only to pause at the last instant. "It—*is* really me?" she said, turning back. "I am not dreaming . . . ?"

Daffy flew to kiss her and swing wide the door. "Off you go, now. And—have a lovely time."

She watched Penelope drift with a shushing of petticoats along the narrow corridor and then closed the door, snatching her apron to her eyes. "She should ought to be used to looking so sweet and lovely," she advised Jasper. "She should have had lots of nice gentlemen admiring her. . . ." She sniffed and whispered tearfully, "My poor dearie . . . whatever lies ahead o' ye, my duck, my sweet lady? Oh—*whatever* lies ahead o' ye?"

XII

Never in her comfortable existence had Lady Sybil Montgomery endured such a nightmare as that wild ride towards London. There was nothing she had wanted less than to accompany the men, for they were all of them in a most ugly humour, even Thomas Beasley, usually at his oiliest with her, having snapped her nose off when she'd dared to complain about being forced to go with them. She *must* come, snarled her lord. She was the only one knew what Chandler now looked like and if by some chance he had abandoned Penelope along the way, Sybil would be able to identify him. And so she'd been bundled unceremoniously into the new carriage, Joseph and Beasley climbing in with her, and Otton with three or four of the grooms riding escort. The coachman had been ordered to spring 'em, and the coach had set off with a lurch, followed by the second carriage wherein rode Simmonds, my lord's man, and Otton's batman.

They were stopped often by the military, as were all travellers, Joseph's chagrin at the interminable delays being eased by the consoling thought that Chandler and his 'great-niece' must also have been thus hindered in their flight. At each stop Otton made enquiries for the runaways, but not until they were

204

coming into Oxford was he successful. A hawk-faced major who looked tired and irritated remembered an elderly gentleman travelling with his niece. The young lady had been most charming, and he was inclined to think she'd said they were en route to Town on some pressing family business. His keen eyes had begun to glint with suspicion when Joseph's glee became apparent, and Otton had been obliged quickly to invent a tale of having discovered some new information that would be of great benefit to the 'old gentleman.'

It was late afternoon before they left this check point, and a short while later they pulled up once more and Otton rode to the window. The rain that had fallen softly for several hours had stopped now, and the air was sweet and fresh as Joseph swore and lowered the window. "Not *another* search?" he growled. "Devil take it, they'll have properly vanished before we can come up with 'em!"

"I doubt it, sir. We've made very good time, considering, and have not once stopped for food, save the few minutes when the horses were being changed."

"How well I know it," moaned Sybil.

"Do you mean to drive on through?" enquired Otton. "We'll likely not reach Hampstead before dark."

"We could overnight at The Spinning Wheel in High Wycombe," Sybil interpolated hopefully.

"Aye, we could," grunted Joseph. "Lord knows I'm ready for some good beef and a raised mutton pie, perhaps. But—we will not, ma'am, so do not refine on't. We drive straight through, Otton. Do you enquire at every stage for our accursed rebel."

"*Naturellement,*" drawled Otton with a contemptuous smirk, and turned his mount so that he might shout up to the coachman.

"But I am tired, and hungry, and nigh black and blue," wailed Sybil, pouting prettily. "'Tis cruel to expect a lady to endure being bounced and tossed about hour after hour on these horrid roads."

"You may lay those miseries at your own door, for being such a gullible maggot-wit," observed Lord Joseph with a marked lack of sympathy.

Beasley, who had begun to nod, yawned and stretched. "Did you mark Otton's sneer just now?"

"He'll smirk on t'other side of his face, if we fail to recapture Chandler," said his lordship. "He'll have neither fortune *nor* Penelope."

Beasley grinned, for he had no love for Roland Otton. "Do you fancy Chandler means to take her to France with him?"

"I doubt that. He fancies himself a chivalrous man and what gentleman would drag a girl along while he's hunted? If she was caught with him, they'd likely lop her head with his. Oh, no. He'll see her safe if he can. But—without we capture him, I've no call to marry her to a penniless Jack-at-warts like Roland Otton!"

"And what if they are not in Hampstead?" asked my lady.

"Then, my dear, there being a full moon tonight, we shall keep on driving until we *do* find them!"

Sybil moaned.

The proprietor of The Flying Dutchman was wont to claim that his was one of the finest posting houses in the south country. All his bedchambers boasted wax, not tallow, candles; the rugs on the gleaming oak floors were thick and colourful; the stairs were always neatly swept; and the dining room was elegant, with many tables of heavy oak flanked by cushioned chairs, and in the centre of the room a dais where sat an accomplished lady of middle years who played a harp while the guests enjoyed their dinner.

Penelope breathed the scents of beeswax and ale and roast beef as she descended the stairs. A gentleman waited in the vestibule, even as Daffy had said. He was inspecting a figurine in a display cabinet, and his back was turned. He wore a French

206

wig tied with a riband of blue velvet that matched his silver embroidered blue coat. Smiling tenderly, Penelope crossed to join him, but as though he sensed her arrival he straightened and spun around. He was sturdily built, and not tall enough, and Penelope gave a dismayed gasp.

"Miss Montgomery," exclaimed Duncan Tiele. "Ah, I had so hoped to see you for a moment."

As dismayed as he was delighted, she stammered, "Oh! I thought you were— That is to say—I—"

His bow was smooth but, she thought, lacked Quentin's grace. Straightening, he said, "You are distressed, I think. If— in any way—I can be of assistance, you must allow it, or do me a grave injustice."

The admiration and the sincerity in this nice man's blue eyes could not but impress her. "How kind you are," she murmured.

He extended his arm. "May I take you in to dine?"

She put her hand on his sleeve. "I fancy my uncle will be coming downstairs at any moment, sir. If we could perhaps go into the parlour for a moment?"

He led her in without a word but, when he had seated her and drawn a chair close beside the cushioned loveseat, he murmured, "Uncle? I must have mistaken it, ma'am. I'd thought you named the gentleman your grandpapa."

"You've a most excellent memory, Mr. Tiele," she said, surveying him from under wrinkled brows.

A slightly austere look had come into his eyes. A smile supplanted it. He said, "Where so lovely a lady as yourself is concerned . . ."

Penelope blushed and lowered her eyes. "I should explain."

"Not at all, ma'am. I am a stranger to you and there is no least reason you should feel obliged to do so."

"I am sure you must wonder why we have been so devious." Her mind groped for something believable. Quentin, in the wink of an eye, would have a tale to account for such erratic behaviour. She must emulate his facility, for his life might well hang in the balance. "You see," she said, taking refuge behind her fan, "of late I have been pursued by a—a most determined gentleman. A powerful gentleman who has fixed upon me as his future wife."

He frowned and leaned nearer. "And you do not desire this man's attentions?"

"I do not, sir. Were my brother alive still, there would be no least problem, but—" She thought, 'Geoff, dear—forgive me,' and went on, her voice a little uncertain by reason of all these lies, "But he is dead, and Sir John deep in this—er, man's debt."

"And you are the price of his ruination, is that it?" Eyes flashing, Mr. Tiele dared in his indignation to grasp her hand. "How abominable! So you ran away? Have you no male relatives to defend you, ma'am? You certainly have admirers, I'd think—"

"My uncle is very strict, as you saw," she said desperately.

He was a little bewildered, but said without hesitation, "My sword is at your disposal, ma'am."

Despite herself, Penelope's eyes twinkled at this grandiose statement. Mr. Tiele, not without his own rich sense of humour, grinned and said boyishly, "Jupiter! That sounds melodramatic, don't it? But nonetheless, I do mean it, Miss Montgomery! Perhaps I should speak with Sir John. He *is* your uncle, I take it?"

Had she said uncle instead of grandpapa? 'Oh, dear, oh, dear!' she thought, but answered that Sir John was indeed her uncle. Both her hesitancy and her agitation were noted and Mr. Tiele's earlier suspicions returned with a rush. "I had best escort you," he said gently. "If this suitor comes up with you, your uncle cannot hope to defend you."

"No! Er, I mean—yes, Uncle John is younger than he may appear, and—and would never allow—I mean—"

"But in such a situation, ma'am, he would surely welcome another ally?"

'Good God!' thought Penelope, and said helplessly, "No—

but he is so proud, you see. And would—would think it an aspersion upon his—er, ability to protect me!"

"He is a fine figure of a man, I grant you," he said, frowning. "But even if he is fond of you—"

"Oh, he is, sir. Devoted!"

His lips tightened. "Forgive me, ma'am, but I rather think your uncle is—"

"Is eager for an explanation!"

Two heads shot around as that demand thundered out. Quentin stood in the doorway, impressive in green brocade, his paler green undercoat richly worked with gold thread, and lace foaming at throat and wrists. His head was held high and proud, his eyes were an emerald blaze under haughtily drooping lids, and outrage fairly radiated from him.

Springing to his feet, Mr. Tiele said, "I assure you, sir—"

Simultaneously, Penelope began, "I was just explaining why—"

"Since we are not acquainted with this . . . gentleman," Quentin intervened with a curl of the lip, "I see no cause for explanations."

Mr. Tiele bowed. "In point of fact, sir, I was assuring Miss Montgomery—"

"As I have told you before," said Quentin at his most disdainful, "my niece requires neither your assurances nor your attentions."

"It appears to me, Sir John," said Tiele, determined, "that your niece stands in need of protection, and—"

His eyes narrowing, Quentin snapped, "Do not fall into the error of supposing me to be so old and decrepit I cannot defend the ladies of my house."

"Please, Uncle," Penelope put in hurriedly, "Mr. Tiele has been only kind and concerned."

"Admirable. And now, m'dear"—Quentin gestured to the hall—"since the concerned young man seems unwilling to take himself elsewhere, we shall do so."

Tiele turned to Penelope. "I beg you will remember what I said, ma'am. I am at your disposal at any time." He bowed over her hand, gave Quentin a perfunctory nod, and strode from the room.

As soon as they were alone, Penelope turned on Quentin, raging. "For heaven's sake—*why* treat him so? He is kind and gallant, and was only trying to—"

"I know very well what he was trying. And let me tell you, miss, that it ain't proper behaviour for an unmarried lady to slink away—"

"I did *not* slink!"

"—to keep a tryst with a stranger, and cuddle up cheek by jowl—"

She uttered a gasp of indignation. "Cheek by—! *Oh!*"

"—cheek by jowl with him, holding hands in an empty room! Do you keep this up, Penelope Anne Montgomery, and I may have to demand the fellow wed you to save your good name!"

"*You* may have to!" she snarled, wondering with some corner of her mind why she was so furious. "By what right—"

Even more furious, and very well aware of the reason, he grabbed her arms and shook her slightly. "By the right that you are in my care," he said, his voice harsh and grating. "Had it not been for your insufferable interference, I'd have had you safe and sound in Hampstead by this time, instead of throwing yourself into the arms of . . . that . . ."

The sweet scent of her was all about him. The great hazel eyes, that scant seconds ago had flashed with rage, had softened and now gazed up at him with a most disturbing expression. He quite forgot the severe lecture he had given himself only a few hours ago, and finished disjointedly, ". . . busy-body. . . . Jove, but you look well in that gown, Penelope Anne."

She said without much conviction, "Let me go at once!" And then, chancing to glance over his shoulder, gasped, and pushed at him frantically.

210

His grip tightened. "No—wait," he murmured. "I must tell—"

A hand of iron caught his wrist and whirled him around. An impassioned countenance glared at him.

"So I guessed rightly," growled Mr. Tiele. "Why—you dirty old blackguard! Unhand the lady at once!" And he slapped Mr. Martin Martin across the mouth.

"If you do not stop," said Penelope crossly, taking soup into her spoon and trying to ignore the curious glances that came their way, "you will likely die of indigestion before Mr. Tiele puts a period to you."

Her cutting remark served only to set him off again. Quentin smothered a final whoop and mopped his eyes with his napkin. "Oh, egad!" he wheezed. "No really, Penny—was ever anything so delicious? To think that silly young fribble—"

"Who is probably not a day older than yourself, Uncle."

"To think he really thought I was . . . conducting an incestuous *affaire* with my own grand-niece! Oh, but I'm *such* a villain!" And he disappeared into his napkin again, his mirth smothered but so hilarious that several heads turned their way.

"People—are—*staring!*" she said between her teeth. "And how you can find it amusing that you have now contrived to be challenged to a duel tomorrow morning, is quite beyond my understanding."

He sighed and sipped at his wine, succumbing to a muffled chortle only now and then.

"Major Chandler," Penelope said with soft but impassioned urgency, "what, pray, do you mean to do about it?"

"*Do* about it?" He tilted his head back and regarded her wonderingly. "Why, oblige the fool, of course. We shall have to overnight here, but the duel itself will be very early and won't take long, m'dear."

211

"Are you *mad?* With that arm?"

"Well, I certainly cannot fight him with my feet!" He chuckled as wrath glittered in her eyes. "No—truly, dear girl, there's nothing I can do, you know. The idiot hit me."

Strangling her napkin, she said an all-embracing, "*Men!* It may have escaped you, sir, but we chance to be making a desperate bid to get you out of the country. You cannot afford to indulge in such irresponsible foolishness. If you care nothing for my safety, you might at least pause to recollect that you've a wound in your arm that is being given no chance to heal."

"Oh, I do recollect, Penny." His voice was low and his smile a fond caress. "But—do you know what I had forgot? How dark and sparkling your eyes become when you're angry."

Both words and look combined to take her completely off stride, and she stared at him, her lower lip slightly sagging. For a hushed, enchanted moment they were very still, not speaking, not touching. It seemed to Penelope that she glimpsed sorrow behind his smile and, guessing that it was inspired by the fact that they soon must part, her dread of that same parting intensified, so that she clung to this moment, lost to the room and everyone in it save this man she so loved.

The waiter rushed past their table, glasses clinking on his tray.

Startled, Penelope glanced up at him, and when she looked again at Quentin he had fashioned his napkin into a rabbit that peeped at her above the edge of the table.

"Hello, pretty lady," said the rabbit in a squeaky falsetto, and waved one ear at her.

"*Will* you be serious?" said Penelope, her dreaming done.

"As you wish," the rabbit replied, bowing sloppily. "Sir Sylvester Serious—at your service."

It was such a ridiculous rabbit, and Quentin's studiedly innocent air so comical, that it was all she could do to keep a straight face. With an effort, she summoned a frown. "I do wish—" she began.

"I can grant any wish for precisely sixty-five seconds,"

squeaked Sir Sylvester. "Dragons slain, excursions through the land of faerie, husbands provided for lovely ladies in pink gowns. . . ."

Penelope caught her breath. Sir Sylvester essayed a pirouette, then waved at a choleric-appearing old gentleman, all whiskers and quizzing glass, who had half-risen from his chair to look with incredulous horror at this performance.

"'Pon my soul!" snorted the whiskers-and-quizzing-glass.

Sir Sylvester waved at him, undaunted; a lady laughed in amusement, and the old gentleman subsided.

Very red in the face, Penelope said, primly, "Please—Sir Sylvester. Go away."

The rabbit turned to peer up at Quentin's empty smile. "Why does she say unkind words when her eyes laugh so?"

"Because you are embarrassing her," said Quentin gravely. "It is very, very ill-mannered to behave so in a public dining room, and likely none of these good people will ever speak to her again."

"Oh." Slowly, Sir Sylvester folded his ears one upon the other, and sank beneath the table edge. Having almost vanished, he suddenly popped up again, so that Penelope and several other diners who had watched his descent, fascinated, jumped. "Have they spoken to her before?" he asked brightly.

"No."

"Then—I do not see why—"

"It is not for you to see," said Quentin.

Penelope interjected, "Besides which, you have no eyes!" and then drew back, her hand clapping over her lips in mortification.

The rabbit gave a small shriek. "She spoke to me! She spoke to me! I shall find her a husband!" He nodded so vehemently that both ears collapsed.

Her pulses leaping about erratically, Penelope saw that by this time approximately half the diners and three grinning waiters were watching them. "I wonder," she whispered, trembling with anticipation of what Sir Sylvester might say next, "that you do not wave a flag with the Scots thistle on it, so as to attract more attention to yourself!"

The rabbit peeped out from between its ears. "Her eyes are very beautiful when she's cross—you were right. She will make some lucky man a splendid wife."

Penelope was motionless, scarcely able to breathe.

"In which case," chirped the rabbit, "you must promise not to hurt her most eligible suitor—Mr. Tiele."

He had done it again. Lulled her into that breathlessly sweet expectancy, and then shattered her with a carelessness that was beyond comprehension. Hurt and reeling, Penelope managed somehow to collect herself and enter this nonsense. "How, Sir Sylvester, if Mr. Tiele succeeds in ridding the world of his foolish adversary? How then?"

"Why," said the rabbit, "in that case your great-uncle won't dance at your wedding, will he?"

Whitening, she murmured, "Oh. What a *wretched* thing to say!"

"Did you not know that rabbits are all wretched?" said Quentin lightly. Much to the disappointment of his small audience, he folded the napkin, sent his brilliant grin to three old ladies who applauded, and took up his wine glass. "Now—speaking of Mr. Tiele, the poor hot-blooded fellow labours under the delusion he has been so brave as to challenge an infirm old gentleman." He waited, but Penelope kept her eyes on her plate and ignored him, so he went on, "In all honour, I should warn him that I'm some forty years younger than he supposes."

"It would seem far simpler," said Penelope, more or less steadily, "merely to leave tonight while Mr. Tiele sleeps."

He gave a shocked gasp. "You never mean it? A gentleman don't run away when he's been challenged to a duel! Good God! Didn't Geoff teach you *anything*?"

She flinched a little. "He taught me that Geoffrey Montgomery would not do so. Neither, I take it, would Quentin Chandler. Mr. Martin Martin, however, being nonexistent, cannot be held accountable."

214

"Why, you little conniver! I vow you could argue me into all manner of improprieties, had you a mind to it."

His voice was hushed, his eyes quizzing her. But that he meant to flirt with death in the hush of tomorrow's dawn, Penelope had no doubt, and she refused to be diverted. "You once told me that your father names you an irresponsible here-and-thereian," she said, her eyes chill. "I think I begin to understand why."

"Ouch," he said ruefully. "No, Penny—be fair. A man must face what comes his way. Not run from it."

"You do not run from trouble, Quentin. You run *at* it! Had you not objected so violently to his simple kindness to me, none of—"

"Simple kindness, my Aunt Maria! The fellow's fairly moonstruck over you, and you know it."

She said demurely, "As Sir Sylvester Serious observed, Mr. Tiele is my most eligible suitor." And she stood, so that he had perforce to rise and pull back her chair.

Leaning over her shoulder, he murmured, "Oh, very well. Since you plead so eloquently for his life, I'll not fight the silly fellow."

Both irked and overjoyed, she spun to face him.

"I owe you a great deal more than to spare the life of your lover," he said with perfect gravity.

"Oh! You are—*impossible!*" she stormed, and turned to the door.

Daffy was already hurrying across the room towards them. She bobbed a curtsey. "The host would like to know do we plan to keep the rooms overnight, sir," she said. "They seem to be full up with—"

"Why, you *fraud!* What the deuce are you got up like *that* for?"

The resonant voice belonged to a tall, well-featured man of middle years who was bearing down on them, grinning broadly. Horrified, Penelope saw that a young officer who had just come in and was seated alone at a table near the dais had turned to watch them.

Also aware of the Captain's interest, and with his every nerve tingling to the awareness of peril, Quentin slid his hand casually into his great pocket, closing his fingers around the butt of the small pistol Gordon had sent him.

"Oh . . . my!" whimpered Daffy.

"If *ever* I saw such a farce," uttered the newcomer, halting before them.

"I think I have not your acquaintance, sir," Quentin said coolly, from the corner of his eyes noting that the Captain had come to his feet.

"I am Philpott," said the tall man, grinning broadly. "Henry Philpott. Certainly you must remember me. I'd know you anywhere in spite of that ridiculous disguise or whatever it is."

It seemed to the stunned Penelope that things were happening very slowly. Again, they were the centre of attention and people stared curiously. The military gentleman had taken a step towards them. Quentin stood very still, but his lean body was poised for desperate action, his face watchful and grim.

Daffy's voice, faint and faltering, cut through the silence. "Y-you must've mistook me fer some . . . other girl, sir."

Astonished, Penelope saw that the abigail's comely face was white as chalk and that she looked petrified with fear.

"Nonsense," said Mr. Philpott, still beaming at her. "The belle of the ballet? How could I forget? You've grown a touch more buxom, I'll admit, but—"

Great tears welled up in Daffy's eyes. She tore frantically at her apron and shrank behind Quentin.

Mr. Philpott, who carried with him a pronounced aroma of brandy, blinked in belated dismay. "Oh—egad! Have I let the cat out of the bag? Look, Daffy love, if I've—"

With a smothered wail Daffy fled, followed by a little ripple of amusement.

Philpott turned to Quentin. "I say, sir. Deuced sorry. Didn't know the girl was—ah, reformed."

"I rather fancy you mistook her for her sister," said Quentin gravely. "Twins, y'know. My niece's abigail is deeply religious, and any mention of Daffy reduces her to utter mortification. She tried very hard to persuade her sister to give up her ruinous way of life, but failed."

"Is that . . . so . . . ?" Eyeing Quentin dubiously, Philpott said, "Jove, I'd not have believed . . . Twins, you say? Amazing resemblance." A gleam came into his eye. "I'd best go and comfort the poor lass."

"Not at all. We shall be glad to convey your apologies. Thank you, sir. And—good day."

There was no defying the old gentleman's chill hauteur. Mr. Philpott bowed. Quentin bowed, and led Penelope into the vestibule.

For a moment, Captain Holt stood gazing thoughtfully after the pair he had already discovered were a Mr. Martin and Miss Anne Martin. Then he sat down and returned his attention to his dinner.

When Quentin entered his bedchamber, Killiam was polishing the hilt of a fine small sword and another lay on the bed beside him.

"Hear you've opened a proper box of worms," said the Corporal with his habitual air of profound gloom.

Quentin frowned. "Help me out of this coat, if you please."

The Corporal stood, eased Quentin out of the coat and carried it to the clothes press. "No use telling him how bacon-brained it is," he muttered audibly. "You want to try a pass or two, Major?" He walked back to retrieve a sword and, not waiting for an answer, tossed it.

Quentin caught the weapon deftly, but he winced, swore, and then said fervently, "Thank God we were able to retrieve this article from Highview."

217

With a scornful grunt, the Corporal took back the sword and resumed his seat on the bed. "Much chance you'll have with it—or any other."

"Damn you," muttered Quentin, sitting beside him and gripping his right arm.

"I wonder what it'll be like," the Corporal said musingly, "to work for a gent as leads a nice, quiet life."

"Got one all picked out, have you?"

"Seems like it's past time I was looking around."

"Indeed? I trust you will at least wait until they bury me."

"Tomorrow," said the Corporal heavily. "Unless that nice young Mr. Tiele has a touch o' conscience."

Quentin sighed. "I wish I was such a fool." And with a sudden wry smile, he added, "I'm not, you know."

"You only want the young lady to think so—eh, sir?"

For a moment Quentin made no comment. Then, staring at his boots he said wearily, "Life's a jest, Rob. And Fate the Jester. You either laugh at it all—or wind up in Bedlam. I choose to laugh."

"And you love to meet Fate head-on and give his nose a pull, don'tcha, sir? Still, may I be boiled if I see something comical in this here sittyation."

"Then think how relieved poor Tiele will be when Sir John Macauley Somerville Martin Martin don't present himself in the meadow at dawn. I've no doubt the poor fellow is reproaching himself for having called out an old man."

With perverse disappointment, the Corporal sighed, "It'll be the first time as *you* ever backed away from a fight. . . ."

Quentin flushed. "I've no choice. My first concern must be to deliver my message."

Killiam was silent, but regarded him with a faintly knowing grin, and Quentin's colour deepened around the edges of his paint. He said sharply, "Blast you! I mean it!"

"I didn't say nothing, sir. I only—er, wondered if that wasn't now your—ah, second . . . concern. . . ."

For a moment they stared at each other; the one all innocent speculation, the other as resentful as he was troubled. At length Quentin said crisply, "There are too many lives at stake for me to reassign my loyalties, Corporal. Even if I could. I cannot. My word was given."

It was the Major speaking, not the friend, and the Corporal responded instinctively. "Yessir. As you say, sir. What we going to do, then?"

"I think," said Quentin, "the time has come for the old gentleman to depart."

"I wasn't never a bad girl, M-miss Penny," wept Daffy, her words rather indistinct by reason of the apron.

"I am very sure of that," said Penelope kindly, sitting beside her on the comfortable loveseat and patting her hand. "I suppose you learned all your skills with cosmetics in the—er, ballet?"

Daffy's shrouded head nodded convulsively. "I had a knack, miss. And I—I was a uncommon good dancer, too." One reddened eye peeped fearfully around the edge of the apron. "Only—the gentlemen was always at us."

"So I've heard." Marvelling that this strait-laced girl had actually been one of Covent Garden's notorious opera dancers, Penelope said, "I fancy the temptations are—overwhelming."

"Oh, no, they ain't!" Daffy mopped at her eyes and lowered the damp apron, blinking down at it as she rolled it between nervous fingers. "It's not what you might think—not by a mile, Miss Penny. Me mum told me to keep 'em off till a really fine gent should come around and make me a decent offer." She sniffed. "The closest I come to a decent offer was a fat old banker, and his last ladybird used to say he was as clutchfisted as a clam! I wasn't going to settle for *that!*"

"I should . . . think not . . ." agreed Penelope, faintly.

"Some of the girls struck lucky," Daffy went on. "One was

took under the protection of a Duke! And one found a chef who started his own gentlemen's club. Bought her a dear little 'stablishment what she called the Salon Satin." Daffy sighed. "I saw what happened to the girls who started to lose their looks, or their figures. . . . So I told me mum it was get out now, or start down that trail. I never thought I'd get a respectable position, but Mum used to be a lady's maid, and she told me how to go on and how to act." She stole a timid glance at Penelope's face and read amazement there. "Oh, miss! Please don't turn me off! I'm begging, Miss Penny! Don't!"

"Good gracious, Daffy—why should I do such a thing? It was thanks to your skill with the paints and powder that Major Chandler was enabled to get away from Highview. I shall never be able to thank you enough!" She gave the girl a grateful hug. "Now—we shall say no more about it. Unless"—a twinkle coming into her eyes—"unless Corporal Killiam chances to hear of it."

Daffy gave a squawk and grabbed at her apron. Very pale, she faltered, "You—you never think the Major would tell him?"

"Would it really matter so much, dear Daffy?"

The girl became scarlet, then disappeared into her apron, from whence came a muffled, "Oh . . . yes, miss."

Patting the spot that seemed most likely to be her head, Penelope said, "I am very sure Major Chandler would never be so unchivalrous. However, I had best warn you that he told that gentleman—Mr.—er—"

"Philpott," groaned the apron.

"Yes. The Major told him he'd mistaken you for your twin sister."

With a squeak of laughter, Daffy reappeared. "What a bouncer! Don't say as Mr. Philpott believed it? He must've been proper foxed."

"Well, do you know—I believe he was. But the Major can be so grave and dignified sometimes. He told Mr. Philpott you had tried to reform your sister, but that 'poor Daffy' had gone her

220

own wicked way. Mr. Philpott was so impressed he wanted to come up and apologize to you."

"I don't doubt *that!*" Daffy's indignant expression eased to a reminiscent smile. "Fancy! Mr. Philpott, of all people. *Such* a naughty gentleman! And him with a wife and six fine children! Oh, but the Major's a rare one, ain't he, Miss Penny?"

Penelope's thoughts turned to the averted duel. "Yes," she said with a grateful sigh. "He's a rare one, all right."

"Mr. Tiele?" drawled Quentin, surveying the other man through his quizzing glass as Tiele opened the door.

Tiele, looking slightly flustered, nodded, his brows lifting enquiringly.

"Allow me to introduce myself. Adam Somerville. I am nephew to the gentleman with whom you were to—ah, meet in the morning."

Tiele stared. Now that he came to notice it, the resemblance was marked. This man, of course, was young and very good-looking with a fine head of auburn hair worn tied back and unpowdered, and thick dark brows which arched over eyes of the same brilliant green as his uncle's. The fine-boned face, the not very straight, but slim, nose, the humorous mouth and firm chin might well have been those of Mr. Martin in his youth, thought Tiele. And there was something else . . . something elusive that stirred at the back of his memory and that he could not quite place. He saw curiosity come into his caller's face and said hurriedly, "Your pardon, sir. Did you say the gentleman I—*was* to meet tomorrow? I trust Sir John is not indisposed?"

Quentin smiled at him in a way that made Mr. Tiele flush. "Gad, what a clunch you must think me," he apologized. "Do pray come in."

He ushered Quentin to a chair beside the unlit fire and provided him with a glass of sherry before drawing up another chair and occupying it.

"Well—he is, I'm afraid," said Quentin.

Mr. Tiele thought back.

"Indisposed," Quentin provided.

"Oh." Much relieved, Mr. Tiele lied, "I'm sorry to hear that."

"Are you?" murmured Quentin, quite unable to resist this delicious farce.

Mr. Tiele stared.

"I'll own," remarked Quentin, holding up his glass and watching the candle flame through the rich gold of the wine, "I was rather surprised that a man of Uncle John's years . . ."

His smile was very gentle but Tiele flushed scarlet. "There were—circumstances," he said stiffly.

"He's a wicked old rogue. I fancy there were circumstances, well enough."

Tiele relaxed. He said with a rueful smile, "To own the truth, Somerville, I'm glad you've come here. Miss Montgomery should not be in the care of so—amorous an old gentleman."

"True. Is that why you called him out? I'd fancied *you* were the amorous party, and that my uncle had run you off." He grinned engagingly into Tiele's angry eyes.

His colour much heightened again, Mr. Tiele said, "I'll admit I find Miss Montgomery a most delightful lady. And that your uncle did not approve of my—er—"

"Flirting?"

"Admiration!"

"I see. So you decided to put the poor old fellow out of the way, did you?"

Tiele, who had just taken a sip of his wine, snorted and choked. Eager to be of help, Quentin pounded him so heavily on the back that Tiele was obliged to duck away from that heavy hand. "By Gad, Somerville," he wheezed, dashing tears

222

from his eyes. "I—mislike your choice of—of words. Damme if I don't!"

"My apologies. I have rather an annoying tendency to come straight to the point, as it were."

"Devil you do! I'd no intention of running your uncle through! Well—that is to say . . . Well, what I mean is . . ." Tiele found it most difficult to meet his caller's steady and faintly amused gaze. His own eyes falling away, he paused, shrugged, and admitted, "To tell you the truth, I've been trying to think of a way to get out of it. I'll own I didn't care for the way your uncle— I—er— Well, I dashed well kept forgetting his age. He's a—most remarkably spry old chap."

"Thank you," said Quentin. "I hope you do not mean to ask me to take his place. I'm not the swordsman the old gentleman is, I fear."

"Good, is he?" said Tiele, all interest.

"Superb," said Quentin modestly.

"Lord! I need not have felt so badly."

"You might have felt a good deal worse, my dear chap. Unless you are a very fine swordsman."

"Who's a fine swordsman?" Captain Holt had opened the door unobserved and now strolled into the room, nodding to his friend and eyeing Quentin with mild curiosity.

Quentin stood and smiled easily through the introductions. Holt had a grip of iron, and Quentin felt it in every nerve of his arm. Every instinct warned that this soldier was a formidable antagonist, and despite his carefree manner, he was very much on guard.

"Have we met somewhere, Mr. Somerville?" asked the Captain.

"I fancy I remind you of my uncle," Quentin replied and then realized with a tightening of his muscles that Tiele knew the 'old gentleman' as Somerville, but that he was registered as Martin Martin. "You may have seen him at dinner," he went on easily. "He escorted my cousin Anne—a most delightful lass in a pink brocade gown."

Holt took the glass Tiele offered and sat on the end of the bed as the other two men returned to their chairs. "Thank you, Duncan. Your health, gentlemen."

"Quite a resemblance, ain't there, Jacob?" said Tiele.

"Remarkable," Holt agreed, watching Quentin levelly over his glass. "You should be abed, my dear Tiele. You've to be up early in the morning. And thanks to your hot-headedness, so do I."

"Well, you're reprieved, old fellow. Won't have to second me after all. My adversary has been taken ill, unfortunately."

"My sympathy, sir." Holt's icy blue eyes remained steadily on Quentin's face. "Would you wish that I send the apothecary up to his room?"

"You are too kind, but it is no more than a bad cold. He took a violent dislike to this inn, and his coachman has taken him off somewhere. I tried to persuade him to stay but—as well talk to the wind. You know how these old martinets are. I only aggravate his gout, I fear."

"Sounds like my sire," said Tiele with a grin. "You don't stand high in your uncle's favour, eh?"

"Somewhere at basement level, alas," sighed Quentin.

"You surprise me," said Holt mildly.

Nerves tightening, Quentin lifted one eyebrow in enquiry.

"I had thought you must be quite a favourite," the Captain said, "since your uncle has given you his ring."

'Damn the fellow,' thought Quentin, glancing instinctively at the cunningly wrought dragon's head ring on his right hand. 'How in the deuce could he have noticed it in those few moments downstairs?' He grinned at Holt admiringly. "Deuce take it, you're observant, Captain."

Tiele was staring unblinkingly at him.

Holt said sternly, "It's an asset in my calling."

"I don't doubt that. Actually, this ain't my uncle's. It's a tradition of my house. There are ten rings, exactly alike. When

224

a male child reaches the age of one and twenty he is given a dragon ring, always supposing there is one available and he the next in line to receive it."

"What a charming tradition," said Holt. "May I see it?"

Quentin extended his hand. Holt gazed with interest at the ring for a moment, then gripped the steady, long-fingered hand. "Do you know, Mr.—er—"

"Somerville."

"Your pardon. But—do you know, I must have met one of your kinsmen at some time, for I've seen this ring before . . . somewhere. . . . Well, I think I'll get to bed. No rest for a poor soldier, you know."

They all stood, Holt a solidly powerful figure in marked contrast to the two taller men. Ushering him to the door, Tiele insisted on paying his shot at The Flying Dutchman. "Had it not been for my—duel," he said, with a grim look at Quentin, "you'd not have racked up here."

Holt shrugged. "As you wish. Thank you—I'll enjoy a comfortable night for once. My bed in the barracks leaves much to be desired. Very glad to have met you—er, Somerville."

Quentin murmured an appropriate platitude.

Tiele closed the door behind his friend and leaned against it, saying nothing, until the brisk footsteps had died away.

Quentin set his empty wine glass gently on the table, then turned to face Tiele. "Get it said, whatever it is," he said in a quiet and grim departure from his customary light-hearted manner.

"You damned liar," said Tiele bitterly. "You're Quentin Chandler!"

XIII

Quentin's hand moved so fast that Tiele saw only a blur before a small pistol with an unpleasantly wide mouth was aiming at his chest. The hand that held the weapon was unwavering, the narrowed green eyes deadly. Markedly undaunted, Tiele strode forward. "By God! I should wring your stupid neck," he declared wrathfully.

"I'm a selfish man," said Quentin, somewhat taken aback by this attitude. "I must deny you. Very bad timing, Tiele. You should have claimed the reward while your military friend was here."

"Reward! 'Twould have to be ten times the amount to reimburse me for all my trouble!"

"Stay back!" Quentin's finger tightened on the trigger. "I warn you, I'll not hesitate to use this."

"And have twenty troopers here in two minutes? Rubbish!" Given pause nonetheless by the determined line of Quentin's mouth, Tiele halted. "What the deuce possessed you to bring a girl along? Did Gordon know you meant to do so?"

Quentin breathed uncertainly, "Gordon . . . ?"

"My former friend. He asked me to bring you a message at Highview and was so ill informed as to describe you a very sick

226

man who was like to turn up his toes at any second. Instead of which I've been badgered and poked at by a crotchety old fidget who added insult to injury by challenging me to a duel!"

Not bothering to make the obvious rejoinder, Quentin counter-attacked, "Why the Lord didn't you say at once that you were from my brother? Did you notice I'd thumbed back the hammer?"

"I did." Tiele glanced at the pistol. "And respectfully suggest you release it with great care."

Quentin did so. Replacing the weapon in his pocket, he put out his hand and said with a twinkle, "Terribly sorry to have run you such a chase. I wonder you did not consign me to perdition and forget the entire business."

"Would have." Tiele returned the handshake gingerly. "Only, it chances that my little brother served under you at Culloden. Sit down and I'll fill your glass."

Quentin sprawled gratefully in the chair and stretched out his long legs. "What name did he use?"

"John House. He said you used to call him—"

"What—young Glasshouse?" Quentin sat straighter, accepting the wine Tiele brought him and asking eagerly, "How is the boy? He lost that leg, I'm very sure."

"Yes. At the knee. And thanks to you is thumping around Brussels on a wooden one." Tiele stood before Quentin and raised his glass in a salute. "Thank you, sir. If you hadn't carried him off the field . . ."

"Tush! It was the only way I knew to remove myself from that damned massacre."

"You lie. Johnny said you were wounded but went back just the same." Tiele saw the flush that lit Chandler's pale face and went on smoothly, "Not that it gave you the right to treat me with such savagery."

They both laughed.

Quentin asked, "Did you go to Highview then?"

"I did. After you'd left, of course. I was supposed to get word to a maid there, but when I arrived she'd run off. I asked to see

Delavale, but a regular block of a butler said he was gone to London. I could only think you'd managed to get away and would likely head for Lac Brillant, so I rode this way, hoping to warn you."

"Warn me?" His voice sharp with anxiety, Quentin asked, "My brother's not suspect, I pray God?"

"Not that I'm aware." Tiele, who had continued to stand, strolled to the bed and sat down. "I am not of your persuasions, I should tell you."

"Nor is Gordie. We had our first serious quarrel over my allegiance to Charles Stuart."

"I fancy Johnny and I did much the same. My elder brother was of a mind to tie him and keep him prisoner until the madness had passed."

Quentin's eyes kindled. "Why is it that if a man does not understand the convictions of another he terms them madness?" He met Tiele's stormy look and grinned. "Only look at us. In another minute we'll launch into an argument that will last till dawn, belike, and solve nothing. However you believe, I'm deeply grateful you have brought me word from my brother. May I know what it is you've to tell me?"

Although they were quite alone, Tiele lowered his voice to little more than a whisper. "Gordon will meet you at The Cat and Kippers. It's a villainous old tavern on the Salisbury Road, about three miles west of Winchester."

"When?"

"I don't know. He said the least I knew, the safer I'd be. But he was most anxious that you find a very good hiding place for the cypher, for he says the southland fairly throngs with ruffians would roast you alive to get their hands on it."

Quentin said cynically, "I'm very aware!" He regarded Tiele thoughtfully. "One thing—your friend, Holt . . ."

"I've known him since we were scared eight-year-olds packed off to school. He's a good man. But . . ." Tiele hesitated, then went on steadily, "God help anyone who runs afoul of him. He's quite relentless."

228

"Yet you're his good friend."

"Yes. One of his few friends, for he's not the gregarious type. Even so, were there a price on my head and he came after me, I'd expect no mercy. Nor get any."

After a short pause, Quentin pointed out, "You risk a great deal, you know. If I should be taken, Holt will know we've talked."

"Hopefully, I could convince him I was merely interested in the lady. Is she really your niece, by the way?"

"*No!* Devil take you! She is not!"

"Oh." Grinning, Tiele said, "I must try not to continue to think of you as elderly. May I ask who the lady is?"

"Whoever she may be," said Quentin, standing and replacing the glass on the table, "I've neglected her for too long, so I'll say good night, and—"

"And tell me—you thankless ingrate!"

A smile flickering about Quentin's lips, he strolled to the door. Tiele was before him, flinging himself back against the panels. "Come on, Chandler—"

"*Somerville!*"

"Blast your eyes! Somerville, then. Tell a poor fellow—unless . . . If she's yours, of course . . . ?"

For a moment Quentin stared at him enigmatically, then he said, "No, she's not mine, Tiele, though she is a very dear friend. I think of her more as—my sister."

"Well, that's a dashed relief, I must say. And—her family?"

It was evident, thought Quentin, that Gordon had judged it safer not to mention Penelope's involvement in their schemes. He said, "She is Delavale's niece, you maggot-wit."

Tiele's eyes took on a glassy look. "You mean . . . she is a lady of Quality?"

"I'd think *that* was obvious!"

Undeterred by Quentin's suddenly icy hauteur, Tiele stammered, "And you—took her away from—from *Highview?* My God! I thought she was your—"

"Have a care!"

"Oh . . . Jove! But—you and she—I mean—you've hauled her all over the countryside? Alone?"

Irritated because Tiele's shocked words merely intensified his own guilt, Quentin growled, "Don't be such an ape, for Lord's sake! We'd her maid and my man along, to say nothing of coachmen and grooms."

"Much that has to say to the matter! You've thoroughly compromised the poor girl, Chandler. That's what you've dashed well done!"

Quentin glared at him, then reached for the door latch. "With luck," he said acidly, "some noble gentleman will come along who is willing to overlook Miss Montgomery's scarlet past and—and make an honest woman of her!"

He marched out and stalked along the hall, his face unwontedly grim.

Duncan Tiele closed the door behind his departing guest, then stood there staring at it, lost in thought.

"I'm tired," Lady Sybil faltered pathetically. "We have been driving for hours and hours and *hours!* Joseph! I want to go to bed."

"You can sleep in the carriage," he grunted.

Sybil bowed her head into her hands and wept.

My lord looked across the grubby table of the grubby coffee room of this grubby inn. "Well? What d'you think?"

Roland Otton, his eyes bloodshot with weariness, said dourly, "That I can scarce blame Beasley for giving up when we reached Hampstead. He's likely found himself a cosier spot than this poor excuse for an inn."

My lord's estimate of Beasley's character caused Sybil to throw her hands over her ears.

"Why a' plague couldn't Chandler go where he said he was going?" he went on broodingly. "If they'd been at Mary's—"

230

"They were not."

"I know that, fiend take you. We were agreed to drive on."

"True. But we're going to have to get some rest some time. Even if we change horses again, the men need sleep, or they'll likely drive you into a ditch."

"Besides," Sybil put in tearfully, "there may be highwaymen . . . or worse."

That horrid possibility had occurred to Joseph. He pulled uneasily at his earlobe, then beckoned his valet, who waited with Simmonds at a side table, and sent the man off to find the host and procure suitable accommodations for the night.

The rooms were the best of a bad lot and, when a complaining Sybil had been deposited in one of them and Simmonds was fluttering about her, his lordship and Otton repaired to the small private parlour Joseph had reluctantly added to his suite, and sat before the inadequate fire. The room was clammy. Rain had begun to fall once more and tapped depressingly against the latticed casements.

"As well I decided to stop here for the night," said his lordship gloomily. "We'd not have got far at all events, as you see."

Otton darted him a contemptuous glance, but only said, "The important thing is that we get an early start in the morning, sir."

"Early start for where? Be damned if I see your logic for heading west. Chandler was running for London, whether to leave my wanton niece with her aunt, or merely to lose himself in the city."

"I doubt he will allow Penelope to leave him. She's his best disguise. The military don't seek an old fellow travelling with his grand-niece."

Lord Joseph frowned broodingly at his ragged fingernails, knowing he should not listen to Otton's arguments but instead hold fast to his own convictions and head in to Town. "I'll hold you personally responsible does he escape us," he said.

'I'm very sure you will, you fat fool,' thought Otton. He said placatingly, "I cannot believe any fugitive would persist with a

231

plan that led him into the patrols we have endured today, my lord. Further, you'll own the last man to describe our disguised rebel even remotely was that Sergeant at High Wycombe."

Joseph's lip curled in disgust. "Blasted fellow stank to high heaven!"

"True. An abominable animal. Nonetheless, he had very definitely seen our quarry, and for all we've been able to learn since, Chandler and your niece might have vanished into thin air. Or changed direction."

A discreet scratch at the door announced the arrival of the waiter, and my lord brightened to the sight of a tray of fruit and cheeses, and a bottle of wine. The waiter deposited his burden on a small table within easy reach of Joseph's pudgy hand, caught the groat Otton tossed him, and departed.

Otton stood to pour a glass of port and hand it to Joseph. He carried his own glass back to settle himself again into the lumpy, musty-smelling chair.

"Has Chandler the brains he was born with," said my lord, appropriating a slice of Cheddar, "he will make straight for the coast."

"Or swing southeast to Tonbridge and thence to Lac Brillant."

"Ha! His sire would show him the door fast enough! I would, under the circumstances. Any man would."

Otton's smile held the twist of bitterness. "My father would, I grant you. But—Sir Brian? I'm not so sure."

"Then you're a noddicock. I only met Brian Chandler twice, but he's properly high in the instep, I can tell you, and Lac Brillant is his pride and joy. I'll lay odds he'd slaughter any man who caused him to lose it. Son or not."

Otton said thoughtfully, "We're now a mile or so west of Stoke Poges. If Chandler realized by the time they reached High Wycombe they'd never come safe to Town, it's likely he'd head west before daring to swing south again. Chances are, he'd make for Reading, and if—" He checked, glancing to the window as a flurry of activity sounded in the yard below. "Some

232

high and mightyness has arrived, it would seem," he muttered, and ambled over to pull back the curtain.

A large and luxurious carriage stood in the yard, the centre of a beehive of industry. Ostlers were removing the traces from the four blood horses; footmen wearing brown and cream livery under their wet, glistening cloaks carried luggage into the building; a gentleman's gentleman with a dressing case under one arm left the vehicle and struggled to unfurl an umbrella. Before he succeeded in this endeavour, another man emerged from the carriage and trod gracefully down the steps. A tall gentleman this, wearing a tricorne over silver hair, his long, caped cloak swinging back as he descended, to reveal a rich *habit à la française* of dull red satin.

"Thunder an' turf!" said Otton softly, his exclamation springing not from admiration of the newcomer's attire, but from the thin patrician features lit by the glow from the wide-open front door. "Only look here, my lord!"

Intrigued by the note of excitement in his henchman's voice, Joseph was already rising. By the time he reached the window, however, the valet below had succeeded in spreading the sheltering umbrella over his master, and all my lord saw was the hurried progress of a tall, cloaked individual and the gleam of gold buckles on high-heeled shoes. "Who was it? Who was it?" Joseph demanded testily.

"The greatest piece of luck! Sir Brian Chandler!"

"Is it, by Jove? What a coincidence!"

"'Twould be a *very* great coincidence were Sir Brian and his son travelling in the same corner of England each unaware of the proximity of the other."

"Ahh-h-h," breathed Joseph, turning back into the room as Otton closed the curtains. "Then—you think he comes to meet that young rapscallion?"

"I do." Otton grinned joyfully. "And our task becomes so much child's play! All we've to do is let the gentleman lead us to his traitorous son!" He took up the bottle and refilled De-

233

lavale's glass. Raising his own, he said an exuberant, "To obliging fathers!"

The glasses clinked together.

"To Sir Brian Chandler," said his lordship.

"You are not cold?" enquired Quentin, guiding Penelope around a wide puddle in the lane.

A little less than truthfully she answered, "No, thank you. I love to walk after the rain."

That, at least, was truth. And if the air was cool it was also clean and bracing, and sweet with the scents of wet grass and woodsmoke. The night sky blazed with brilliant stars, and one long cloudrack glowed luminously as it hoarded the moon's glory to itself. Few people were abroad at this hour, for it was near ten o'clock, and country folk went early to bed. Lamplight gleamed from an occasional cottage window; somewhere nearby a man's voice was raised in hearty laughter; a white cat with long silky hair was sitting on the post of a picket fence and offered a friendly mew as they passed. Quentin paused to stroke it. Penelope watched him obliquely, wondering why he had asked her to walk out. Earlier, she had thought to see fatigue in his eyes, but he had denied it, and indeed no one would suspect he was tired, for his stride was as supple, his manner as light-hearted as ever. She should not have agreed to come, of course, for he should be resting after such a long, tiring day. But—oh, how wonderful to be alone with him; to feel the occasional gentle touch of his hand on her elbow; to be guided carefully around obstructions as though she were something infinitely precious and her skirts must not be brushed by muddy fences or wet foliage.

They went on, but after a moment, "Your friend is following," she said.

The white cat was treading daintily along the narrow pickets, its long plume of a tail waving high in the air.

"What a fine fellow you are," said Quentin, scratching beneath its chin as it came up to them. The cat uttered an amiable trill and rubbed against his hand. "Now, you must stay here," Quentin ordered. "If you're good and obey me, I'll bring you a fat yellow bird for your breakfast."

"Villain," cried Penelope. "I shall tell Daffy what you plan for her beloved Jasper!"

"Beloved Jasper, indeed! That bird is the noisiest, messiest pest I ever saw. A canary is supposed to sing sweetly—not screech like a banshee! I wonder where Daffy found the wretched creature."

She chuckled. "A gift from one of her admirers, perhaps. Oh—see, Quentin! How pretty the moon is now."

The yellow orb was sailing majestically from behind the cloud to light the velvety blackness of the heavens with its radiance. Penelope's hood fell back as she gazed upwards and, for a small space, Quentin studied her profile bathed in that gentle light. The look in his eyes would have astounded her, but when she turned to him he also was admiring the celestial display.

"A smuggler's moon," he murmured nostalgically. "The lads will be busy along the coast tonight, I'll warrant."

"And you wishing you were with them. Oh, never look so innocent, sir. I well remember the tales you used to tell Geoff and me of your forays with the Free Traders, and how your papa pretended to know nought of it."

He grinned, took her elbow and led her across the cobbled street. The white cat, ears back, tore after them and hurled itself into the graveyard of the serene little Gothic church.

"Good heavens!" exclaimed Penelope, startled.

"Mad cat," said Quentin whimsically. "He'll scare all the ghosts to death."

Laughing, she asked as they went on, "Did Gordon share your illicit pursuits?"

"Lord—no! He has too much sense for that kind of lunacy. I

235

pulled him into it eventually, of course. Poor old fellow. I've been a sore trial as a brother."

"He doesn't seem to mind very much. How did you 'pull him in'? Were you able to persuade him to sail with you?"

"Small chance of that. He held it to be all folly and bravado."

"Was it so?"

"Not . . . exactly." He hesitated, then said with a shrug, "But I don't repent my deeds. I came into the game by accident and found them to be good men, Penny. Hungry men. I mislike our stupid tax laws and—well, life was curst dull during the Long Vacation. Smuggling was jolly good fun."

Aghast, she thought, 'Fun!' and said, "But you have not explained how your brother was involved."

"Oh—well, we'd made the run from France one night and were almost home when a squall blew up. We were capsized and, if you can believe it, one of the lads couldn't swim. By the time—er, we got to the cove, the excisemen were hot after us. I'd managed to wrench my ankle a bit, and Paul had swallowed half the Channel, and we were a sorry pair. Luckily, Gordon had been out looking for us. He arrived just in time with some fast horses and off we rode through a hail of shot." He chuckled. "Poorly aimed, fortunately."

"Good gracious! What terrible chances to take. How lucky you are to have such a fine brother."

"Yes." His white grin gleamed at her. "I think I'll keep the chawbacon. Shall we cross here?"

Two farm labourers came towards them, returning wearily from some late task. They touched their caps respectfully, and said, "Evenin', zur and marm," in their soft, pleasant country accents. The white cat scampered past again, then jumped on to the ledge of a deep bay window. Penelope stopped to caress the playful animal, and Quentin peered in the mullioned window. It was a confectioner's shop. "I wish they were open," he murmured. "I'd buy you that big lollipop."

Penelope laughed and scanned the pleasant shapes of red and

236

white rock canes, marzipan and nuts, comfits and dishes of toffee. Quentin straightened, his gaze shifting to the reflection of a girl with a warm smile and clear, resolute eyes. Penelope looked up, met his eyes, and could not turn away. They stood thus, unmoving, through a hushed, enchanted moment, while diamond drops splashed softly from the eaves, and the white cat twined, purring, around their feet.

A cart rattled up the street. Quentin turned about rather hurriedly and ushered Penelope back the way they had come.

For some moments neither spoke. The sounds of the cart died away and the night was still once more, the wet cobblestones silvered by the moonlight. They approached a larger house set back in a pleasant garden across which drifted the pure notes of a violin playing a poignant and familiar love song. Quentin began to sing in a soft, clear baritone.

> *"I prithee send me back my heart*
> *Since I cannot have thine.*
> *For if from yours you will not part*
> *Why then shouldst thou have mine?"*

It was the final touch of delight, and Penelope seemed to float along in a daze.

A big dog came from nowhere to charge at the fence beside her, barking furiously, and she recoiled with a little cry of shock.

The white cat, which had been keeping pace with them in a sedate fashion, shot into the air with a yowl of fright, then was gone in a white streak across the darkness. In the same instant, Quentin's arm had whipped around Penelope's waist and swung her aside.

"Be quiet! Bad dog!" he snapped in an authoritative way. But the dog only barked more wildly than ever. Amused, he said, "He knows he's not really a bad dog, you see, but protecting his master's property as he should. Did he frighten you? My apologies, but I'd not seen him until he sprang. Here—" He took up her hand and tucked it into his arm. "We shall go on better like this, I think."

They walked on, Penelope's heart still beating very fast, but no longer from fright. The dog's frenzied barking died into a growl, then he ran off in answer to a whistle from the house.

"Now, about Gordon," said Quentin. "I'm to meet him tomorrow."

With an exclamation of excitement Penelope demanded, "Where? When? How did you learn of it?"

"Question one: At The Cat and Kippers, near Winchester. Question two: When he shows himself, I collect. And as for Question three: My friend Duncan Tiele told me."

Penelope halted and her jaw dropped. "Your . . . *friend?*" she echoed feebly. "B-but you were to *meet* him until— I thought you despised him."

"Oh, no. He seems a very good sort of man. In fact"—he trailed one fingertip absently around her lips and, his eyes dreaming, murmured—"it turns out that . . . his brother served under me. A splendid young—" He broke off, drew back and finished abruptly, "All in all, I think friend Tiele may do very well for you, my bright little Penny."

She had quivered responsively to the soft touch of his hand on her face. She had, in fact, been leaning slightly towards him although not until this moment had she realized it. She felt as though she had been struck and for a second could not catch her breath. Then, "Do you indeed," she said tartly, walking on. "Would you suggest I wed him tonight, sir? Or might the ceremony wait until morning?"

'I am *not*,' thought Penelope, watching the moonlight slant serenely through her window, 'going to cry all night. Not again!' She blinked, groped under her pillow, sat up, and blew her nose. They were to part tomorrow. *Tomorrow!* Quentin had told her on the way back here that it was most fortunate he'd sent Killiam and Dutch Coachman on ahead, because Captain Holt had gone prowling about the stables to determine if, in fact, the old gentleman's coach had left. She was afraid of the cold-eyed Captain, and when she'd reacted in a scared voice, Quentin had soothed her by saying that tomorrow she would see the last of Holt because Gordon would take her to Hampstead. "I mean to instruct him," he added firmly, "that if he don't think your aunt capable of protecting you, he's to carry you to Lac Brillant. My father will know what to do, rest assured."

Well, she was not resting assured. She was not resting at all. She had been such a fool as to give her heart to a man who not only had no fondness for her, but was so cruel as to play wretched little games. He had probably, she thought, shivering her way under the covers again, been the sort of little boy who tied kittens' tails to the boots of stagecoaches, and— She checked, frowning into the darkness. Only, Quentin had *not* been like that. And even all those years ago at Lac Brillant, she had once or twice caught him watching her in an oddly speculative sort of way, as if— She gave an impatient little snort. Ridiculous! Why must she keep on torturing herself? Quentin Chandler, her dear papa had implied five years ago, was a rascal with the ladies. Just because those green eyes said "I love you," while his lips said "I don't want you" did not mean— Unless . . . ? She sat up again, pulling the eiderdown around her chin and gazing with dawning suspicion across the moonlit room.

It was silly, really. She was only deluding herself. But looking backwards she could call to mind several instances in which she had thought to see a breathtaking tenderness in his eyes, that look invariably followed by some carelessly unkind remark. He had risked his life without question when he'd been so close to escaping Highview, and had stayed rather than leave her to face terror alone. Her brows puckered thoughtfully. Any honourable gentleman would have done the same . . . no? Again—

239

there had been that moment when poor Killiam had gloomily predicted her possible execution, and Quentin had flown into such a towering rage. And there were more recent incidents. For instance, how furious he'd been when Daffy had dressed her so prettily and he'd found Duncan Tiele holding her hand in the private parlour; their bitter-sweet encounter with Sir Sylvester Serious in the dining room; the wistful sadness of his expression when their eyes had met in the reflection of the shop windows; the exquisite delight when he had gently traced around her lips, and the nonchalantly dismissing words that had followed.

She was trembling now, her eyes wide and staring. Surely only a most quixotic chivalry would demand that a man in love thrust his lady into the arms of another, to protect her? She gave a gasp. And surely Quentin Chandler was the very figure of chivalry! He was the same man who had plunged wholeheartedly into a doomed cause and never once whined because of what had followed. He was the same man who, weak and suffering and helpless, had yet fought against accepting his one hope of escape for fear of the possible consequences to her. He was the *very* type of dear simpleton who would, loving her with all his heart, push her away—to spare her!

"Oh, lud! Lud!" she whispered, both hands tight clasped about her knees. "It *could* be so. And if it is—how *silly* I have been! I've handled it all wrong!"

The morning dawned fair with a brisk westerly wind setting the inn sign creaking on its chains and chasing a few wispy clouds across the pale skies. Penelope was up early, as Quentin had requested, and joined 'Mr. Somerville' and Mr. Tiele for breakfast in the coffee room. Quentin had little to say beyond the usual pleasantries, leaving the field clear for Mr. Tiele who, delighted, engaged Penelope in a brisk conversation. They were neither inclined, as was Quentin, to be still drowsy at breakfast, and they soon found they had many interests in common, including a love of dogs. Quentin interrupted a deep discussion over the temperaments of the various setters to suggest it would be as well to get on the road as soon as possible.

Corporal Killiam having left them, the coachman and groom carried down the luggage and packed it in the boot. Daffy hurried out to the yard carrying Jasper's cage, well shielded from the wind. Quentin's spirits had been restored by his morning coffee, but his mood was not sufficiently improved to support the notion of sharing the carriage with Jasper. The bird, he declared firmly, must ride on the box. Indignant, Daffy refused to entrust her pet into the doubtful care of the groom who had been temporarily elevated to the status of coachman, and whom she had described to Penelope as "a proper block." Dutch Coachman she had taken a great liking to, but Dutch Coachman had been obliged to drive the nonexistent Mr. Martin and his man to their next destination. She was, however, dismayed when Quentin relented and said Jasper might stay inside the coach, but that he himself would ride on the box. A lively discussion ensued, but Penelope had no intention of allowing Quentin to ride outside and, between the deft manipulations of the two girls, he was at length persuaded that Daffy would manage very nicely with the extra rug that was to be wrapped about her knees.

Much to her delight, Duncan Tiele lifted Daffy to the box, to the accompaniment of her small scream of maidenly modesty. The wind sent Penelope's skirts billowing, and Quentin gave an appreciative grin as he handed her up the steps and climbed in beside her.

"Delightful morning, m'dear," he said, watching her adjust her gown.

"If one cares to be ogled," she returned. "I wonder my betrothed did not land you a facer, the way you stared at my ankles."

He pulled the door shut but did not at once reply, and Penelope was struck by the thought that he looked rather heavy-eyed. He had refused to allow her to change his bandages last evening, saying that Killiam had made such a good job of it before he left that there was not the need. It struck her, then, that Rob himself had seemed somewhat concerned for his master, and she asked anxiously, "I wish you had let me look at that arm. Are you feeling not quite the thing? I'd not meant to—"

"Shock me?" he interpolated gravely. "I'm afraid you did, you know. It don't matter if you utter such gaucheries with me, Penny. But—as I've tried to point out, Duncan's a very proper sort of fellow."

The 'proper sort of fellow' chose that moment to ride up to the window. He looked very well in a blue riding coat, spotless breeches, and high knee boots. He called a greeting, bowed to Penelope, and went on ahead.

"Tell me please what I have done now," said Penelope. "I cannot afford more mistakes, for I do not think Mr. Tiele is quite as besotted as you suppose."

Quentin looked mildly surprised, then answered, "There's no doubt in my mind on that score. Even so, Penelope Anne, I think Geoff would want me to point out that a lady should not use cant terms—such as landing someone a 'facer.'"

"'Twas Geoffrey taught me the term."

"Perhaps so, but he was younger then, and—"

"And alive," she put in bitterly.

"*What* did you say?"

That sharp question brought her head around, and she beheld an incredulous expression that she judged to be for once an authentic mirror of his feelings. Bewildered, she replied, "I said that my brother—" And she broke off, glancing to the window as the carriage slowed and stopped only a short way down the lane from the inn.

Quentin opened the window and peered out, then sat back, gave Penelope's hand a quick squeeze, and murmured, "Easy, child."

Tiele came to the window again, his eyes holding a warning. Following him, neat and solemn as ever, rode Captain Holt.

"Give you good day, Mr. Sommerville," called the officer. "Making an early escape?"

Despite herself Penelope gave a gasp, and her hand clamped convulsively upon a fold of her gown.

Not waiting for a reply, the Captain saluted her and smiled expectantly.

"I think you've not met our gallant soldier," said Quentin. "Miss Martin—Captain Holt."

The Captain acknowledged the introduction politely and remarked, "I fancy you're off after your uncle, eh, Somerville?"

Quentin stared at him. "Are you subject to these mental aberrations? Why the deuce would I want to follow the old curmudgeon?"

"Misjudged you, have I? I'd thought you would be eager to obtain restitution."

Every nerve tensing, Quentin asked, "For what? I'm not vastly put out because he required me to escort my cousin home, if that's what you mean."

"I fancy any gentleman would find that a pleasant task," said the Captain blandly, but with a little gleam in his eyes. "No, I'd referred to the fact that I hear *you* paid Mr. Martin's bill this morning."

The cold clarity that always enveloped Quentin at a moment of extreme danger made him intensely aware of Penelope's terror. He could cheerfully have strangled Holt, but he laughed and replied lightly, "Oh, the old fellow's not quite that bad, you know. He left me sufficient funds to pay our shot—and that's dashed well all he left me!"

"I wonder you could be surprised," said Penelope, somehow keeping her voice casual. "My uncle guessed why you wanted to meet us. And how you could have made such a request of him when he was in gout . . . ! Really, coz!"

"How the devil was I to know that? And with all his blunt I do not see—" Quentin broke off and looked wryly at the two

243

men. "Well, never mind about that. Tiele? Do you go with us or not?"

"One moment, if you please," said Holt, unconvinced. "I had fancied your arrival at The Flying Dutchman a chance matter. Were you in fact *expecting* to meet your uncle, Mr. Somerville?"

Quentin frowned at him. "I do not see that it is any of your bread and butter, sir, but—yes. I learned my uncle was to escort Miss Martin home and that he meant to stop here, so I sent word I'd meet him." Anticipating the next attack, he went on in an aggrieved way, "I'd fancied the old skinflint would at least have reserved me a room, but when my friends set me down I found I was expected to share *his* room!"

Holt said, "So you did not drive your own equipage. I had wondered by what means you arrived."

"Devil you had! Nosing around were you, sir? Well, if you must know, I can no longer afford my own equipage, as my curst uncle refused to—"

"Cousin!" exclaimed Penelope, looking outraged, and having failed utterly to remember by what Christian name Quentin was presently known. "How can you speak so of your own family before strangers? Uncle could very well have refused to let you use his room at all."

"Not if he wanted me to escort *you* back home, m'dear."

"And—where exactly is—home, Miss Martin?" Holt said at once.

Quentin could feel Penelope shaking. "Well, if you ain't bold as brass," he said indignantly. "You only just met the lady!"

"I ask in my official capacity," snapped Holt, irked at last.

"A likely story! Tiele—if this fellow's a friend of yours, I can tell you I don't care for his way of courting a—"

"I was *not* courting the lady," Holt gritted, quite red in the face.

Keeping his mouth grave with an effort, Tiele said, "He is but trying to do his duty, Somerville. You must know there's a widespread search for Jacobites, and—"

"Well, if Captain Holt fancies my cousin fought at Culloden,

244

he must have maggots in his head! Be damned if I don't mean to complain to old Mariner about this ridiculous harassment!"

Again, that name proved a magical one.

Holt stiffened. "You are acquainted with Major Fotheringay, sir?"

"You may believe I am! His papa and mine were school-mates." Quentin paused, as though struck by a sudden inspiration and, as if to himself, muttered, "Come to think of it, old Mariner broke my shins some time back. . . . Jove, I fancy he'll be glad enough to fork over the dibs now!" He turned to Penelope. "Would you object if we turned about, coz? I've a notion Mariner's stationed near Oxford and he owes me—"

Correctly interpreting his slight frown, she pouted, "Well, I *would* object! This has been a horrid journey and already taken much too long. I am promised to the Nashes at Coombe Bissett tomorrow, and I want to go home—*now!*"

"Then I shall detain you not another moment," said Holt. "My apologies for any inconvenience, Mr. Somerville. But—duty is duty." He reined back and hailed the coachman and the carriage rumbled forward, Tiele waving as he rode past beside it.

Captain Holt did not at once ride off, but looked after the carriage, deep in thought. His intuitive mistrust of Adam Somerville had evidently been unwarranted. His mouth twisted scornfully. A typical, selfish young wastrel with no thought for anyone but himself, and not the backbone of a pullet—far less a fighting rebel. Still, the girl *had* gone as white as a sheet when he'd first stopped them. . . . And that business about the old gentleman rushing away so suddenly had been more than a touch havey-cavey. He pursed his lips, debating with himself as to whether to send a trooper to keep an eye on them. Although—Tiele was with them, of course. . . .

The Captain turned about and rode slowly towards The Flying Dutchman.

In the carriage, Penelope's nerves gave way at last. With a muffled sob she closed her eyes, shaking uncontrollably.

Groaning, Quentin pulled her into his arms. "Do not! My poor, sweet soul! My God! What have I dragged you into! Please—I beg you—*please* don't cry."

But she wept helplessly into his cravat, and he held her, pleading that she cease, stroking her hair and eventually drawing out his handkerchief and dabbing clumsily at her tears. "I am so very sorry," he murmured distractedly. "It's all my fault! That *damnable* head-hunter—to frighten you so."

"Only," she gulped, "because I was—so afraid I m-might . . . let you d-down. . . ." It seemed to her that the hand clasping hers trembled at this, and she raised her brimming eyes hopefully.

He looked rather too cool. "Oh, no fear of that," he said with a bracing smile. "You were very believable."

Penelope sighed shakily. "That man terrifies me. He seems so inhumanly zealous—so cold."

"Zealous, certainly. In pursuit of promotion rather than an ideal. Never mind, my niece. Between us, we properly bamboozled him."

"Cousin . . ." she corrected huskily.

"Gad! It becomes more and more difficult to remember! At all events, with luck we'll not see the creature again." He leaned to the still open window. "Hi! Tiele!" he called, and pulled on the check string.

Alarmed, Penelope asked, "What are you going to do?"

"Nothing treasonable, for once. Hello, Tiele. Change seats with me, there's a good fellow. I feel the need for a ride." He turned to Penelope and said just above a whisper, "It'll give you a chance to trap the poor gudgeon."

'Coward,' she thought, but she managed to look pleased, and whispered back, "Oh, thank you!"

She would have sworn that Quentin's mouth was tightly compressed as he let down the steps and left her.

XIV

It was not easy to find The Cat and Kippers. Duncan Tiele's optimistic "about three miles west of Winchester" turned out to be almost six miles west of that fair town, and "the Salisbury Road" was found to be Salisbury Lane, this muddy, pot-holed atrocity winding for another mile northwards before the inn came into view. Long before they reached Winchester, Quentin had regretted his noble impulse in allowing Tiele to sit with Penelope whilst he rode one of the most jolting-gaited hacks it had ever been his misfortune to bestride. He was forced to the admission that he was not as fully recovered as he'd supposed, and had seldom been more pleased to come to the end of a journey.

Tiele's description of the place had erred on the side of optimism, and Quentin viewed it with growing astonishment. The inn sign was of itself sufficient to cause any traveller possessing an ounce of self-preservation to beat a hasty retreat. One must hope, thought Quentin, amused, that whoever had painted the sign had some other employment to sustain him. Certainly, his work could not be in great demand. The Cat was a tabby of most unusual hues, blobs of near vermilion alternating with stripes of white and bright yellow. The head of this unlikely

247

feline was several sizes too large for its body and, although it was smooth-coated, a gigantic and very fluffy white and yellow tail curled up behind it. This latter feature might account for the fact that the enormous round eyes of the creature were so surprised and stared at the visitor as if to say, "Why on earth are you coming in *here?*" Of the second half of the name there was no trace, for although the Cat pranced upon a red velvet cushion, nothing even faintly resembling a kipper was evident.

The inn itself was little more than a hedge tavern, and one of the most unprepossessing that Quentin had ever beheld. A collection of structures of varying heights and appearing to have come together more by accident than design, it possessed mullioned casements, whitewashed walls, and a thatched roof. The latter, although in seemingly good repair, had never been properly trimmed and hung like unkempt hair over the dirty windows. The wagon wheel atop it was in a disintegrating condition, several of the spokes hanging precariously, posing a potential threat to any unwary traveller who chanced to be beneath when they fell. The whitewash looked to have been applied at least a decade since, and now gave every appearance of an advanced case of mange. The paint hung in shreds from the front doors, and even the steps leading to the unimposing entrance were broken and uneven.

"Reckon you'll know it if you 'appen ter see it agin," grunted a surly voice.

Quentin brought his incredulous glance around and beheld a tall, slouching ostler who watched him without enthusiasm. A straw hung from the mouth of this disreputable individual, his greasy coat was worn over a grimy shirt, his breeches were a disaster, and long, lank black hair straggled down from beneath what might once have been a hat.

"I pray I never have the opportunity," said Quentin fervently, but curiosity getting the better of him, added, "Where are the kippers on your sign?"

A broad and oddly familiar grin spread across the lean, unshaven countenance. "Cat et 'em," he said, and let out a loud hee-haw of a laugh.

The carriage came rattling up. The ostler looked at it with resentment. "You with that lot?" he asked.

"I might be," said Quentin thoughtfully. "And you might be an ostler." A pair of singularly beautiful grey eyes flashed to him with a twinkle in their depths he could not mistake. "Treve!" he exclaimed.

"Quiet, you block," said the Honourable Trevelyan de Villars without rancour, and spat out his straw. "If it took *you* a minute or two to place me, I'm fairly safe. You best go round in back," he advised the coachman *pro tem* with a careless stab of one finger towards the side of The Cat and Kippers. He added softly, "We heard you were at death's door. You look almost alive."

His spirits soaring, Quentin said, "More than I could say for you, old lad. Have you words for me?"

"Several. That's a good scowl. Keep it up. Can you stay on that nag long enough to follow the carriage?"

Quentin said he could, advised Mr. de Villars in a loud and disgusted tone that he was an insolent clod, and urged his bone-shaker along the muddy path to the rear yard.

Two surprisingly luxurious carriages were in the roomy barn, and ostlers argued loudly as they rubbed down a team of matched bays. A stableboy ran to take Quentin's reins. His climb from the saddle was stiff, and the boy watched him shrewdly, then enquired with a grin if he was having a specially good day. Quentin tossed him a coin, told him to stow his gab, much to the boy's delight, and turned wearily to find Killiam at his elbow.

"What's *that?*" enquired the Corporal, eyeing Tiele's hack with disbelief. "And why was you riding of it? I thought—"

"Oh, stop fussing," said Quentin shortly. "Mr. Tiele is—enamoured of Miss Montgomery."

"Then you shouldn't of—"

"So I gave them a chance to get to know one another," Quentin went on, the ring to his voice and the stern look in his eyes that said there would be no further discussion.

He walked over to hand Penelope down the steps of the carriage, but Tiele, laughing merrily at some shared joke, jumped out and turned back to assist her. Quentin at once changed direction. Dutch Coachman was running from the stables, a great grin of delight on his weathered features. Long ago he had seemed a giant to the very small boy he'd taught how to ride and care for his first pony. Now Quentin towered over him, but whatever else had changed, the bond between them was unwavering, and they greeted each other with an affection that went far beyond that of master and servant.

Penelope had enjoyed a delightful drive, for Mr. Tiele was a man of easy address and a keen sense of humour. She had blossomed under the warmth of his attentive admiration, so that had he not been captivated by her at the start of the journey, he certainly was by the end of it.

Glancing around anxiously as she trod down the steps, Penelope saw Quentin absorbed in conversation with Dutch Coachman. Her worries had evidently been unwarranted. He stood with his back to her, one hand resting against the coach, all graceful nonchalance, betraying no least sign of weariness.

Mr. Tiele was remarking lightly that she would be surprised by the bill of fare at this shocking old place, and that she must have a bedchamber where she could rest and refresh herself. She gave him a grateful smile and went on his arm into the rickety old building entertaining little hope of finding comfortable accommodations or decent food inside.

The hall they entered was long and dim and dusty. They passed a closed door leading to what was—to judge from a waft of ale and a buzz of hearty conversation—the tap. The next door was opening, and the same deplorable ostler who had waved the carriage around from the front came through it to meet them. He was quite tall and had a fine wide pair of shoulders. Uneasy, Penelope drew nearer to Tiele, wondering if he

250

could handle this rascally fellow should the need arise. She was astounded when the ostler bowed gracefully before her, shook the hand Tiele extended, and said in deep, cultured accents, "He looks better than I'd feared. Were you followed?"

"I don't believe we were. But there was an officer in Reading who made a dashed nuisance of himself and I've a notion he ain't easy in his mind about us. Oh—my apologies, ma'am. Allow me to present Trevelyan de Villars, who is normally something of a dandy. Treve, this is Miss Montgomery."

A wide, white smile came her way. "A very gallant lady," said de Villars admiringly. "I beg you will forgive my dirt, ma'am."

"Forgive it," she exclaimed, overcoming her astonishment. "I honour you for it, Mr. de Villars. Are you also— Oh, dear. Forgive me. I should not ask."

"If you was about to ask if Treve was a Jacobite—he ain't," said Tiele.

"Lord, no," de Villars confirmed, breezily. "Cannot abide the silly fellows, but it annoys me to see them so savagely hunted. This way." He led them along the murky corridor until they reached an even murkier flight of stairs. "What was the name of your troublesome officer?" he asked as they progressed upwards. "Not Fotheringay, I sincerely trust?"

"No. It was Jacob Holt. A friend of mine—which will avail us nothing, I'm afraid."

Penelope inserted quietly, "Major Mariner Fotheringay stopped us near Oxford, sir."

De Villars halted for an instant, a frown making his dark face even more villainous. "Did he, by Jove! I'd not thought him this far south as yet." He glanced at Tiele. "He's hounding another poor devil, and I'll tell you frankly, we'll be lucky can we bring *him* safely off."

They had come to a small landing and a long hall leading off to right and left, and even dimmer and dingier than the downstairs passage had been. De Villars turned to the right, stopped at the last closed door, flung it open, and bowed Penelope inside. She passed him and stopped, amazed. She stood in a charmingly appointed parlour. Thick rugs were spread on gleaming oak floors, and chintz curtains hung at the windows. The furnishings included several comfortable armchairs and a sofa, a long mahogany table with covers set for luncheon, and a credenza which held a silver tray full of decanters and sparkling crystal glasses. There were two more doors; one on either side of the room. De Villars led Penelope to the right-hand door and opened it to reveal a bright and pretty bedchamber. Even as she trod inside, however, a shriek rang out and something whirred past her cheek at a great rate of speed.

De Villars dropped into a crouch, a long-barrelled pistol appearing in his hand as if by magic. Tiele gave a startled cry and jumped aside, and Penelope, despite her acquaintanceship with Jasper, found the beating of wings very close beside her face unaccountably frightening, so that a small shocked cry escaped her.

There came a quick light step. She was seized and spun around. Quentin scanned her face frantically. "What is it?" he demanded. "By God, Tiele! I gave her into your care! If you've—"

In the nick of time Penelope restrained her instinctive reassurances and snatched at the fine opportunity Fate offered. "No, no . . ." she gasped faintly. "It was . . . only . . ." And she swayed, drooping.

"Look out!" cried Tiele, alarmed. "Allow me, Miss—"

His outstretched hand was brushed aside.

"Oh, no, you don't," snarled Quentin.

Penelope felt a pang of contrition as he swept her up into his arms, dreading lest he hurt himself again. But she consoled herself with the thought that she, too, had a battle to fight and win, and she lay limply against the cushions when she was tenderly deposited on the sofa.

Another scream rent the air. Daffy pushed between Quentin and her mistress and cried a tremulous, "Let me help her! Why has she swooned, poor soul? Likely wore to a shade!"

"Brandy—quick!" snapped Quentin, rounding on the aghast Tiele.

"Daffy—*go away!*" whispered Penelope between her teeth as her devoted maid bent over her.

For a split second Daffy stared, then tossed her apron over her head to conceal her sudden comprehending grin, and withdrew, wailing.

"Devil take it!" cried the frantic Quentin. "What the deuce happened?"

"I—ah, think the bird frightened her," said de Villars, his clear grey eyes glinting with amusement.

"Me poor Jasper got away," moaned Daffy, having discovered that her unpredictable pet was sitting on top of the curtain rod, leering triumphantly down at them.

"Stuff," said Quentin, taking the glass Tiele hurried over with. "Penny is the bravest girl I ever knew. She'd not be scared by that stupid little pest."

"I assure you it is not unusual for people to become alarmed when wings flutter in their faces," said de Villars. "I've a friend who's fairly besotted over the feathered varmints, and even he instinctively ducks if one of his small friends zooms at him." He added deprecatingly, "If you will forgive the play on words . . ."

Tiele grinned. Unamused, Quentin held the glass to Penelope's lips. "Here, love," he said in a caressing tone she had never dreamed to hear. "Just a little sip, Penelope Anne."

"You're spilling it down her neck," Tiele criticized. "Let me . . ."

"Be damned if I will! Stay back! She's fairly exhausted, sweet lass, and no wonder. Penny—please, my darling girl. Try to take a little."

Penelope knew a soaring joy when the man of her heart designated her his darling girl. However, the brandy trickling down her neck was not very comfortable, besides which she had an uneasy feeling that de Villars was at any second going to laugh aloud. She therefore sighed deeply, fluttered her lashes, and opened her eyes.

253

Quentin had moved very fast. It was Duncan Tiele who leaned above her, the glass in his hand and a troubled look in his honest eyes.

"Oh, dear," murmured Penelope, sitting up with one hand to her sticky throat. "How very silly of me." Under her lashes she slanted a glance to Quentin, who now stood at the window, hands on hips, glaring up at Jasper. "Much more of you, my fine feathered friend," he said darkly, "and you will be served up to a very amiable white cat who waits hopefully in Reading."

De Villars came up beside him. Quentin turned, hand out-stretched. "My dear old boy, how very good of you to stick your silly nose into this bumble broth."

"Isn't it," drawled de Villars. "I would hope you see the error of your ways, Chandler, but I doubt it."

"What I see is that once again you risk your neck to—"

"Oh, stubble it, for Lord's sake. My Uncle Boudreaux got me into this, and were I not seeking to turn him up sweet—"

"Liar! His feelings for you have not changed one whit. Do not try and gammon me."

Lowering his voice, de Villars said, "You're the one gammon-ing, friend. I fancy that lovely lady is—"

"Never mind about that," Quentin interpolated hastily. "Tell me only—is my brother here?"

"Yes. And I've to ask if you have the cypher."

"I do. And well hidden."

"Do you care to tell me—where?"

Quentin regarded him steadily. "No." He saw de Villars' head tilt upwards in prideful resentment, and reiterated, "No, Treve. I'll not add your life to the rest. If I cannot bring it to its destination, it will be lost with me." He glanced broodingly to Penelope and to Duncan Tiele, who bent solicitously above her. "God knows, enough innocent lives have been endangered and I'll—" He paused as a scratch sounded at the door.

The host came in with three maids carrying bowls and plat-ters, which they proceeded to arrange on the table.

Daffy led Penelope into the bedchamber, de Villars took

himself off, and Tiele wandered over to Quentin, who had sprawled wearily in a chair, put back his head, and closed his eyes.

"See here, Chandler," Tiele began in a low, urgent voice. Quentin looked up at him.

"I'd not thought," Tiele went on awkwardly, "that you—that Miss Montgomery—"

"Good," said Quentin. "We're not."

"But—deuce take it, man, I saw the way you . . . I mean—I heard you call her your—er—"

"I was merely distraught. That is—er, I'd not have said it save that I'm rather tired. But—she did not hear it, which is all that matters. And—" Quentin hauled himself upright. "Where the plague did you find that miserable bone-shaker of a hack?"

Tiele chuckled. "Rented him. My own mount picked up a stone bruise. Terrible gait, what?"

The host said politely, "Your pardon, sirs. We have put out the cold dishes. We'll fetch the hot food in ten minutes—shall that suit?"

Quentin told him it would suit very nicely, and he and Tiele went into the second bedchamber to refresh themselves for luncheon.

Penelope was the first to return. Daffy had worked wonders with her windblown curls, a snowy fichu had been placed about her shoulders, and she looked fresh and quite recovered. She had no sooner entered the parlour than the far door opened and Tiele hurried in, shooting the lace at his wrists, his eyes lighting up when he saw her.

"Are you better, Miss Penelope?" he asked, coming quickly to her side. "That wretched bird! After all you've been through, one can but sympathize."

She allowed him to lead her to the sofa. "I am quite all right, thank you. Did Major Chandler tell you, then, of our—troubles?"

"More than I'd known before, at all events." He pressed her hand shyly. "How splendid you have been."

Blushing, her gaze slipped past him. Quentin stood in the open door of the bedchamber, in the act of looking away from them. "That wretched beast!" he cried, exasperated. "Only look at what he's about now!"

Four covers had been set. In the center of the table was a bowl of sliced cucumber and beetroot. Beside it, a board of fresh bread. And next to that, a shallow dish that had contained celery stalks, radishes, and raw new carrots. Most of these items had, however, been removed from the dish and deposited on the table. Tugging with determined energy at the last remaining stalk of celery was one small canary. Even as they watched, Jasper succeeded in his mission. He hopped eagerly to the now empty bowl, perched briefly on the edge, then launched himself into the water that had gathered there. While three astonished humans stood watching, he proceeded to splash busily about, making quick little chirping sounds and flapping his wings industriously, sending water in all directions.

Tiele murmured, "Jupiter! What d'you mean to do about that pest?"

Quentin's eyes flew to Penelope. She was watching him, hands clasped, her face mirroring his own amusement. Quite forgetting Tiele, he crossed to her. Her hands went out and he took and kissed each in turn, then asked intensely, "Are you better? Gad, but you scared me half out of my wits."

She smiled up at him. "Yes, I am quite recovered. And what of you? You should never have ridden for so long, you know. You look very tired."

"Tush," he murmured, still holding her hands and gazing into the wide hazel eyes so tenderly regarding him. "Had it not been for Tiele's—" The name recalled him to the present. He fairly flung Penelope's hands away and turned about, his colour much heightened. "Tiele! Oh, what a fellow you must think me! Did you say something?"

Resisting a strong urge to comment upon the depth of the bond between Chandler and his adopted 'sister,' Tiele said dryly, "I asked what you propose to do about our shameless public bather, though I can perfectly understand why you did not hear me."

Penelope blushed and felt repentant.

Quentin's laugh was strained. "What we *should* do," he answered, "is to wring its blasted—"

The outer door opened. Instead of the maids with the food the host had promised, Gordon Chandler stepped quickly into the room.

With a glad cry, Quentin rushed to hug and be hugged. "Gordie! Thunderation, but I'm glad to see you!"

Gordon gripped his brother's hand and scanned his thin face narrowly. "You look a deal more alive than when last I saw you, you great looby." He turned to bow to Penelope, take her hand and press it to his lips. "For which I have you to thank, Miss Montgomery, though I shall never be able to do so properly."

Her smile was, he thought, intriguingly mischievous, but she evaded, "How grateful I am that you sent Mr. Tiele to us. He has been simply splendid."

Poor Tiele was at once inundated with thanks, Quentin, additionally driven by guilt, becoming so humbly earnest that Tiele declared an intention to leave at once, did they not "stop all the faradiddles! Only look at the time you are wasting!"

"True," Quentin agreed, leading Penelope to the table and pulling out a chair for her. "We'd best start. Do sit down, Gordie."

Staring thunderstruck at the bather, Gordon gasped, "Good God! Should he not at least be plucked?"

The breeze had become a wind that was busily filling the sky with threatening clouds. Beyond the temporary haven of this strange old tavern, death and danger lurked, their grim shadows growing ever darker. But in the cosy first-floor parlour, six people ate, drank, and were merry, and the shadows were balked for a while. The food was excellent and, once the rosy-cheeked maids had brought all the dishes and crept away again, the conversation swept along fast and furiously, for Gordon was as full of questions as Penelope, Quentin, and Tiele were eager to share their adventures. They all had insisted that Killiam and Daffy join them. Daffy was too shy, however, to sit at the same table, so she and the Corporal took their plates to the small round table by the window, and joined in whenever they were called upon to contribute to the chatter. A brief lull occurred when Jasper, who had returned to the top of the curtains when the maids came in, swooped back and began to strut among the dishes, pecking curiously at this and that until Tiele objected and one lustily screeching canary was seized and thrust back into his cage. Jasper vented his outrage in his customary manner and Tiele, his indignation heightened, beat a hasty retreat from the deluge.

Quentin's Highview masquerade as Sir John Macauley Somerville drew shouts of laughter from his brother and Tiele, and Penelope, managing to seem unaware of the sly wink Quentin directed at Gordon when Lady Sybil was mentioned, could only be happy to see him so relaxed and at ease. "I cannot but be grateful," she said, looking around at them all fondly, "that so many brave people have been willing to aid Major Chandler. But why should Mr. de Villars help? He made it clear he has no fondness for Jacobites, and—" She broke off in confusion as she realized what she had implied.

Gordon said with a chuckle, "Oh, you must never pay heed to what Treve says, ma'am. The entire family is rather off the road, to say truth. His uncle—Lord Boudreaux—was enraged by the persecution of the rebels, and has gone to considerable risk and expense to help wherever he can. I think he was never more surprised than to find that his notorious nephew was similarly engaged." He slipped a fine enamelled watch from his waistcoat pocket and glanced at it. "Quentin . . . ?"

"Should we be off, now?"

"Yes. I regret to break up such a pleasant gathering, but

258

Treve has—" He glanced expectantly to the door as the latch was raised, then sprang to his feet with a horrified exclamation.

A tall, thin gentleman stood on the threshold. Elegant from the top of his immaculate wig to the buckles of his high-heeled shoes, he seemed to Penelope the very essence of aristocratic hauteur. She was conscious of a sense of familiarity, but not until Gordon hastened to kiss the regally outstretched hand did she realize who he was.

Quentin, who had sat for a moment as though turned to stone, jumped up, his chair going over with a crash. "Father!"

"So it is truth. . . ." His face livid, his eyes sparking with rage, Sir Brian Chandler stepped to the centre of the room, dominating them all with his presence. A grey-haired, impeccably clad retainer followed, his anguished gaze flashing from one to the other of the dismayed brothers. Lifting his quizzing glass, Sir Brian scanned Quentin from head to toe. "Good God!" he muttered. "How I'd prayed it was a lie."

Quentin hurried around the table and reached for his father's hand, bowing respectfully above those frail white fingers. "Sir— I know you do not approve of—"

Sir Brian snatched his hand away. "You may be sure," he said in a voice of ice, "that I do not approve of deceit, sir! Of treachery, treason, and lies!"

Quentin paled and, knowing what must follow, stood very still.

"Father," Gordon interceded, "at least allow him to—"

"To do—what? Add to the falsehoods I have been told? That *you* have been cajoled into repeating to me?" Ablaze with wrath and hurt, his fine green eyes swept back to his younger son. "You look ill," he said, still in that harsh, strained voice. "Did you manage to get yourself wounded?"

"Yes, sir. But thanks to Gordon and—"

"Oh, by all means! Let us thank the poor dupes you have gulled into helping you!" Ignoring the anxious entreaties of his faithful valet, Sir Brian advanced on Quentin, his hands clenching. "Are you *quite* without shame, that you can stand

259

before me and brag that they have been so gallant, so unselfish as to risk death just so that *you* may escape the consequences of your crass recklessness?"

Very white by now, Quentin said, "I make no apologies for fighting in a Cause I believed best for Eng—"

Sir Brian gave a snort of disgust. In a contained but terrible voice, he grated, "You fought *against* England, sir! Can you guess what it means to me to have to name you a damnable rogue and a traitor?"

Penelope shrank with a horrified gasp.

Quentin flinched, and his head went down.

Gordon had known from childhood that although he was loved, his flamboyant brother was closest to his father's heart. And if at times he had been wounded by that awareness, never had it seemed less important than at this moment. "Sir," he pleaded, "you do not give him a chance."

"Chance?" His face twisted with grief, Sir Brian cried, "What chance did he give you? Do you deny that you have risked arrest, questioning, disgrace, and a death beyond words hideous, for this rascally young here-and-thereian?"

His head still bowed, Quentin said before Gordon could respond, "He may deny it, but it is quite true, sir."

"Thank you," raged his father. "I might well have lost both my sons to your mad folly! Dare I hope you have some small vestige of contrition for what you have brought down upon your friends? Look about you, brave rebel. Have you given one single thought to the jeopardy in which you have placed this gently bred child of my dearest friend?"

"My God!" Quentin whispered, his anguished gaze flashing to Penelope. "Can you think I have *not*? Father—I beg you will believe—"

"I *believe*," rasped Sir Brian, taking another step towards him, "I *believe* that you did not give a button for the fact your brother might well be called upon to pay the supreme penalty! I *believe* that now you must pay the price of your braggadocio airs and graces, you do not hesitate to imperil your poor faithful bat-

260

man, or any other man or woman necessary to your protection! God knows I am aware you've no shred of affection for *me*, but—"

"No, no, sir!" Quentin reached out imploringly. "Do not say such dreadful things! Rake me down if you must, but—*please*, you know I love you! You *know* I always—"

"'Fore God, *stop* with your protestations and muling falsehoods! The last letter I had from you was sent from Rome, I was told. From *Rome!* And where *did* you write it, my loving liar? After the grisly battlefield whereon you raised your sword against your countrymen? Did you know that young Bremerville fell at Prestonpans? Your lifelong friend! Was *yours* the sabre that cut him down?" His voice rose. He thundered, *"Was it?"*

Tiele, horrified, had retreated to the wall, but when Quentin's attempt to respond resulted only in a choked incoherency and the helpless gesture of one unsteady hand, he ventured a faltering, "Your son s-saved my brother's life at Prestonpans, Sir Brian."

"And thus claims yours in exchange?" The older man gave a mirthless laugh, and staggered.

Quentin sprang to support him, only to be repelled by a fierce shove. The valet threw an arm about his master, and Gordon ran to pull up a chair. Terrified, Daffy seized the opportunity to slip into the hall, followed at once by Killiam. Appalled by this terrible confrontation, Penelope hastened to pour some wine and carry it to this remorseless gentleman she remembered as having always been the soul of kindly courtesy.

Sir Brian accepted the glass with a trembling hand. "My poor girl, how came you to be tricked into aiding my worthless traitor?"

Penelope looked down into eyes ravaged by heartbreak and disillusion. Glancing to the side, she saw the man she loved, his shoulders very straight, his white face expressionless, his pain betrayed only by the hands tight-clenched at his sides. She felt oddly strengthened and, throwing pride away, said calmly, "I love him, sir."

261

Quentin gasped. He looked fully at her. Then, as though this was the last straw, he averted his face.

"Sweet innocent!" Sir Brian exclaimed. "I pray you will not pay a terrible price for your devotion. How proud you must be, my son, to have endangered the lady who has given you her heart!"

Shattered, Quentin was quite incapable of a response and could only shake his head in numb helplessness.

Gordon glanced at his brother. Frowning, he said, "Quentin did not *want* Miss Montgomery involved, sir."

"Oh, that is true, Sir Brian," said Penelope in a shaken voice. "He begged—"

Once more Sir Brian laughed, the sound a racking travesty of mirth that made his hearers shrink. "Oh, I know how well *he* begs, m'dear! Why do *you* not beg him to tell us what was in his mind when he embarked so blithely on this insanity? Did he think, I wonder, that his brother would stand by him, no matter what happened? That Gordon would die willingly enough rather than—"

"In the name of . . . God!" Staring at this man he always had idolized, his eyes glittering with tears, his face twitching and convulsed with horror, Quentin gasped, "*No!* Sir—you *surely* cannot think me so cruel and unfeeling?"

His father rushed on bitterly, "And what was *my* portion of your concern, Sir Galahad? You must have known that your actions were in violation of everything I honour and cherish! Did you console yourself by thinking I'd soon get over it? Did you suppose I'd not grieve to see your brother's head adorn Tower Bridge . . . beside your own . . . ?"

Quentin's head bowed low and he was silent.

"Did you for one instant consider," said Sir Brian, his voice shredding painfully, "that . . . that Lac Brillant has been in our family for almost eight hundred years? *Eight . . . hundred . . . years!* All the Chandlers and the Fromes before them. . . . My parents died there. Your dear mother, who so loved the old place, is buried there. And you—*you* would whistle it down the

262

wind for a pretty princeling whose cause was doomed before ever it began!" He came to his feet, leaning heavily on the arm of his servant who appeared almost as distressed as he himself.

"Look at me, Quentin Frome Chandler," commanded Sir Brian in a cold, harsh voice.

Quentin closed his eyes very briefly and took a deep breath, nerving himself. Then he turned to face his father squarely.

For a moment that seemed an eternity no one moved or spoke, and the only sound to break the silence was the patter of rain against the casements.

"I am done with you!" Sir Brian drew a fat purse from his pocket and flung it at Quentin's feet. "Get yourself out of England. I do not want to see your deceitful face—"

The door was flung open unceremoniously. De Villars thrust in his lean countenance, darted a narrow-eyed glance around the dramatic group, then said urgently, "Your friend Holt is less than half a mile away and coming at the gallop. Quentin—into the basement with you, before—"

Quentin sprinted for the bedchamber. Snatching up cloak, tricorne, and small-sword, he ran back, dropped to one knee beside his father, seized his nerveless hand and pressed a kiss upon it. Throwing a desperate glance at Penelope, he jumped to his feet and ran into the hall.

His voice almost suspended, Sir Brian whispered, "Quentin . . ." and sank into the chair.

Penelope ran across the room, but Gordon leapt to restrain her. "No, my brave lady," he murmured. "Not this time."

From the hall came de Villars' distinctive voice, raised in alarm. "Chandler! You damned idiot! Not *that* way! *Quentin!* Oh—for Lord's sake!"

As if an unseen hand had turned them all to stone, they waited, tense and silent, while in every heart lurked the same terrible dread.

As from a very great distance, Penelope heard a sudden tattoo of hooves on the cobblestones below the window. Wrenching away from Gordon's slackened clasp, she ran to the casement and flung it open. She was in time to see a horseman, crouched low in the saddle, racing at breakneck speed northwards along the lane, only to pull his mount suddenly to a rearing halt and turn back to the south. Seconds later, she heard a brittle crack, followed quickly by another, and then saw Quentin return in a blur of speed, galloping northwards again, closely pursued by a group of red-coated riders, sabres drawn and flashing.

Frozen with fear, she realized that someone stood beside her.

"The *damnable* gudgeon!" groaned Trevelyan de Villars savagely. "The ungrateful clod! After all my blasted *work!*"

On the other side of her, Gordon muttered, "He's leading them away. He's trying to protect us, Treve."

De Villars swore.

XV

By four o'clock the rain was a downpour, beating so strongly against the windowpanes that some of the accumulated dirt was washing away. The skies had darkened and the parlour was dim. A fire had been lit in the grate to combat the plunging temperature, the light from the flames flickering over the four glum faces of those clustered about it, and shining less brightly on the three equally glum-faced servants seated nearby.

No one had spoken for quite some time when Sir Brian broke the silence, murmuring almost to himself, "I wonder why it is that no matter how vexed he makes me—however ashamed . . . I cannot stop loving him."

Penelope smiled mistily at him, the ache in her heart lessened slightly by those forlorn words.

Gordon sighed. "I have not asked you, sir, how you found us."

"I knew you were worrying. I began to suspect Quentin was in another scrape. . . . I knew if that was so you would try to help him—as usual. So—I had you followed. When we began to encounter all the patrols, I became suspicious . . ." He shrugged wearily. "Justifiably."

265

"I see." Gordon said with a wry smile, "He is a hopeless case, sir."

Predictably, his sire's eyes sparked resentment, the handsome head whipping upwards, but before Sir Brian could speak, Gordon went on reflectively, "Do you recall when he was ten, how he took on those village louts who had tied the puppy to the water wheel? He didn't give a straw that there were six of them—all bigger than he. The cause was there—so he fought."

"And got himself properly knocked up! The cause he fought for this time was a less worthy one, though I doubt he gave it any more consideration!"

"He could not defend himself on that score, sir," argued Gordon quietly. "He fancied you too ill for him to put his political convictions in your dish. The truth is that he feels very strongly on the issues, and has nothing but contempt for the House of Hanover."

"As I have nothing but contempt for a cheat," snapped Sir Brian, his wan face flushing. "Had he come to me honestly, and told me of his beliefs, I'd—"

With a courage that awed Penelope, Gordon interposed, "You would have flown into the boughs—as you did today; raged at him, as you did today; and fretted yourself into horse nails every hour he was away. No, sir. Quentin dared not ride off to his loved Scots and leave you grieving. You were still recovering from your surgery, and I doubt would be sitting here now, had he done so."

Staring at this usually taciturn son in astonishment, Sir Brian growled, "You're mighty eloquent in defense of your brother, seeing that all his life he has taken advantage of you and persuaded you always to what he wished. Do you think I have not seen how he uses and abuses your good nature?"

"Your pardon, but"—Gordon's voice hardened—"that is not true, sir. In point of fact, Quentin is straight and above-board in everything. I am more . . . devious, I fear." He raised a hand, slightly smiling as he saw his indignant father ready to defend him. "No, no, it really is the case, sir. It was as a rule

266

comparatively easy for me to—ah, persuade Quentin that we did as *he* wished, when in many instances I had first implanted the idea in his mind, then argued so forcefully against it, he was convinced it must be the only thing to do." His smile faded away. With a regretful shrug, he added, "On one issue I could not sway him, however. The most important issue of his life. I was so desperate that we came to blows over it. Quentin tried to fend me off, for he had no wish to fight me. He had lowered his fists when I . . . struck him." He bit his lip and added reluctantly, "I broke his nose."

His jaw dropping, Sir Brian gasped, "*You* did? But—but he told me—"

"He told you whatever he felt would cause you the least distress, Papa. He was afraid you would be less than pleased to know that perfect nose of his had been ruined by your heir."

Sir Brian glanced at him sharply, for the first time wondering if this young man he had always secretly judged clever, but rather dull, was aware of his opinion. He said in new anxiety, "Gordon—you know, lad, that my love for you is just as deep as that I hold for your brother."

Reddening, Gordon said gruffly, "Thank you, sir. But if you truly love Quentin, you will do as I ask and leave here now."

"No! How can you ask me to go—not knowing whether he is alive or dead?"

"I ask only that you go as far as Winchester. We will get word to you as soon as we hear. Treve has men out now, trying to find out what happened. Sir—" Gordon leaned forward, saying intensely, "He is risking his life—do not make his sacrifice for nought."

"Then you *do* think it a sacrifice!" Remorseful, Sir Brian said, "He looked so tired and ill, and—God forgive me! If he dies with my last words to him having been so . . ." His voice broke and he bowed forward, one thin hand wavering up to cover his eyes.

With a little cry of pity, Penelope ran to kneel beside his chair and take his other hand between both her own. "Oh, my dear sir—do not! Can you suppose Quentin does not know of your love for him? You were deeply hurt and shocked, and disappointed—as much for all of us as for him. What could be more natural than for you to rail at him? If . . . God forbid . . . he should be killed, why he—he would die with no other feeling for you than devotion. It is not his way to hold a grudge. His heart is too . . . too generous. . . ." Her own voice broke, and the hand she clasped was dampened by her tears.

"Good God! What a damp-nosed lot!"

The insouciant charm of the deep voice brought them all to their feet. Penelope was across the room in a flash, sobbing into Quentin's drenched cloak, his cold, wet arms fast about her. He tilted up her chin and kissed her very gently on the brow, with lips like ice and water dripping from his soaked hair. Reaching around her, he returned his brother's strong handclasp.

His gaze turned to his father. Penelope stepped away from him. Apprehensive and uncertain, Quentin waited.

"You . . . damned rascal!" croaked Sir Brian, and held out his arms.

Quentin gave a small sigh of relief and stepped into a crushing embrace.

Her eyes blurring, Penelope had to turn away.

"*Peccavi—peccavi*, sir," gasped Quentin, drawing back. "Egad, for—for a sick gentleman, you're vastly strong."

"In my denunciations, at least," said his father, then scowled and added ferociously, "Not that you didn't deserve most of it!"

"I'll not argue that, sir. But . . . ." Tilting his head to watch his sire with a tentative smile, he asked, "Am I—just a little forgiven?"

"No!" snarled Sir Brian. And seeing that anxious smile fade, he said, "Why did I have such a rogue for a son? Blast you, Quentin, you could charm the fangs from a snake, I swear!"

"I'd never have drawn such a simile, Father—I do assure you."

Sir Brian laughed. "Come over here by the fire, boy! You're soaked through. Ah! Have I hurt you again? The arm, is it?"

"Hanging by a thread," said Quentin solemnly, a twinkle creeping into his eyes as Gordon rushed to draw a chair closer to the fire, Penelope brought him a glass of wine, and the Corporal took away the dripping cloak.

"How did you get away, Rabble?" asked Gordon, gripping his shoulder.

"Very bravely! If you did but know the misery I endured whilst I led that fumble-footed troop in circles. . . ." He laughed suddenly, the wine and the fire warming him. "Lord, but they were a muddy mess! I left poor Holt struggling to free himself from a lovely bog on Salisbury Plain! Faith, you could hear the man curse for miles! Tiele! You stayed, then. My dear fellow, how very good of you."

He stood to shake Tiele by the hand and, noting the joy in the faces of Killiam and his father's speechless valet, wrung their hands also.

"Let's get you into some dry clothes, sir," said the Corporal, blinking rapidly.

"What he needs is a good long sleep," Sir Brian muttered.

"No time for that, sir. I must be on my way. With your permission, I'll go and change my clothes."

He took Penelope's hand and started for the bedchamber, Killiam hurrying ahead. At the door, Quentin looked down at her tenderly. "You're a bold hussy," he murmured softly. "But I fancy my papa will be glad enough to care for you until I can come back home and claim you."

"It makes no odds, love," she said, just as softly. "I go with you. You'll not be rid of me so easily."

He smiled and lifted her hand to his lips. "Nothing would please me more. But I've a task to complete." His eyes very soft, he murmured, "And then . . . my darling girl. . . ." He glanced up. The others were gathered about the fire, having apparently seen or heard nothing of this tender exchange. He bent and kissed her full on her willing mouth, drawing back to murmur, "Then you will have yet another name." He kissed her hand and left her.

269

Penelope, her heart full, rejoined the gentlemen at the fire, and a moment later the hall door opened to admit de Villars.

Without preamble, he said, "Your carriage is ready, Sir Brian. We've no time to lose. That confounded Holt is quite likely to come here, although your idiot son very dangerously made it appear he'd come past—not from—our scruffy tavern."

"Just one moment, if you please," commanded Sir Brian autocratically, and then proceeded to express his gratitude so humbly that de Villars, renowned rake and duellist, fled in disorder.

Amused, Gordon asked, "Tiele? Do you ride with us?"

Ever the gentleman, Duncan Tiele said it was as Penelope wished, and volunteered to escort her. Penelope thanked him, but announced her intention to remain with Quentin. Gordon said that she must travel under his escort, and Sir Brian insisted she ride to Lac Brillant with him. "It will be my opportunity to become better acquainted with my future daughter," he added with a fond smile.

They were still arguing when Quentin returned, looking weary despite his best efforts, but considerably less drowned. His caped cloak, which Daffy had appropriated and spread before the fire, was steaming but still very wet. Gordon offered his in substitution, since it had now been decided he would ride in the coach with his father.

Tiele said, "We have been trying to convince Miss Montgomery to accompany one or other of us, but I fear yours is the only word she will heed, Quentin."

"In which case she will travel with you, Tiele." Over his shoulder, Quentin called to the Corporal to arrange for the hire of a carriage for Mr. Tiele. Penelope's hand, already fast caught within his own, tightened. He said gently, "If Holt should come up with you in company with my father and brother, m'dear, he'd be a noddicock not to put two and two together and arrive at an approximation of my true identity."

"Come along—do!" urged de Villars, again sticking his head around the door.

Carrying Quentin's valise Killiam hurried to join him, and Daffy, also laden, followed them out.

Sir Brian stood. "You will follow by another route, Quentin?"

"Regrettably—no, sir. Oh, never look so alarmed. When my task is completed, I—"

"Task?" At once uneasy, Sir Brian said, "I'd fancied your only task was to escape with your head!"

"Would that it were. But I've a message must be delivered."

"We'll have one of the grooms deliver it." Frowning as Quentin shook his head, he went on impatiently, "Very well, then—I'll deliver it! But—"

"Father," said Quentin gently, "I cannot."

"Why not? Because it has to do with those miserable damned Jacobites? 'Fore God! If this task of yours has to do with igniting the whole hellish mess again, I'll see you—"

Quentin's laugh rang out. "No, really, sir—you must not be pinching at me again. I'm still not recovered from your last scold."

Torn between rage and anxiety, Sir Brian's face was a study. Quentin gripped his hand and said with ready sympathy, "I am such a trial, I know it. But I do swear, sir, the message I carry involves nothing more than a fortune—and the lives of a great many frightened people."

"Am I then not to be trusted?"

"With my life, sir. But"—a whimsical grin tugged at Quentin's mouth—"you are not markedly in sympathy with the Jacobite Cause."

"Not . . . *markedly?* By God, I am not! Even so— Boy, you're in no state to jaunter about the countryside. Give me the curst paper and, against my better judgement, I'll guarantee—"

"Sir, I cannot."

"*Cannot?* Why the devil—"

"No, sir," Gordon put in. "He cannot, because the message he carries is death."

Paling, Sir Brian gasped, "Now heaven aid us! Must we still suffer this nightmare, then?"

"For a very little time, sir," said Quentin earnestly. "I've only to leave the message in a certain place. Then, I shall come at once to you."

"Dammit—I still do not see why—"

Quentin said with quiet inflexibility, "Because I gave my word, sir."

It was unanswerable. Sir Brian swore under his breath, fumed, groaned, and gripped Quentin by the shoulders. "Wretched offspring! Someday, when you are safe out of this, you and I will have at your peculiar political persuasions. Till then—I cannot agree with you; I cannot help you. But—" his tone softened—"no more can I put you out of my heart, so I fear I shall have to grin and bear it."

They embraced, and without another word Sir Brian left, his valet saying a fervent, "God bless you, Master Quentin," before following.

Gordon came to wring his brother's hand and claim a farewell kiss from a shy-eyed Penelope.

There were just three left after the door closed once more, and Tiele said aggrievedly, "I am surprised you trust me with your lady, Chandler. Especially since you encouraged my courtship of Miss Montgomery before you stole her away from me."

"It was very bad, I know," Quentin admitted. "But, you see, I did not think she would have me."

Tiele laughed. "*What* a rasper! You thought rather that you had only danger to offer her."

Her heart in her eyes, Penelope looked up at her love.

Watching her, Quentin murmured, "Which is purest truth, after all, my dear."

"It is no use trying to escape," she warned. "You are quite trapped, sir."

He smiled and pulled her closer. "Indeed I am. But tell me, you little rascal—for how long were you aware of my noble martyrdom in pushing you into the arms of another, more worthy gentleman?"

272

The room was quiet and dim, the pleasant light of the flames dancing upon Penelope's shining hair and revealing the adoration in Quentin's thin face. It seemed to Tiele that they had quite forgotten his presence, and he thought that not until this moment had he glimpsed the abiding wonder that is true love. Reluctant to intrude in so priceless a moment, he backed quietly away.

"I suspected it for some time," Penelope murmured, her hand going up to caress Quentin's cheek. "You were so nonchalant with me, but now and again you made a little slip."

"For instance, when the dog frightened you during our walk, and I almost kissed you," he said with a rueful sigh.

She nodded. "That was one of your worst mistakes. And when I fainted, and you called me your 'darling girl.' Oh, yes, I heard." She smiled saucily. "I thought it might indicate an emotion rather more than friendship."

He caught her hand and pressed a kiss into the warm palm. "Rather more, indeed," he said tenderly. "That blasted bird frightening you so caused me to quite forget—" He started, looked up, and had the grace to flush darkly. "Oh, Tiele—er, there you are. I was so—distracted I did not notice what Daffy carried downstairs just now. Has she taken Jasper?"

Recovering his voice, Tiele said, "No. I believe she took Miss Montgomery's dressing case and a hoop bag. And the Corporal carried your valise, I know. You do not really mean to scrag the little blighter?"

"I should! Your pardon—I'll be back in a second." Scarcely able to tear himself away, Quentin caressed Penelope's soft cheek, then walked quickly into her bedchamber.

Returning to the sofa, Penelope sat down and looked in an embarrassed way at Mr. Tiele. "You have been very kind, and we have treated you badly, sir," she admitted. "I beg your pardon for it."

He came forward and smiled down at her, awe still very apparent in his eyes. "I am more grateful than I can say. I know now that I'd not had the remotest idea of such devotion as you

273

and Chandler share. I only pray it is not so rare I'll have no hope of finding it for myself."

It would be, she thought, a real tragedy if he did not do so, for he was the very best type of man, and she said earnestly that there was no doubt such happiness waited in his future.

Neither of them noticed the hall door slowly inching open. . . .

From the instant Quentin entered the bedchamber, Jasper had fixed him with a baleful eye, and when the tall man crossed to open the cage, the canary went into his war dance, shouting his rage and scattering debris in all directions. Quentin narrowed his eyes against the dust, told the bird in soft but explicit terms exactly what was his probable ancestry, and reached into the cage to grasp the swinging perch as Jasper fluttered about, screeching.

With a deft twist Quentin disconnected the bar from the swing. Whether this apparent destruction of property he considered his own offended Jasper, or whether he was terrified would be hard to tell. Whatever his motivation, the canary took drastic measures. With a shrill squawk he alighted on Quentin's withdrawing hand and gave it a good peck.

The beak of a healthy bird is more powerful than the uninitiated might think. With a startled oath, Quentin pulled his hand back, and Jasper, triumphant, swooped out also and began to zoom giddily about the room.

"Damn and blast your feathers," growled Quentin. But he had neither the time nor the inclination to engage in what would certainly be a prolonged struggle to catch the bird. The light was dim in the room and he went over to the window, took out his penknife, and carefully inserted the thin blade into the hollow bar he held. After only a moment's probing, a corner of parchment appeared. Quentin wound it carefully until a long thin cylinder was eased from the bar. It unrolled in his hand and he gazed down at the innocuous poem inscribed there, again marvelling that hidden within it was so vital a message—or part of one.

He folded the precious fragment carefully and slid it into a cunningly hinged plate along the grip of his small-sword. Jasper continued to scream defiance as Quentin replaced the weapon in its scabbard, and he looked up at the bird speculatively. Rob would be able to get the confounded little brute, he thought. Still, he must be careful in closing the door. He walked over and opened the door cautiously, watching the canary. Turning about, he halted abruptly, all thought of the need to confine Jasper driven from his mind.

How it could all have happened without his hearing, he could only set at the canary's door, for all that screeching must have drowned the inevitable sounds.

Duncan Tiele lay sprawled either dead or unconscious in front of the sofa. Across the room, Roland Otton stood behind Penelope, one hand clamped over her mouth, the other aiming a pistol at her head.

"Nasty business, isn't it?" he said regretfully, shifting his grip to her wrist and pushing her forward. "But you brought it on yourself, you cannot deny."

Quentin drew a deep, hissing breath. "Then your quarrel is with me," he said, flexing the fingers of his right hand and wondering for how long he could manipulate a small-sword if the opportunity arose.

"Yes, of course it is. But—my dear fellow, whatever else, I am a patriot. Our estimable Captain Holt has put out a warrant for Miss Montgomery's arrest." He shrugged, his black eyes glinting mockery.

That terrible news reduced Quentin to stark panic. With a mighty effort, he managed to conceal it and to sound undismayed. "Even so, you will make more money off my head than hers."

"Oh, yes. But do you know, Chandler, I really do not enjoy—er, questioning a wounded man."

"Or burning him?" said Penelope with disgust.

"C'est la guerre, my sweet love . . . as I have told you before."

Quentin uttered a smothered expletive and lunged forward. Otton twisted Penelope's arm up behind her. She managed to refrain from crying out, but the pain made her gasp and at once Quentin threw up a hand in acknowledgement of defeat and stepped back. "Don't hurt her! Please don't hurt her. I will surrender my sword."

Struggling frantically, Penelope cried, "No! He cannot get away, Quentin. Rob will come, or—"

"But no one will come, my pretty," Otton purred. "Your aunt and uncle and most of the men went tearing off after Captain Holt and his merry men. I knew your lover would elude them. I've seen him ride. So I stayed here and waited. My man, an estimable chap, and one of your grooms, Cole, stayed with me. We watched your father leave and the direction from which he came. My people are holding your servants at gunpoint in a nice quiet room below stairs. Not that they will dare raise a fuss because . . . well, only look outside, Chandler."

Quentin walked to the window and glanced into the fading afternoon. Military uniforms were everywhere, troopers sauntering cheerfully into the tap or chatting with comrades in the yard.

Otton volunteered, "There's a regiment quartered just this side of Winchester. They favour this decrepit old place. One shout from Cole—one pistol shot, and they'll be up here quicker than a rabbit can twitch its nose."

Quentin glanced to Tiele, who still lay motionless. "Did you kill him?"

"If he has a thin skull." Otton shrugged. "One takes no chances."

Penelope said in a strangled voice, "He hit him terribly hard."

"Even so," Otton pointed out, "I am easier to deal with than Delavale will be. He is a very jealous man and, do you know, Chandler, I believe he suspects you had a little—er, dalliance with the fair Sybil." He shook his head chidingly. "Such a naughty fellow—who ever would have thought it in your condition?" His taunting voice hardened. "The cypher. Quickly. I shall hand her over, else."

Quentin said contemptuously, "Whether I give it to you or not, you'll likely do so. What guarantee have I that you'll spare her?"

"My word of honour."

Quentin said nothing, but his lip curled in an eloquent appraisal of the worth of that offer.

"Whatever else I may be," said Otton, flushing, "I do not break my given word. Give me the cypher and she goes free."

"And what of Quentin?" asked Penelope frantically.

With a slow smile Otton said, "I only want the cypher. Chandler can take his chances."

Quentin knew better. If he was left alive he might be recaptured, and there would be nothing to prevent him telling his inquisitors that Otton had the cypher and had allowed him to escape. Otton was not the type to risk his own head. But— Penny would be clear. That was all that mattered now. He reached slowly for his sword.

Otton levelled the pistol at him. "If I fire, she will be taken and you'll die easier than she does."

"The cypher is in the grip."

Still aiming the pistol steadily at him, Otton growled, "Unbuckle your sword-belt then, but—have a care."

Moving smoothly, Quentin obeyed, alert for any least chance to attack. He unfastened the hinged plate and removed the cypher. The long deadly pistol in Otton's hand held very steady, the barrel gleaming in the firelight. Quentin held out the cypher and for a second everyone stood motionless. Except Jasper. Having been deprived of his own perch, his beady eyes located another. Elated, he zoomed across the room to alight on the barrel of the pistol.

Captain Otton was apparently no more proof against the shock of whirring wings beside his face than was Penelope. With a startled yell, he swayed to the side.

Penelope wrenched free from his loosened clasp and ran clear.

Simultaneously, Quentin sprang forward and, not daring to delay for the instant it would take to unsheath his sword, with one savage swipe of the scabbard slammed the pistol from Otton's grasp.

Otton howled a curse, but made a very fast recover, his sword seeming to leap into his hand. Quentin unsheathed his own weapon by the simple expedient of whipping the hilt to the side so that the scabbard flew off across the table, in the process sending a vase of flowers toppling. He was barely in time to parry Otton's furious attack. In that first powerful engage he knew that not only was his opponent a master of the sword, but that he himself had very little time. The shock of the blow on Otton's pistol had sent a lance of pain through his arm, and now, for every movement he paid a savage penalty. Numbly, he thought, 'If only I was left-handed . . .'

"It's as well," jeered Otton, his blade circling warily. "I'd not have dared fire the pistol, at all events."

On the last word he lunged, lightning fast. Quentin's parry of that thrust was barely strong enough. Drawing back, panting, he stumbled a little and Otton laughed. "Do not expect me to kill you at once, Chandler. I'll first have that cypher and be sure you've not tricked me."

Quentin's desperate attack in sexte was unavailing, Otton parrying so strongly that he was obliged to use both hands to hold on to his sword. Grinning, Otton drove him relentlessly, his adept attack challenging Quentin's increasingly feeble defence again and again, the repeated violent shocks wreaking such havoc with Quentin that he was barely able to fight on.

278

Knowing he must soon fall, he cried gaspingly, "Penny . . . the cypher! Into . . . the fire!"

Penelope had been watching the struggle, gripped by the terrified awareness that Quentin could not possibly hope to win. Her fear for her love far outweighed her concern for the cypher and, ignoring his desperate plea, she ran to the fireplace and snatched up the poker. The swords were ringing in a flurry of steel on steel but, disregarding the danger, she waited her chance, then darted behind Otton and swung the poker high.

With a shout of anger he sprang out of range of Quentin's faltering attack and Penelope's flailing poker. His left hand whipped out, the back of it connecting hard across the side of Penelope's head and sending her flying.

Frozen, Quentin saw her collide with the table and crumple. A red haze drifted before his eyes. A rage such as he had never known possessed him. With a primeval snarl, he swung up his sword.

Otton, whirling to cut down his disabled adversary, found himself facing a madman, and an attack that, astounding him by its power and brilliance, sent him reeling back, his offence abruptly changed to a desperate defence.

Quentin was oblivious of anything but a consuming drive to kill. He no longer felt the throbbing of his hurt arm, and his weariness had been swept away by the searing fire of his fury. Teeth bared, eyes narrowed, he advanced, his sword a glittering menace that seemed to the bewildered Otton to come at him from every angle, ringing savagely against his blade in sexte, switching to quatre before he could rally, darting in a malevolent blur for his throat, so that, breathless and outmaneouvred, he fell back and back. Quentin's sword sang down his blade in a glizade that almost disarmed him. He riposted angrily, but in the perilous stroke down as the time thrust, Quentin advanced into Otton's attack and, barely eluding the plunging steel, thrust to the full length of his arm.

His face suddenly ghastly, Otton staggered, his weapon falling to the floor with a ringing clatter. Quentin disengaged hard and clean and stepped back. Otton clutched at his chest and sagged to his knees, staring up at Quentin's white, frowning face. Blood streaked through his gripping fingers, but he gasped, "By—God . . . but you can . . . fight!" And, coughing horribly, he sank, face down, to the floor.

"Well done! Oh, jolly well done!" cried de Villars, who had watched the last seconds of the ferocious battle from the doorway.

Out of breath, but having managed to stand up, Penelope tottered to Quentin's side. He flung down his reddened sword and took her in his arms. "Are . . . you all right . . . love?" he panted.

She nodded, her appalled gaze on de Villars, who had knelt beside Otton and turned him onto his back.

"Fumblefoot," he said, with an admiring grin at Quentin. "Give me your handkerchief. You didn't kill the pest." He accepted the handkerchief Quentin gave him, and glanced at Duncan Tiele, who sat up, groaning and holding his head. "One up. One down."

Quentin staggered, suddenly feeling like a wet rag.

Leaping to support him, de Villars said, "Correction. Two down!"

"Down . . ." muttered Quentin, sinking gratefully onto the sofa, "but not—out, Treve."

"Oh, no, dear boy. Most definitely not out."

Roland Otton was bandaged and borne off to some unknown destination by a pair of grimy ostlers, neither of whom said a word, although Quentin was perfectly sure he recognized the twinkling green eyes of one of them as belonging to a dashing young peer named Horatio Glendanning.

His own wound had not been improved by the violent duel

and, although he made light of it, Penelope had come to know the white look about his mouth and she insisted upon inspecting the injury while Quentin fortified himself with a glass of brandy and de Villars tended Tiele's broken head. Her fears that Quentin's wound might have reopened proved unjustified, but it was very angry and swollen. Coming over to view the damage, de Villars swore under his breath and said in a voice of ice, "I pray I may someday have the pleasure of meeting your uncle, Miss Montgomery."

Penelope winced, and Quentin said quickly, "Not today, I hope, Treve. Tell us if you will, how Otton found us, and what happened to our friends."

"We were able to overpower Otton's men with no harm to your people," said de Villars, returning to the table and bending over Tiele, who sat in a dazed silence. "Your abigail, ma'am, was in such a state that I've ordered her to rest until you are all able to leave. As for finding you—I gather Otton and Delavale followed Sir Brian here. Most of the scurrilous crew charged off after friend Holt. I suppose they thought if he didn't catch you, Chandler, they would. Didn't you see 'em?"

"Well, it was raining, you know. I knew there were a devil of a lot of men pounding along after me, but this is my country, Treve. I know the Plain like the back of my hand. We'd a governess who lived in Salisbury, and Gordon and I spent several summers with her while my father was abroad. I led them towards the stickiest spots and left them swearing."

Penelope asked, "What about my groom, Cole? He has a—a deep dislike for the Jacobites, but he's a good man. I hope he wasn't hurt?"

"Oh, no," said de Villars, winding a makeshift bandage expertly about Tiele's head. "We had a little chat and he's gone haring off to Scotland, as you might expect. Shall you be well enough to travel, Quentin?"

"Of course. Thanks to you and to my lady's valour, I'm right as a trivet. We should leave at once, I gather?"

De Villars said with a rather grim smile, "Five minutes ago would be better."

Quentin stood and took Penelope's hand. "Well, love—I fancy you're bound to go with me."

Still puzzling over why Cole should be going up to Scotland, Penelope gathered her cloak and reticule. "I've no choice," she said demurely, "since I am also a wanted fugitive."

Quentin scowled. "If one is to believe Otton. What d'you mean to do with him, Treve?"

"I doubt he'll be causing anyone any trouble for a while." De Villars grinned. "However, we'll keep him tucked away. By the time he recovers, I fancy an amnesty will have been declared and his fangs thus pulled. Well, let's get you on your way."

Tiele's floundering attempt to accompany them was firmly suppressed, and his protestations that he had promised to escort Penelope were cut off when she kissed his pale cheek and thanked him profusely for all his gallant efforts in their behalf. Quentin wrung his hand, and Tiele subsided to watch regretfully as de Villars ushered the pair into the drab hall.

In a comfortable downstairs sitting room, their parting from Daffy and Killiam was more painful. Daffy was distraught at the thought of being separated from her beloved mistress, and even offered to leave Jasper behind if she could but go along. Killiam put his arm about her in a proprietory way and told her to stop fretting. "We ride alone, do we, sir?" he said. "I should've knowed it."

"Not you and I, old friend." With quiet finality Quentin said, "They know us now. If we travel as a group, they'll have us in no time. You must take Daffy to Lac Brillant and wait for us there. I'll ask that you swing north and come into the estate by the east road. Take care of your lady, you old villain. And keep your eye on that blasted bird!"

Penelope ran to hug Daffy, and the abigail sobbed heartbrokenly. "Oh, miss—you cannot go orf like this! I—I mean it—it ain't *proper!*"

Quentin put his arm around her and gave her a hearty buss

on the cheek. "Your *Miss* will be my *Mrs.*, Daffy, m'dear, just as soon as may be." He took the Corporal's hand in both his own. "Rob—Godspeed. Pray tell my father what happened here, and that we shall wait at the old lighthouse until he sends word the coast is clear."

His distress very obvious, Killiam said huskily that he would do as the Major wished. "And—good luck, sir," he added gloomily. "Gawd knows—you'll need it!"

Quentin grinned at him, took Penelope's arm and ushered her from the room.

Outside, the wind howled around the old inn, but the rain had stopped. Dutch Coachman had driven the carriage to the back door and a porte-cochere which had survived an earlier and more affluent period. Her hood flying, Penelope was handed up the steps. Quentin climbed in beside her, then turned to let down the window. He reached out to wring de Villars' hand. "You'll be protected, Treve?"

"Oh, never worry for my carcass. For Lord's sake try to get some sleep. You look worn to a shade! You've your famous cypher safe, I trust?"

Quentin patted his sword hilt.

"Do you mean to overnight at Farnborough?"

"Not if we can reach Guildford."

"You'd best take these." De Villars handed some papers to Quentin. "A bill of sale for a horse you bought; a letter addressed to Mrs. Bainbridge—that's you, ma'am; and an estimate from a landscape gardener for renovation of your grounds. Your estate is Bainbridge Hall, in Kent, and you are a prominent surgeon, Edward Bainbridge. No—don't thank me. Goodbye—and God go with you."

Quentin raised the window, sat down and gathered Penelope into his arms. The carriage lurched into the start of its journey. "Bainbridge Hall," murmured Penelope, with a little sigh. "How wonderful it would be was there really such a place. And you and I returning to it with friends and loved ones awaiting us." She sighed and, receiving no answer, said, "Quentin . . . ?"

But he was already fast asleep.

XVI

hey were stopped three times during the long drive south and eastwards. Quentin slept like one dead, and fortunately the soldiers were tired and, having endured much vilification by irate gentlemen, were willing enough to accept Penelope's identification papers and her plea that her husband not be wakened since he was a doctor and had sat up with a sick patient all the previous night. The sun was beginning to be obscured by clouds and the violent jolt as the carriage wheels encountered a large pot hole finally awoke Quentin. He was at once fully alert and tensing to the possibility of some new threat. Penelope touched his hand and murmured, "What a good nap you have had, darling."

This fond observation inspired him to devote the next ten minutes to convincing his affianced bride of the depth of his love for her, at the end of which time they were both so enraptured that he put her from him hastily and said, "That had better be enough of that, my girl! Lord, but you drive me wild!" He peered out of the window. "Where in the deuce are we?"

Considerably shaken, Penelope managed, "A little way east of Aldershot, I believe. We have made not very good speed, love. The roads were so muddy and we have been thrice stopped."

Astonished that he had slept through it all, he next drew forth the watch Gordon had left with him, and was shocked to discover it was nearly quarter past seven. "Oh, egad! And from the look of the sky we'll not get much farther tonight." He turned to Penelope again, but contented himself with taking up her hand and pressing it to his lips. "Have you been able to rest at all, Mrs.—er . . . Oh, the plague! Who the devil are we this time?"

She laughed. "Bainbridge, love. And I am much too happy to be tired."

Her chin was tilted upwards. He kissed the end of her nose and murmured, "Dearest Penelope Anne Montgomery—how little I have to offer you. My future is questionable; my estates may be forfeit; and I am a younger son without a splendid fortune to lie at your feet. I have brought you into the shadow of the axe and the gallows, when all I wished to bring you was joy and contentment."

"Foolish creature," said Penelope, her eyes misting. She tucked her head under his chin and snuggled into his cravat. "For how long have you wished to bring me anything at all?"

"For a very long time," he said dreamily, his cheek against her fragrant hair. "But I suppose, with absolute certainty that first moment, when I saw you standing in that hellish room while your uncle was—questioning me. I couldn't make out what it was you were saying, but you seemed to me like an angel from heaven. For a moment . . ." He paused, then said very quietly, "Do you know, Penelope Anne—for a moment I really thought I had died."

Too moved to say anything, she hugged him tighter and pressed a kiss into his cravat.

He smiled and went on, "I'd felt very close to you while you and Geoff were at Lac Brillant. It was because I told my papa I would not marry until I'd seen you again, he insisted I take the

285

Grand Tour. Not that he didn't approve, but he thought me too young to have made up my mind. I met Charles Stuart in France and very soon gave him my allegiance. He kept me busy. The years slipped away so fast. Then, when I saw you again . . ." He kissed her hair and finished simply, "I knew."

She said, her voice tremulous with emotion, "And so began to call me your sister! Wretched man."

"Yes. When I'd come to my senses. At first, I was so giddy with love. Each time you came to tend me I could scarce refrain from seizing you and telling you how I felt. I was so selfish, in fact, that I actually crept from my bed once and came to the door to woo you."

"What stopped you, love?"

"Daffy." He felt her stiffen, and said, "Not intentionally. It was on the morning Otton had pawed you and I was beside myself. Daffy scared us all out of our wits by rushing in and wailing about them taking Jasper away, and you left Rob and me whilst you calmed her. Rob hadn't enjoyed very much sleep the previous night—"

"For some odd reason," teased Penelope.

He pulled her earlobe. "Wretched Bainbridge. Anyway, he sat down and soon dozed off. I lay there, thinking of how splendid you'd been, and how cleverly you'd managed to fool Sybil with your 'cold.' And I began to long so to hold you. I crept to the door and opened it. Only—you and Daffy were not quite done. She was on her knees, clinging to you as if you were her last hope, and you—"

Penelope's eyes were very wide. "You—heard what she said?"

"That I would bring you nothing but fear, sorrow, and a cruel—"

"Oh, my dearest, I am so sorry! How you must have felt."

"I felt a worthless wretch because she was perfectly right, and I should have thought more of my prospects. Neither of you saw me. I closed the door and vowed I'd do nothing again to cause you to suspect how much I loved you." He sighed. "It was far

286

more difficult than I'd imagined. And now—look at me! I've brought you to—"

"You have brought me the greatest gift life can offer, my darling. Love."

There was only one answer to that, of course, and it was several dizzying moments later that he sighed and, still holding Penelope very close in his arms, murmured, "What a life we will have, you and I. I shall take you to a little village outside Paris. The very loveliest spot. There is a *pension* where we can stay until we hire a place—only until the King grants an amnesty, of course."

"What kind of place?" she asked dreamily.

"I'd thought a cottage, perhaps. Not too large. A cosy cottage with a patch of garden where I can grow vegetables and—"

The thought of this firebrand digging vegetables reduced Penelope to a squeal of laughter.

"Rascal," he grumbled, kissing the top of her head. "I am a great hand with a shovel, let me tell you."

"I wish I may see it! And I must have a corner of the garden patch for flowers, if you please?"

"Of course. And in the evenings when we are worn out by our labours in the patch we'll come in to a cheery fire. . . ." He yawned.

"Before which you will fall asleep whilst I make dinner, I suppose."

"Gad, what a marplot! No, madam. Mrs. Quentin Chandler shall have a cook and a pretty little French housemaid who will—"

"Who will do very well to keep her saucy eyes from *Mr.* Quentin Chandler!"

He chuckled. "And we'll have a cat, of course. And a dog . . ." And suddenly, the picture he painted brought such an intolerable longing that he turned up her face and, running his fingertip along the hollow of her cheek, said, "Oh, Penelope

Anne—how I love you. Do you think you could endure to take me to husband?"

Blinking away happy tears, she said huskily, "With joy and pride, and . . . forever, my darling. Oh . . . my darling . . ."

Relinquishing her mouth dazedly, Quentin was at last brought to an awareness of the sound that had been agitating at the edges of his mind for some moments. "Good Lord!" he groaned, and reached for the check rein.

The trap was swung up, and Dutch Coachman's face, dripping, peered in at them. "You all right, sir and ma'am?" he enquired, grinning.

"My poor fellow! You're fairly drowned. Find us a nice inn, quickly. We'll all be the better for a rest and some hot food."

Very soon afterwards, her wet cloak having been carried off by the pretty chambermaid who had brought hot water and clean towels to the neat bedchamber of The Three Quails Inn, Penelope turned to where Quentin sprawled sleepily in a chair before the small fire. "Wake up, sleepy-head," she admonished, tugging gently at his hair.

He blinked up at her. The green gown was creased and rumpled, and her hair was dishevelled, raindrops glinting here and there among the tumbled curls, but meeting his gaze a deeper pink glowed in her cheeks, and shyness caused her lashes to droop. He stood, and said very softly, "How lovely you are, my lady."

"Oh, pooh," she said in a rather uncertain voice. "Do you mean to go on tonight?"

"If the weather clears. I must push on, dearest."

"To where, Quentin? Can you tell me?"

He pulled her closer, paused thoughtfully, then chuckled. "You'll know the instant you see a signpost with the name. No, love—for your own protection I'll tell you no more than that it lies near the Ashdown Forest, and—" He slipped both arms around her waist, looking at her in a way that caused a strange tension to interfere with her breathing and set her heartbeat

288

racing. "Penelope Anne," he sighed, "how very much I wish I could wed you now."

Despite the knowledge that her face must be quite pink, she met his yearning gaze steadily. "And I. Is—is it possible?"

"Oh, yes. If the banns had been called for three Sundays. If I had a special licence." He kissed her eyebrows lightly, feeling her tremble. "Small chance of that."

"But—we *will* be wed. Tomorrow, or . . . the next day." She saw desire turn his eyes to green flame, and she put her arms up around his neck, her skin tingling as she gave up her mouth to his. She was breathless and shaking when he lifted his head. "I want . . ." she whispered, "to belong to you, darling. Now. Tonight. I don't want to wait another day."

'Another day,' he thought, and his heart sank. What might happen tomorrow? What if he was taken, and Penny hounded? What if he went to his death, and she was left alone and un-wed—perhaps carrying his child? "No!" he said harshly. "'Fore God, have I not done you enough harm that I must now tempt you to do this?"

"You do not tempt me," she argued.

"Oho," he cut in, with a rather uncertain grin. "I repulse you, do I? Now mark this, Mrs. Bainbridge—"

She put her hand over his lips. "Stop. I belong to you. Whatever happens. Don't you . . . want me?"

He groaned and crushed her close again, kissing her hair, smelling the sweet faint scent of the perfume she wore, feeling her soft body pressing so enticingly against him. "*Want* you? *Lord!* How can I tell you—" He thrust her from him and turned away, drawing an unsteady hand across his eyes. With a really heroic effort, he faced her again and said lightly, "Just at the moment, m'dear, I want my dinner more." And seeing her suspicious frown, he added quickly, "Besides—my arm is deuced troublesome."

"But," she demurred reasonably, "you'd not need to—"

"Penelope Anne!" Laughter danced into his eyes. He said

289

primly, "I was never more shocked!" and retreated to the adjoining bedchamber.

Left alone, Penelope sighed and did what she might to restore her appearance. She missed Daffy's expert assistance as she dressed her hair, and even more when she put on a simple travelling gown of cream muslin, embroidered in shades of blue and with many little buttons down the back. She was still struggling with those fiendishly elusive buttons when a scratch at the door announced Quentin's return. He looked rested and elegant in his coat of burgundy velvet, with snowy lace foaming at throat and wrists, his hair powdered and tied back neatly.

"How well you have done, dearest," said Penelope. "If you could possibly manage some of these irksome buttons . . . ?"

He managed willingly, but the business of the buttons became considerably extended since he found it necessary to kiss her back with each button he secured. Penelope's skin began to shiver with that new electric excitement as his lips touched her bare back. His hands were very cold and she could feel them trembling. She spun around as he finished, reaching out to him with eager arms, but he retreated, gasping threadily that he must not, dare not kiss her again.

"Coward!" she murmured. "That's not fair."

He agreed. "I'm a selfish rogue, I own it, and fairly famished!"

The dining room was occupied by only one other couple, a middle-aged pair with the stamp of *nouveau riche* upon them and an odd habit of either not talking at all, or bursting into impassioned utterances at the same instant. The lady's wig was much too elaborate to be properly worn in a hedge tavern, and her wide hooped gown of magenta taffeta gained nothing from an elaborate garnet necklace. The gentleman's chair faced away from them and he did not look up as they entered, but the woman's narrowed eyes took in Penelope's gown, shawl, and hair in one quick sweep, then passed on to Quentin. After that, she scarcely looked elsewhere save when engaging in the sporadic outbursts with her husband. Beyond having offered a polite bow when first he walked into the room, Quentin paid no attention to this behaviour. Penelope, however, was vastly irked by it.

The serving maid hurried to their table with a bowl of watery and lukewarm chicken soup in which were dumplings that Quentin glumly pronounced no heavier than cannon balls. Penelope discovered she was hungry, and forgot their ill-mannered fellow diners as she struggled with the soup. "Dear one," she said softly, "are you not too tired to press on tonight?"

"You forget I had a good nap on the way here. I'm very weak, however, for I'll be dashed if I can get my fork into this thing! How are you—Good God! Small wonder that lady stares so. Here, love . . ." He reached across the table to cover Penelope's hand with his own. "Put this on as soon as you can manage it without causing the starchy creature to faint." He pressed his dragon's-head ring into her hand and, as she closed her fingers around it, he murmured, "If you wear it back to front, it should resemble a wedding band—temporarily, at least."

Unobtrusively, Penelope managed to slide the ring onto her finger. It was much too large, but to wear his ring brought a tightening of her throat and the sting of tears to her eyes. Quentin saw her distress, promptly misinterpreted it, and chatted easily, recounting some nonsensical episode he had involved his brother in when they were children. The waiter came to take the bowls and bring a basket of bread, a platter of cold pork, a half of a mutton pie, and a bowl of water in which huddled some pallid carrots. Looking up, Penelope found Quentin's concerned gaze on her. A relieved smile lit his face. He said, "I don't wonder that soup upset you. Dreadful stuff. You should do better with—" He glanced down, saw the drowned carrots and moaned, "Oh . . . egad!"

Penelope smiled at him. "Geoff was the same. He despised vegetables."

"You will find it hard to convince me that those deceased objects are vegetables. And as for your brother, I wonder Lord

Hector did not take that lad in hand. If he don't pay less attention to his sweet tooth, he'll be fat as a flounder before he's—"

The glass Penelope had been lifting crashed down. The woman in the magenta gown sent a supercilious glance her way, and her spouse turned to direct a curious glance at Penelope, then continued to stare at her, frowning. The waiter came running to mop up the lemonade and bring a fresh glass.

"You're tired, poor girl," Quentin said worriedly. "Gad, I wish I'd not to drag you on, but—"

"What did you mean about Geoff?" demanded Penelope urgently. "Can it be that you didn't know he was killed at Prestonpans?"

"The devil! How could—"

"'Pon my soul, but it is!" exclaimed the magenta lady's husband. Undeterred by the annoyed frown Quentin slanted at him, he stood and advanced on their table. "Your pardon, sir, but I believe I have the acquaintance of your companion. It is Miss Montgomery, is it not? Permit me to jog your recollection, ma'am. I am Sir Leonard Epps. Your papa and I were old friends. I trust I see you well?" His brows lifting, he glanced at Quentin, who had risen politely.

Aside from a vague sense of recognition, Penelope had no memory of a close friendship existing between this gentleman and her father. Confused, she lied, "Of course I remember you, Sir Leonard. May I present my husband, John—er, Somerville?" And she could have sunk as '*Bainbridge*' rushed belatedly into her flustered mind.

Sir Leonard shook Quentin's hand, but he had noted Penelope's hesitation and that, added to her vivid blush, brought the glint of suspicion to his eyes. He returned to his wife after the slightest of courtesies and bent forward to mutter to her. Lady Epps' smile seemed to creak as she pinned it on her thin lips and, although she bowed to Penelope, her eyes were glacial.

Agitated by the inexplicable reference to her brother, horrified by her blunder, and sure that Quentin would explode

292

with mirth at any instant, Penelope concentrated upon her food. It was mediocre. She ate lightly and refused dessert.

Very aware of her discomfiture, Quentin said, "We'd best go, love," and rose to pull back her chair. At the same moment, Sir Leonard and his lady started past, murmuring farewells.

Penelope reached for her reticule and her *pro tem* wedding band slipped from her finger, bounced to the floor and rolled to lie at Sir Leonard's feet.

Quentin moved very fast, scooped it up, and bowed to the astonished knight. "Old family heirloom," he said with oblique honesty. "My love, since you've become so thin, it would behoove us to have this resized. I'd not like any gentleman fancying you to be unattached." He winked outrageously at the shocked Sir Leonard, bowed to Lady Martha, swept Penelope from the room, and giggled hysterically all the way up the stairs.

"Oh . . . Jove . . . !" he gasped, striding across the bedchamber to collapse on the bed with a shout of laughter. "Did ever you see two such quizzes? I thought the old fellow would swallow his eyeglass, and his lady looked about to burst her staylaces!"

"Very well for you, sir," said Penelope, mortified. "I was embarrassed to death, and am quite disgraced."

"Well—don't blame me if you cannot remember your own husband's name! John Somerville, indeed! I dashed near told 'em you were confusing me with your first husband!"

"Oh! Quentin! You never did?"

But he was off again, laughing so heartily she could get no sense out of him and at length sat beside him and pulled his hair.

Lying there, laughing up at her, his eyes softened, and he reached up to touch her lips. "Such a sweet mouth."

She kissed his fingers, but when he sat up and slipped an arm about her, she said, "No, love. Not now."

His lips quirked. "Do you mean—no *love*? Or—'*no*, love'?"

"Quentin, please—this is so important to me. What did you mean about my brother?"

He sobered at once. "Deuce take me for a fool. Of course it's important. However came you to make such an error, Penelope Anne? You surely must have had his letters?" Scanning her face, he saw the colour leave it, and said, "Good Lord! You really *believed* him slain?"

"Y-yes," she whispered, her heart pounding dizzyingly. "Is— he . . . not?"

"By God, he is not! How do you think I came to Highview, except that Geoff— Oh, no!" His arms were around her wilting form. Terror-stricken, he moaned an imploring, "Do not faint! Penny—you would not do so dreadful a thing! Lie down." He tried to pry her hands from around his neck and, failing, looked frantically to the pitcher of water so near and yet so far, on the bedside table.

Penelope tucked her head under his chin, the room distorting strangely about her. "I'll be . . . all right . . . in a moment," she whispered.

Somehow, she was lying back against the pillows, and Quentin, his hand shaking, his eyes wide and dark with fear, was holding a flask to her lips and begging that she take a sip.

She obeyed, coughed, and sipped again, a warm glow spreading through her to dispel the dizziness. "Oh, thank you, love," she said, smiling tremulously up at him.

"Now you mean to cry," he groaned. "My dearest girl, what would you have done had I told you old Geoff was as dead as you'd thought? And how the plague *could* you have thought such a thing?"

"I received a letter from Whitehall, telling me he was—was wounded at Prestonpans."

"Well, so he was, poor fellow. Out of his head for weeks, but he didn't slip his wind."

"But—they sent a second letter, saying he had been killed and buried by the Scots in an unmarked grave."

"Damned idiots! My God, Penny, do you think if that were so I would have come to you for help?"

She refused the flask he offered. "I—I didn't know you *had* come to us. I thought it chance that my uncle had taken you. And I knew that Geoff would have deplored the treatment handed out to escaped rebels."

Quentin stoppered the flask and set it aside. "After their defeat at Prestonpans, Scotland was an unsafe place for King George's soldiers, as you can guess. Geoff was taken in by a kindly Scots family, but for months his life was despaired of. He began at last to improve, but the family had come under suspicion and it was necessary that he be moved. They tried to smuggle him to the Border, but were balked at every turn and eventually were obliged to carry him to the northeast and Inverness. Soon afterwards, we suffered the tragedy of Culloden." He frowned and left her to pace to the window and stare broodingly into the night. "The tables were properly turned. We suffered a crushing defeat and *Jacobites* were hunted, not the English."

"Thank heaven you got away! So Geoff helped you?"

"He did indeed. The lady with whom he stayed chanced to be sister to Lord Boudreaux and great-aunt to Treve de Villars. Geoff discovered that she was also a staunch Jacobite and involved with Treve and many others, in helping fugitives to safety. You can guess he plunged in—up to his neck!"

"But surely there would have been an English army garrison there after the battle. Did he not have to report his survival?"

"Well . . . yes, and no. He reported his survival, but—not as Geoffrey Delavale." Quentin saw her bewilderment and explained, "You see, there had been a typical army mix-up. There was an officer in Geoff's Brigade named Geoffrey Delacourt who was killed at Prestonpans. They reported poor *Delacourt* missing, and your brother slain and buried. Geoff knew nothing of his premature demise until after Culloden. He was by that time deeply engaged in helping fugitives and decided, for the sake of

295

his family, to keep his false identity. In that way, should he be caught, you would not be endangered, nor the estates confiscated."

"My heavens!" Sitting up, Penelope cried anxiously, "Is he now a fugitive also?"

Quentin came back to reassure her. "No, no. But he's running some blasted close risks, I can tell you. To all intents and purposes, he's a hopeless invalid. Actually, he's busier than a dog with two tails, arranging escape routes. That's why he hasn't come home." He sobered. "I know for a fact he has sent several letters off to you. Why you haven't received them—" His eyes narrowed. "Your uncle . . . ?"

Shocked that her own family would have kept such news from her, she nodded wordlessly.

"That miserable bastard! I'll warrant he kept you thinking Geoff was dead, hoping to ensure it and inherit!"

"But, it would have been so easy to get rid of my brother. Uncle Joseph need only have told the authorities of his Jacobite involvement, and—"

"And the estates would have been confiscated," he interpolated grimly, sitting beside her again, and taking up one of her trembling hands. "No, he dared not do that. He probably hoped to receive word that Geoff was coming home, and could then have had him ambushed. Blast, but he's a filthy swine! To think of them keeping you in those hideous blacks all these months and letting you grieve for Geoff—as though it were not bad enough to have lost your father."

"I remember," she whispered distractedly, "that on the first day you were hidden in the dressing room, I surprised my aunt reading a letter. She seemed so guilty, and whipped it out of sight. I fancied it was from one of her cicisbeos. I never dreamed it might be from Geoff."

"Likely it was, love. Lord knows how many letters they've intercepted. I fancy that's how they knew I was on my way."

"Oh . . . !" She bowed her face into her hands. "How shamed Geoff will be when he learns how his own relations have betrayed him. Only think—if you'd given into them and

296

let them have your message—or cypher, as you call it—we would have been responsible!"

He patted her shoulder comfortingly. "Well, I didn't—and at all events, I only carry part of the cypher. Just the first stanza."

"I saw that it was a poem. There are other verses, then?"

"Yes. I don't know how many, but when they all are pieced together the whole will tell where the treasure is to be taken, and to whom the list may be entrusted."

Penelope was quiet for a moment. Then, she said slowly, "What a fearsome responsibility. Dearest—heaven forbid the need should arise, but—if anything should go wrong, what must I do?"

Quentin frowned and the faint premonition of trouble that had dogged him all day returned, stronger than ever. He said curtly, "Nothing. I will not involve you."

She dried her tears. "My brother risks his life to be involved. I am involved because I love you. And I am involved because had it not been for my family you might have safely completed your mission by now. Tell me, dear."

For a long moment he was silent, common sense battling the instinct to protect her. Then he stood and crossed to take up his sword-belt and carry it to the bed. He showed Penelope how to open the little plate on the hilt of the sword, then drew out the small piece of parchment upon which rested the lives and fortunes of so many. "If I should be taken and there is any chance for you to do so without endangering yourself, my heart, get this to Treve or my brother, or to Geoff. They'll know what to do."

"May I see?" She took the parchment and read:

I

Cattle sleep at night
Walls of darkness round them.
Songs of owls affright, but
Cannot confound them.
Break of day will brighten.

297

Stiff and chill the wind,
Zealously to waft away
Bat and elfin-kind.
Banish every fear, my dear.
Summer's almost here.

"Good heavens," she muttered, bewildered. "Who on earth could make any sense of that?"

"Someone evidently. It makes no sense to me, I grant you. Unless perhaps it refers to an estate having walled pastures, and Lord knows there are plenty of those, particularly in the North."

"Hmmnnn," she said dubiously. "But what about the bats and the elfin-kind?"

He chuckled, took back the parchment and replaced it in its holder. "It wasn't written so as to be easily deciphered, that's certain. Perhaps the key is in the other stanzas—who knows? At all events, we must be on our way. It seems to have stopped raining and we dare travel a few miles farther, I think." He scanned her features keenly. She looked tired, despite that valiant smile, and there were shadows beneath her trusting eyes. She had lived a nightmare since he had re-entered her life. The insidious whisper of danger warned that she would be so much safer if he left her here. . . . "Penelope Anne," he said softly, taking her face between his long sensitive hands and gazing down at her, "how much do you love me?"

She took in every line of the beloved face and, her eyes soft with love, whispered, "Oh, my dear. Do not you know?"

"Then—for my sake, do as I ask." He sat beside her and holding the hand that at once came out to him, went on, "This is taking too long. I cannot wait for the coach. I can cut across country if I ride."

Fear rested its cold and now familiar touch upon her heart. She said with resolution, "I ride very well across country."

"Darling girl—be reasonable. Only see how tired you are. Penny, I *must* leave you."

Her grip on his hand tightened. "You are far more tired than I. And if you go, I shall follow."

"Dear heaven! Must I tie you to the bed, woman?"

She said demurely, "For what purpose, dear sir?" But when he frowned, she put up her hand to smooth away the furrows in his brow. "'Whither thou goest . . .'" She tilted her head. "Listen . . ."

He heard a soft pattering as of many tiny feet rushing across the windows. "Oh, no!" he groaned, and strode to fling open the casement.

Running to his side, Penelope looked gladly into the rainy darkness, sniffed the sweet clean air, and leaned to him as his arm slipped so naturally around her waist. "Admit you are thrown in the close," she said.

He was silent, knowing that he should go on, rain or no rain.

Reading his thoughts, she twined her arm about him. "Dearest, you cannot. We'd have you ill again. Your arm was more inflamed after that awful duel with Otton. It would be the height of folly to ride any more tonight, especially in the rain. And you are so very tired."

He was tired, and it was true that his arm was a bit of a nuisance. He glanced down at her face, so full of concern and love, and was lost. "Delilah," he murmured huskily, pulling her to him. "Very well, but we must be up with the dawn, so— early to bed for both of us."

Her face upraised, she said with a small sigh, "Whatever you wish. *Whatever.*"

Whatever he wished . . . He kissed her gently and then not so gently, her eager response so sweetly passionate that he fled like a craven, closing the door hard and leaning back against it, eyes closed, breathing hard, the flame of desire fighting his nobler impulses.

Left alone, Penelope tottered to the window and flung the casement wide, allowing the night air to cool her blazing cheeks. Leaning there, feeling the rain now and then splash on to her skin, she whispered a heartfelt prayer of thanks for her brother's survival and begged that this valiant and honourable gentleman who had won her heart not be taken from her; that his so precious life not be sacrificed and she left alone in a void of grief and loneliness.

She was a good deal more tired than she had realized, and almost fell asleep while bending over the washbowl to clean her teeth. And yet, once her head touched the pillow, she could not sleep and lay there, staring into the darkness, battling the intrusive images of horrors that might be, attempting instead to concentrate upon the dear vision Quentin had pictured: the pretty French cottage with its vegetable garden; the dog and cat, and perhaps, God willing, other companions in the fullness of time . . . a little boy, maybe, with his father's laughing eyes and indomitable courage. But always the fear crept back, and the yearning, until she could stand it no longer and, throwing back the covers, sat on the edge of the feather bed. She gazed at the connecting door, feeling wretchedly lonely, knowing that he was so short a distance away. Only a few yards separated her from the solace of his nearness; the blessed comfort of his strong arms about her. . . .

Scarcely noticing that the wooden floor was icy against her bare feet, she wandered over to the door and laid one hand on the panel. There was no sound from within. If he was sleeping he was being very quiet about it. Perhaps he was as wakeful as she. Perhaps he, too, was lying staring into the dark, longing to hold her.

With trembling fingers she reached for the latch, but in that moment it lifted of its own accord. The door swung open. Wearing Geoff's black dressing gown, Quentin gasped as he saw her.

They faced each other across the threshold, neither moving, their earnest faces lighted faintly by the glow of a single candle beside his bed.

"You, too?" he murmured at length.

"I needed you so."

His hands clenched. "I know. I seem to have not as much

willpower as—as—" He groaned and held out his arms. Penelope melted into them, and he held her close and stroked her long hair and whispered huskily, "Can it truly be sinful and wrong, I wonder, to love so much?"

She could feel the hurried beating of his heart and knew her own heart was answering that passionate summons. And yet . . . She lifted her head and by the dim light he saw the look in her eyes.

"What is it, my darling? Are you afraid of me?"

She shivered, and held him tighter. "No. But—sometimes, I am so very scared. Oh, Quentin—hold me. Hold me!"

He held her very close, trying to soothe her, wondering as she had wondered earlier if this would prove to be all the time they had. Only tonight. Over her silken hair he saw a gleam from the bedside table. He put her aside and went over to pick up the dragon ring. He stared down at it, his eyes troubled, then looked up at her. She waited, where he had left her, standing there, patient and trusting, like some pure and shining angel, the long hair framing her expressive face, the white nightgown with its dainty little pink satin bows seeming to him to accent her purity . . . her vulnerability.

Feeling humble and unworthy, he stretched out his hand. "Come, my dear Delilah."

At once she hastened to rest her soft warm hand in his. He led her to the window and opened the casement. The rain had stopped again, and the moon was emerging from behind a shredding cloud mass, painting silver edges on trees and cottages, making the lane into a ribbon of light.

Quentin turned Penelope to face him squarely. With grave and unknowing dignity he said, "I can offer you no great cathedral, Penelope Anne. No other church than this little room; no other witness than our Creator. But—will you do me the very great honour of becoming my wife?"

"You know I will, my dearest," she answered fervently.

"Now?"

She looked up at him wonderingly, and he took her hands

and sank to his knees, drawing her down with him. Still holding her hands, his eyes fixed on her face, he said in a hushed, reverent voice, "Here before God, I, Quentin Frome Chandler, take thee, Penelope Anne Montgomery, for my lawful wedded wife. And I do swear to love and to cherish you for so long as I may live."

Penelope's throat tightened so that for a second she could not speak, then she murmured, "Here, in the sight of God, I, Penelope Anne Montgomery, take thee, Quentin Frome Chandler, to be my lawful wedded husband. To love, honour, and obey. For as long as I may live."

He slipped the dragon ring onto her finger, then bent to kiss it. With his head still bowed low, he said haltingly, "Lord, thou knowest how deep and reverent is my love for this gentle lady. Grant that—that I may never give her cause to regret this true and holy marriage. Amen."

Quite unable to speak, Penelope blinked at him through a blur of happy tears. He lifted his head and looked rather shyly into her radiant face. With ineffable tenderness he said, "In the eyes of God we are now man and wife, my dearest girl. And I swear to you that, so soon as may be, I will wed you again, so that the laws of man may be satisfied."

He helped her to her feet and asked with a slow smile, "May I kiss the bride?"

With a joyous sob, she yielded to him. He kissed her thoroughly, closed the casement, then walked with her to the feather bed.

Trembling, adoring, trusting, Penelope took him to herself as a woman takes the man she loves. She knew no sense of shame or regret, only an initial shyness soon banished by Quentin's expertise. He handled her very gently, but was soon able to bring her to excitement and thence to a quivering passion. Briefly, she experienced a frightening pain, soothed by his loving whispers of explanation, and then she was caught by a soaring ecstasy, a wondrous binding of hearts and minds and bodies. Returning dizzily to earth, she lay curled snugly in his arm, her hot cheek against his bare chest, her body pressed close against his. And, imbued with a sense of completeness such as she had never known, she sighed purringly.

Drowsily content, Quentin planted a kiss rather erratically on her eyebrow. "I can hear your mind spinning," he murmured. "Go to sleep, love." But then, a thought striking him, he asked anxiously, "Of *what* are you thinking?"

Her voice came to him, soft and sweet out of the darkness.

"I was thinking that—surely, there was never a more holy marriage than mine."

Another brief silence. Then he said, just as softly, "Mrs. Chandler . . . have I chanced to mention that—I love you?"

"And I you. Quentin—oh, my darling, I love you so very—"

But what with one thing and another, she never did finish that sentence.

XVII

enelope awoke to sunlight and a sense of great excitement; a bewildered knowledge that something wonderful had come about, and that this day was supremely important. For a minute or two she could not recall the cause, but then she became aware that something was digging into her shoulder. She retrieved the dragon ring and memory returned with a rush. She knew an awed disbelief as she returned the big ring to her finger, and her cheeks felt hot as she remembered the events of the night. Her wedding night. . . .

She heard a muffled rumble and darted a laughing glance to the connecting door that Quentin had considerately closed when he left her. She stretched, smiling happily at the faded bedcurtains, the garish floral stripes of the wallpaper, able to find fault with nothing. She was Mrs. Quentin Chandler, and whether or not the laws of man would acknowledge that fact, she knew beyond doubting that her beloved was as irrevocably bound by the vows he had spoken upon his knees in a wayside inn as though they had been spoken in the greatest cathedral in the land, with an archbishop officiating and hundreds of guests to bear witness.

Her joyous eyes roamed the little room, alighting by chance

on her treasured clock. She gave a gasp of dismay. A quarter to nine! And Quentin had wished to leave at dawn! She sprang up in bed, throwing back the blankets and pushing her feet into her threadbare carpet slippers. Running to open the connecting door, she was greeted by the stentorian evidence that her beloved slept soundly. She thought, with a giggle, 'Very soundly!' and she ran to kiss his cheek, not caring that it was flushed with sleep and stubbled by a growth of beard.

He opened one eye, stared in momentary shock, then gave a great grin of delight. "Mrs. . . . Chandler . . ." he said, yawning and reaching for her.

Penelope danced clear, then leaned to ruffle his tousled hair. "Wake up, sleepy-head! It is near nine o'clock!"

"Good God!" He leapt up, begging her to ring for hot water. She did so and left him cursing under his breath because the maid had neglected to wake him.

By the time he had washed, shaved, and dressed, Penelope was ready, a fact that stupefied him. Coming into her bedchamber and crossing to the window seat where she sat waiting, he pulled her into his arms. "Is there no end to your perfection, wife?" he asked, kissing his way from her brow to her throat. "Who'd have dreamed I would find beauty, courage, and promptitude all in one delicious package?"

Surrendering to his tantalizing kisses, Penelope wondered dreamily if he really thought her beautiful, and drifted in a golden haze until he regained sufficient of his wits to remember the time.

They ate a hasty breakfast in the coffee room, and Quentin went to the front desk to pay their charges. Penelope, who had paused in the hall to stroke a large and handsome collie basking in a patch of sunlight, straightened to find Lady Epps turning disdainful eyes from her. Smiling a greeting, Penelope started forward, but the woman pointedly snubbed her, and Sir Leonard, his face a study in outrage, looked at her grimly, shook his head, and marched on. Blushing, Penelope thought, 'I suppose they must think us a shameless pair,' and wondered

305

what they would say if they suspected in what unorthodox fashion she had been married last evening. Her eager eyes sought out her husband. There seemed to be some problem with the host, and Quentin's handsome features were flushed. Hastening to his side, Penelope became the recipient of a shocked stare from the host, and a gasped "Well, I never!" from his plump spouse.

Quentin gripped Penelope's arm and hurried her outside. "God help us all," he moaned, under his breath. "Of all the ghastly things!"

Dutch Coachman was supervising the loading of the luggage into the boot. Their groom, a family man, having been once more warned of the ever-present danger, had reluctantly declined to go on with them, so that Dutch now had to manage alone, but Penelope doubted Quentin's distress was by reason of this circumstance.

"What is it?" she asked anxiously. "Did someone recognize you?"

He handed her up the steps, then sprang in to sit beside her, throwing his tricorne onto the seat and running a hand through his hair in exasperation. Glancing out of the window, he came eye to eye with the host, standing arms akimbo on the front steps, truculence written all over his stalwart self. Quentin turned his scarlet face away and breathed a sigh of relief as the coach lurched and started off into the sunlit morning. "Thank the Lord for that!" He pulled Penelope's hand through his arm and smiled wanly at her. "What a pair we are! Do you know, my mind was so full of my adorable bride that when the host asked to be reminded of my name, like a perfect gudgeon I started to answer truthfully! Luckily, I stopped when I realized what I had done, but then I couldn't remember our present alias!"

"Oh, heavens! Whatever did you say?"

"The host snarled at me, 'Quentin—is it? I thought as how you'd said you was Edward Bainbridge!' and looked at me as though I was Bluebeard, unmasked. And just to sweeten the pot, up comes your nosey Lady Epps. 'Good morning, *Mr. Somerville,*' says she!"

"Oh—no!" moaned Penelope.

"The host pointed to where I'd signed the register last night, and said in a voice of doom, 'You mean Mr. *Bainbridge,* don't you, ma'am?' and she went so stiff I wonder she didn't splinter! Egad! I thought all three of me would sink right through the floorboards!"

"Poor darling! Little wonder I received such censuring looks just now. They fancy me a fallen woman."

He slid his arm around her. "You are," he said tenderly. "Fallen right into my trap. Are you thinking better of it this morning, sweetheart?"

She was able to convince him that she'd had no second thoughts and, after a delightfully improper interlude, she straightened her cap and advised her reluctant husband that they should talk sensibly. "I must write to Geoff at once, dearest," she said, allowing her hand to be recaptured.

"I can give you his direction, but you must remember he is Captain *Delacourt.* And you shall have to be very careful as to what you say."

"Yes, I shall. And—he *is* better? Where was he wounded?"

"Took a piece of shell casing in the chest, and his lung was pierced."

She gripped her hands, distressed. "Oh—how awful! I should have gone at once to him, had I only known."

"That would have been impossible, I'm afraid." He added quietly, "Geoff has had a nasty time of it, but there are many men today, Penny, who owe their lives to his efforts."

"Including your precious life! How proud I am of him! But—it is two months since Culloden. Surely he can come home soon?"

"There are still many rebels in hiding, and now he has a small band of brave fellows who will likely keep at it—God bless 'em!"

She said thoughtfully, "And—this treasure—is it still in Scotland?"

"It has been divided into several shipments and sent to various temporary hiding places. What we want to do is transport it all to a place of real safety and keep it hidden until it can be either returned to the original donors, or put into a fund to help those of our people who survive. Many of my own men were stripped of homes, farms, everything they owned. If we can keep the treasure safe until amnesty, it could mean the difference between life and starvation for hundreds of people."

Penelope sighed. "Oh, how very dreadful it is."

"Why, a man must fight for what he believes best, Penelope Anne. And be prepared to take the consequences. The dreadful thing is when his loved ones, innocent children perhaps, suffer because of his actions." He looked sombre, and she knew he was remembering what his father had said during that terrible confrontation in Reading.

She said loyally, "Yes, you are right, of course. If every man was afraid to defend right and justice for fear of what might happen to his loved ones, we would still be in serfdom."

"Very true." But he still looked troubled, and muttered, "If it weren't for that damnable list, I'd not be so concerned."

"List? Of the items contributed?"

"Yes. And the contributors."

"My heavens! Quentin—*you* do not—"

"No, no. You've seen my only message. But the poor devil who does carry the list bears the heaviest responsibility of us all. I'd not be in his shoes."

"Do you know him?"

"Very well. A splendid young chap. What worries me is that the officer assigned to take him is that devil Fotheringay."

"The man you snored at so convincingly."

His smile was fleeting. "He's the one."

"And you fear this Major Fotheringay."

"If all I hear of him is truth, he's a man to be feared."

He lapsed into brooding silence, Penelope not interrupting

his thoughts, content to put back her head and watch his profile against the swiftly changing scene of the far window.

He turned to her. "Lord, what a clodpole! To be sitting here muttering in my teeth, when I could be loving you . . ."

Lady Leonard Epps was, she informed her husband, more than shocked to find that a girl of Penelope Montgomery's breeding should be so flagrantly flaunting about the countryside with a strange man. "For that he is her husband, my dear Sir Leonard," she expounded, spreading marmalade on her toast, "you will never convince me! Quite apart from that ugly ring, which was not in the slightest like a marriage band, I knew the instant I laid eyes on that young"—she lowered her voice, glancing around the almost deserted coffee room before continuing—"that young rake—the *instant* I laid eyes on him, I knew that he had seduced the chit!"

"I noticed last evening how you stared at him," murmured Sir Leonard, not above getting in a little snipe when the occasion offered.

"Of course I stared at him!" She fixed her spouse with a militant glare. "But do you think he had the grace to be discomfited? He did not! Bold as brass! The tavernkeeper should be publicly chastised for permitting such disgraceful conduct. I, for one, shall never set foot in this place again! Such a nuisance, for it is not as dear as most of the other inns hereabouts. And as a Christian woman, I feel it my duty to tell him so."

Sir Leonard did not share his wife's crusading spirit, his thoughts having run in another direction. "Do you recall how cool old Delavale used to be when we called?" he asked reflectively. "Always managed to make me feel I was beneath him."

"*I* certainly received no such impression! I hold myself quite the equal of any Montgomery ever born, so he'd not dare take such a tack with me! To the contrary, I thought him excessive courteous."

"Exactly so. Went out of his way to be polite. *Noblesse oblige,* I used to think. Not at all like his manner with Marbury."

"Of course not. His grace is of much higher rank."

"Dammit, that's just what I'm saying, my lady. Delavale thought nothing of arguing with Marbury. Why, I once heard him address him as a cod's head!"

She stared at him, aghast.

"'S truth, I assure you. But with me it always was punctilious civility. Used to get my hackles up, I don't mind telling you. And now—to think his pious daughter has turned out to be little better than a lightskirt!" He laughed suddenly. "Rich—eh?"

"It is disgusting," his wife declared, tossing her napkin on the table and taking up her reticule. "Come, Sir Leonard. We have a duty to perform!"

Thus it was that a few moments later the hapless proprietor of The Three Quails Inn stood at the desk in his own lobby, wringing his hands and protesting miserably that he'd had no idea anything hanky-panky was to do. "They seemed like such a well-bred couple, ma'am," he wailed, "for all they had no personal servants. I'm a God-fearing man, as is my good wife. I assure you I'd never have allowed—"

"The fact is," my lady interpolated in her high, shrill voice, "you *did* allow it. That wicked young rogue had clearly seduced the gel, and in renting them a room here, you contributed to her downfall!"

Since Lady Epps made no least attempt to lower her voice, the discussion attracted several interested listeners and, glimpsing a red coat amongst them, the landlord swore under his breath and declared in a more forceful way, "You've no call to accuse *me* of anything, ma'am. The gent claimed they was married, and I'd never a' knowed no different save that when he left he forgot what name he'd given me. I told him just what I thought, then!"

Bored by this dispute, the young officer made his way through the gathering. "Host," he began, "I need—"

"You need to remember your manners, Captain," interrupted Sir Leonard tartly. "My wife is speaking."

The Captain frowned, but my lady gave him no chance to respond. "And despite the rude interruption," she shrilled, "you must be either blind or a halfwit to have thought them wed, host! I hope I am not a busybody, but the ring no more fit the gel's finger than would have a bracelet!"

"Nor was it a wedding band," her husband put in, adding hurriedly, "Not that I'd have noticed, had it not fallen off, right at my feet."

"A most hideous thing," his wife confirmed, "for all he claimed it to be a family heirloom."

The Captain's ears perked up. "Did it look like an heirloom, ma'am?" he asked.

"Well, if it was, I can but be glad it is not in *my* family! It was shaped like the head of a dragon with horrid evil red eyes, and certainly—"

"Your pardon, ma'am," the Captain intervened, the harsh note of authority in his voice. "I regret the necessity to interrupt, but it chances we seek a man who wears such a ring." He jerked his head, and the Sergeant who had followed him into the room at once began to herd the onlookers away with the demand that they "move along, now, move along."

They obeyed with reluctance, while the Captain obtained the identities of the now uneasy trio before him. "My name is Holt," he said briskly. "The register, if you please, host."

The host swung the dog-eared book around, maintaining that he was always most careful and ran a good Christian house, no matter what anyone said.

Holt's keen eyes flickered down the page. "Nothing here. What name did he use?" The host pointed, and Holt muttered, "Bainbridge. Hmmnn. The lady who wore the dragon ring, ma'am. Was she a tall young woman? Quite attractive, with very fine eyes and a rather unaffected manner?"

"Bold, more like it," said her ladyship huffily. "My husband is

311

acquainted with her family, and I know them slightly. I vow I was never more shocked!"

"You know the lady?" said Holt, slanting his cold gaze to Sir Leonard.

The older man hesitated. He wasn't above a bit of gossip, especially about the family of so high-in-the-instep a fellow as Hector Delavale had been. But if this was serious business, the matter took on a different colour. "I—er, cannot be certain," he said warily. "What business have you with the girl?"

"She is believed to have given aid to a Jacobite fugitive."

Lady Leonard gave a gasp and turned very pale.

"You mean—she is wanted for . . . *treason?*" gasped her husband. "Oh, I was certainly mistaken, then. I've not seen the chit since she was a child, and might very easily—"

"As you say," the Captain intervened, familiar with the reaction. "A description of the man, if you please, host."

Thoroughly frightened, the host wet his lips and stammered, "Why, he was very tall, Captain, and—and his hair was brown, but reddish . . . and his eyes so green as—"

The Captain spun on his heel. "Sergeant! Mount up! We have him, by God!"

He ran into the yard, scattering the awed crowd around the doors. "Get the stablehands over here! One of 'em must have seen which way that coach went."

"I see 'em, sir," volunteered a shifty-eyed ostler, much relieved that this ugly customer wasn't here because of last week's little difference of opinion about the pistol that had been stole by wicked gypsies out of the Sergeant's saddlebags.

"Speak up, fellow!" snapped Holt. "Which way?"

"They took the left fork at the crossroad, sir. To Godalming."

"South! I knew it!" Holt swung into the saddle, his eyes alight. "That damned rebel's heading for the coast! At the gallop, Sergeant!" And he was away with a creak of leather and pound of hooves, the troop clattering after him.

In the suddenly quiet lobby, Sir Leonard Epps threw a dismayed glance at his wife.

"Well . . . well, *we* are not to blame," she said defensively. "After all, she brought it on herself."

"So that's why he changed his name." The landlord mopped a handkerchief at his sweating brow. "Poor lad. Poor lad."

"And they did seem very devoted," muttered Sir Leonard. "God help them!"

For once, her ladyship had nothing at all to say.

There really was no cause, thought Penelope, to be so nervous. They had come very far, very fast, with relatively little trouble, only once having been stopped as they approached the New Forest. The young lieutenant in charge of the troopers, obviously disliking his task, had been sufficiently conscientious as to demand identification, but had then engaged in a pleasant banter with Quentin, and had waved them on within a few minutes. Quentin had seemed strained, his good humour unfailing, but an underlying tension in his manner that had not escaped her. They had obtained sandwiches at the posting house where they'd stopped to change horses, but he had pressed on immediately and they'd eaten their luncheon in the swaying carriage.

It was quite warm now, and there was nothing odd in the fact that Quentin had wished to ride on the box for a little while. "Like to get a breath of air, if you don't object, love," he'd said cheerily. She wrinkled her brow. He had been so tender with her, so jealous of any incident that separated them for even a few moments. And now—to leave her alone like this, seemed . . . But she was being silly. They were almost safe, for he'd told her with a grin that she soon would have a clue to their destination. They were driving through the New Forest even now, the sunlight dappling the quiet road ahead with ever-changing shadows, and the trees providing a cooler temperature. Very soon, Quentin would be able to deliver that terrible little piece of parchment. There would be only the final run to Lac Brillant, and then—a ship, France, and a new life. Penelope smiled dreamily. She would look back on all this one day, while Quentin dug around his cabbages, and she would think it only—

She was flung to the side and reached out to steady herself. They were moving at a great rate, for the coach began to rock wildly, and the trees flashed past. Alarmed, she started up, then quailed as she heard a sudden sharp crack, like a brittle tree limb snapping. Before her startled mind could identify the sound, three more retorts shattered the peace of the drowsing forest. The trap was swung upwards, and Quentin's face peered down at her.

"They've sniffed us out, I'm afraid, m'dear," he shouted. "No—don't talk. No time." He ducked as another shot rang out, but went on, "You must do exactly as I say. There's a side road about a mile up ahead. We shall turn off there and stop very suddenly. Jump out just as fast as you can. Dutch and I will drive on a little way, then swing back for you. As soon as you alight, run and hide, and stay there until we come." He threw down his purse. "Just in case we become separated, this will help you get to my father at Lac Brillant, and—"

"No! *No!* Quentin—let me—"

"Do as I say, if you please!"

And he was gone, the trap slamming down to blot out his unwontedly stern face.

Cold with terror, Penelope took up the purse and put it into her reticule, her mind struggling to cope with this sudden but so long dreaded disaster.

She gave a little cry as she was hurtled to the side, her shoulder making bruising contact with the door frame. She heard the screams of frightened horses. The carriage was leaping crazily, but they were stopping. Somehow, she got the door open and, without lowering the steps, sprang out. The vehicle was still moving, and she fell heavily. She could hear Quentin's voice, sharp with anxiety. "Get up, Penny! Hurry!"

She scrambled to her feet. She saw Quentin's face, white and anguished. Then, obedient to his fierce gesture, she stumbled off the road and into the trees, blinded by tears, her knees bruised and scratched, but that pain a small and distant thing, as nothing to the grief and terror that pierced her. Looking back, sobbing, she fell again and, even as she tried to struggle up, she was deafened by another shot. Terrified, she lay pressed against the damp earth, biting back her sobs, feeling the ground tremble to the thunder of many hooves, praying in a whispering near-hysteria for God's mercy on her beloved.

The violent sounds faded. The silence of the forest settled down again, broken only by the heartbroken weeping of the girl who lay huddled among the ferns.

"You can order yer lady, Master Quentin," shouted Dutch Coachman, manipulating the ribbons with skilled desperation, "but ye bean't able to order me. Not on this." He gave a gasp as a musket ball whistled past his ear. "You—you just be trying to get me orf safe."

"You old fool!" Quentin's hands clamped onto the reins. "Let go, damn you!" And as the coachman swore at him, and the coach leapt and plunged along the winding lane, he shouted, "Dutch—for the love of God! She must not be left alone, and I've this blasted message to deliver. I beg you—go back to her. Help her! For my sake, Dutch. For the sake of—"

The shot was closer this time. Dutch Coachman yelped and his hands were suddenly slack on the reins. Quentin flung a steadying arm around him and with his free hand gripped the reins desperately. "Dutch! My poor fellow—are you—"

"I be so . . . fine as . . . fourpence ha'penny," quipped the faithful man weakly. "Just . . . my side. A graze, likely."

He was clutching his ribs with crimson-stained fingers. Quentin flashed a quick glance behind. One of the trooper's horses had gone down in the mud they'd just splashed through, and the men were milling in confusion. The carriage raced into a good lead. "This next curve," shouted Quentin. "You'll go back for her, Dutch?"

"I—I will that, sir. I'll bring her to you . . . I do swear."

"*Now!*"

Again the poor horses were wrenched back. Again, the carriage rocked and lurched. The coachman became a Flying Dutchman indeed as he leapt into and annihilated a tall clump of shrubs.

The carriage rolled on. Quentin shouted, "Get on! Giddap! Giddap!" slapping the reins against the foam-streaked backs of the team. After a minute he glanced behind. The troopers had re-formed and were coming up fast. He grabbed the whip and sent it swinging out to crack loudly over the heads of the horses. It was the last straw. They took the bits between their teeth and bolted. The carriage flew. Quentin braced his feet and prayed. The lane swung in a wide left curve through the trees and as they came out onto the straight-of-way again, he saw a hump-backed bridge looming ahead. He thought tensely, 'Only a few miles to go.' But then he realized that Holt must know this road, and had done exactly as he himself would have done in like circumstances. A trooper had been sent through the trees to cut him off, and now rode in from the side, musket levelled. The coach roared past, heading for the bridge. Quentin ducked as the trooper's musket belched flame. There was a shattering crack. One of the horses screamed and staggered as they thundered on to the bridge. The carriage leapt crazily into the air. Quentin was hurled from the box. He had a brief impression of slowly spinning trees and sky. He was falling. Something dark and big was coming down over him. Water glittered and a tree loomed up, a stone wall beyond it. Instinctively, he threw out his arms to protect himself. A violent impact brought

316

pain that was too intense to be borne and wiped everything into emptiness. . . .

It was hours now. Hours of prayer and pleading and nightmare imaginings. And still he did not come. Penelope's tears seemed to have dried up with her hopes. She stood at last, and brushed mechanically at her skirts. A small rabbit, who had watched her for some time, made no attempt to run, but crouched there, its long whiskers twitching, its bright eyes fixed on her. Almost, she thought dully, as though it could feel her despair and was staying to keep her company. She took up her reticule. Her little hand mirror was smashed, but there were two large pieces left and, by resting them side by side in the crook of a branch, she was able to see herself. She was shocked, not by her mud-streaked face, swollen eyes, and dishevelled hair, but by the dull hopelessness of her expression; as though the light of life within her had been turned out and she was already dead.

"Mrs. Chandler—have I chanced to mention that I love you . . . ?" The words were so clear that she could almost hear them, almost see the worship in the fine green eyes, the half-smile on the beautifully shaped mouth. Mrs. Chandler . . . A widow, perhaps, before she was legally a wife. She lifted her hand. The dragon ring gleamed in the sunlight, and pausing to touch it tenderly, she marvelled again that despite her falls it had somehow stayed on her finger. Her shoulders stiffened. What would her dear husband think of her now? He once had called her a valiant lady—she was not being very valiant at this moment. She began to tidy her hair as best she might, and to wipe the mud from her face. Quentin would have been here by now, had he been able to get away from the soldiers, but he'd said that if he was delayed she must make her way to Lac Bril-

317

lant. It *was* possible, surely, that he had been driven so far out of his way that he dared not swing back for her? It *was* possible that he was now making a desperate attempt to get closer to Lac Brillant, even if he would not dare go directly there with the troopers hot on his heels. If he was able to escape, eventually he would seek her there. There was no point in waiting here any longer. Somehow, she must make her way to Lac Brillant.

The rabbit hopped unhurriedly away when she began to search about for her cap. She found the lace-edged patch of silk hanging on a lupin and carefully restored it to her curls. At least it gave her some slight aura of respectability. She removed twigs from her shawl and draped the torn silk across her shoulders. There was a large rent in the hem of her gown and the muslin was rumpled and muddy. She tidied it as best she could and made her way back to the road.

She walked along slowly at first, then more rapidly, her mind busying itself with the invention of a plausible explanation for her plight, in case some Good Samaritan might drive by and rescue her. But she realized with a faint sense of shock at her own stupidity that she must not walk so openly beside the road. The troopers might come up behind her long before she heard them, and they'd have no doubts as to what had befallen her especially if the terrible Captain Holt was with them. A fine thing it would be if dear Quentin made good his escape and she was taken purely through carelessness! She turned off the deserted road and began to walk parallel to it, through the trees, finding the going tiresome in the extreme, her skirts catching on the undergrowth and the thin soles of her half-boots seeming to find every pebble however carefully she tried to avoid them.

On and on she trudged. The afternoon was waning, but the sun was still hot and the hooped skirts and constricting corsets she wore added to her discomfort. These miseries were felt, but relegated to a distant part of her mind, most of her concentration fixed upon Quentin and where—and how—he might be at this moment.

Quentin's return to consciousness was as puzzling as it was painful. He was lying down and yet he could see water some distance below him, and a grey rock marked by vivid red splashes was directly beneath his gaze. He was most uncomfortable, and when he moved he discovered miserably that he seemed to be one large bruise. Not until his hand came within the field of his vision did he comprehend that he was draped ignominiously over the branch of a tree and that the slowly spreading stain on the rock was dripping from his own fingertips.

That shock brought full recollection. He must only have been unconscious a very few minutes, for he could hear soldiers grumbling and, lifting his head, saw them scrambling down the banks in search of him. He began to drag himself up, a more difficult task than he'd imagined, and one that must be accomplished as swiftly and silently as possible, if the troopers were not to discover the source of the stains on the rock. Moving with desperate caution, he managed to straddle the branch and rest his back against the tree trunk. He was enormously relieved to find that his sword had not been torn off when he'd crashed through the branches, and that the panel concealing the cypher was intact.

The troopers were coming closer. He wrapped the skirts of his coat around his hurt arm and tightened the folds, cursing with soft and anguished fluency as he tried to restrict the bleeding. He'd obviously reopened the wound when he'd zoomed through the tree, but a glance to the side told him he'd been very lucky. The stone arch that supported the approach to the bridge was scant feet away. If he'd smashed into *it* instead of the branches, his problems would have been permanently settled.

The troopers were investigating the wreck of the coach, which lay on its side half in and half out of the stream. They were also indulging in a low-voiced and extremely profane assessment of the probable ancestry of their Captain. Quentin was in full accord with their opinions; he was also aware that at any instant one of them might look up and see him, and he was very relieved when a noisy commotion arose in the nearby woods. Startled birds were shooting up with a great outcry, probably flushed by some wild creature, but convincing the soldiers their quarry had blundered that way. With much excited hallooing they all went tearing off.

Quentin lost no time in descending the tree and hobbling stiffly toward the east. After a while, there being no sound of pursuit, he paused beside a quiet pool and, kneeling to drink, beheld his reflected face so covered with welts and scratches that it was a miracle his eyes had escaped injury. Apart from his many bruises and the damage to his arm, a raw scrape across his left knee was his only other injury. Trifling annoyances compared to what might have befallen him. Congratulating himself on his narrow escape, he was startled to hear distant shouts and the noisy approach of horses. He made a run for it, but they gained rapidly. He plunged into the most densely overgrown areas where it would be difficult for a horseman to follow. It soon became obvious that the soldiers had also abandoned their mounts and were again closing the gap. Holt, thought Quentin, being the efficient officer that he was, had no doubt sent a man on ahead so that the net could be spread beyond the forest to snare him should he get through. His one hope was that they would expect him to aim south, whereas his way lay eastward. He dared not continue in that direction, however. Penny would certainly know his destination when she saw the name on the signpost, and he had no intention of leading this curst pack to his love.

And so he ran where they expected him to run, making no attempt now to cover his tracks, refusing to slow his pace until he was staggering with exhaustion and so light-headed that he knew he was cutting things too fine. He must change direction, or he would be too far spent to complete his mission.

He took to the trees again, struggling to quiet his sobbing breathing as they came into view; shocked because they'd been so close behind him. Again, he was spared. They ran past without a pause and the sounds of their progress faded into the distance. Down he clambered, and set off at a steadier pace towards the northeast, taking care this time that he left no telltale splotches of blood to betray him.

The sun was low in the sky and he was parched with thirst when he came to a hurrying stream. He plunged gratefully into the deliciously cold water, drinking with the restraint that experience had taught him was vital, and bathing the wound in his arm that had once more become an unremitting agony. It came to him rather dimly that he must do more. He went back onto the bank and risked the time it took to struggle out of coat and shirt. With his teeth and his left hand, he managed to tear off the left shirt sleeve. His handkerchief served for a pad, and he bound it tightly over the wound. His efforts to tie a knot sent him to his knees, but he fought off the faintness and after a short rest managed a bulky knot to keep his awkward bandage in place. Scanning the result, he was reminded of Penelope's gentle and competent hands. "You'd take a very dim view of this botch, love," he said wryly, then checked, his head jerking up in panic as he heard the sounds of pursuit once more.

Cursing, he struggled into his shirt and coat, then began to run. The faster he ran, the hotter and more breathless he became, and the more consuming was his dread of capture. Soon he had only two thoughts: firstly that he dare not slacken his pace, and secondly that he must keep the sun ever behind him. He ran on madly, until every breath sent a flame through his lungs and a sword into his side. He was reeling and spent and half-blind when he wavered through thinning woods in the heat of the waning afternoon. He saw blurrily that a great oak loomed against the golden skies and that there was a lightness beyond it. Drawing in great rasping gasps that seemed to tear his lungs to shreds, he staggered to the old tree and clung to it, soaked with sweat, consumed by an overwhelming need to lie down—to be done with the whole damnable business and let Jacob Holt haul him wheresoever he would.

His knees gave out under him. He crumpled and slid down the rough bark. They were all about him, but they would give him some water . . . surely, they would at least let him quench this hellish thirst . . . ?

"Come on . . . then," he croaked. "Damn you, Holt . . . come on!" And he sank to his face and sprawled there, beyond caring.

Penelope's heart gave a leap of hope when she heard hooves approaching, but the vehicle that came into view was heading west, and of such dilapidated appearance that she would not have dared accept a ride, even had one been offered. The narrow road wound on and on. At length she turned a rather sharper bend and saw a bridge ahead, and the rippling sparkle of sunlight on water. In anticipation of a cold wet handkerchief against her heated face, she hastened her steps, only to check, appalled. A dead horse lay beside the road, and one side of the stone bridge had been smashed away along the top. Frantic with fear she ran up the curve of the old structure and peered over the damaged wall. Below, resting half in the stream and half on the bank, lay a carriage, one wheel gone, and the water lapping softly at its crushed side.

The scene swam before Penelope's staring eyes. She clutched the ragged stones and dazedly became aware that she was whispering "Dear God . . . Dear God . . ." over and over again. She made herself stop, and only then did she hear someone calling softly, "Miss Penny . . . he ain't here. Miss Penny!"

Her heart leaping, she scanned the scene again. "Dutch . . . ? Is that you? Where are you?"

322

"Down here, miss. Under the bridge."

She ran swiftly down the far side of the bridge and clambered around the bank. Dutch Coachman, his coat and shirt lying nearby, had been attempting to bathe a deep wound across his side. With a cry of mingled relief and sympathy, she ran to grasp his outstretched hand. "Oh, I am so *glad* to see you! Let me help."

"It ain't nothing much, miss," he said apologetically. "Just sorta knocked me sideways as yer might say."

She could have kissed his pale, rugged face, and she made him sit down on the bank while she cleansed and bound the ugly gash, using a strip torn from one of her petticoats for a makeshift bandage, and assuring him that she herself had suffered nothing more than a few bruises. "Never mind me. Please tell me what happened to Major Chandler."

He told her as much as he knew. "I must've been struck silly arter I jumped off the coach, Miss Penny. Master Quentin had begged me to go back and help you, and I thought I was going the right way till I come to the bridge. All I could think of then was to find if he was here." His eyes slid away from hers. He went on awkwardly, "And he ain't. Either the troopers got him, or—" He paused, biting his lip.

Staring at him, her hands stilled, she whispered, "Or—he is . . . dead."

His greying, curly head ducked lower. He groaned, "Don't ye say it, miss! Don't even think it! I've knowed the Major since he was a boy. Such a mischievous, high-couraged lad he were. And growed into such a fine man. I cannot bear to think as—as . . ." His voice trailed off.

Still staring at him, Penelope said, "But you do think it. Why? Did you find something you've not told me of?"

He shook his head, not looking up.

"Dutch Coachman," she said in a voice of remote, unnatural calm, "I must know. You see—I am the Major's wife."

He gave a shocked gasp and jerked his head up.

Penelope held out her hand. The coachman gazed down at the dragon ring. "Strike a blooming light," he muttered.

Penelope finished her bandage. "I must know."

He sighed heavily. "All right, ma'am. Just let me get a bit more respectable like."

She waited quietly while he put on his shirt, and she helped him ease his way into his torn coat. He took her arm and guided her gently to the stream. "See here, ma'am." He gave a quick, reluctant gesture. "On the big rock, there. I'm afraid as there—there bean't much doubt . . ."

Penelope stood unmoving.

Watching her, the little man thought he had never seen so tragic a face, and nerved himself for the sobs, for the faint. But neither came.

She said in a whisper, "It—couldn't have been from one of the horses, perhaps?"

He shook his head. "No, ma'am. One was killed up on the road—still there, poor brute. And I could see where the other three was led off. The pole musta snapped when the coach went over."

Her wide eyes fixed on that ghastly stain, Penelope whispered, "Was there more . . . ? L-leading off , perhaps?"

"No, ma'am. It's—it's the only thing what give me a bit a hope."

Her gaze darted to his face. "Why?"

"Well, I reckoned that if the Major was killed, ma'am, or bad hurt, with him bleeding like that you'd be able ter see where they'd carried him orf. But—if he fell and hurt hisself not so bad but what he could still get up and run, why—he wouldn't leave a trail like that there. Lead 'em right to him; and he's been hunted, ma'am. He knows. Leastways . . . I thought as it might be that."

"You mean he would bind up his hurt, so there would be no trail to follow. Yes. Yes, of course." Her eyes bright with new hope, she asked eagerly, "Which way would he go, Dutch Coachman? Do you know?"

The desperate hope in her eyes wrung his heart. Not caring to dim it, however slight the chance that it was justified, he said that he did know. "I saw a signpost up the road a bit. Likely it'll point our way, though I fancy the Major will try to lose they sojers 'fore he goes there."

He helped her up the bank again, and they went along together, an unlikely pair, the short, powerfully built man, slightly stooping, and treading with careful strides, and the tall girl, limping markedly, but with her head high, her eager gaze fixed on the distant signpost.

When they were close enough to distinguish the words, Penelope halted. To the coachman's astonishment, she broke into a quavering little peal of laughter. "Oh, yes," she gasped. "That's where he was going, all right. He told me I'd know, the moment I saw the sign." And suddenly, she broke down, bowing her face into her hands and weeping for a brief, racking moment.

Slipping an arm about her slender shoulders and comforting her as best he knew how, the coachman realized his doubts must be unwarranted. If this fine young woman knew that particular trait of Master Quentin's, she certainly must be his wife. A faint smile came into his strained eyes as again he glanced at the signpost.

One sturdy arm of that useful contrivance directed the traveller northwards to the green slopes of The Weald, and was inscribed 'To Tunbridge Wells.' The other arm pointed to the southeast, and upon the weathered wood some skilled hand had painted with a flourish, 'To Little Snoring.'

XVIII

The Church of St. Francis of Assisi lifted its four-hundred-year-old Gothic tower benignly above the even more ancient village of Little Snoring. Picturesque thatched cottages lined the single street, interspersed with tiny shops and the single tavern. A few ducks foraged on the pond in the middle of the village green, and some children were making a great business of throwing pieces of stale bread and shrieking with glee when the ducks hurried noisily to snatch up their offerings.

This pleasant scene of rural peace and beauty was, however, marred by an argument. Even more incongruously, the argument was being conducted on the front steps of the church, the protagonists being the black-robed young vicar and a grim army officer whose troopers waited with faces variously glum, or bored, or impatient, until Captain Holt should have his way. Inevitably, he did. With an angry toss of his fair head, the vicar stepped aside. The Captain beckoned, the Sergeant dismounted and led the troop inside the hallowed old building.

A few villagers drifted over to watch these proceedings and, when the troopers reappeared some five minutes later, responded with bovine stupidity to the questions directed at them, and grinned as the thwarted military men mounted up again.

Holt turned his tired horse and called a warning. "If the rebel *should* come here, Father, I'll remind you the penalty for sheltering a fugitive is a fearsome one. This man is wanted for high treason and anyone helping him or his lady friend will share his fate. You are duty-bound to detain him—or both of them—and send word to your nearest military post."

A steady stare was his only response. He swung his horse around, then tossed over his shoulder, "There is a large reward for this pair, you people!"

"Is there, by gar!" exclaimed a gawking individual who appeared to be the village idiot.

"You want us to scrag the lady, 'fore we give her to 'un?" enquired another man with an innocent lift of the brows.

A laugh went up, and Holt flushed angrily.

"Be better'n what *he's* got in store for the poor lass," contributed a fat and scornful woman, wiping soapy hands on her apron.

A trooper came in at the gallop, and Holt turned to him eagerly.

"We got on his trail, sir," shouted the trooper, reining up. "The men be hard arter him, and he's running like a rabbit and bleeding like a stuck pig!"

A growl went up from the assembled villagers. Ignoring it, Holt led his men out at a canter, hoots and catcalls following.

"Bloody damned hounds," grunted the village idiot in unexpectedly cultured accents. Then, glancing to the priest, added, "Sorry, Charles."

Young Father Albritton, his blue eyes stormy, made a gesture of impatience. "They make me ashamed of my name," he muttered. "Don't waste your time apologizing, Chandler." And he walked back into the old church, opening both doors wide as though to air out the sanctuary.

A few moments later, mounted on a sturdy donkey, Gordon Chandler also left Little Snoring and turned to the south.

Two hours later, the brief flurry of excitement was still being discussed over cottage dinner tables. The street and green were deserted now, the children had gone home, and the ducks had abandoned the water and were grouped companionably under the weeping willow tree. The hush of the warm early evening was broken as a dog barked in a desultory way and then stopped, and all was quiet once more.

Quentin opened his eyes to find the pain in his lungs had eased away, although his thirst was a raging need. The soldiers were very quiet. He frowned at a nearby snail. He was very weak now, and his mind might be playing him tricks. On the other hand, it might have played him tricks earlier. Perhaps there had been no further pursuit after he'd reached the stream. He dragged himself into a sitting position and looked about. Not a red coat in sight and all was quiet except for the distant and civilized sound of dishes rattling. He could smell delicious cooking smells, and the cooler air of early evening restored him somewhat, but his thirst must be assuaged, even if death was the price to be paid. He hauled himself to his feet and leaned against the oak tree. The lighter space beyond the oak was red now—the sunset bathing a broad meadow, dotted here and there with clumps of gorse, and ending at the railings of an old churchyard.

"Now . . . 'pon my soul!" he croaked. "Chandler—I think you've done it!"

Heartened, he wavered forward. The meadow seemed very wide indeed, but if he could just get to that first patch of gorse, it would be a start. Solemnly, he warned the meadow that 'the journey of a thousand miles begins with a single step.' His own step was wobbly, his legs uncertain beneath him, but he knew his condition would not improve if he waited.

He crouched and set off in an erratic, weaving run. The

patch of gorse obligingly lifted and floated towards him, and at last he was kneeling in its shadow, breathing in painful, rasping sobs, clutching his throbbing arm, and peering desperately about for any sign of having been seen. There was no outcry, no running men with clubs or pitchforks, no red uniforms and bayonets to cut him down. He recruited his energy and tried again.

How he at last came across that meadow, he could not have said, but after a period that seemed as unending as it was appalling, he was amongst the gravestones. The back door of the church was open, and the cool dimness within beckoned, offering a blessed surcease from effort, if only he could get to it, for the Leper's Door must be close by. And—surely, there would be water . . . ?

He picked his way amongst the headstones, but they were perverse objects, alternately vanishing and materializing directly in his path so that he blundered into them. Panting and exhausted, he hung down his head and found the earth only a few inches from his nose. This seemed a very odd circumstance. He realized at last that he had been crawling, but one did not go to church on one's hands and knees. With a mighty effort he clambered to his feet again and staggered determinedly for the elusive door. A great slab of black marble loomed up, and the white angel above it jabbed him with one of her wings.

It was, as he told her, the outside of enough. He sat down on the marble slab and gave the angel a piece of his mind.

Dutch Coachman was quite sure that if the Major had survived he would by this time be making his way through the forest towards Little Snoring, for he knew that somewhere in that village was the point at which the vital message was to be delivered.

"But surely," Penelope argued wearily, "he will be too weak

and hurt to worry about that now. He shall have to look to his own safety."

The coachman smiled faintly. "Not Master Quentin. He give his word, ma'am. He'll die sooner'n break it. Now, do you see that little hill yonder, where the trees poke up?"

Penelope shielded her eyes against the sunset and made out the heavily wooded hillock. "Yes, I see it. Do you really think he might be there?"

"I'd not be surprised if he runs rings round they sojers, then comes to where he can give the village a look-see. I be going up there, ma'am."

Twice on this interminable journey, he had fallen. The second time it had taken her a great time to revive him, and she had insisted he rest and try to regain his strength. Now, she tugged at his arm, protesting, "No! Dutch, you cannot! You'll never be able to climb up there. And I am so hot and tired—I know I could not."

"Lordy, Lord, Miss Penny," he said with faint chiding. "As if I'd 'spect it of ye. No, miss. There looks to be a nice little church in that there village. You wait fer me in there."

She argued against this and said resignedly that she would go with him in case he should fall again, but when he pointed out that Master Quentin might just as likely have took refuge in the church, she thought it quite possible, and so at last watched his sturdy figure disappear in amongst the trees and turned her own steps towards the drowsy village and the quiet peace of the ancient church.

When she trod timidly through a wide-open side door, the interior was cool, dim, and deserted. She found it rather odd that there was no one about, but at this hour of the evening she reasoned that everyone was indoors for dinner.

The high vaulted sanctuary was bathed in crimson, the sunlight making a glory of the west windows. The oak pews, dark with age, invited her, and she went to the rear and sank down with a sigh of relief where the light was dim. She stretched out her aching legs and leaned back gratefully, but it came to her that she was in God's house and had spoken no word for her beloved. She pulled over a cassock, sank to her knees, bowed her head reverently, and prayed.

Her prayers were disturbed by an odd sound, a sort of muted shuffling punctuated by little thumps and heavy breathing. Penelope opened her eyes. The church was as empty as it had been when she entered. It was, in fact, so silent that she began to think it strange. Surely the vicar or the curate should be about, or someone cleaning, or arranging flowers?

"Oh . . . damn . . . !"

She gave a gasp, and sprang to her feet. Those so unexpected words had been groaned out, but the voice was wonderfully familiar. Holding up one hand against the glory of the west windows, she hastened to the aisle and walked along towards the altar, scanning each pew with desperate anxiety. She stopped abruptly.

Quentin had managed to crawl inside and had spotted the Leper's Door at last. The old church had been designed in the shape of a cross, and in the southeastern corner at which the shorter section of the building bisected the main sanctuary, a small door had been built long and long ago: a door little more than a foot in height and less than that in width, inserted into the wall at eye level, outside which the unfortunate lepers might stand to see the altar and hear the services. It was in that little recess in the thick wall that Quentin had been instructed to leave his cypher. He had tried so hard, but now, however he struggled, he lacked the strength to get to it. He could not even crawl any more, for his legs were like lead and he was so very tired and he hurt so badly, but worst of all was his thirst.

He thought, 'Come on, Chandler!' and, gripping the heavy end of the pew, heaved with all his strength and managed to pull his failing body another inch or two. He groaned despairingly, and his head bowed onto his outstretched arms.

He heard, then, a little cry and a whisper of draperies, and looking up incredulously, saw a vision coming towards him. Her hair was dishevelled, mud streaked down one cheek, and her gown was torn and a mass of creases, but he saw her with the eyes of love and thought her the most beautiful sight he had ever beheld.

Penelope sank to her knees in the wide pew, and Quentin fought his way up, whispering her name and reaching out for her. She gathered him into cherishing arms and kissed his brow, his scratched face, his dry cracked lips. And between kisses, she whispered, "Oh, my love—my poor darling. Where are you hurt?"

"Just . . . this foolish arm," he croaked, gazing at her adoringly. "How did you ever . . . find me?"

"Because I was meant to, dearest heart. Oh, but you are all blood! I must go and find—"

"First—my sword, love. The—the cypher."

He looked so spent that she was frightened, but respecting his wishes, she opened the little compartment in the hilt of his sword and took out the cypher.

"Over . . . there. The Leper's Door in—the corner. Just lay it . . . on the ledge."

She obeyed, then ran to the font and, with a hasty plea for forgiveness, immersed her handkerchief there, then flew back to Quentin.

He gasped with relief when she bathed his face and moistened his dry lips. He said with faint elation, "We've *done* it! Penelope Anne, we—"

Her hand clamped over his mouth. Paling, she turned towards the main door. Hooves sounded outside, and wheels rumbled over the cobblestones. For one glorious moment she had dared to hope they might escape. That the little cottage in France really did await them . . . that Quentin would have his vegetable garden. Now, she shrank as a man bellowed, "What's to do here? Is everyone in the blasted place dead as dust? Treadway—take some of the men and search the village. Don't stand for no nonsense from the yokels!"

Shivering, Penelope whispered, "Uncle Joseph . . ."

Quentin pulled her hand away from his lips. "*Go*, love! *Please*—go now. You can hide if—"

"No, dear."

Frantic, he started to beg her, but heavy footsteps were stamping through the front doors. Lord Joseph growled, "Empty as a politician's head! Oh, well. Best look, I suppose."

Quentin struggled vainly to stand, only to sink helplessly into Penelope's arms. Holding him close, she watched with frozen dread as her uncle's shadow began to come into view along the roseate floor.

"Delavale?" called Lady Sybil. "Are you in here? Oh, there you are. Treadway has found an oaf in the tavern who seems to know something."

The shadow, which had stopped, now retreated. "Well, Jove, it's about time! We're close, Sybil, I can tell you that. We'll have 'em before nightfall. I knew we'd only to follow that Holt creature, and he came straight here."

"And left again, my lord."

The shadow was gone now. Penelope breathed raggedly, hoping against hope.

"See here, Sybil," grunted Joseph. "You make sure. I've got as far as that pew by the pillar. Can't take no chances. That rebel scum might be skulking there."

"*What?* You never mean to leave me alone? What if Chandler *is* here? You said yourself he will stop at nothing!"

"Oh, for God's sake! From what I hear, the fella's half dead, but—very well—take this if you like. It's cocked—have a care."

Quentin reached up one unsteady hand to caress Penelope's cheek.

She smiled and held him tighter, pressing a kiss onto the wet tendrils of hair that had curled against his forehead. Her eyes widened with dread as Sybil's shadow began to appear, and she gazed with unblinking fascination as the shadow lengthened until she could see the long sleek shape in her aunt's small hand

333

that was Joseph's pistol. She could hear the rustle of Sybil's gown; hear her moaning little grumblings. The tension increased to such a pitch that she could hardly breathe, and it was almost a relief when the tip of the black velvet cloak came into view, and then Sybil's lovely face, framed by the fur-lined black hood, was staring at them.

My lady gave a little squeak of shock. Paling, she swung up the long-barrelled pistol and aimed it, her eyes taking in Quentin, sprawled in Penelope's arms, his bloodied, sweat-streaked face resting against the girl's bosom. He lifted one hand in a feeble wave, and the corners of his pale mouth twitched into the same whimsical grin she had first seen on the face of an older gentleman. Her eyes shifted to Penelope. There was a deep sadness in the face she had never judged pretty, but that now had an oddly proud beauty. Penelope said nothing, but bent a little lower over the man she cradled so tenderly, in an instinctive gesture of protection.

"Joseph . . . !" shrilled my lady faintly.

From behind her, Father Albritton said, "The quality of mercy, my child."

Sybil squawked and spun about, her pistol covering the priest for an instant.

Watching the inexperienced finger that wavered on the hair trigger, Charles Albritton judged accurately that he had never stood in greater peril, but he stood firm.

"They—they brought it on themselves, they are traitors," gasped Sybil.

"Perhaps. But you have only one immortal soul," he pointed out with a grave smile.

"And only one life to live!" she retorted. And not glancing again at the silent lovers, she fled, her croaking voice calling, "Joseph! Joseph!"

Albritton moved rapidly along the pew. "My poor fellow! Here, let me help you." He managed to half-lift Quentin onto the pew, but the wounded man sagged, and Penelope sprang to support him. Quentin's head sank onto her shoulder. "If he might please have some water," she begged.

"Of course." The priest turned away.

"No!" gasped Quentin. "Please—Father . . . will you rather . . . marry us?"

A wry smile twisted the clergyman's mouth. "Have you had the banns called, my son? Have you a special licence?"

"I'm not your—son," said Quentin fretfully. "Dammitall, you look to be younger than me!"

Penelope flinched, looking at this man of God in a silent plea for understanding.

Albritton grinned. "You were up two years before me, as I recall, Chandler."

Horrified, Quentin's strained eyes searched the fine young face. What he read there reassured him. "Do you know," he said wearily, "I doubt Christ would have asked for . . . a special licence."

Albritton hesitated. "I doubt He would have, either." He moved closer. "Your name, ma'am?"

Penelope told him, her heart racing, her eyes gemmed with tears, praying that Uncle Joseph not burst in and drag them off before this was done.

"This must be a quick ceremony, I fear," said the priest, over a sudden tumult that had arisen outside. "Quentin Chandler, do you take Penelope Anne Montgomery to be your lawfully wedded wife . . .?"

Their responses were spoken softly. Their eyes, banishing pain and sorrow and dread of the ghastly fate that must separate them all too soon, met in so tender a look that the priest's gentle heart ached for them, and he spoke the final benediction in a voice that broke. The lovely young bride bent to kiss her husband, and Chandler's left arm lifted weakly to embrace her, then sank again.

His eyes misting, Albritton looked away and, hurrying to the organ, began to play Bach's beautiful "Jesu, Joy of Man's Desiring."

Nestling his head closer against the sweet softness of his wife, Quentin said, "Whatever they may . . . do to us—I shall never stop loving you, my Penelope Anne."

She kissed him again, and murmured, "We must not let Death part us, my darling."

"Why should it?" he said, his words faint but his eyes fixed on her expressive face. "It never has . . . before."

"So you have felt that, too?"

"Yes. Since first I—"

The pure organ music stopped suddenly. Quentin's hand tightened on Penelope's.

Many feet were running along the aisle.

Her teeth chattering, Penelope closed her eyes and prayed for courage.

"I love you," said Quentin, quite clearly.

"Well, of all things," exclaimed Trevelyan de Villars. "Here we ride all day, *ventre à terre*, trying to come up with you— while *you* lounge about taking your ease!"

Wrenching her head around, her heart thundering, Penelope saw Gordon Chandler, de Villars, and a beaming Dutch Coachman watching them. "Oh . . . my God!" she sobbed. "Oh—*my God!* Are you all taken . . . as well?"

"They're all gone, brave girl," said Gordon, hurrying along the pew behind them to peer over at his battered brother and reach down to grip the hand that so waveringly tried to reach his. Blinking rather rapidly, he scolded, "You see what happens, do I but turn my back on you for an instant!"

"But . . . but my aunt . . . *saw* us!" stammered Penelope, trying in vain to comprehend.

"Did she, by God!" said de Villars. "That beauty in the black lace?" His dark brows lifted appreciatively.

"Then she certainly did not tell your uncle," said Gordon. "We watched them ride out—the very picture of frustrated fury. Perchance there is some good in the woman, after all."

"There is good in all of us," said Albritton in quiet reproof.

De Villars spun around. "Devil take you, Charles," he said, laughing as he recognized the young man he'd not seen since university days. "Why the deuce are you done up in that . . . ridiculous . . ." And he faltered to a stop, his crimson face a study. "Oh . . ." he moaned. "Egad! You really *are* a priest!"

Albritton threw back his head and shouted with mirth.

Too stunned to be able to grasp this miraculous reprieve, Penelope looked down at Quentin.

His eyes were bright with tears. He turned his face against her breast and wept.

She bent and kissed his untidy head, then looked up, her joyous gaze moving from one loyal face to the next. They all looked so fond, so understanding, and perhaps a little awed. Her gaze slipped to the Leper's Door.

The cypher was gone.

Dutch Coachman leaned forward in his chair and said low and urgently, "We must get them away, sir." He glanced to the side of the vicar's study where Quentin lay on a sofa while his bride gently tended his arm. "They'll come back here. Soon, like as not."

Albritton sighed and lifted his eyes to the man who leaned against the desk beside him. "You agree, Treve?"

De Villars nodded. "Either that rapscallion of an uncle of hers, or our ambitious Captain Holt." He bent his dark head closer to his friends and murmured, "Whatever we are to do, it must be fast, gentlemen. If they take old Quentin again, I'm thinking it's his lady wife's funeral we shall attend, as well as his. We have—" He checked, his grey eyes widening. "Hey, now . . ." he muttered, and then, grinning, repeated, "Hey, now! A *funeral*, by Gad!"

The small cortege wound slowly along the rutted country lane, the hearse in the lead, drawn by black horses with tall black feathers bobbing above their heads; the mourners' coach behind, escorted by two sombrely clad outriders.

Inside the coach, her veil drawn back from her wan face, Penelope clung tightly to the hand of her new brother-in-law. Her fingers were icy cold and trembling, despite the warm afternoon. Gordon placed his own free hand over them and said reassuringly, "Hang on, brave little lady. Only twenty more miles."

"Two hours," she whispered. "Oh, Gordon—*why* did it have to grow so hot? My poor love must be roasting in that dreadful c-coffin!"

His grip tightened. "Courage, m'dear. Quentin's come through all this, and though he's a bit pulled at the moment, he's tough as nails, never fear."

"But I do fear. Indeed, I cannot help but fear that we—we tempt Fate. All these hours, jolting and bumping over these dreadful roads!"

"Why, it is more than fifty miles, you see. And we dare not travel at the gallop, for it must look very improper were we to do so."

His attempt to make her smile failed. She said, her voice breaking, "I declare I am black and blue in this well-sprung coach. But—Quentin . . . oh, if only he'd taken the laudanum as Trevelyan suggested, I'd not have to think of him enduring such anguish."

Gordon's lips tightened. His own imagination had been plaguing him these endless hours, although the Rabble had grinned up at them so cheerily when they'd closed the lid on his pale face. He said quietly, "He dared not, Penny. If he is naturally sleeping and we are stopped, Dutch will pull up the hearse sharply enough to waken him. But had he taken the

338

laudanum he'd likely be snoring his head off were a search party so crude as to demand the coffin be opened."

She gave a gasp. "My God! I never thought of that! But— but surely they would not? Especially if Treve were to tell them he died of the pox."

Gordon thought grimly that he'd be not in the least surprised was such an outrageous demand to be made, and prayed that his brother was not stifling, despite the air holes they'd drilled in the wooden coffin.

The object of their concern lay panting in his cramped quarters, wondering why his sadistic friend de Villars had chosen a route that led through the Sahara, or hired a hearse equipped with square wheels. He swore as he was jolted against the side for the thousandth time, and concentrated desperately upon all the things he would say to his benefactor did he ever escape this torture chamber. . . .

They were passing a little north of Woodchurch and almost home when they were stopped again. This time, the Sergeant was a pompous, authoritative individual with a florid complexion, beady brown eyes, and a loud bray of a voice.

Sick with dread, Penelope heard him question de Villars and Albritton and shout down their indignation at the suggestion that the coffin be opened. She clutched Gordon's arm. He said in a clipped voice, "Time for you to put in an appearance, m'dear. Can you deal with this block, d'ye think?"

"I will . . . I must!"

By the time she and Gordon came up, the troopers had already opened the hearse door and were lowering the coffin to the ground. She uttered a genuine shriek. "What are you doing to my poor husband?"

De Villars put in quickly, "I warned 'em, dear lady. Wouldn't believe me. So be it. You stand well away, for your own sake."

The troopers moved back uneasily. The Sergeant said with his loud laugh, "Aye, we've heard that tale afore! We be sound, sturdy men, we be. Not afeared o' no pox. Open the lid, you chaps, and quick about it!"

339

"You *cannot!*" wailed Penelope, desperate. "Ohh—it is *sacrilege!*"

Again, the troopers hesitated, eyeing their leader with marked trepidation. The Sergeant, dismounting to stand beside the widow, bellowed, "Open, I say! The poor gent will not object, be he really dead."

The lid was swung open. If Quentin was breathing it was not apparent. He looked ghastly, his features waxy and so pallid he seemed a corpse. With a little moan Penelope swooned into the Sergeant's unready arms.

"Unhand her, you savage brute," roared Gordon, appropriating Penelope's convincingly limp form.

Relinquishing his burden nervously, the Sergeant yelped, "I never meant nothing. I never done—"

"I'll have your stripes for this, damme if I don't," de Villars put in with enthusiastic ire. "You're all witnesses, you men, of how this beastly clod brutalized and assaulted this poor grieving widow!"

Well aware that one or two of his underlings might have old scores to settle, the Sergeant protested, "I didn't do no such thing. I was just a'doing of me duty." At this point his eyes alighted again upon the corpse and he gave a bellow of triumph. "*Dead,* is he? Stap me if ever I see a cadaver sweat like a ox! Only look at him—fair wringing wet, he be!"

Gordon, fanning Penelope, whitened.

The irrepressible de Villars nodded solemnly. "Death dew," he declared.

Charles Albritton, still mounted and preparing for desperate action, jerked his head around to direct an incredulous stare at his resourceful friend.

"Death dew?" echoed the Sergeant, sneering. "What the hell's that? And how be I never heard of't?"

"I am a mortician," said de Villars. "I doubt you've dealt with as many corpses as have I. It's the natural condensation in the body, especially on a warm day, d'ye see, when the cadaver's been shut up in a closed box." Warming to his theme, he added

340

ghoulishly, "Lord, man, I've seen the death dew spray up like a fountain when a lid was raised." He reined his horse a few paces away. "They do say it clears the germs from the cadaver and that they transfer to the nearest warm body. I'd move the lady back, was I you, Mr. Gordon."

The troopers leapt clear, as one man. The Sergeant, finding it difficult to quiet his horse, which Dutch Coachman had unkindly pierced with a pin, decided enough was as good as a feast and swung into the saddle. The troopers were deserting rapidly. It was clearly his duty to lead them. He applied his spurs. "Get that there hearse clear of His Majesty's highway," he roared over his shoulder, and galloped off along the dusty lane, shouting redundantly, "At the double, you men. Forward . . . !"

De Villars strode to the coffin and bent over the cadaver. "You all right, dear old boy?"

Quentin blinked up at him blurrily. "*Death . . . dew?*" he gasped feebly, the suspicion of a grin twisting his pale lips. "Damn you, Treve! As—as if I've not enough misery, you . . . have to make me laugh!"

The effort to open his eyes was taxing, but Quentin was warm and, except for an unpleasantness in his arm, relatively comfortable. He turned his head drowsily and beheld immaculate sheets, familiar bedcurtains and an empty but obviously recently occupied trundle bed. He was gazing thoughtfully at this object when a side door opened and a vision in pink and white gauze crept into the luxurious bedchamber.

"Penelope," he cried, his voice a croaking whisper, and struggled to sit up.

With a sob of joy Penelope ran to sit on the bed and place a cool hand on her husband's brow. "Thank heaven! The fever has gone at last!"

"Never mind that, woman. Kiss me!"

She obliged the invalid so tenderly that several wonderful minutes passed before he muttered uncertainly, "At last? We are at Lac Brillant, I think?" And in quick anxiety, "No military about? Otton did not—"

She placed her soft palm over his lips. "No, my darling. Thanks to your brave friends we are quite safe. We brought you here three days since, and you've been fast asleep, although with such a dreadful fever—" She broke off. "But now you're better, praise God!"

He kissed the hand that caressed his cheek and, glancing to the trundle bed, said, "So you stayed beside me, faithful as ever, my dearest love."

"Not I. Your old nurse took charge the moment they carried you in." She had really thought him dead at that point, and shivered at the memory, then went on hurriedly, "I tried to tend you, but she would have none of me and I was bundled off to be pampered while she cared for you as if you were a babe. What devotion you do inspire in your dependents, dearest."

He smiled at her, his sunken eyes so eloquent that she bent to kiss him again.

The outer door opened. Nurse, her uniform glaring cleanliness, her eyes militant, paused on the threshold.

Quentin murmured, "What does my father mean to do, love? I'd not bring disaster down on him."

"De Villars has a yawl waiting. So soon as you are strong enough, we'll be away." Slipping to her knees beside the bed, Penelope took up Quentin's thin hand and pressed it to her cheek. "Oh, darling—only think. We are safe together at last, and yet my aunt *must* have known that Geoffrey is alive."

"Most assuredly she must. You'll recall you caught her reading his letter that first morning at Highview."

"Then she must also have known in Little Snoring that she and my uncle would lose the title and the estate."

Quentin did not voice the grim qualifying remark that came to mind. "And yet," he mused, "she did not betray us. Perhaps Albritton's reminder of her immortal soul struck home."

"Hmmmn. Or perhaps Sybil had a soft spot for a certain elderly gentleman."

He grinned at her with a marked lack of repentance.

"Rascal." She kissed his hand and murmured, "I had all but given up hope, but do you know, my dearest dear, I do believe that very soon we shall be safely in our little cottage near Paris."

"Where I shall grow my cabbages, and"—he gave her an arch look—"we might even produce . . . other things."

Joying in the return of that mischievous glint in his green eyes, she asked shyly, "Such as . . . ?"

"Well . . . I've been thinking it would be nice to have a—er, cat. Do you think, Penelope Anne, that we might be able to find a white one . . . with long silky hair . . . ?"

Penelope laughed merrily. "Odious creature! You know very well that is not what you meant."

"Managing female," he retaliated, his eyes adoring her. "I wish you will tell me then, what else I *should* mean."

She crept back onto the bed and snuggled cautiously in his good arm. And she whispered in his ear exactly what he had really meant to say.

Nurse heard his deep chuckle ring out. Smiling, she closed the door and, singing softly, went down the hall.